RYAN KURR

SAGE SMOKE & FIRE

A NOVEL

Sage, Smoke & Fire/ Ryan Kurr. -- 1st ed.
ISBN 978-1-7347245-0-9 (Hardback)
ISBN 978-1-7347245-1-6 (Paperback)
ISBN 978-1-7347245-2-3 (ebook)

Jacket and cover design by Allison Layman

Visit the author's website at **www.ryankurr.com**

Those who don't believe in magic will never find it.

Roald Dahl, The Minpins

Also by Ryan Kurr

Sugar Burn: The Not so Hot Side of the Sweet Kitchen

For those with fire in their blood
Those who draw circles in the mud
The keepers of sage and pine
The ones who feel the divine
Those who use three eyes to see
The ones who experience life differently
The collectors of rain, and water from streams
Those who explore the landscapes of their dreams
And for those who shaped, inspired, loved, and challenged me
Without *you*—this would cease to be

CONTENTS

*Elucidations for text marked with this symbol are located at the back of the book in the Esoteric Compendium.

SAGE

SMOKE

&

FIRE

Central Asia, 1338

Yesun's magic created the black plague and killed his brother. Both were accidents. After years of being cloaked by his brother's shadow, Yesun had grown cold. He was neither strong nor well mannered but rather had about him a commendable craftiness and intensity that spoke of a man of nobility. Yesun, being from the upper crust of society, naturally admired his brother's keen sense of justice and uncompromising code of honor. Nevertheless, envy doesn't respect patriarchy or family bonds. It was known to many that Yesun had taken a particular interest in privacy, and with that came a sense of entitlement, as he took pride in the mysteries he uncovered in his solitude. Especially the secret he had discovered a year earlier.

Yesun had a gift far more extraordinary than any of his brother's talents: he *was* magic. He had deserted the ideology of family and been initiated into a new dynasty that involved only himself. His chambers were filled with linens stitched with mysterious symbols, small bones, antelope horns, dried organs and jars of dried herbs. Along with the tools and objects came a sense of urgency and responsibility to use them toward a goal, a destiny—to create and promote balance in the world. That was his assumption, anyway, after interpreting messages he had received inside altered states of consciousness. In his time spent outside of meditation and magical experimentation, he obsessed over the messages he received in solitude, the visions he would see on the backside of his eyelids and the death-rattle whispers that gave him insight about his gifts. He was undoubtedly emerging from the depths of his brother's shadow, which in and of itself was something to be celebrated—but it consumed him. He accessed parts of his mind and spirit that proved he would have been a tremendous ruler, if it hadn't been for his desire to put himself first. In his newfound confidence, he was no longer just the younger brother, a less admirable member of the family who is noble only through blood and nothing else. He was now a formidable force, someone strong and worthy of respect and able to manifest change, all through sheer will.

No one had introduced him to his gifts; no one was there to guide and educate him on the purpose of the miraculous abilities he possessed other than the ethereal bodies he communicated with. Yesun, being the only one (to his knowledge) with abilities, abandoned the tasks whispered to him in the higher consciousness. He marveled at the power that had arrived with the full moon, one that surged from a source he couldn't see but could only feel. The earth's crust shifted in and out, east and west, north and south in response to the lunar and solar gravitation that activated his power. His strength grew with the vigor of a raging storm. Yesun moved forward, compelled by mania, ambitious and ravenous for power like a beast craves blood.

The morning sun rose into the sky and spilled its light beams through the window of Yesun's chamber. He was immediately anxious about the evening, even upon waking, for that would be the moment when everything would change. Locked inside, without food or water, he prepared. First, a long meditation that ended at noon. Then he opened the solid wood chest adorned with silver that was close to his bed and looked over the silvery embroidered sheet that covered all of his tools: five small golden bowls, an understated knife with a bone handle and bundles of fresh gray mint, cream narcissus and branches trimmed from a juniper tree. His rough fingertips buzzed with excitement, and he stared inside with great restraint. He plucked out a sufficient handful of herbs for the spell, and while the thought of his brother falling to his knees to worship him filled the back of his mind, he placed the bowls around himself in a circle, filling each one with broken juniper branches and herbs. He lit each bowl with the flame of a nearby candle and listened to the wood pop. The invigorating scent of mint filled his nose, one that always inspired thoughts of the beautiful patches of flora and fauna near their home where mint grew wild with effortless splendor—the same natural and gentle grace that his brother possessed. He dipped his finger into a bag filled with powdered eggshells and traced intricate patterns across the floor. He heard a knock at his door, too heavy-handed to be ignored but too unimportant to answer. Yesun slipped off his linen smock, tossed it away and continued with the ritual.

Knock! Knock! Knock!

Another set of raps at the door was followed by his brother's request to open the door. Although Yesun ignored his brother's beckoning, he responded with a smile. His hands reached over to the floor and lifted a small bouquet of cream narcissus flowers. He picked the blossoms, discarded the stems and tossed the petals into the bowl of burning herbs in front of him, along with a single strand of his brother's black hair. He muttered a chant—quietly—so that it couldn't be heard outside the room. Yesun could smell his brother outside the door. He could smell his intentions. He knew his brother had come to check on him because he hadn't left the room all day. The evening had finally come and the sun had set, bringing with it the crisp change of air from the landlocked country. *Now was the time.* The pile of ashes in the bowl in front of him was no longer smoldering, and he reached into the depths and pinched up the blackened cinders. Tracing along his forehead with his gray finger, he carved a circle through his sweat and then a line down to his chest, where he drew another circle of ashes.

"Ashes, ashes. Give me the crown. Ashes, ashes. Changshi, bow down," he chanted to himself.

He pushed on with his magical experiment and pulled over the tiny rat he had captured and kept alive for this very moment. The room was dark and smelled like the devil's breath. He breathed deep, filling his lungs with valor, and held the rat out in front of him. The rat squeaked at the pressure of his hands and the looming death. The greasy prickles of fur poked out over the top of Yesun's fist, and he tightened his grip. He was close to completing the spell, although he wasn't even sure what the result would be. In the blackness of the room he narrowed his eyes on the rat in front of him, and within seconds the head burst into flames. The squeaks became shrieks as the fire burned through the fur and melted the skin off the rat's head. Yesun gasped at the magnificence of his manifestation and breathed in the smoke of the burning flesh as the head popped.

He placed the dead rat on the floor and with his right hand picked up a knife and stabbed the rodent in the chest, splitting the flesh. As the blood pooled out over the sides of the body and onto the floor, he reached his enthusiastic fingers into the mess. Looking up, he rubbed the blood across his face and chest. Even through the thick walls of his room, he could feel his brother's heartbeat slowly changing its rhythm. He could smell the stink of his flesh beginning to rot like a butchered street rat. For a moment he considered the reality of what he might have accomplished—by accident. It was power he wanted, not death. Above all else he wanted to be the one in control, the one to rule, the prized visionary whom people admired and praised for his ingenuity. As he stood over the blood and ashes, he soothed his hands in a bowl of cold water. Intention was everything. He repeated to himself, *It's what I intend that makes a difference in the outcome.* But he was unaware of the difference between what his soul actually wanted and what his conscious mind *believed* he wanted.

After he cleaned up the remnants of the spell, he left his room to find his family and found them gathered in his brother's chamber. His eyes fell upon Changshi for the first time since the spell had been cast. Changshi's fingertips, especially around his nails, were black as soot. His neck, arms and torso were covered with bulbous, pus-filled swellings of rotten flesh. The sheets around him were covered with blood that was slowly being excreted from his mouth, even after death. His body had fallen victim to an unknown poison, one that no one had ever seen before and brought about a heinous death. And Yesun had willed it into existence. Yesun's desire to be respected—that he had wished so hard for and with such childlike ignorance—had come true. Immediately, Yesun rose to power as the next in line. With his eyes locked in awe over the manifestation of his sheer will, he immediately felt regret.

He yearned for power and not death, yet he had received both. It was only then that he realized that using magic required caution.

SAGE

CHAPTER 1

Louisiana, September 2019

Over the twenty-minute taxi ride from the airport to the plain farmhouse in Destrehan, Nina believed one thing for sure: Louisiana was not a place she would've chosen to start over, yet she was about to with a new family—a coven. The California-born taxi driver referred to the Pelican State as a "swampy shithole," with irrationally proud locals who treated alcohol like a meal, partied endlessly, obsessed over the removal of Confederate statues and celebrated antiquated traditions. Nina, not quick to judge, decided she'd see for herself. If any of what he said was true, Louisiana would be a great place to begin the task of restoring some balance to the world.

Nina stepped out onto the soft, spongy soil of the long driveway that led up to the Barrow House where she would be living for an undetermined amount of time. It was a house with a history and a name, one that she had learned about only a few weeks ago. From the trunk, she retrieved two bulging suitcases, which held her entire forty-four years of life. She stood five foot six, straight and poised. The soft soil became gravel as she drew closer to the house. She was overdressed for fall in the South, where the oppressive heat was hardly at an end come September, the height of hurricane season: high-waisted, wide-leg white pants with contrasting stitching and a high-collar, semi-sheer violet top with balloon-like sleeves. The only relief she had from the humidity was the possibility of central air inside the house.

The six oak trees that lined either side of the driveway tossed thick wisps of Spanish moss in the slow air as if waving hello. The taxi turned around and crept away at a pace that she would have to get used to. Things moved slower in the South, almost backward—NOLA time, they called it in New Orleans, Louisiana. Her strappy, heeled sandals crushed the tiny bits of gravel as she moved toward the house, the air so dense that reaching the front door was almost a form of aerobic exercise. The beads of sweat covering her umber skin glistened like shiny jewels in the afternoon sun.

She reached the steps and stepped into the shade of the front porch. She had only heard descriptions of the place she was going to call home. Her immediate impression was that it was, much like everything else she'd seen, so far on the edge of decay that it was about to slip off. Yet it held a certain amount of idyllic charm, a maintained type of shabbiness, except for the potted fern, with leaves so brown they blended in with the terra cotta. That wasn't rustic elegance; that was just dead. However, nothing that a little magic couldn't fix. Perhaps some pruning and repotting along with some energized incantations or stormwater charged with moss agate. She fluffed her long, voluminous curls and tossed an armful to one side, returning a side part back to the left side of her head.

"Welcome home, Nina," she said out loud. She retrieved a key from her front pocket and slipped it into the lock. With a crank of her wrist, shove of her foot and push of her full body weight, the heat-swollen door moved begrudgingly into the foyer.

Brrrrrrrrrunk!

It was cleaner and much larger than she'd expected, partially furnished and with lots of natural light. The foyer led into a hallway that ran perpendicular to it, with three bedrooms and two bathrooms to the right. To the left, a small study, one small bedroom, the master bedroom and bathroom, and a dining room. Continuing straight into the house was the great room, where four large pillars created a divide between the great room and the hall. The great room would be perfect for gatherings, rituals and meetings for the coven, with its high ceilings and airy feel. The fireplace was a delightful addition. Nina did love fire. Adjoining the great room was a boxy dining room and a farmhouse kitchen with a breakfast nook to the left and another bedroom on the far right corner. The large floor-to-ceiling windows that filled the wall at the back of the great room exposed a small back porch with steps that led to the back lawn. The yard ran farther than her imagination had anticipated, with a single magnolia tree at the end.

Her feelings of uncertainty turned to delight as she began to consider what she could achieve in the house, a place where she could manage people in a way she felt would truly help create some positive change. It had been a long time coming, after years of entering the Somnium* plane during deep sleep and learning about her gifts from other witches and celestial spirits and guides. It was in that altered state where she was able to learn, practice and accept her gifts in addition to assuming the role of Proctor of Louisiana.

She had known the day would come when her powers would spring to life, and the day had finally come and with it, a perfunctory smile as she gazed out over the backyard. Since learning of her gifts ten years earlier, she had practiced only divination and meditation, because they were the only arts she could truly access outside of her soul's expeditions to the Somnium plane. First, she learned the archetypes of the tarot, practicing spreads and methods of interpretation in her spare time, as a writer with a full-time job would craft a novel. Then, she moved on to scrying, gazing into flames, crystal balls and bowls of water. It was difficult at first, as most things are, but through dedication, discipline and daily meditation, she improved her connection to the higher consciousness, opened her third eye and came into her psychic awareness. The ripening of her soul had cost her all of her old life: the boyfriends, the social circles, the meaningless social media connections and professional relationships. The dismantling hadn't been easy, but it had been necessary, because it was that very upheaval that allowed her to grow beyond the limitations of what she knew she had already begun to outgrow.

She rolled her two pieces of luggage to the master bedroom on the left side of the house and immediately changed into something more weather appropriate. In the zippered front pocket of her suitcase was a large bundle of California white sage. A box of long kitchen matches sat on the nightstand next to the bed. Nina lit the sage and let it burn for a few moments before blowing it out with a gusty breath, letting the smoke billow out around her. Moving her arm in a large circle, she smudged the house as she uttered a mantra:

Sage, smoke and fire, burn away,
Cleanse and purify this home,
free the way.

Taking special care to reach all the high corners in the house, she ran the smudge stick along the walls, the wooden floorboards and in front of each warped-glass window. She held her hand underneath to catch any loose ashes as she treaded over the eggplant-hued, well-worn, antique rug in the great room. She removed her shoes to experience how comfortable it was underfoot, and continued to chant. As she stood in the center of the room, she glanced over its magnificence for the second time. Creamy, semi-transparent drapes underneath English violet-colored valances with gray tassels, an old mahogany bookcase with six shelves and half filled with books, a smaller wooden side table in front of the floor-to-ceiling windows that overlooked the straw-colored afternoon sun beaming through the glass and over the dark gray sofa and chairs near the fireplace. It was indeed the greatest room she had ever lived in. There was even an upright piano along one side that she hadn't noticed the first time through.

Nina pulled at her top, fanned her chest, switched on the air-conditioning and went outside. Around the right side of the house was a four-door Toyota Prius—cerulean blue—with the keys on the driver's seat. All of the obnoxious administration that goes into securing a car had already been taken care of by Nix, the Advisory's Keeper of Books and Assets, when he purchased and partially furnished the house for her. The Advisory had proved to be incredibly helpful, covering all her expenses from New York to Louisiana. She grabbed hold of the door and flinched when her hand hit the sun-scorched handle. Nina had never been to the South and was unprepared for all of its characteristics. In the manner that one rips off a Band-Aid, she threw open the door and hopped inside, only to feel the supreme heat that had been held hostage in the confines of the car. For a moment, her whole life flashed before her eyes. She had never experienced anything so hot. A husky sound escaped her mouth as she gasped for air.

She caught her face in the rearview mirror. It was the face of someone very new to the South, shocked and terrified, her mouth hanging wide open. The heat—uncompromising, her body—stunned. Her skin had already generated enough sweat to thoroughly saturate the fresh shirt. She slammed the door shut like a petulant child, started the car and blasted the air-conditioning. Louisiana would take some getting used to.

She hadn't needed a car in New York, so the luxury of being able to do what she wanted and when she wanted was a refreshing blessing. Nina was also unaccustomed being so far out in the country that the closest grocery store was thirty minutes away. The closest neighbor was a five-minute drive. Unaware of what foods to fill the kitchen with, she made a mental list of all the spices, herbs and oils to buy during the half-hour drive. She even took some time to satisfy her curiosity about why there was an entire aisle devoted to roux.

It would be foolish of her to believe that she could check out quickly. After all, things did not pass in a hot minute like they did in New York City. It didn't make any sense: the customer in front of her had fewer than fifteen items, and it took nearly fifteen minutes to complete the transaction. Nina wasn't as impatient as an Aries, but she was about to be. She blinked, tucked her tongue into the roof of her mouth and inhaled deeply, holding her breath in her lungs. Being a Transcendent* witch meant she was gifted with the power of influence. It was something unpracticed outside the Somnium plane, and perhaps a tad self-serving to perform now, yet it was already underway before she could talk herself out of it. She smiled and then it began, the swirling sensation from behind her forehead. It had a sound in the real world—the physical plane—like the sound of a gas stove before it ignites. Then, her power of influence erupted and the cashier's face appeared livelier and more accommodating. The whole process took less than a few seconds, and with the cashier's expedited manner of service, Nina avoided all small talk and her order was bagged in less than half the time it would have taken otherwise.

It was half past three when she arrived back at the house. She unpacked the sixteen double-bagged plastic grocery bags. A wasteful amount of plastic bags, one that puzzled her: some items, like the carton of eggs and the jar of crunchy (never creamy) peanut butter, were in a bag all by themselves. Was this a southern idiosyncrasy or a result of her spell? She couldn't be sure. Perhaps she would know after the next grocery trip. The kitchen was the warmest room in the house and had the second-best view. Nina was a mastermind when it came to organization, and everything was put away as if she'd already known where it was going to go. In the pantry was a large wooden salad bowl. She placed it on the center island and filled it with apples, bananas, satsumas and a pair of nearly ripe avocados.

Nina fixed herself a salad and then, like the crackling of autumn leaves at the end of a breeze, became still. She ran her tongue along her teeth, cleaning out bits of candied pecan, and held her breath for a moment. A thought rose up from the unknown, pure and unfiltered. She was compelled to blend and crush some herbs, boil them in oil, anoint a candle from top to bottom and unleash her request into the universe. The images came clearly to her and were much more precise than visions had ever appeared to her in the past. It was time for magic. It was time to call forth the coven.

I can do this. Doubt slipped away from Nina's mind as she carried out magical preparations with skill and ease, like a well-practiced baker making chocolate chip cookies. Her front teeth bit into the flesh of her lip in speechless admiration of her natural talent. Nina threw back her curls, rubbed her hands together vigorously and allowed herself to abandon any sort of pragmatic approach to how she'd continue, allowing the voice of her intuition to instruct her. It was a warm and enigmatic voice, one that she had grown to trust and rely on in the most precarious of situations. Every now and then she would try to tune her intuition in response to everyday situations that ranged from which baggage carousel her luggage was at to what time the first witch would arrive. That voice was like a muscle, and like any muscle, it needed to be exercised to grow strong.

The center island was covered with tiny bowls, each filled with a different ingredient for her summoning oil. She held the energized palm of her left hand over each bowl and recited a charging incantation:

I cast away all that is not in harmony with its own nature.

I amplify your characteristics,

I instill you with the power of magnetism, for the good of all.

Let me see what is not seen, let me hear what is not heard, let me feel what is not felt.

In a marble mortar and pestle that lived on the kitchen counter, she pounded and mashed together datura flowers, dandelion roots, sage, rosemary, chamomile and the peel of an apple she had stripped away in one long spiral. Her conviction—unswerving. She placed a pot on the stove and poured in enough olive oil to cover the bottom. As the heat warmed the oil, the peppery and grassy scent hit her nose, and she inhaled deeply. *There's nothing like an excellent, fresh olive oil.* Nina's love for a simple pasta in olive oil came flooding back. Although an innocuous and fleeting thought, she let it go as quickly as it came and continued to focus on the task at hand—magic, not dinner. Certainly not with the assortment of ingredients she was about to add, ranging from calming to toxic, if ingested. Nina dumped the ingredients into the hot oil and gave the pan a few swirls with a flick of her wrist. The makings of the summoning oil muddled together and hissed in the pan.

While the oil was coming to room temperature, she grabbed hold of a four-inch indigo candle and held it to her third eye to connect with it. She lowered the candle to her mouth, closed her eyes and licked up the side to the wick to form a deeper bond with it, something she never could have imagined herself doing back when she was completing her MFA at Yale twelve years earlier, right before she became aware of the magical role she would embody shortly afterward. Nina strained the oil and discarded the sautéed components, leaving a deep ochre-colored oil behind. She dipped her finger into the oil and anointed the candle from the bottom to the top, around the entire circumference. Onto a pewter saucer, she poured a mound of sea salt and secured the candle in the center of the white hill. She brought the saucer into the great room and sat upon the floor, facing out toward the backyard. From her pocket, she drew out four chunks of cerussite and four shards of magnetite and encircled the saucer with the crystals. She lit the candle and gazed into the fire's hypnotic fluttering. Within an instant, the flame stopped flickering and stiffened. Nina, stone-faced, succumbed to the mysteries within the flame, closed her eyes and ascended into the higher consciousness.

The cicadas faded from her awareness, as did the dampness of the southern climate that usually managed to penetrate any defenses against it. She tuned in to the broadcast that streamed through her mind and trusted it to tell her what to do. Faint echoes and whispers from ancestors, angels, spirit guides and all the wonders of the divine filled the space in the infinite hollow of consciousness. Ego—abandoned, as spirit assumed control. Connected—moving in and through space and time harmoniously, with complete trust and synchronistic synthesis amidst all cyclic patterns and ebbs—into a flow.

After the first five minutes, the black abyss became glittered with spots of purple that bloomed into tide-like waves. Nina flushed with euphoria as she explored the depths beyond the restraints of the human mind. Slowly, very slowly, a vibration hummed inside her consciousness. The purple orbs began to cluster together like bees in a swarm and take shape. An iridescent image of a paintbrush—no, a makeup brush. Then it changed shape and became a rectangle, then an envelope, and then finally, with a little creative interpretation, a postcard with the word *CHICAGO* across the top. Denying herself the chance to overthink her interpretation, she searched for the next experience. Her senses awakened, listening for the next clue, in whatever form it took—a gut feeling, a buzzing in the hands, a rush of chills up the length of her back. Any information she received wouldn't be denied or rebuffed based on how it emerged—a common reaction to those with a highly rational and logical mind. After all she had seen and encountered during her enlightenment period in the Somnium plane, she knew it was irrational to assume that information could be received only through one's ordinary senses and analytical mind. After all, all humans are psychic, but not all are motivated to peel back the layers of camouflage that often hide psychic information, or are adept at doing so.

Then, like a match that has suddenly caught fire, a new set of images surfaced. The name of a makeup store in Chicago: *Warpaint*. The name of a Nigerian woman: *Bisa*. Along with the name came a wave of emotions. For a moment, Nina considered if these emotions and feelings were her own, but after checking in with her body, she realized they belonged to— Bisa. She could feel her emotions beyond the limitations of distance. A white flash passed over her range of psychic vision, and a detailed representation of the woman's face manifested. Smooth skin, high cheekbones, dazzling eyes surrounded by sapphire-blue eye shadow, skinny dreads wrapped into an ornate topknot. Spirit quickly led her to the next burst of information—no name, no images, just a gut feeling, one that implied she would find what she needed when she saw the first woman in New Orleans with an actual paper map clutched in her hands, and to trust in that.

The final group came in a firecracker burst of sounds. Nina continued to breathe deeply as her body softened and remained receptive. With each inhale, she heard a first and last name, and on each exhale, she heard a location. The voice, so subtle, so familiar that it was difficult to tell if it was her own voice inside her head. *Trust*. Nina often carried on conversations with herself, but this was different. This wasn't laced with judgment or criticism.

The voice repeated itself with confidence and simplicity until it became abundantly clear that the message was true. *Oliver...Oliver Kemp. Mitch...Mitch Wickleby. Avery...Avery Scott.* The boundaries of awareness are not rigid and structured like algebraic formulas. It is kaleidoscopic alchemy where the rules and senses combine and mix.

Nina opened her eyes and remained still, her body and mind absorbing the leftover thoughts of her experience. She was slightly disoriented, as if waking from a nap in the late evening. Exultant and ready to begin, Nina uncrossed her legs and stretched. The candle had burned straight down to the salt and extinguished itself. The odor of burnt wick hung fresh in the room. She wrote down the names and details that had come to her during her meditation. She had one more task to do before the list was complete: she needed to find the woman with the map, because she would lead her to the final member of the coven.

CHAPTER 3

The late afternoon was orange and hazy. An impenetrable, syrupy blanket of moisture still filled the landscape, making it no different from earlier in the day, apart from the one-degree drop in temperature. Nina looked at the weather app on her phone: *89°F, 91% humidity*. It wasn't the deep meditation that sapped her energy, it was the heat as she walked to the car. She cranked the air-conditioning full blast and switched the radio on. She hadn't owned a car in a very long time and was used to modern conveniences like Spotify and Pandora. She hit the Scan button and allowed the radio to help her choose. Oldies. Old-school hip-hop and R & B. The university's station. Christian music. Christian music. Country. Public radio. More country. Jazz. Nina hit the Scan button to stop the scrolling and heard the distinct sound of Junior Kimbrough's "Pull Your Clothes Off," from an album she remembered vividly from her college years when one of her roommates, who'd had a passionate fascination with Delta blues, played it endlessly.

It wasn't the song itself that drew her attention, although she did enjoy Junior; it was where her mind led her. She searched through the rough and dissolving memories of that spring of 1993 (or was it 1994?), when she awoke and fell asleep to his music most days of the week. She tapped her fingers on the steering wheel as she pulled out of the driveway. Nina tried to remember the name of the one song that was eluding her at the moment. She pulled over to the side of the road, not knowing where she was going to go. Her eyes closed, and the music filled her ears. Another soft sound, that of the title. "Meet Me in the City." Her eyes opened, and if they'd been able to smile, they would have. Hot sunshine beamed down on her arms as she turned back onto the road. New Orleans was only thirty miles away, far enough to allow the air-conditioning to fully cool the interior of the car. She drove toward the city without purpose or a destination in mind, guided by instinct and intuitive navigation, not something one can download to their phone with a push of a finger.

Nina entered the city and drove along the edge of the French Quarter, east on Decatur Street. The Big Easy's strength is in its prideful sense of charm and tradition and being a city resilient in the face of change. Nina had never been to New Orleans, and it wasn't exactly how she had envisioned it from all the movies she had seen. She rolled down the window as she passed Café Du Monde and smelled the hot grease from inside where they fried the world-famous beignets. Touristy shops lined the ground level of every building, each selling the same things: T-shirts, hats, masquerade masks. Traffic came to a standstill at a green light as drunk tourists wobbled like newborn babies into the street, their iconic hand-grenade cocktails sloshing around in the tall neon-green tubes their hands barely held on to. People were everywhere—all in defiance of the New York minute Nina had become so accustomed to.

She continued to drive at an obnoxiously leisurely pace and turned left onto Elysian Fields. The car fit into a spot along Washington Square Park, where it was shielded from the sun by the leaves of the tall trees. As she stepped out of the car and onto the uneven sidewalk, cracked and slanted from years of being poured over swampy wetlands, she could hear the bustle of nearby Frenchmen Street. She rounded the corner of the park and headed toward what people called "the locals' Bourbon Street." Each short building, stacked directly up to the next, had its own personality. A five-man brass band was stationed on the corner, performing for the sake of performing, and crowds of people shuffled through the streets, wet from what she assumed was liquor, vomit and piss, judging by the smell wafting through the air. She walked down the road, looking over the crowd. The neon signs of the local jazz clubs fell away as she rounded a curve. The street was like a vein, carrying lifeblood from one place to another. The sounds of jazz and blues collided as they spilled out from the numerous music clubs and bars that decorated the street. A casual stroll turned into an obstacle course as she maneuvered around trash bins, tourists, groups of street folk and puddles of unidentifiable liquid that lived inside potholes. She realized it was a mistake to wear open-toed shoes.

The road curved toward Esplanade Avenue, and that's when she saw what she had been looking for. Across the street, standing on the corner of Esplanade and Decatur Street, was an older woman holding a map. An actual paper map. Nina craned her neck and blocked the sun from her eyes to catch a better look. It was as if the wind was knocked straight out of her lungs; she was so excited. With a few skips and a rush across the street, Nina approached the woman, who was obviously lost. Her brows were knitted, and her flaxen hair, which had begun to turn gray, fell out of her sun hat like vines from a tree. The woman held the map like a steering wheel, turning it every so often in circles, sorting out the streets. As Nina drew closer, the glare from the sun was less of a threat than the woman's fluorescent pink shirt with the words *New Orleans* across the front that glowed hot in the sunlight.

"Do you need some help?" Nina asked politely as she gently patted the woman's shoulder.

"I have no idea where I am right now," the old woman said, peering out from behind rectangular glasses.

"May I have a look? Let me show you."

"I rented a car and parked on Dauphine. And Elysian."

Nina nodded. "I know exactly where that is. I just passed by there." She pointed on the map to where the woman's car was parked and then turned around and pointed in the direction of Dauphine and Elysian. As her arm extended to its full length, her finger outstretched like an arrow, she saw something else. Above a building in the direction she was indicating was a plume of soft gray smoke. Not a wildfire kind of smoke, but more along the lines of cooking smoke. In that instant, she felt she was on the right track, on a sort of treasure hunt for the last remaining name. The single spiral of smoke provided all manner of possibilities, but she knew it was a sign. She felt it like she felt the sun on her face. Being present and becoming more comfortable with recognizing signs only served to make her day—life—more interesting, more whole and fully realized.

With a gentle caress of the old woman's shoulder, Nina pointed her in the right direction. As soon as the woman thanked her and began to cross the street, Nina took her first step toward the smoke. The honking and bright buzzing of trumpets and trombones mixed with the warm tones of clarinets and a drum became louder as she approached the corner of the building across the street.

A sea of people bounced to the beat of the brass band, and she followed her nose to the source of the smoke, a plump, bald man sweating in front of a portable barbecue pit. *I could eat,* she thought, but that's not what she was there for. *That smells amazing*—but maybe it was. She jounced through an opening in the crowd and stood in the queue for the vendor. Her foot tapped along to the beat as she gawked wickedly at the portions of barbecued spare ribs and Cajun-spiced shrimp skewers. Nina unknowingly licked her lips and looked over the makeshift paper menu sign with two items listed in blue ink. *Cajun-spiced…What makes something Cajun?*

Nina leaned closer to the person in front of her, tapped his shoulder and asked, "What makes something Cajun?"

The man pointed to a large cylindrical tube of commonly used Cajun spice mix near the barbecue pit and guessed, "Tony Chachere's?" Nina looked confused until she realized that it was the brand name of the spice mix. The man pulled out his wallet to pay, and with it came a crumpled two-dollar bill that spilled out onto the ground. Nina bent down to pick it up.

"You dropped this," she said, unfolding the bill between her index and middle finger.

"Thank you!" the man beamed back.

Nina's finger brushed against the man as he retrieved his bill, and she had another flash of information. This time the name Leo sparked before her eyes in gold light.

"I haven't seen one of these in years!" Nina exclaimed.

"I've never had one before. I'm gonna hang on to this one. The guy at the shop over there just gave it to me." He nodded toward the hot dog shop on the corner behind her.

Without question, Nina removed herself from the queue and darted toward the shop, completely forgetting the sizzling, juicy ribs she wouldn't get to taste. When she pushed open the door to the hot dog-focused restaurant, a blast of warm, spicy air smacked her in the face. She glanced at the chalkboard menu, the empty tables littered with napkins and sprays of ketchup, the overweight man in a tank top sitting on the bar stool. The restaurant was void of patrons, but it wasn't entirely empty: there was an energy hanging in the air. An important incident was about to take place, she just knew it. She pushed aside her awareness that it looked peculiar for her just to be standing in the path of the door, not intending to order or find a seat. The fat, stubble-headed man looked over at her and made eye contact, just long enough for her to hear that he didn't like her kind, a thought so deeply ingrained in his makeup that even he didn't consciously know he felt that way. It was a small, albeit important, detail for her to realize, because it was not only a direct example of discriminative hatred but also an indication of the work cut out for her and the coven. There was an enormous amount of hate and imbalance in the world, and it was going to take a lot of effort to reverse its progression. Especially in the South, where things, including broad and tolerant thinking, progressed at a much slower rate. But this wasn't the time to mess with all that. It was small potatoes compared with what she was concerned with now. Suddenly, someone immediately to Nina's left spoke.

"Leo Sullivan. L-E-O…S-U-L-L-I-V-A-N," a young man spelled out into his cell phone. More of a man, really, but youthful in appearance, energy and attitude. He was a scrawny beanpole with entrancing eyes the color of evergreen fossilized in amber and sloppy, straight, cinnamon-colored hair that fell just above his eyebrows. Dainty ears with lobes that joined directly into his head, a tiny nose with no pores, and a wispy, I-wish-I-were-a-beard beard that grew in patches and mostly around his mouth. Somewhere between twenty-five and thirty years old, with white skin, but toasted-bread white. His fingers like butter knives, straight and blunt-tipped, nails bitten beyond the quick as if he had tried to crawl out of a cave with his bare hands. His stick-like frame hidden under a T-shirt two sizes too large and baggy cargo shorts that exposed his skinny secret from his knees to his ankle socks.

"I already paid the late fee. Check my payment history, dude!" Leo commanded. An accent that was southern, but mysteriously so, as if it had been learned or blurred by living somewhere else or being around other types of people. He looked up at Nina, who had been staring at him. "Yeah…yeah, see? On the seventeenth. That's when I closed the account and switched providers cuz y'all suck!" There was a short pause, just long enough for him to bite his nonexistent nails before continuing his rant. "Dude, this is y'all's mistake, not mine. I'm not gonna pay for a late fee when it's your fault you didn't process my payment right the first time. I went into the store to do it in person! Actually, I went to two stores. The first one they told me I couldn't close any accounts from that location and I had to drive to the flagship store all the way across town. So, I drove myself all the way over there. Their system was down, so I waited for thirty minutes until it came back up. The manager processed my payment and closed my account…*and* she charged me an extra thirty bucks for a cracked screen. No way, dude, screw you guys!" Another pause, which was accompanied by a nod. "Yeah. That's right. Fix it. Tell the manager she sucks," Leo sneered as he hung up his new phone.

Nina used the situation to her advantage and dropped herself into the conversation. "Who was your provider?"

Leo looked up and shook his head before he responded, "Fuckin' Sprint, man. Worst customer service ever."

"I had them for years too," Nina said painfully. "They tried to pull the same thing with me when I switched providers." *Give me a hint, Leo. How can I get you to meet with me?*

"You hear that shit about me having to drive to another store to close the account too? That was the last thing I wanted to be doing. It was so hot, and I had just lost my job that morning."

"Oh, Lord! What kind of work do you do?"

"Construction stuff, but they laid me off. I'm just living with a friend right now and sleeping on his couch until I can figure something out."

Nina jumped at the opportunity, and as the words slipped off her tongue, she added a little touch of spirit that made the offer sound more realistic, appealing and above all, completely natural. "What about painting? Do you paint houses too? I'm just starting a new bed-and-breakfast, out in this really quiet spot in Destrehan. It needs a little work and I'd been planning to do most of it myself, but painting isn't really my specialty. The last time I painted a room, the ceiling ended up looking like a Picasso."

"Yeah, you need something like painter's tape—stops you from painting places you don't want. If you need help, I could help you out."

"I could give you a room at the B-and-B, too, and you could be a little more comfortable while you finished up. No rush." In an ordinary world, under ordinary circumstances, the offer would have seemed quite peculiar, but this wasn't an ordinary world and Nina certainly was no ordinary person. Her connection to spirit and her ability to infuse words with the air of influence allowed her offer to come off sounding as common as someone asking a stranger for a cigarette on the street.

Leo began to nod in acceptance but had not entirely responded to her proposal.

"Why don't you come by next Monday, around noon? We can start then," Nina said, and at the same time, she realized that next Monday was the new moon. A perfect time to begin something new.

"Well, all right, then!" Leo said.

Nina gave him her contact information and made sure it was correctly stored in his new phone before she left.

Only a few more days until the new moon, and she still had four more people to secure. She returned home and gathered a few purple wildflowers, possibly weeds, from the backyard before the sun sank behind the trees. She knew the people's names, and within a few solid minutes of deep concentration, she knew the type of witch they were and what motivated them most. Nina kicked around a loose bit of grass in the backyard until there was nothing but a rusty brown patch of dirt and pebbles under her feet. On the back porch, next to the many empty flowerpots and planters, were a few wedges of old firewood. Three, to be exact. The wedges of wood were a sad trio—damp and termite ridden—that flaked away upon being grabbed, like a piece of well-cooked fish.

Nina carried the pieces of wood to the clearing she had made in the dirt and arranged them in a pattern closely resembling the letter *A*. She collected a box of matches and the grocery receipt from earlier, tore it into pieces and twisted it into long, pointed strands. The paper slipped in between the logs like thin white snakes, and Nina struck the head of the kitchen match as she recited the names she had learned earlier. The flickering yellow fire from the match caught the paper receipt and slithered down into the pile of wood. Nina raised her eyebrows in surprise as the wood caught fire faster than she'd expected. She quickly crumbled the purple flowers in her left hand and cast them into the fire.

Angels, ancestors, energies, light beings and guides, in love and light, I ask you to bring them to me for the good of all.

However it may be, make it their journey.

On the new moon, let us attune.

A guttural sound came from her throat as she finished her incantation. She closed her eyes and instantly fell into a trance. For a moment, she saw all that was about to happen. She knew what the universal life force energy would do to bring them to her. She had faith in spirit, and as her eyelids opened and her eyes cleared of the visions, she cleared her throat. Her voice was still deep and low. It was done. They were coming. She ruffled her hair and stared into the flames of the fire, the wedges of wood now crackling into pieces of orange ember. The evening sky darkened around her, and as the final log fell to pieces, she turned her back to the campfire and headed inside.

CHAPTER 4

The next few days passed as quickly and Nina added a few luxuries to the house to make it more of a home. Things like dimmer switches, pillar candles, a large chunk of rose quartz and some patterned throw pillows for the great room. She took it upon herself to refresh the bedding, and washed all the linens before everyone's arrival. The dampness of the southern air found its way into the sheets and left them uncomfortably clammy and heavy. The fresh bedding was soft and cozy, but it was significantly improved with a few sprays of an aromatherapy blend for insomnia. Traveling was always hard for Nina. It disrupted her sense of comfort and therefore upset her ability to sleep soundly. Her all-purpose insomnia mix was a blend she was proud of discovering a few years earlier and had been using ever since.

> Six drops clary sage
> Four drops vetiver
> Two drops valerian
> Four drops lavender
> Five drops ylang-ylang
> 1 Tbs. grapeseed oil
> ¼ c. witch hazel

Nina sprayed the atomizer three times over the surface of every pillow in each bedroom. The space was expertly prepared, and all that was left was to invite the members of the coven to stay. It wasn't going to be an easy task.

To begin with, these were members of her new magical family, not unassuming guests. Guests were people who were invited to a home or stayed at a hotel of some sort and eventually left. They weren't permanent residents—not usually, anyway. She supposed there was the occasional permanent resident in high-profile hotels—celebrities, artists or prestigious icons. She had known a few stars in her time, mostly old classmates, but the people on their way to her home were not celebrities. Further, these ordinary people had no intention of staying long term. They wouldn't be quick to assume that Nina was part of their new magical family, let alone accept without question the idea that they were in fact—witches. These guests were being led to her home to become part of a coven. They would all be leaving lives they might not want to leave and would be asked to be a part of something bigger, and the success of their union depended entirely on Nina's ability to convince them of it all.

The grandfather clock that stood next to the front door soundlessly struck noon. Nina had turned the switch that silenced the chime sequence that normally accompanied the top of every hour—it had proved to be disruptive to her meditation time. Perhaps she would change it once everyone arrived.

Nina had been sitting patiently in the great room with her legs crossed and hands clasped together over her lap. At the stroke of the hour, she stood tall in her black heels and straight-neck jumpsuit with its buttoned straps, patterned with large white and yellow flowers and ivy-green leaves. Her collarbones were exposed, apart from a single gold necklace with a large piece of raw quartz. Golden hoop earrings with a single piece of malachite hanging inside each hoop dangled over her smooth shoulders. She looked like a piece of chocolate cake covered in ganache, one of the really expensive slices from one of the fancy bakeries back in New York, where a single slice could easily cost more than admission to the Museum of Modern Art. Nina inhaled deeply and recognized the changes in the air. It smelled different, like magic—it smelled like witches.

An enthusiastic expression fell across her face as she moved to the front door. Her hand grabbed hold of the handle and she pulled the door toward her. The exchange of air rushed through her hair as she fixed her eyes on the cars driving down the driveway. A few cicadas buzzed in the trees outside, singing a song of welcome. She stepped out onto the front steps and closed the door behind her. A massive gust of hot air danced across the driveway and rippled the small puddles that lived alongside the path. Five cars made their way down toward the house where Nina stood gazing back at them. A few free-spirited leaves cast themselves into the air from the oak trees and over the windshields. Four of the cars, each carrying a passenger in the back seat, came to a standstill about thirty feet from where Nina stood. The fifth car had only a driver.

Moments later, the passengers exited the vehicles one by one, almost as if they had choreographed the whole thing. She recognized the man on the far left from the quarter the other day: Leo, a vape in his right hand and pressed tightly to his lips. A whirling crackle came from the device, and as he pulled it away from his face, his features were momentarily lost in the cloud of strawberry-custard smoke he blew from his mouth, opaque and fragrant. Nina jerked her eyes to the next car, where a woman much younger than expected squinted from the sun, the frizzy tips of her straw-colored hair blowing into her mouth. She smelled of sulfur, not from perfume but because of the power she possessed. Her skin was like cream, so youthful that it looked like it would spring back like a down pillow if pressed. Avery, Nina presumed, the traveler. The woman standing in the middle was dressed to impress with a sense of style that would have intimidated salespeople at Chanel. Nina recognized the same sharp cheekbones that she had seen before, cut like edges of a rock, tourmaline even. Where Nina was simple and natural, this woman was decorative and extraordinary. Bisa, Nina established.

Bisa removed her large sunglasses to reveal a pearlescent pop of canary yellow surrounding her eyes. She was more vibrant than anyone within a fifty-mile radius—five hundred, even. Nina blinked and turned her eyes toward the next person in line. A man in his early thirties, short, solid jet-black hair, slightly greasy or perhaps overconditioned. Brown eyes, scruffy beard and weighing in at about 145 pounds, which made up his entire unathletic, slender body. His face was symmetrical and ridiculously handsome. As for his clothes—an outfit of mismatched textures: burgundy socks, gray shoes, aquamarine cotton twill jogger pants and a smoky gray T-shirt with the sleeves cut off and in their place, spaghetti-thin white threads. That was Mitch.

The last on the right was the most entrancing of the men, slender yet fit, nourished both physically and spiritually. Another burst of wind swept over the driveway and carried the scent of Oliver toward Nina, the smell of cucumber and rain. His unruly, wavy locks, brown like a coconut shell with hues of light brown sugar, danced in the breeze and lit up his wide indigo eyes. He was dressed in all black, the light hitting his face and reflecting his generous spirit. Oliver rested somewhere in the balance between what one would consider masculine and feminine.

Nina pulled her lips back into a smile and nodded. "Welcome! I'm Nina. I'll be running the show around here."

Everyone waved and said hello as they retrieved their luggage. As the cars pulled away, apart from Leo's, the front lawn was littered with bags of various sizes and levels of wear.

"Everyone, please come inside," Nina said. "It's too hot to be standing out here, and we have so very much to talk about. Please." She backed up against the front door and pushed it open with her leg. "Make yourselves at home."

There was an exchange of looks between the members of the group, the kind of curious, exploratory look one often has when entering a new group situation like an unfamiliar classroom or a new gym. Leo was the first to grab his luggage, a tattered and oversized green duffel bag. He sucked his vape and walked past everyone else without making any eye contact. He wobbled into the house, his torso cranked to one side as he tried to balance the weight of his bag. He handled the load well even though it contained his entire life up until that point. Leo often resorted to doing things himself and usually with his bare hands. From working in construction, he had built up calluses on his palms. The toughness of his skin made it easy for him to handle his luggage, unlike the rest of the group, whose soft hands made it more of a struggle. Leo set his duffel bag inside the doorway and walked back outside. Bisa was stepping up on the front step with her pretty black suitcase when Leo blocked her path.

"Want some help with that one?" Leo asked. Without waiting for a response, he grabbed hold of the handle of Bisa's bag.

Slightly surprised at the unexpected help, she said, "Thank you!"

Within what Nina would have referred to as a New York minute, the house was filled with her new guests. Once they were all inside, she instructed them to leave their bags at the front and follow her into the great room. The house was quiet, and the sound of their footsteps echoed into the high ceilings. Nina glanced back behind her and saw the group members looking from side to side, soaking in their surroundings. In the quick instant that she looked over them, she could see that they were curious and fascinated with where they were. She had a distinct impression that the house wasn't anything like they expected, and neither were the other people. She smiled and, with a sharp twist of her neck, turned her head back toward the great room. Nina remained silent but kept her smile warm as she placed herself in the center of the room. Her hands lifted into the air, and with open palms, she pointed at the plush couches and chairs, an open invitation for them to be seated. She hadn't fully considered what she was going to say. After everyone had situated themselves comfortably, she cleared her throat.

"Welcome to the Barrow House. I appreciate all of you being here, and very soon I will show you to your rooms and get you checked in. First, I'd like to give you a little general information about the house. It's small here, as you may have noticed on your way in. We can accommodate only a few people during our season, and all of you are very lucky to…be a part of this. I know you all probably have a lot of questions, and understandably so. Before I get into some details, I will address all your questions, and I'll probably have a few answers to questions you didn't even know you had." Nina studied their faces, trying to determine what each of them was thinking. For a brief moment, her mind tuned into the ether, and she could feel each of their emotions and thoughts.

Nina clapped her hands. "I'd like to start with something I like to call *celebrations*." It was a ritual she had learned during the daily corporate meetings at a leadership conference a few years back when she was fresh out of Yale. She found the exercise quite useful in place of an icebreaker.

Leo shuffled forward on the couch. "Should I..." he said, motioning with his thumb to the back room.

Nina shook her head. "Oh no, please stay. This is for you too."

Leo stared back at her and began biting his nonexistent nails.

"So, thank you all for making it here in this crazy heat. I hope everyone is comfortable and cool. Let's start with the celebrations! All of you are from different parts of the country and have different interests and backgrounds, and I can safely say you have different perspectives on things. That will become very important going forward, because it will be a challenge for us—for all of us—to work together."

The thoughts were scattered among the group members. Bisa thought Nina was too wordy and that perhaps the others were less skilled with makeup and color than she was. To Avery, Nina's speech smelled suspicious, and she suspected she had been led astray somehow. She had trusted her spirit, which she would call her gut, when her hostel had accidentally and puzzlingly canceled her booking reservation and then offered her a full week's stay at a bed-and-breakfast just outside the city as consolation. Mitch, with his background in liquor production, thought he was going to learn a fresh way to blend mindfulness with alcohol distillation from a company that had probably been founded by hipsters with a bunch of cash and even more conceptual ideas. Oliver heard his own voice in his head, asking, *What the hell is this?*

"So, let's begin," Nina burst out. "I'd like to go around the room and have you say your name and where you're from, and add a celebration. By that I mean I'd like you to say something about someone else here—something positive about them. Make it special, make it unique. Step outside the box and beyond the limitations you have already set in your mind since I've given you this instruction."

"I don't know anyone here," Leo said, and laughed. A few others nodded in agreement, baffled by what they could possibly say about strangers they had barely introduced themselves to.

"Nobody here does," Nina said. "Relax, breathe into your mind and pay attention to what you hear."

Yup, this is totally a new-age attempt at a distillation workshop, Mitch thought to himself.

"I'll start," Bisa said candidly as she raised her hand high into the air.

"Beautiful," Nina exclaimed.

Bisa smiled and sat up tall. Her eyes scanned the group for a moment until she verbalized the first thing that came into her head. "I don't fully know if this is what you're looking for, but…"

"Don't question it. Say what you feel!" Nina said.

"I'm Bisa, and I live in Chicago. I'm a—well, I'm many things, but professionally, I'm a makeup artist. I'm excited to see what new things I will learn in the workshop." Confusion drifted across everyone's face. "I didn't even catch his name, but when I was carrying my bags up toward the house, he came back out and helped me carry them inside. That was helpful and really nice. I don't remember the last time someone has offered to help with bags without being paid to do it." She looked over at Leo. "I still don't know your name, I'm sorry."

"Leo," he said, and then shot her a tight-lipped smile.

"Leo. Nice. Short for Leonardo?" Bisa asked.

"Nope. Just Leo."

Bisa looked into his eyes and nodded. "Cool."

"That's a good start, Bisa, thank you," Nina replied.

Mitch raised his hand and said, "My name's Mitch. Mitchell. But I go by Mitch. I was born in California, and I've lived all over the place. Right now, I live in Salt Lake. I get bored a lot, and so, like, I try to, like, keep up with my ever-changing interests and I'll just dive into something new and start something different. I was studying art therapy for a while. I'm sure some of you can tell I have a sort of...imaginative temperament." He laughed and then continued with his rapid-fire momentum. "Um, the body has always fascinated me, just how it works and how it, like, functions and everything, so I started going to school for chiropractic care, but some things fell through and a job kind of landed in my lap working for a distillery, and yeah, that's kind of where I've been and what I've been doing."

Mitch scratched his arm nervously. "I crochet a lot too. Like, whole outfits sometimes. And even for trees, like, outfits for tree trunks sometimes. I really like doing that." There was a short pause before he continued enthusiastically, "I'd like to celebrate this girl over here." He pointed to Avery. "I'm really, really into your energy." Then a moment later, "I can just tell that you have a sort of natural drive to live your own truth and you seem really, like, guided toward, like, the higher good. It's like…" Another sudden start and stop as he began to fidget with his fingers and expand his arms as if trying to expel words from his chest. "I don't really…" Another pause. "I don't know where that's coming from, and I don't really have anything to, like, back it up or anything." Another break. More finger gestures. Wider arm expansions. Suddenly he pulled his arms back in and crossed his legs, settling on a thought. "But I can tell you're a really aware and empathetic person, and that's really cool. I know I sound crazy, but it's just what's going on in my brain." He laughed.

"Those feelings and thoughts are valid, not crazy," Nina reminded him.

"I guess I'll go next?" Avery said. "First, thank you, that's really cool to hear. My name's Avery, from Wisconsin. I travel a lot, I kind of let myself go where I want and when I want and trust that my gut won't steer me wrong. I have trust aplenty in my gut." She pulled her hair, which was sandy blond and snowy white in places, into a messy ponytail with an effortless swoosh of her hands. A few pieces fell forward over her ears and across her cheek. She inhaled and stared into space as if conjuring up what she was about to say out of thin air. "I'd like to celebrate this woman with all this style—Bisa. Beautiful skin, confident, wears clothes I could never pull off. You smell amazing too. I don't know what that is, but it's pretty great."

Nina looked over toward Oliver. "How about you? Oliver, right?"

"Yeah, or Ollie. No one really calls me Oliver except my parents. Well, some people do. I live in L.A. I was born in Argentina, but we moved to California when I was three. I'm a pretty curious guy. Whether it gets me into trouble or brings me to something really fascinating or leads me to break my leg, it doesn't matter, I'm just naturally inquisitive. I find life and people really interesting, so if I don't delve deeper into things, I get bored." His eyes drifted to the center of the room and fixed on the emptiness there. His head flicked back and forth as he organized his thoughts. "I really love photography and being able to be part of a collective for an exhibition, so I just feel lucky that I'm able to be here and do that. So, I'd like to thank you, Nina, for allowing this whole thing to happen. I'd like to celebrate your vision of this whole experience and seeking people out who have that same sort of vibe." He looked at Nina with his big eyes, brows raised, forehead creased with expression. "I'm actually really interested to see what happens here, in this landscape for me, because it's so new. Lately, I've been doing this thing, unintentionally, where I will take a nap or find myself daydreaming or something and I'll start thinking of new angles to shoot or ways to shoot something differently, and then I'll go and do that. Some of the best pictures I've ever taken have come out of doing that, so I'm really curious to see what will happen here in a totally new place in a new part of the world for me. Especially with the collaborative group part, and seeing what kind of improvisation and collaboration comes out of working with strangers."

The room was silent, but there was enough internal chatter among the group that they could have drowned each other out had they actually been speaking. Oliver looked over the faces of everyone he thought was there for a photography workshop, but their expressions told him something different.

Nina cleared her throat and broke the silence. "Leo, would you please wrap up the celebrations for us with yours?"

"Do I really have to do this? I mean, I'm not—"

"I would really appreciate your input," Nina interrupted. "Please, Leo."

Leo leaned back in his seat, shook his head and let out a sigh. He lifted his right hand to his mouth and bit at the nail bed of his middle finger as he thought. There were people who bit their nails and people who ate their nails. Leo was one of the latter. For years he had done it out of an anxious habit, as a way to use up excess energy. It eventually spread to his feet and picking at his toenails, sometimes clipping them and eating the clippings. There had been quite a bit of nail biting since he'd sat down in this room full of people he had nothing in common with, and now he was being put on the spot.

With his wide-open, bewildered eyes, completely confused about what he was going to celebrate, he scanned the faces of everyone present. Each person stared back at him, waiting for him to speak or spit out the piece of nail he was rolling between his teeth and across his tongue.

"You know, I'd like to celebrate this guy, Mitch," he said finally. "He seems like a cool guy. I don't think I've ever met someone quite like you before." Leo leaned all the way back into his seat as if he had finally accomplished something he hadn't been sure he'd be able to do. He spread his legs wide, taking up more space than necessary to make sure he was comfortable.

"All right, thank you, everyone," Nina said with a smile. "I think we should be able to get started now."

"Excuse me," Avery said as she raised her hand high in the air, stopping Nina's words in their tracks. "I have a lot of questions. I thought this was a bed-and-breakfast. It is, right?" Her words came out in crackly sputters.

Leo nodded: he had been told it was a bed-and-breakfast and that he would be painting it. A scoff-like laugh rose up out of Mitch's throat before he spoke. "What? Wait." He laughed again and shook his head. "What? I thought this was a distillation workshop. Isn't that what, um, everyone is here for? Or, what's going on?"

"I don't even know what distillation is," Leo said.

Bisa lifted her chest and straightened her spine. "So, this isn't the makeup workshop then, either…right?"

"Makeup?" Oliver questioned.

The room began to rile up, and a murmur of questions and anxiety filled the space.

"What are we doing here? What is this?" Bisa asked while moving to the edge of her seat as if ready to pounce, seize Nina's throat and demand answers.

In a loud but controlled tone, Nina said, "I can explain everything. All of you came for something very different…" She paused, broke through her apprehension and stood up confidently. "This is not any of those things."

"I knew there was something wrong when I was told about this place, I just knew it," Avery hollered.

Everyone began to shout and talk over one another so much that no one could discern what anyone else was actually saying. Oliver and Bisa stood up to grab their bags and leave.

"It is something *more* and something that I think each of you will appreciate once you fully understand why you're here. This is not a trick," Nina bellowed.

"Then what is this?" Bisa asked as she turned around toward Nina with a dagger-like gaze, hands on her hips.

"Let me explain. Everyone, please calm down!" Nina demanded.

"Don't tell me what to do," Bisa responded, pointing at her chest.

Nina stiffened, and her eyes mirrored Bisa's intense stare. "Sit. Let me explain."

Bisa paced toward Nina, her steps steady and slow, her hands curled up against her side. "Do not…tell me what to do."

"You are all here to—"

Bisa raised her voice and repeated her words, so swollen with defiance that she seemed about to burst. "Do not tell me what to do!"

"I'm here to help all of you," Nina said.

"What is this? I'm about to…" Mitch trailed off.

"Are you just going to leave?" Nina asked, and then turned to Bisa.

Oliver chimed in, "Why are we here?"

Bisa began to realize how enraged she had become at the rug being pulled out from underneath her. She stared directly at Nina. "Tell us the truth."

Nina walked back toward the center of the room and turned to face all of them. She put her hands together in front of her chest as if in prayer and then began to speak. "All of you have something in common, and that is why you're here. This is not a distillation workshop, and we won't be learning about makeup techniques or photography. We will be learning things, and at its core, it will be art, like all of those things that brought you here in the first place. But it will be honest, and it will be unique, and it will be sensational and fantastical. Above all, it will be magical, because each of you has a gift and was brought here to explore it, develop it, and understand its limitations, dangers, rules and reasons for it being yours to begin with. This is not a house designed for a bed-and-breakfast, although you will be staying here if you choose to do so. You aren't a prisoner and are free to leave, but I guarantee you will want to stay."

Mitch stood up and held out his hands in front of him. "I was really trying to invite something new into my life, and I was gonna, like, give myself a pat on the back for moving forward with something and start to work, but, like, what are you even talking about?"

"You are a witch, Mitch," Nina said forcefully.

Avery's mouth opened, and she lowered her voice and leaned toward Oliver. "Did she just call him a bitch?"

"No—Mitch…That's his name."

Mitch laughed, rubbed his palms over his forehead and spun around on his heels. "What? Okay, I don't know about all of you, but this woman is crazy and I'm going to leave right now, before she starts to slice us up and put us in the oven. People do that sort of thing. I see weird shit like that all the time on the news and I don't intend to be one of them, so, who wants to, like, share an Uber, because I'm not gonna be stuck here. And I also can't afford it all on my own."

"And so are you, Bisa," Nina continued. "And you, Oliver. Leo. Avery. All of you. You were brought here to form a coven and work together to bring about balance with the gifts you all have. And I know that resonates with some of you, because at some point, very recently, something occurred that you couldn't explain. There's more of that to come, only I can explain and offer you some answers, and a home, and a family without judgment, one based on nurturing and understanding yourselves and the greater good. We have a purpose. Together, we create change, and it will echo out into the world."

"Sounds a little culty," Leo quipped.

"It's not a cult, it's a coven. And I'm guessing the reason that all of you haven't walked right out that front door with your things is that what I'm saying makes sense to you."

Bisa let her arms down and took a few steps back. "What gifts are you talking about?"

"You, Bisa, and Oliver as well, have very spiritual gifts, and empathetic ones. Granted, we are all empathetic and psychic beings, but you two have a little more of that inside of you." Nina squinted as if she were trying to read something far away in the distance. "Bisa, you most recently had a string of incidents that you knowingly embraced and tested. The first involved a woman with a short stubby nose and a moony face. She didn't like you, just because you were black. She didn't say it, but you felt it, you heard it. You hesitated for a moment when she began to become difficult when you helped her pick out the skin care products she wanted, but then it happened, am I right? It was like a prodigy playing Beethoven effortlessly when they had never played the piano before in their entire life. But you knew you had control, you felt it, you knew you held sway over her decisions, her impulses. You led her to buy the whole damn line of, what was it"—Nina kept her head fixed, but her eyes flickered to the ceiling as if the answer were above her— "Kiehl's. Right?"

Bisa's jaw began to fall like a rusty drawbridge, slowly but surely. "Yes."

"The next was another woman, the same day, maybe half an hour later. A woman who never wore makeup, never knew anything about beauty at all, just wandered into your store and you found her browsing. You weren't just a helpful employee—you felt it. You felt her sadness, her pain, her wanting to see the beauty in herself but not being able to do it.

It wasn't about the makeup you applied. You did a full face, and although it was"—Nina smiled and visualized the woman's face—"resplendent, you infused something into her astral field. Sure, the beauty enchantment went on to attract what she wanted to attract—which was self-worth, by the way, not men—and she began to build confidence in herself and take care of herself for the first time in a long while. She nourished her soul. Not because of what eye shadow you sent her home with or the foundation you applied to her face, but because you willed it to be so, because you wanted her to heal."

Bisa's face tightened as if something were caught in her throat. "It's true. All of it. I knew I felt something. It was different. I felt different."

Nina nodded and then turned to Oliver, "You, handsome man, are already way in touch with the divine. It may sound like you're talking to yourself from time to time, but you know what you hear in your head isn't just random chitchat. You have one hand in this world and another dipped into the spirit world. You were sitting having coffee when you learned about what you thought was a workshop, and as you tapped your finger on the coffee mug and stared out into space, you asked yourself if you should do this. The answer wasn't just yes—it came to you like a premonition, didn't it? A flash of emotion that you associated with something good coming out of you going to the workshop, and then you heard it. You heard a voice, and it said, *Your soul needs this*. You heard those very words, didn't you?"

Suddenly a strong, earthy and fresh aroma, rich like perfume, filled Avery's nose. "Would it be crazy if I said I could smell that you're telling the truth?" Avery asked Nina.

Nina slowly rotated to face Avery. "Green? Leathery? Woodsy?"

Avery's face was excited and amazed. "Yes! I don't know how to describe it, or why green comes to mind, but it does. It smells green, and like tobacco and tree bark!"

"*Evernia prunastri*—oakmoss. That's what you're smelling. I can't smell it—not many witches can—but that is for sure one of your many talents."

Avery shook her head in disbelief. "I've smelled it four times in the past month. The first few times it happened, I thought it was just something in the air. Then I got to talking to some girl at this yoga class I was at, and she told me she was forty, and I didn't believe her, she looked so young. But then I smelled it…that"—she sniffed and inhaled deeply a few times—"that…smell. I didn't believe her! Her skin, face—everything about her screamed she was not a day over thirty at the most. And she pulled out her driver's license, and there it was, clear as day, the truth. She was forty. I hated her for a minute, but then I loved her again. I mean, I considered it some kind of weird fluke, but then I noticed it kept happening more and more. I knew when people were telling the truth even when I doubted them, and I couldn't tell anyone about it or I would seem crazy. But if that's what this is, then I'm staying." She took another deep sniff and then her eyes opened as wide as the sky is vast. "What does a lie smell like?"

"Because the spectrum of lies is so vast, and emotional distress and emotional intelligence factor into how it's formulated, it's incredibly difficult to determine what a lie smells like. If I knew, I would tell you," Nina assured her.

"Man, what a bunch of bullshit!" Leo said. He looked at Avery and Nina, his eyes full of both contempt and alarm. "You can't smell the truth!"

Avery ignored Leo and threw out another question. "Why does it smell like that?"

"Derived from Old English. Its roots, no pun intended, are from what the word *true* looked like and was pronounced like some thousand years ago. *Trēow*, meaning good faith, trust...and also, tree. The origins of these meanings stem from some of the first representations of the notion and theory of truth itself, which is associated with the uprightness of a strong, solid oak tree."

Leo laughed and turned his tart, skeptical expression back to Nina. "No, it's not, dude! How long did it take you to think of that one?"

"A few of these species are still standing strong and upright, and those roots are more than five thousand—hell, even more than eighty thousand years old if my math is right," Nina said. "Prophets, painters, philosophers and poets dating back to the origin of mankind have sought answers in the trees, worshipped them, written stories about them, treated them as a sacred home for spirits. They have stood the test of time and survived the moods of Mother Nature and even worse, humans. Yet even now, they stand steady and straight, tall as buildings and with more honor than those who continually mow them down to make room for another Lululemon store or block of high-rise condos. I'm telling you now, everything I'm telling you now, about all of you, is the truth."

There was a fleeting moment of silence followed by a buzz of cicadas from the trees outside.

Avery took a deep breath, held it, and then exhaled through her mouth. "She's telling the truth. I can...smell it...but I just can't believe it."

"There is no way that you can smell whether she is telling the truth! Okay?" Leo said. "Truth doesn't have a smell. The only thing that smells is that bullshit story."

Oliver took a few steps forward and shoved his way into the conversation. "Test her." He looked at Avery and then over at Leo, enthused over the exchange. "Tell her something. Something that only you would know to be true or not. That way she can tell us if you're telling the truth, and if she can't, then we know it's just all in her head and it's the power of suggestion and we can all go from there."

The idea made sense. It would undoubtedly prove whether Avery could, in fact, detect the smell of things that others could not, if she really could smell what could not be smelled. And if she could do that, is that where it ended? What were her limitations? Could she see what was not seen? Could she feel things that others could not?

"Avery? Are you up for this?" Nina questioned with one eyebrow arched.

A slow, exaggerated jaw-drop was the only way Avery could manage to respond for what seemed like ten minutes but in reality was only a few seconds. "What? I learned only a few seconds ago that this was even a thing! I didn't even know what oakmoss was, and now I'm suddenly being asked to perform like some kind of trained dog on command. Like, *Speak, Avery! Roll over, Avery! Good girl—you won best in show!* What if I can't even do this?"

"You can; you just did," Nina said soothingly. "No one is going to force you to do anything you don't feel comfortable with. But if you prove Leo wrong, it will help all of us settle in with each other that much more easily."

"I got three for you already," Leo quipped.

The three statements—which Leo gathered in a matter of seconds, as if he had been prepared for this to happen—were so far-fetched that he hadn't even considered that they might seem too outrageous to be true, even to a complete stranger.

"Okay. Fine. I'll do it," Avery said with a new wind of confidence.

Leo patted Avery's shoulder condescendingly. "You sure now? You don't need to blow your nose or anything? Clear out those sinuses? There's a lot riding on this!"

Avery stood unimpressed, stoic and silent.

"Nothing? Not even a smile?" Leo asked.

"Ask," Avery said lifelessly.

Leo nodded, laced his fingers together and cracked his knuckles with a slow bend of his fingers before crossing his arms tightly in front of his chest. Eyelids half closed, head cocked back and slightly toward his shoulder, legs spread wide, he said, "I'm Canadian."

As quickly as his statement rolled off his tongue, Avery responded like the crack of a whip. "Lie."

Leo fired his second shot. "I've never had a cavity."

Again, like lightning, "Lie."

Nina rolled her eyes and tossed a chunk of hair that had fallen over her cheek. "Something deeper, more personal."

Leo changed his third statement and continued with another proclamation. "My daughter's name is Krystal."

The silence before the storm fell across the plains of Avery's lips, and she hesitated before answering. She closed her mouth, lifted her head ever so slightly and inhaled deeply enough to catch the scent of oakmoss in the air between her and Leo. For a brief moment, she thought it could be the scent of something else, maybe something he had eaten or whatever dessert-like vape juice he had been sucking on. At first sniff, she second-guessed herself, but then she quickly and confidently decided that what she was smelling was in fact what she had known it to be many times before when she heard the truth, that bright and lively scent. "Truth."

"Well, that one was obvious!" Leo said.

Mitch spoke. "How was that obvious?"

"Because, dude, she made it seem like I needed to throw her something she would be able to sniff out! So yeah, of course the next one is going to be something that smells like what she says it does."

"Again," Nina demanded politely.

"I had Cheetos for breakfast."

Sniff.

"True."

"I have fifty-two cents in my pocket."

Sniff.

"Not true."

Nina pointed to Leo's pocket. "Empty your pockets."

Leo dug his hands into each pocket, pulled them out and revealed a sizable mass of lint, a starlight mint, two quarters, one dime and three pennies.

"One more," Leo said, hoping that he sounded like more of a good sport than he actually was.

"I thought we were only doing three," Avery said.

Leo continued, "What was the last sickness I had?"

"I'm not psychic!"

"Okay, one more. It was scarlet fever, by the way."

"Scarlet fever? Really?" Avery mocked.

"Yeah, dude!"

"What were your symptoms?"

"A headache," Leo answered quickly. Avery and Mitch exchanged a few puzzled looks before Leo cleared his throat with the intensity of a garbage disposal.

"One more," Nina interrupted.

"No—screw this," Avery said. "Let me ask *him* a question and *he* can answer. It's only fair, since he keeps testing me and testing me like I'm making all of this up!"

"Go ahead," Leo said, and he took a deep drag from his vape.

"Do you know what scarlet fever is?"

"Fuck yeah, dude! I told you I had it."

Sniff.

"Lie!" Avery burst out.

"Fuck!"

"All right, enough," Nina said authoritatively. "Those aren't the only gifts here. Mitch, you have perfect eyesight, am I right? Your parents couldn't see a flashlight at midnight between the two of them without their glasses, but you can see beyond perfect vision. Sharp. Alarmingly clear and exact."

"Well, sure, I can see pretty well, but I don't see how that is, like, a power or anything. Lots of people can see!" Mitch responded.

"That's not an ability, but rather a side effect or benefit of being a certain type of witch. It's a bonus. Most of your senses are heightened and have become stronger and more intense lately. But that isn't what's puzzling to you, is it? That probably just seems like a fun bonus, but what really has you wondering if this is all real is your gift with animals. You've always lived on the periphery of your peers, constantly misunderstood, overlooked and mocked when you were just being the only way you knew how to be, which is entirely yourself—which, frankly, is more important in the grand scheme of things. Yet as you continued to float from job to job, regretting your decisions, constantly questioning your purpose, you told yourself that you've done many things except experience success. Which is only because the one area that you haven't explored hasn't been available to you, the one that would allow you to be fulfilled beyond what any career or relationship would ever be able to do."

Mitch sat quietly and gaped at the story unfolding from Nina's mouth. His skepticism was slowly fading and being replaced with validation. Nina's sizzling words blazed right through his doubt. He didn't want to chance sending her off course by saying something that would deny what he had been seeking for months now—an answer to the mystifying occurrences that had entered his life recently. Instead, he tried to think of all the incidents that had caused him to question everything he knew, all the strange happenings that contradicted what he knew to be reality. If the next words out of Nina's mouth could detail what he thought was a psychotic episode, then he could rejoice and embrace it and perhaps be as fulfilled as she promised he would be. His blood pulsed in his ears, which felt like two throbbing microphones desperately waiting to pick up sound.

"You must have thought you were crazy," Nina continued. "Maybe even started to believe everything that people had been telling you all these years—that you were nothing more than an eccentric hipster in a colorful, crocheted festival coat. But I cannot tell you how soothing your gift can be for everyone, especially when you're so misunderstood by so many of those around you."

"Is anyone else still waiting for her to specify what the hell she's talking about?" Leo barked, as he would when things were out of his control and he was no longer able to quell his anxiety.

"First, the birds: it started with the bush near your apartment window, which was cluttered with about a dozen birds. Every morning they chirped and chatted and woke you up. Even if you shouted, banged pots and tried to scare them off, they never shut up. Then you told them you had a headache and you needed them to be quiet, and just like that, they stopped. Then the stray cat that came to visit you outside work. You could feel what it was thinking, you could *communicate* with it."

"So he can read their minds? He can read animals' minds?" Leo said darkly.

"I said communicate. He's not a mind reader. He can hear their thoughts in a nonverbal way. Like when you know someone very well and you can understand what they're thinking just by looking them in the eye. It's like that." She turned to Mitch and could see that he believed her. She watched a wave of validation roll over his face. "The cat told you he liked strawberry ice cream, not vanilla. You tested it and set a pint of both in front of him one day, and he stuck one greedy little fat paw in the melting pint of strawberry. You chatted back and forth—well, so to speak—for days, and then he said you should take this opportunity in Louisiana…and that's why *you're* here."

Mitch didn't dare contradict or challenge Nina, because she was right. He let out a gentle sigh, too precious to mean anything other than he felt understood and, above that—seen. He no longer had to worry about being insane or living under a bridge as an outcast who talked to animals. It was legit. Heavy silence remained in the air after Nina finished speaking, and everyone seemed afraid to break it with their voice. When a fair amount of time had passed, not unlike the time a comedian waits after delivering a joke to let the audience laugh, Nina tossed her humidified hair as far as she could behind her shoulder. Tapping into the higher consciousness was exhausting, and she had grown tired, yet she remained steadfast.

"Now, Mister Leo. Of all the people in this room, you give off the most puzzling aura. We are in a sort of magical crisis. That is why all of us have come together, to cooperate and create something better. We have to extrapolate from our world what is really going on to make a difference. You're stubborn, skeptical and hot-headed." Nina walked toward the fireplace and picked up a bundle of white sage. She walked over to Leo, controlling her impatience, and held the bundle out away from her chest. "Light this for me."

"I never have a lighter on me anymore. I vape."

"Not with that. Set fire to it like you did to that bundle of rags in the wheelbarrow."

Leo backed up a few steps. "What the fu—"

"Everyone thought you were careless and accidentally set the rags on fire, but was it really an accident, Leo?"

"It was! I didn't set fire to them! I didn't have any matches, no lighter, nothing! I don't know how the fuck that fire happened!"

"So, what did happen?" Nina inched the bundle of sage closer to Leo.

"I chucked my fuckin' rag into the pile and it caught fire like outta nowhere!"

"It was you, Leo. Your energy manifested the fire. Your intention, albeit ill-guided, willed it into being."

"Should we really be encouraging this?" Mitch hissed. "We're in a wooden house surrounded by, like, flammable everything. What if he, like, misses and, like, I catch on fire?"

"You're already flamin', aren't you, Sally?" Leo said, and then laughed at himself.

"Grow up," said Bisa as she walked toward Nina.

"Quiet, everyone!" Nina shouted. "Leo, concentrate on the tip of the bundle."

"Just the tip?"

Nina rolled her eyes, clucked her tongue and shook her head. "I know it sounds crazy, but focus your intention, imagine what you want, manifest it into being."

Leo took a deep drag from his vape, held his breath for a tick and then exhaled artfully toward the smudge stick. The plumes of sweet-smelling smoke curled toward the tip of the sage bundle, and when the smoke hit the top, there was a crackle and pop, followed by a tiny fizzle, then a flame. A solid, healthy, bright orange flame ate away at the dried leaves in Nina's steady hand.

"Dude, what the fuck!" Leo shouted.

Nina tilted her body backward and flipped an armful of hair behind her shoulder with conviction. "All right..." she said firmly, "there's a lot of ground to cover, so if we're done playing *This Bitch Is Crazy,* we can actually get started and you can get some answers." Nina crossed her arms in front of her chest, grasping each biceps tightly. "Things are going to be very different from this point on, and we all have a lot to learn if we are going to survive." A lengthy pause and a heavy tension filled the air. "Now…" she began, squinting, "who wants some iced tea?"

CHAPTER 5

Shortly after they had cooled their anxieties with some iced tea—unsweetened—Nina softened her hands with some lotion, sat down in the largest of the gray armchairs and took some time to read their expressions before she began to speak.

"The Barrow House, where you are now, is very old, but pretty well maintained—well, at least in comparison to many other buildings in the area. It came into being under the ownership of Olivia Barrow, a widow with several children, when she and her children began building homes and large plantations around 1800. Shortly afterward it was sold to a nearby sugarcane farmer and was in his family's possession until it went up for auction after the last legal heir had passed. The house was bought by a man named, ironically, Arthur Barrow, unrelated to the previous owners. He bought the house in 1979 but never lived in it. It's known as the Barrow House among the locals. When he finally passed two years ago, it was bought by Nix De La Fuente, a member of the Advisory, of which I am also a part."

"What's the Advisory?" Bisa inquired, her legs crossed, the fingers of her right hand delicately brushing her chin as her left hand clasped a sweating, half-full glass of iced tea.

"The Advisory is a small group of witches who govern and, in a way, oversee the use and education of magic." Nina adjusted herself in the chair and sat up straight. "We strive to uphold natural spiritual law—the law of balance—which at its crux is the balance of all aspects of life in our world. Groups of witches, which are called covens, are formed to help concentrate the magical output as a collective. It's a way to augment our power. The covens should have some sort of leader, or one a little wiser than the rest to help guide—not necessarily a master of any sort, just someone who knows a little more than everyone else. There are, of course, solitary witches, ones who have no interest in or are unable to become part of a coven. It's surely not for everyone, like this heat."

"Seriously," Mitch scoffed.

Nina closed her eyelids as if doing so allowed her to hide from all tones of mocking and hot-headedness. When she reopened them, she continued, "It's not for everyone, but there are many benefits to a coven."

Avery clicked her tongue and asked blandly, "Like what?" as if she were intrigued by the idea but not completely sold on it, and didn't want to give the impression that she was totally interested.

Nina brushed a cloud of hair away from her temple and tussled it a few times in her hand before letting it live its own life free of control. "Well, there's always the advantage of being around people who are having the same experiences as you, who have the same questions as you. People with whom you can share your experiences and discuss or even debate your beliefs. Covens, like the one I am asking all of you to form here, is about acceptance, a place where we can feel safe and valued. No judgment—only support."

Leo felt a cynical grin grow across his face. "A self-help group."

Nina jabbed back, "Community."

Leo's toothy grin, with its slightly tobacco-stained enamel, grew wider. "A cult."

Nina looked back at Leo coolly. "Spiritual family."

"Groupies."

"A coven," Nina finished stiffly.

Nina assumed Leo's wordplay was only a cover-up for his defeatism, masking itself as derision. "There is nothing fanatical about a coven," she said. "Witches aren't obsessives or holy rollers or devoted extremists. We aren't trying to bomb something in the name of some irrelevant god or archaic belief. Covens have a purpose and a place in this world."

Leo's face looked uncomfortable—pained, even. Definitely put in his place.

Oliver cleared his throat and said, "So the celebrations thing we did earlier? Was that like some sort of initiation thing?"

"That's entirely different," Nina said thickly. "The celebrations exercise was something I felt would help encourage a bond between us all early on. The energy of celebrating something, celebrating each other, can positively bend our reality. We are so conditioned to celebrate something only when we reach some sort of milestone or goal…instead of realizing that we are alive, we are part of this mystical universe and get to participate in something so fleeting, yet so special. In the grand scheme of the entire universe, we as humans don't have the role our egos think we do. We mean so little and so much at the same time. Forcing that glitch in your expectations of what you thought would happen brought you closer to that celebratory frequency that lets in joy and pushes out fear and judgment. It began the acclimation process to this new level of being, which, whether you like it or not, you all now have."

Leo slid forward on the couch. His butt was a little numb from having sat in the same spot since he'd finished his iced tea. But more importantly, Leo had no idea what Nina was talking about, and the more she tried to explain, the more his willingness to understand slipped away. The bewilderment on everyone's face seemed to spread faster than any of them had anticipated. The rug of reality had been pulled out from underneath them, and they were all left scrambling for something solid to hold on to. As their guard walls melted away slowly, Nina got to see a glimpse of each of their true selves. They began to change the way they asked questions, and loosened up.

"Why now? Why all of a sudden are these *powers* surfacing?" Bisa asked.

"Well," Nina said as she exhaled a deep breath, the same way she did in the middle of the night when she couldn't sleep and had been staring at the ceiling for hours, "a lot of it has to do with gravitational pull. Our world—the universe—works with balance. It's all very scientific, and sometimes I have a hard time truly remembering all the specifics of it. Earth tides and terrestrial tides affect the entire earth's mass. The earth's crust shifts in response to lunar and solar gravitation and ocean tides."

Leo, a bona fide astronomy nerd, began to tune in to what Nina was saying. Magic seemed fictional, but science was real. He stopped biting his nails and opened his ears, waiting for Nina to say something that didn't make sense or that he could disprove, but also taking note of what she said, in case it actually did make sense.

"Now, these tidal forces, they generate currents in conducting fluids that are in the earth's interior. They, in turn, affect the earth's magnetic field. Tides can affect and cause all sorts of things. They can even trigger earthquakes. The earth tides affect the earth energetically and physically in all directions—north, south, east and west—which is normal and nonmagical, but it all comes back to being in balance. What we do has a vibration. What everyone and everything on this planet does emits a vibration, and those vibes carry with it a sort of—charge. Positive and negative, like the sides of a battery." Nina held out her hands and wiggled her index fingers back and forth as if signaling the sides of a battery. "Our world, our species, we as humans, are out of balance, and it's getting worse. There will always be light with dark, but the darkness that is manifesting on this planet right now is getting worse by the day. Think about it. Think about the hate, the anger, the ignorance. Murder, poverty, power, greed. It's all connected. It affects the whole."

The group was hooked, even Leo, the most skeptical of them.

"The poor honeybees. Our whole ecosystem is being thrown off because of the pollutants and pesticides we create. What happens as a result of that—that simple decline in the number of bees?" She felt a bit like an elementary teacher giving a pop quiz to her students—like the kind of teacher who is passionate about things her students couldn't care less about, like famine, deforestation and extinction. "Many crops are no longer being pollinated." Nina paused a moment. "Everything is made of energy—even things that are solid, right? This chair, for example. That glass in your hand. It's all made of energy. All fruits, nuts and vegetables are made of energy and radiate at different frequencies, much like possessing different nutrients. When there is a sudden drop in the number of bees, there is a drop in pollination, which means there is a drop in the amount of food produced, which means there is—"

"An energetic imbalance," Leo finished.

Nina glanced over at Leo and nodded warmly. "That affects the energy in certain areas. Energy can't really be created or wiped out; it can only change from one form to another. A few months ago, the energy on this planet shifted and fell way the hell out of balance. That's probably when you all noticed your gifts. That isolated gravitational pull was the tipping point, and it triggered a gene in our bodies, making us magically inclined."

Mitch sat still and expressionless. "Wait. So, everyone, like, on this planet, is a witch? Like, even my mom?"

"No," Nina said patiently. "Not everyone. It's a gene in the human body—not all humans—that is dormant. That gene is what allows us to have these gifts. It is in our cells, but it doesn't actively affect the body until it is triggered." Nina could tell this was an overwhelming amount of information for them to soak in, and she remembered when she first heard it herself. It all seemed like material from an insanely detailed fiction novel. She, however, had had the luxury of being led into this world step by step, slowly over time. These people were being thrown into a new way of living faster than gasoline can catch fire. "When the gene is activated, it's like plugging in a hair dryer. It's not on, but it has power. That energetic tipping point is like being plugged in. Turning the hair dryer *on* comes when you're triggered. It kind of functions like a virus, the triggering aspect. It can be activated by stress, changes in temperature, menstruation and even everyday things like exposure to sunlight. It's different for everyone."

There wasn't much debate over whether this was accurate— for Oliver, anyway. It seemed to make complete sense in a way that he couldn't explain. It was as if he had heard it before, although that was impossible. He hadn't heard this information before, yet it was shockingly familiar. He was almost paralyzed by the amount of information Nina was giving them. His first feelings of denial and disbelief were being replaced with amazement and intrigue. It was all happening so quickly that it was hard for him to settle down. His heart began to flutter with excitement as he contemplated what his life would be like soon, what mysteries he would unearth, what talents he would develop. There was no sense in trying to understand it.

The more he tried to rationalize what he had heard, the more bewildered he became. How could something that didn't make any logical sense feel like it made complete sense? He delved back into his past, reaching into the corners of his memory, retracing his life to the present moment. Was everything before this only a stepping-stone leading to this new world? He remembered very little about his time in Argentina; most of his memories were from California. He had grown through many phases in his life, tried many things, traveled many places and eaten a large range of foods, yet none of it felt as fulfilling as hearing that he had just hit the tip of what he was truly capable of. Nothing that had come before was able to invoke such a spark of meaning as what he had just learned about himself. It instilled a sense of purpose.

Oliver had naturally been successful at most things he attempted. He was a bit of a natural when it came to just about everything. It was a characteristic that many people admired but had been problematic for him. He would rarely describe himself as passionate about the things he was able to pull off; he was just naturally able to grasp concepts and techniques without any trouble. He could have taught yoga if he'd wanted to. His body acclimated to advanced poses without ever having to practice them first. He had made an anti-pop pop album after he taught himself GarageBand on his computer; the finished album existed only on the hard drive of his computer and had been played only as a joke for friends, even though some music critics would have gushed over its ingenuity and freshness. He could fix a carburetor in the same amount of time he could install a small fishpond. He was a creative thinker, one who liked to explore all options with an open mind. Like he had told Nina earlier that day, he was just an inquisitive person. He never felt satisfied or fulfilled by any of his accomplishments because they weren't passions, they were merely interests and activities that he happened to be good at. He suffered from a crushing feeling that he had peaked and nothing would ever bring him the sense of accomplishment—fulfillment—that he so longed for and was fearful of never experiencing. This new spiritual truth felt like the final piece in a puzzle, only he wasn't quite sure what the finished puzzle looked like. He still had many questions.

"Why do only certain people have this gene?" Oliver asked, his fists clenched, thumbs slowly rubbing the edge of his knuckles.

Nina rubbed her hands together and then allowed a moment of silence. She reached over to grab her glass and polished off the last watered-down swallow of iced tea. Her lips smacked as she set the glass back down.

"Magic has been around since there were men and women. In the beginning, it was outrageously strong, truly a force to be reckoned with. It, of course, activated during an energetic shift and they passed it down, and the gene spilled further down the line, becoming less and less active, or rather, more rare, practically on the verge of extinction. The numbers are very low compared with times in the past. I imagine the first witches were terrified of the powers they had! Confused and frustrated as all hell—although sometimes those witches were venerated by their community, treated more like gods and worshipped rather than shunned."

"So it's genetic? Passed down from generation to generation?" Oliver asked, his voice soft and whispery like cattails.

"Exactly. Over time, the approach toward magic and its acceptance has changed. Religions complicated things quite a bit, making magic look wicked and evil, often as a way to cover up their own madness or control people. Think back to the Salem witch trials, think about the fear they instilled in people and how, at their height, practically the drop of a hat would signify that you were a witch and you would burn for it. Time went by, science and technology flourished and magic was suppressed as mere myth." Nina took a breath and broke eye contact with the group to stare off into space. Her eyes fixed on the emptiness of the air above them. "Science has replaced what was once known to be truth, and those ancient beliefs faded away. Magic…a phenomenon that serves a shared intention, to create balance, isn't incompatible with the world, it's a part of it."

Bisa's lips coiled and puckered as if what Nina had just said had put a foul taste in her mouth.

"What about Wicca? And Wiccans? Aren't they *witches*?" Bisa asked hotly.

"Wicca is a man-made religion, with a set of rules to follow and guidelines for practice. The general term for a practicing Wiccan is a witch, yes. You can say Wiccan phrases like 'Blessed be' and 'Merry meet' all you want, but it won't allow you the same powers that we innately have. Having said that, they still can access parts of the higher consciousness. Everybody can do that. We are all psychic, and the more you develop your psychic skills, the stronger your connection becomes. The same applies to those with this magical gene. Your powers—I hate using that word, it sounds so hokey—are like a muscle, and they'll get stronger if you use them and train them. If you ignore and neglect them, they will weaken and atrophy. And subsequently, being in touch with them enough can also aid in awakening your offspring to them. Which is also an issue: the more our blood is diluted, the lower the chances are of someone having this unique gene."

Nina cleared her throat and looked outside. The sun had lowered in the sky, and she tried to deduce how long she had been talking. "When I go into a bookstore, I always have to laugh when I see a copy of the Bible not in the fiction section. It's a pretty solid fairy tale. Adam and Eve…were witches."

Leo pursed his lips and rolled his eyes. He was back to being his hardheaded self. A tiny rumble in his throat turned into a grunt as he tousled his hair. He sometimes acted like a whiny, impatient, teenage boy, and Nina's monologue wasn't helping. "Adam and Eve were not witches," he said.

"They were," Nina said reflectively. She stared into the depths of Leo's eyes, making sure that he was aware of how serious she was. "Then religion happened. Religion was created to control society and people's awareness of these powers. Out of fear. Fear that someone could be more powerful than those who call the shots. That's when pride came into play. Every now and then there is a surge in the number of people paying more attention to spirit, and that's when the gene evolves during the next shift."

Leo, Mitch, Avery and Oliver all looked into Nina's eyes. Bisa did not. Her eyes were lost somewhere between Nina's last sentence and the cusp of her next one. Her gaze snapped up toward Nina's eyes like a fisherman had pulled on a rod after a bite.

"Bisa?" Nina asked delicately. "What's on your mind?"

Bisa stared back at Nina. Stoic and contemplative, she tilted her head.

"What's a shift? You said the gene evolves? What does that mean? Are all of us here different?"

Outside, the clouds covered the blazing sun, and the light in the room faded slowly to a hazy gray.

"Like I said earlier, the world functions on being in balance energetically, and when enough is out of balance, the gene activates to help restore balance and set the world back in a more constructive direction. It's not just about us here on this planet. There is much more than just Earth—so much that we can't even comprehend and will never understand. Sometimes when that tipping point occurs, a new type of witch will emerge. Often, some of the more experienced or gifted witches will have a premonition about it. The last emergence happened a very long time ago, back in Asia. A man named Yesun tapped into his powers, but because he was uneducated about who and what he was, he caused all sorts of shit through his magical experimentation. He didn't really know what power he had, or how great his gifts were. His ignorance and juvenile carelessness led him to accidentally start the black plague. His brother was the first to suffer from it. Of course, it weighed on him, and he didn't know how to cope with what he had done. It eventually led to his downfall, and his dynasty was overthrown a few years later. He was what we call a Transcendent—a spirit witch. That was the birth of that nature of witch. They're incredibly empathic, clairvoyant—adept in all the clairs."

"Who are the Clairs?" Avery asked timidly.

"Clairs, as in the type of psychic senses," Nina said. "Clairvoyance, clairaudience, clairsentience, claircognizance and clairempathy. There are other types too, but they're not as common. Things that relate to smell and taste."

"What else can they do?" Oliver asked eagerly.

"Astral projection—the ability to separate your spirit from your physical body and travel to other places in the physical world. They have a strong influence over others and are very much in touch with the divine."

"Divine?" Avery asked.

"The spirit world, the higher consciousness."

Nina looked over at Oliver. She felt her next statement was especially for him. "Because of their set of gifts, they make great emotional healers. They are the ones who can usually connect and communicate with spirits. For example, I'm a Transcendent witch. My abilities helped me during my spell to get you all to gather here at this place to learn about your gifts."

Oliver looked toward Avery and then back at Nina. There were many thoughts in his head, and they drowned out the cicadas, which had been growing louder with every passing minute. He leaned forward and rested his elbows on his knees, clasping his hands in front of his mouth.

"Do you know what we are?" Oliver asked.

"You're a Transcendent, Oliver."

A look of approval fell across his face as he leaned back in his seat, the sofa creaking a little under his weight.

"You and Bisa are both Transcendents," Nina declared. "Mitch, Leo and Avery are Primordial* witches, or nicknamed the Elementals. They are the oldest kind of witches, like Adam and Eve. They were both Primordials. They are the ones able to manifest actual physical healing to the human body. Also the most in touch with nature and animals. Many of them have been able to manipulate the elements, which is helpful for things like divination, because it doesn't come as naturally as it does for Transcendents. The big, fun ability is to communicate with animals." Nina waved her hand around her face in a circle. "Your senses are heightened too. You can smell, see and hear things that others wouldn't ever be able to do."

"I can do all of those things?" Avery asked excitedly.

"Well, not yet. Maybe not all of them, some maybe not ever. Some witches develop only a few powers linked to the type of witch they are. You may not be able to summon elements, but you can see really well, and you can communicate with animals. Mitch may be able to manipulate the air or the water but not be able to summon animals. It's different for everyone. And no matter how strong your powers become, you'll develop them only as fast as your brain allows. That's why it's crucial to practice that sort of mindfulness, to get into that headspace."

It took less than a few seconds for Leo to shout out gleefully about his powers. For the first time all day he felt excited about something. He hadn't even noticed that his hands were trembling from a lack of nicotine. Leo heard about his powers and thought it sounded like fun. It sounded—exciting.

"Now, that's why it's important for us all to be here. You need to know what you are and how to control your gifts so that they don't control you. All of them can be very dangerous."

Leo's ears perked up. It was as if the single word *dangerous* had hit him like a needle full of adrenaline straight to the heart. He had an addictive personality by nature and was hooked on it all: drugs, people and, more significantly, danger. The world and its banality stifled him. If something was dull, he found a way to make it more interesting at whatever cost necessary. If he wasn't able to go beyond the boundaries of something, it felt like being inside a straitjacket. He stalked dangerous things, even if they scared him—especially if they scared him. The flood of sensation that rushed through his veins from experiencing danger was as close as he ever got to feeling fulfilled. His love of danger made his natural fears that much more prevalent, and in turn, made them more exciting and—more fulfilling. He applied this system to everything he did. If he wanted to see the inside of an abandoned building, he would break in, embrace his fear of heights and climb the unstable structure all the way to the roof. Leo couldn't just drive over the bridge—he had to speed across it and push the limits to feel something, anything. A day completely sober was about as enjoyable as an unsalted rice cake.

He constantly amended his life to include a substance that changed a sink full of dirty dishes into an enchanting jambalaya of astonishing alternatives. He didn't need to be on drugs to go about his day, but he wanted to be—everything was just a little shinier. How much reality could one man take without feeling the ocean of boredom drown him? Leo was certain that he was a functional addict. He got everything done that he needed to get done, sometimes even faster and with a few more laughs.

He was content with his lifestyle even after the death of his daughter. That was the first day he tried heroin. A friend of a friend had introduced him to the needle as a sort of antidepressant. Eventually, he weaned himself off of it, but only after he had tried methadone, then gone back to heroin, then taken more methadone, then acid, then acid and molly, then just acid again, then weed and acid, and then only acid and weed on their own. Now he was a risk-chasing pothead with a predilection for psychedelics who vaped in between. He felt like himself the most with that combination: acid, marijuana and nicotine. It buried the emotions surrounding his daughter until he barely remembered that she'd ever been born.

"Leo," Nina said.

Leo's eyes flickered at the call of his name. "What?"

"This isn't something for you to run wild with, not here," Nina said as she uncrossed her legs.

"How do you know all of this?" Bisa asked, her eyes probing.

"That's a whole different story. To make it short, I was, in a way, chosen to become a Proctor. Which is really just a leader of a coven, a mentor. Like all of you, I wasn't able to use any of my gifts until the shift activated them."

"So, what? You just knew all of this?" Bisa asked.

"Hell no. I was born like the rest of you. I just had the advantage of knowing before the shift happened."

"How?"

"While I slept, my soul slipped into the Somnium plane—"

"Okay," Mitch interrupted, his hands flailing like fishtails. "This is, like, so much information, it's out of control."

"Let her finish," Bisa exclaimed.

Nina was just as overwhelmed as Mitch was. It was as exhausting to divulge all of this information as it was to absorb it for the first time. She was on the edge of her seat now, and one foot had already begun to feel the weight of her body as she aimed to stand up and end the conversation.

"The Somnium plane is where dreams take place. It was where I was met by the other members of the Advisory, who had the same thing happen to them. Every night, for years. It was where I was able to practice magic, learn about it, and use it. It was like a sort of lucid dream, until the activation occurred. Then I was able to actually perform everything I had prepared for." Nina pushed her weight into her other foot, slipped off the sofa and stood tall.

"Didn't you think you were crazy?" Bisa asked. "How did you not think you were crazy? I would have! I mean, I'm still trying to decide even now if I'm crazy for entertaining this idea right now."

"You're damn right I thought I was crazy! You think I told anyone about that? Absolutely not! It took me a couple of weeks to realize that I hadn't just had some mental break. It was real. It really hit home for me when I insisted on testing them and asked for proof. I had to. I asked them to show me something tangible in the real world, my waking world, where I was conscious, that everything in the so-called Somnium plane was real."

Nina looked around at the soon-to-be coven and smiled.

"What did they say?" Avery asked.

"They told me…*there is a reality beyond tangible matter, it's all made of energy, and that is all the truth you need.*"

Leo's hands grasped his vape, and he brought it to his mouth. He sucked in and breathed out a solid plume of smoke toward Nina. "What the fuck does that mean?"

"Think of it like this…That phone in your pocket, all those apps and touch-sensitive icons, the button that says Photos, for example—is that what is really inside your phone? Or is it a bunch of metal arranged in a complicated way that gives the illusion that that solid app icon or that selfie is actually inside that phone?"

Leo scratched the underside of his chin. "What?"

"Yeah, it was all playing out during a dream, but it's still real. There is a reality that exists beyond what we can identify through our everyday senses. When we access altered states of consciousness, like that of dreams, we are able to encounter *facts* that are beyond anything our physical senses would understand, because it's beyond actuality, beyond concrete matter. It's different…Why should that be any less real?" Nina paused for a moment and considered what she could tell them that would resonate with their souls, beyond skepticism, doubt and uncertainty. "You are all exceptional. And I have had the humbling advantage of being nurtured and educated by people and spirits who truly understand the magic of this world, and one of the biggest virtues that they taught me was balance. So, I aim to give you grounds to build instinct, because instinct is something that isn't taught in a single school on earth, and the power of instinct is that it will show you how to find your own path, your own voice, and it won't be anyone else's but your own. It will be your strongest tool going forward."

Suddenly no one was arguing or attempting to debunk Nina's statements. They were accepting them.

"That's enough for today," Nina said. "I'm getting as bored as someone waiting for slow Wi-Fi, and we have a lot more time." She walked out of the room and toward the kitchen. "Grab your things, pick a room, make yourself at home. I'm going to start dinner, and then we can talk some more tomorrow morning. I hope everyone likes pasta."

CHAPTER 6

Although nothing was official, Nina already considered the group a coven by means of her own personalized version of an initiation: a meal. She wasn't particularly well versed in the kitchen, but she could make a few things pretty well. Learning to make a few dishes in college persuaded her to put a little more effort into learning the basics. It wasn't because her dishes were basic; it was because her closest friends weren't able to eat what she prepared. For the most part, she was a good sport when it came to taking criticism. Telling her that her roast chicken was bland was one thing, but running to the bathroom to throw it up was just rude.

Nina was determined never to have to witness bits of raw chicken and chunks of her wounded pride again. However, she didn't know anything about seasoning or how to tell when meat was done. She was somewhere between knowing how to boil water and not knowing what a bay leaf was. It took some time, along with some horrible food, before she was able to nail down some basics and actually cook something that wasn't half bad. Nina liked to learn, and she applied the same ethic to her studies that she applied to learning to cook. She wouldn't be in school forever, but she would have to feed herself for the rest of her life. Over her final year at college, she had gone from being a packaged-ramen connoisseur to an unsophisticated amateur home cook. Of course, it's hard to teach yourself how to cook from scratch, so between studying for classes, she studied the recipes and stylized photos in magazines like *Bon Appetit*.

Her culinary education ended when the magazine subscription addressed to a former resident stopped showing up, probably because of an address change. She couldn't figure that part out. Whenever she tried to cancel a magazine subscription, she had to practically beat someone to death to do it. Then a magazine she found useful and actually wanted suddenly disappeared forever, leaving her to fend for herself in the kitchen. It felt like a sick cosmic joke.

She started visualizing her perfect dishes, making them look just like the photos in the magazines. She had read somewhere that visualizing what you want helps attract it to you. Now, looking back, she didn't know how she had managed to become a little kitchen witch. Then she thought a little harder and remembered that instead of accepting defeat, she had opened up a world of opportunities with a library card. The New Haven Free Public Library was still missing six cookbooks and was owed a hefty late fee under her name. It hadn't been her intention to steal the books; she had forgotten to return them when she moved. Her favorite was an unfashionable yellow, hardcover cookbook called *Chunk Cooking*, about a cooking style that encouraged one to cook by not fussing with exact measurements or perfect cuts. The idea was to simply cut everything into chunks and throw it in a pot. *One day they will come for me*, she would say to herself every time she made Chicken Piccata* on page 78, and, *I wonder how much my late fee is* whenever she made Poached Salmon in Tarragon Cream* Sauce on page 43. All petty theft and possible misdemeanors aside, she made one damn good bucatini all'amatriciana*.

The coven members sat together at the large pine dining table. Much like the imperfections and variations of the table itself, the people who sat around it, with their own imperfections, only added to the charm. The scene looked like a commercial for a progressive Coca-Cola ad campaign, one that encouraged diversity and community. Leo refrained from vaping at the table, much to his annoyance; it was hard enough to actually sit at an actual table and have a meal. He was used to standing, or sitting at a coffee table, or not eating altogether. He sat across from Bisa, who had been giving him weird vibes ever since they'd found out about their powers. Mitch was the only one who had a second plate of pasta, and he was able to finish it before the rest of them even finished their first plate. Avery sat closest to Nina, who was at the table head, and Oliver sat across from Avery, listening and observing.

There were only a few questions about witchcraft, and even fewer answers from Nina. She thought she had conveyed that she wanted to take a break from answering questions for the evening, but a Proctor's job was never fully done. It wasn't a job she had expected or was being paid for, but it seemed to suit her. She was levelheaded, nurturing and more aware than most. Her ability to find the beauty in all things was something she prized above many of her other admirable qualities. The questions were fired at her like machine gun bullets, but even though her mind said she was exhausted, her heart disagreed. She felt great satisfaction in helping others become more spiritually aware, and it was that fire inside her that allowed her to never truly be depleted. She understood the balance between giving and receiving, and one day she would be able to see the rewards of her care.

When the plates were empty and the sounds of metal attacking porcelain dwindled, Nina went over some of the duties that needed to be done around the house and the responsibilities of living there. It wasn't the most fascinating conversation, and no one was particularly thrilled about it, but it had to be said. The house grew quiet as the moon rose higher into the sky. The air was warm and moist. Outside the house, the grounds seemed to disappear into blackness. The group members could hardly remember what the backyard looked like, and they could see only as far as the lights and candles from inside would allow. Even through the closed doors and windows, one could hear the familiar sounds of the South, the songs of insects and other creatures that most of them hadn't ever seen or known about.

Sometime after the scent of hot tomato sauce was replaced with that of lemongrass-ginger dish soap, everyone retreated to their new private space. Granted, they didn't have all of their belongings—after all, no one had intended to stay long term—but they would be arriving shortly. Nina was excellent at arranging and organizing things, even other people's lives. In another life, she would have made a terrific event planner, one who unapologetically brought all requests to fruition while managing the moods of every personality like it was easier than learning to clap. It was her organized approach that made her so popular so quickly among the coven members, in addition to being approachable. Had Nina not already figured out how to tie up the loose ends of their former lives before they walked through the door, the chances of them staying wouldn't have been quite so good.

Nina understood the concept of sentimental value as much as she knew when it was time to purge and let things go. There were items in her suitcase that she wouldn't have wanted to leave behind if she were tricked into living in the South—things like her floppy black hat, with its brim like the rings of Saturn. There was something unusual about the fabric. It wasn't just black. It was so black that it seemed to absorb all the light around it. It really made her face pop; that was something she would never leave behind. She prized it over the piece of paper in a fancy frame (her diploma from Yale), which was in storage. To be fully honest, it was a toss-up between the hat and her personal space, both of which she could fit into a suitcase. She understood that some things you just needed to have with you, and she assumed the other witches were just like her. After all, they were all still people. Their jobs were on hold, their rent mysteriously never had to be paid, and their belongings were being looked after or had been shipped or put in storage. She knew how to make someone feel at home.

Oliver had settled into the room closest to the back of the house on the right. The door to his room connected to the great room, and a separate door led out to the back patio. He was drawn to the rear of the house mainly because of the easy access to the back patio, which he envisioned turning into some kind of greenhouse. He had acquired a green thumb right before traveling to Louisiana, and it was something he wanted to continue to explore. Bisa took the smallest room, the first room on the right, followed by Mitch in the front right corner of the house, and Leo chose the room between the bathroom and Mitch.

Avery, the one most guided by spirit and impulse, decided to build a home out of the room closest to Nina on the left side of the house. Avery liked to read. She was a traveler, after all, and the best way to pass the time on planes and buses was to read. She thought it was no coincidence that she felt the most comfortable next to the small study, with its eclectic collection of books and deeply varnished shelves. The room had the distinct smell of leather and toasted marshmallow, with undertones of chocolate truffle—not the typical musty odor of a used-book store. If there hadn't been books on the large bookshelves, one would have thought one was walking into a bakery.

Just before bed, Avery peeked outside her room and down the hallway. A single sconce light was illuminated near the first bathroom door at the corner of the foyer and the hall, and the hall was empty. Her fingers clutched the frame of the door as she timidly waited for someone—anyone—to appear, but no one did. She slipped a bare foot out into the hallway, which caused a rickety creak reminiscent of the janky wood floor in her last apartment in Madison, Wisconsin, only a lot warmer. She inched gingerly a few paces and entered the study. It was slightly romantic, like a dinner date between her and the books. A single side table near the door held an expensive-looking stained-glass lamp. She reached down for the dangling golden cord, and with a gentle tug, the light snapped on. The mahogany lamp stand resembled a twisted tree branch that had grown up into the lamp's remarkable dome. Colors of pond green, rich amber, dusky blue and Provencal violet beamed to life. She could now make out the blue-bodied dragonflies with their crimson eyes and mustard-yellow wings. It was as beautiful as reading good poetry, and she gasped. For a brief moment, in the late evening hours in a mysterious room in the Deep South, her whole world seemed suspended in time. Everything had changed, yet at this very moment, among all this change, she had a moment of stillness.

Avery slowly made her way to the bookshelf and ran her index finger along the dusty shelves. When her finger was the color of freshly cracked pepper, a shade that reminded her of the skies back home in winter, she picked up the first book that spoke to her. It was an unimpressive selection if she were to judge it by its cover, something one would weed out of a garden if it were a plant. The buckram cover was tattered and peeling apart at the edges. It looked like it used to be red, but now its coloring was something like a blemished persimmon. The grimy gold title read *The Secrets of Magic and Other Curious Practices*. There was no author. Avery tapped her fingernails on the binding like a string of percussionists, flicked off the lamp and headed back to her room to read at least the first chapter before bed.

Everyone had taken the first steps toward erasing stagnancy. The first thing that needed to happen was to get out of the pattern they had all been a part of. The simplest change in action and movement created a domino effect so everything else could flow in. Their movement created a magnetic pull from the higher consciousness and rested in the one common anchor they were most familiar with: their physical bodies. Their bodies were the home for all the energy to reside in. The energy would manifest itself in their bodies, because nothing changes without active movement.

CHAPTER 7

It was a little past nine the next morning, after the first night all the witches had stayed under one roof. Nina had made it very clear that they would survive together as a unit and should function as such. This meant that each person had to do their part, both magical and nonmagical. Learning the delicate art of divination was just as important as keeping up with the chores. There was only one scheduled meal, and that was dinner. They would always prepare it as a group unless otherwise specified. If someone wanted to do their own thing, skip dinner or have a meal elsewhere, they needed to let the others know in advance. It was like putting in a request for time off at a job. It wouldn't always be approved, but you didn't have to pretend you were dying of a sudden case of walking pneumonia or colitis, either.

Breakfast was a time when everyone had to fend for themselves. One could either make something for the group, skip it entirely or eat whatever one wanted. Some of them had kitchen skills, and a few others got by with doing as little as possible. In due time, they would realize that breakfast usually consisted of fewer than ten ingredients between them all together. It would be a severe stretch to say that their morning meals were well-balanced feasts.

Nina and Bisa were the first to wake. They met each other in the kitchen, both fully dressed and ready for the day by eight o'clock. Nina started a pot of coffee, and Bisa prepared a light breakfast of toast with honey and a sliced Honeycrisp apple. Avery was the next to come into the kitchen, the scent of brewed coffee having pulled her out of bed faster than she would have wanted. Barefoot and in pajamas, she smiled at the other women as she floated toward the coffeepot. Still half asleep, she managed to go through her somewhat rigid style of coffee prep: a splash of cream followed by the coffee—unstirred. She liked how it mixed itself that way. Mitch, Oliver and Leo entered the kitchen and all made toast. Bread was going to be a hot commodity around the house. As Leo walked over to the table, he passed Mitch and gave him a light slap on the cheek. Leo's hands were rough and always had been, so when his palm came in contact with Mitch's soft skin, it felt like the type of abrasion one gets when they skin their knee on concrete.

"Why would you do that?" Mitch asked.

Leo laughed to himself and sat down at the table. The laugh was the only response he gave Mitch. His attention was focused on the coffee he lifted to his mouth. It was hot, but no match for Leo's liking.

Nina cleaned up the mess of paper towels, bread crumbs and spilled coffee that littered the kitchen counters. By the time she had thrown the trash into the bin, she realized that she shouldn't have to clean up after them. Maybe it was too late to say anything. Now they would expect it. "When everyone's finished eating, I'd like to see you all in the great room," she said.

Leo smirked bemusedly as if Nina had said something asinine, but then tried to force his raging cynicism aside.

When everyone had finished their toast and half finished their cups of coffee, they walked into the great room to meet Nina. Everyone took the same seat that they had instinctively taken the day before. Nina smiled at everyone and crossed her legs. She sat up straight in the chair and looked across each and every one of them before uttering a single word.

"How did everyone sleep?" Nina asked.

Everyone replied with the usual *fine, okay, good*.

"We aren't going to have this every single morning, but we will have it once a week, to start."

"What's this?" Mitch asked.

"Just a meeting, as a coven."

"Like AA has meetings?"

"There won't always be a specific agenda, but there will always be open discussion on a variety of issues. Anyone can address a concern or talk about something specific to their own spiritual journey. It will be guided, though."

"By you?" Leo asked.

"By me."

Bisa watched the exchange between Leo and Nina with the clever movement of her eyes, her body still and statuesque.

"This is going to continue from where we left off yesterday. I'd like to share a few more things with you. I encourage you to start keeping a journal. This isn't going to be something that you will share with me or anyone else, but it will be useful for you."

"What do you want us to journal about then?" Avery asked. Her eyes lit up at the idea of creating a physical representation of her journey.

"Is this like a Book of Shadows kinda thing?" Mitch asked through pinched lips.

"You can call it that. A Book of Shadows is more of a…Wiccan thing, or Pagan-ish. It's also called by other names—Book of Light, Book of Mirrors. I like to use the term *grimoire*. We witches have fallen in love with that term. This will be your own personal codex. It's intimate, and because we on earth have a sort of romance with books, it makes perfect sense that this is just an extension of your life."

"What the fuck is any of that?" Leo bellowed.

Nina inhaled and quenched her immediate response. "I'm explaining it to you," she said. "Find a book, any book with free, blank pages. It doesn't have to be sexy or some sort of facsimile of something you've seen in the movies. It doesn't have to be bound in leather or wrapped in human skin. Get what you want. What speaks to you, what you *want* it to be."

"What do you have?" Bisa asked.

"Mine is leather bound, with a lock. Handmade. But that's mine; it doesn't have to be yours. I encourage you to make this book your own and consecrate it in your own way. Sleep with it, cleanse it under the sun or bathe it in the moonlight. If you are drawn to smells, make a blend of essential oils and use that in the pages. Smudge it with sage. Stain the pages using coffee or tea. But you don't have to be that artsy with it. It can also be as simple as pen and ink. And it may change over time. I know all or some of this may seem bizarre. *At first.* But it all imbues your book with purpose, with meaning, and creates a bond between you and your journey."

Oliver cleared his throat and tapped his fingers before he said, "So what do you actually put in the book? Just thoughts?"

"It can be a multitude of things. Mine started out as a journal, with entries about my thoughts and dreams. Then as things became more…real, it changed. I included drawings, recipes, I began to write in multiple directions, I started using color, embellishments like gold leaf, salt, thread. Write down spells, rites, experiences, entries about whatever you want. Don't worry about the order or making it perfect or trying to make it something specific. It will be a meditative space, essentially. Like I said, you don't have to do any of this, but you will find what you want to do as you get further along. You will find your style. It's much like how a writer finds their own voice, or how a band forms their musical style."

"How will we even know what to learn about?" Mitch asked.

"We are going to be doing lots of work here, together. You are also encouraged to work on your own. Inspire yourself, push yourself, learn on your own. There are lots of books and resources here in the study that are just for that purpose. The more we develop and explore your powers, the more you will want to *play* with them. The grimoire is a good way to keep track of that."

Nina could tell that Leo was starting to doze off and Oliver wasn't amped up over the idea. She shifted the topic into another arena, one that concerned them all and would inadvertently encourage them to explore their magical personalities.

"What is your biggest fear?" Nina asked quickly.

The room fell silent, but they all came up with answers in their heads.

Oliver had always been good at everything but was afraid he would never truly find purpose.

Leo's biggest fear had already come true: he had outlived his daughter. With the hopes that his offspring would have a full life beyond his own now dead and buried, he didn't have much else to live for, and fear wasn't really an issue for him, even if he was sometimes frightened.

Bisa was afraid of many things. Her biggest fear was simply loss.

Mitch considered many factors in the few moments of silence after Nina's question. Even though he had a hard time admitting it to himself, he knew he was afraid of being alone and dying alone, without ever having found a partner who really made a difference in his life. It seemed irrational to believe that everyone found someone for them. It seemed to him that people settled. But he didn't want that. He wanted what the culture shoved down his throat, albeit in a heterosexual way. He believed it was possible but elusive.

Avery, so enlightened already without any awareness of it, still feared that she lacked purpose and would never find the meaning of her being on earth. She wasn't afraid of snakes, or drowning inside a car that had driven into the water, or having her throat slit. Those things were high on the list of many other people, but they weren't on hers. She saw beyond that and therefore had a more deep-rooted fear.

"Now that we've covered that, I'd like to talk about what you can learn," Nina said lightly.

"But, we didn't, say anything," Mitch stuttered.

Nina only smiled, looked over each of their faces and then said, "The list of things we can do is pretty long. There are shared powers and abilities that are available to any witch. Things like spellwork, power via intention, potion and tincture making, acquiring familiar spirits."

"Dragonflies are totally, like, my spirit animal. Well, insect, I guess," Mitch said in a breathy voice.

"You may even be able to shapeshift one day," Nina dropped quickly.

"Shut the fuck up!" Leo said.

"It takes intense, dedicated practice. You'll learn a lot more in the future, but before we get too far ahead of ourselves, we will focus on the smaller aspects and build up to the ones that are a little more difficult or dangerous."

"Dangerous?" Leo asked.

"There are dangers involved in witchcraft. It's no different than it is for others who create. Architects must know what they are doing if they are to build something that doesn't fall. Machinists need to know how to properly work a machine so they don't hurt themselves. There's also the element of humans. Being a witch is a secret. Some know, but you should not go parading around what you can do and what you are capable of. That's not how we achieve our goals."

"Can you like, reiterate what our, like, goal is?" Mitch said seriously.

"Balance. Put things into mental, emotional, spiritual and physical balance."

Bisa heaved up her shoulders and with the utmost respect asked, "Is there anything we can do to expedite this balance?" For a moment, there was a little doubt in the back of her mind. A suspicion that this particular group wouldn't be able to pull off something so sensitive.

Nina's cheeks flushed as she considered telling them about the Union of the Divine Dualities*. Her mouth salivated at the thought of discussing it. The ritual was something she found intriguing, one that was of a great deal of importance in the witch community, but it was also considered a myth. Her mouth opened, and her tongue flickered against the back of her teeth, edging closer to spilling the thoughts in her head.

"What about psychedelics?" Leo interrupted. "Ayahuasca ceremonies, LSD, things like that? How do those affect our powers?"

Bisa rolled her eyes, but Nina was happy to change the subject. She didn't feel they were ready to know about that type of magic quite yet.

"Acid really screws with your body," Mitch said. "It, like, stays in your spinal cord, like forever."

Leo laughed and shook his head. "No, it doesn't dude. That's made up."

Mitch tapped his fists against his bare knees to emphasize his perspective. "No, it's not! I used to know this guy, he dropped acid, like, every single day like a breath mint, and now when he like, cracks his back, he sees blue angels!"

"He's making that shit up, bro," Leo said harshly.

Irritation and some sexual attraction slipped out of Mitch's mouth in the form of an "Ugh!" sounding like a stack of papers hitting the wind. "I swear! I was with him one time when it happened! I remember it like it was *yesterday*!" Mitch's head bobbled back and forth with conviction. "It was like one o'clock, it was September twelfth, he cracked his back and said, *Holy shit, look, blue angels!*"

"The Blue Angels are a flight squad. They do air shows, you dumb bitch."

"Uh…I've never heard of that before. How am I supposed to know that's what he was talking about when I'm on— while I'm trip— flipp— took a hit of ac— *fuck you!*"

"Leo, leave him alone, just stop," Avery said.

Leo leaned back in his chair, spread his legs wide and, with a hard pump of his fist, pointed at his crotch. "Man, stop deez nuts."

"You're ridiculous," Avery chirped.

In response to Leo forcing everyone's attention to his bulge, Mitch felt entirely obligated to look. He was wearing sweat pants, and it didn't matter if he was standing, sitting or crossing his legs: everything always seemed to be outlined as though his pants were tracing paper. The sweats were baggy everywhere but the crotch. The whole thing seemed like a sick, cruel joke. Mitch always gave straight men crap for ogling women on the street when they were just wearing normal clothes, and here he was on the verge of needing a restraining order for unwanted voyeurism. It was confusing, because he couldn't decide if he thought Leo was trashy or hot. He didn't look promiscuous. He looked like a shiny new prism that someone had rolled down a rocky street and picked back up out of a muddy gutter, only Leo threw himself down the street. Leo was closed off, sarcastic, cold and bitchy, but if he were sanded down, dipped in soap, wiped clean and polished up a bit, he could be something really special.

Mitch liked helping people. He was quiet and sensitive, and generally didn't like conflict. He had a deep appreciation for art in all forms within his heart. It was his goal to focus on the positive and help himself and those around him by doing that. In the flutter of a passing second, the abrasive, rough edges of Leo's personality seemed like a challenge well suited to his goals. Mitch often saw the beauty in all things, including, now, the bulge Leo had so graciously pointed out to him. Perhaps objective number two could be to convince Leo that he should sleep with him, regardless of his sexual orientation. Even though that seemed wrong. Even though he would perpetuate the stereotype that all gay men wanted to convert straight men.

"I don't really understand what you're asking, Leo," Nina said politely.

"Do those things affect us? Do they prevent us from doing things, help us, or what?"

"He wants to know if he can still do drugs," Bisa said.

Leo leaned back into his chair and nodded. "That's right," he said smugly.

"They have their place in the spiritual community, although maybe not quite like how you intend them to be used. Shamans are guided toward certain plants that allow them to access a higher awareness and expand perception beyond the traditional senses."

"Like ayahuasca?" Leo asked.

"Exactly. So one could say that drugs—hallucinogenic and psychotropic drugs that were created, discovered or used specifically for heightening one's spiritual awareness—were a part of that journey, the evolution of spirituality and enlightenment. That's different from man-made drugs, though."

"So like DMT or LSD aren't good?"

"As far as your powers, that all depends on how you are affected by the awareness that becomes you. Like I said before, everything is made of energy, and those energies give off vibrations. The vibration of that natural plant or substance isn't going to be the same after it's harvested and transformed. The natural essence of it is manipulated. You drink milk, right?"

"No, milk freaks me out."

"My point is, you can't have a glass of milk and then understand—experience—a cow."

"Cool," Leo said. He felt he had heard the answer he needed. He could continue to take whatever drugs he wanted, when he wanted, and as much or as little of them as he wanted, and he could still evolve as a witch.

"Now, that aside, any drug, natural or not, when used as a form of escape, recreationally, isn't going to be one bit of use to you. What's your intention when you take these drugs? Anything in high amounts isn't good for you. Sodium, a nutrient that our body needs, isn't good for the body in high doses."

Oliver's eyes flickered and he said, "Positive and negative intentions."

"Yes," Nina said. "If you use drugs as a means for entertainment, or to escape, or to distract yourself, the results won't be positive. Positive results come from an intention to expand your awareness. Things like you are talking about, like dropping acid, can be useful in breaking down barriers in your mind and gaining profound insight, but they are not by any means necessary. Take ayahuasca, for example. Experienced shamans leading those ceremonies no longer need it as a tool to reach that type of awareness. They have access to those vibes already. They can induce it themselves."

"Wouldn't it take a really long time to reach that state without it?" Avery asked.

"Of course it would. The danger is just like what happens with modern religion, which is really just another form of drug for some religious people. They experience something, a feeling of belonging, a sense of purpose, a reason to be alive, a way to live with themselves; they chase after it, that doorway to whatever, and they see it as the only way they can get…whatever it is they found in the first place. It becomes the only way they can live their life."

"How is being a religious person dangerous? Not all religious people are crazy bigots," Avery said.

"It's dangerous only when one becomes obsessed—to the point that it governs every choice they make and every thought they have. When it becomes a substitute for actually living life."

Mitch understood exactly what Nina had said, and in a way that was beyond what she intended. His entire family was Christian. Mitch was the oddball, the reason other parents in his family's church had looked at his parents sorrowfully every Sunday. The leader of their youth group had suggested that he attend more often, and the pastor had insisted that he be more involved. Something—a godsend, Mitch would joke, although it was more like a fluke—prevented him from believing in the Christian version of God. It didn't seem to make sense, and he refused to follow suit and incorporate the ideals of a faith that claimed to be loving yet rejected who he was as a gay man. The stroke of luck that Mitch jokingly referred to as a godsend was what he called the most unremarkable personal highlight of his teenage years. He had told a friend at public school (his parents always said those kids weren't good influences on him) that so much had gone awry in the world that he didn't think God—if there was one—cared whether he wanted to suck dick or not. His father had overheard him and called him into the kitchen to talk about it immediately afterward, right after sending the wicked public schooler home.

The conversation wasn't as terrible as some coming-out stories Mitch had heard, but it wasn't exactly something he would choose to go through again. It had kind of been like sitting through a Sunday sermon. There was a lot of yelling from someone with less hair than him, and he was trying hard not to roll his eyes or picture the pastor's son naked, only the pastor's son wasn't there. His father had wiped his forehead with his fingers as if trying to soothe a migraine and then reached down to grab hold of the kitchen table like it was going to get up and run away. The sequence of statements had gone something like this: *Are you gay? Have you always been gay? Why have you kept this a secret? How could you do this to us?* His father wasn't upset that his son was gay; it was that his son hadn't trusted his parents enough to tell them.

When all was said and done, the reaction Mitch had expected wasn't the one he received at all. The last thing his father told him before he kissed Mitch's pale forehead was "It doesn't matter to me if you're gay or not. It doesn't change how much I love you. I wouldn't trade you for anything or change anything about you. You're my little boy, my youngest boy. When I look at you, even now, I have a hard time realizing you're not eight years old." And that was all he ever said about the subject. It was as if the memory of the event had been chopped right out of his brain. Everything changed, though. Mitch no longer had to attend church, go on mission trips or engage in youth group lock-ins where he and one of the other boys snuck off to the basement to jerk each other off. It was okay, the kid told him, because it was dark and God couldn't see. It was a refreshing change of pace. He was free to live life his own way, from his own perspective.

His older brother, Chad, wasn't quite as tolerant. When he heard the news that Mitch was gay—an abomination—his temperature rose, his hope for normality plummeted and he lashed out in extensive ten-minute intervals of hate speech with only a breath of air between each session. Mitch didn't really believe in demonic possession, but if there was ever a time he felt his family needed an exorcist, it was right then. He had never been witness to such venomous, insane rage. Chad vomited up disgusting slurs and did everything but levitate and make his head spin. Mitch attributed his brother's animosity to being force-fed Christianity and food at the church potlucks.

People could have been spiking the food with mind-controlling drugs. After all, no one really knew what was in Amy's macaroni salad…If there was no mayonnaise, why was it so creamy, and why were there grapes? Amy always quoted the Bible when people inquired about the velvety texture and mysterious zippy tang. "He asked for water, and she gave him milk. She brought forth butter in a lordly dish." That never answered the questions, but it never seemed out of character for her, either. Amy was the ultra-pious type, the type of woman who thought not attending Sunday service was an act of terrorism in the name of Satan. She made a hobby of being pregnant, which only made the secret ingredient in her creamy contribution to Wednesday night potlucks all the more unsettling.

Watching Chad on a rant was scarier than watching a horror movie. At least with those he knew it wasn't real and the lights would come back on. The rift between them was irreparable, and their relationship as brothers dissolved faster than a bone can break. His father understood less and less how some Christians believed Mitch would go to hell for living in sin when he believed the crux of Christian values was unconditional love. The divide caused tension between his parents, because his mother was still active in their church. Eventually his parents divorced. The catalyst for the separation could have been Mitch's coming out, but the truth was that they had just fallen out of love with each other when it became so evident that their values were different. The distance between them was uncomfortably wide, and it made little sense to stay together once the kids were older. His father was happier, his mother was better off, Chad married and started a family. It was the beginning of a whole new world for all of them, one where everyone was free, albeit with a few scars. Mitch understood how easily people could chase after the single thing that held them together and gave them purpose. He understood very well how people used crutches to get through life.

"We're getting a little off track," Nina said, brushing her hair out of her face. "Our time here is uncertain. I'm not sure how long all of us will be here together, but before we get any further, I think it's important that we move forward—together. Like anyone else's family, we may not get along or like each other all the time, but we are joined. It's time for the initiation."

CHAPTER 8

Technically, the new moon had risen at 1:22 p.m. earlier that day. The initiation was to begin after sunset and before moonset, meaning they had exactly twenty-three minutes. And that meant they had to prepare everything ahead so they wouldn't waste any time. Being fully prepared for any spell or ritual was very important and a learned skill. It was much like mise en place in cooking, where everything is in its place before you even begin so you can complete the dish from start to finish without interruption. Spell and ritual work functioned the same way. It required one to be organized and methodical, and encouraged one to think ahead. Nina had finished preparing the anointing oils, creating the salt blend, picking the magnolia flowers, and lighting the piles of white copal in abalone shells—all for the initiation ritual—before half past six, showing the characteristics of a true leader by setting a good example. She had to act with total confidence and dedication, or no one would follow suit and take anything seriously.

The sun had set, and the slate-blue color of twilight had blanketed the backyard. Nina had cleared a sacred space out in the back field near the flowering magnolia tree that was uncharacteristically in bloom in September rather than early summer, which was perfect for the initiation. She grabbed the silver pail of the initiation salt she had hand-blended earlier that day: sea salt to encourage harmony, black lava salt for protection, pink salt for grounding, dried rose petals for love, pink peppercorns for friendship, white peppercorns to manifest their goals and yellow peppercorns to promote healing.

Working with a handful at a time, Nina poured the mixture in the shape of a large circle on the ground. With her hands still salty and covered in debris, she adorned the salt circle with the magnolia blossoms, letting the petals fall freely along her path. The chunks of white copal were left to smolder in the abalone shells as she placed them equidistant from one another around the circumference.

The group members stood by and watched her set the space. A few mosquitoes buzzed around their heads and tried to find a bare ankle. After placing each shell along the circle, Nina reached into her pocket and revealed a tiny glass vial of anointing oil. She twisted off the cap and put her index finger over the opening, followed by a series of shakes of her wrist. The herbs and spices in the bottle bobbed around before settling at the bottom in an unidentifiable pile. The fire in the center of the circle was small, and it crackled as if singing to them, beckoning. Nina called them over to the edge of the circle one at a time and smudged their bodies with white sage before tracing a small circle between their eyebrows with the anointing oil. She approached Bisa first, wrapped a white blindfold over her eyes and pulled her toward the edge of the circle.

"What you seek, you already are," Nina said in a melodious voice. "Under the darkness of the new moon, in love and light, I welcome you home. You have arrived. Will you cross into the coven of the divine?"

Bisa moistened her lips and opened her mouth to speak. "I willingly cross into the divine and accept my fellow brothers and sisters as one, and will create balance for the good of all."

Nina grabbed hold of Bisa's hands and escorted her over the threshold of the divine circle one bare foot at a time. She placed her like a chess piece and went to retrieve the next person in line. Slowly and meticulously, each of them was blindfolded, questioned and led into the circle. A few winged insects buzzed around the perimeter of the circle before leaving entirely once everyone had crossed over the salt. From inside the circle, the sounds of the Deep South had all but dissolved away. The group members couldn't hear the buzzing of the insects, and the sound of the central-air unit on the house was inaudible. Within their new sacred space, the realm of divine ritual, came only the sound of burning wood and incense and their own breath.

Nina had told them very little about what they would experience during the initiation, because she wanted the effect of the unveiling of mystery to be a large part of their own experience. It wasn't about keeping it a secret; it was about making it sacred. In the lives they had led up until that point, there was little mystery and very little if anything was sacred. She wanted to encourage them to embrace the mystery, to feel the journey they were about to begin. The surprise, amazement and uncertainty was part of discovering their path—their power.

Nina nestled her feet into the grass and took one last look at all their blindfolded faces before closing her eyes. "You are home, but you are not finished. There will be challenges, and you will be tested, continually. This is an ongoing relationship, a partnership with yourselves and with each other. Your relationship to one another will shift, and you will have to shift along with it." Nina walked to her left and opened Bisa's palms to form a cup. She dropped a single petal from a magnolia blossom and tapped it lightly three times into her palm. As Bisa's fingers closed over the petal, Nina removed the blindfold from Bisa's eyes. They exchanged a quick glance with Bisa's new eyes, and then Nina continued clockwise around the circle. Once everyone had their petal from the same flower and everyone was freed from their blindfold, they stepped forward a few paces and dropped the petals into the fire simultaneously.

A sudden shock shot through their bodies. They all felt it, but no one mentioned it. It was subtle but too electric to ignore. They were now a coven.

Mitch looked around at everyone, who wore the same blank expression he did. "So, like, is that it?"

"We don't have to raise our hands to the sky and all that?" Leo said.

"Not today," Nina declared sharply.

As the petals turned to ash in the fire, the sounds of the natural world surged back to life: the cicadas, the air-conditioning unit, the rustling of the marshy brush in the distance. Mitch looked over at Leo. He immediately wondered if the experience was as grounding and significant for Leo as it was for him. He held his breath for a few beats and contemplated the strength of the bond between them. It was as if he could feel them in the air, under his feet and inside his heart.

Oliver reached down to brush off his feet and retrieved a small heart-shaped leaf from in between his toes.

"I think you should save that," Nina said to Oliver as he examined the shape of the leaf.

"What? The leaf?"

"Make a plant essence out of it. Preserve the energy of tonight. It's a great way to reexperience a moment in a very subtle way. There are a few books about it in the house." Nina walked around the circle and picked up all the abalone shells and brushed the circle of salt away with her foot. On her way back to the fire, she grabbed the last piece of wood. Then she threw it onto the orange embers and watched fire lick the sides of the log. A sense of accomplishment washed over her, and she kneeled down next to the growing light.

"So, what happens now? What do we do?" Avery asked as she looked beyond the illumination of the fire and into the depths of the grounds.

"Now we can start, as a unit, to learn and use our powers," Nina said.

Avery's eye caught a small white box in the distance. She squinted and tried to make out what the object was. *Is that a dresser? No, a mailbox. Wait, why would there be a mailbox back there? A shed?* She craned her neck toward the object and asked aloud, "What is that out there?"

Nina twisted her neck to look off in the direction Avery was staring. "Oh! That's an old beehive. Someone used to keep bees on the property. It's empty now though. Never been tended to or taken down."

"Oh my God, I am so all over that! I volunteered at the insectarium back in Wisconsin for a summer, and it was amazing. Can I use it?"

Nina grinned. "Of course, Avery. This is your house now too. It would make perfect sense for you to do that. You're a Primordial. Nature is part of how you communicate and establish balance in the world. Your modus operandi."

"Did you ever get stung?" Leo asked.

"Not once! I mean, I was in full beekeeping gear, you know, with the suit, the hat and all that." Avery paused, rolled her eyes back into her head and then shook her head in disbelief. "Well, it did happen once. It was my second day, and the head entomologist was really into these stylized pins and brooches and things like that. Like the first day, she wore a big spider and it looked totally real. It might actually have been real at one point, but at this point, it was an accessory. She always had one pinned to her coat just above her name tag. I went to compliment her on how she liked to match her brooch with what we were studying and reached out to touch it, but it turned out to be just like, a really angry wasp."

Nina lifted her voice to address the whole group. "We are a coven, and although I don't know how long we will be here together, I think it's important to not lose sight of your own wants. What does your soul need? As much as the entire purpose of us being brought together is about something much larger than any one of us, we're still a part of it, and your journey is yours and no one else's, and so it's as much about your own path as it's not."

"That doesn't make one bit of sense," Leo declared. "How can something be about us and not about us?"

"She means, like, yeah we have a purpose and we have a job to do, sort of, but like, also like, that's not all we are," Mitch said. "We're not, like, machines or whatever, so like, okay— like you have a job, right?" He opened his arms out wide and talked through body gestures as much as he did his mouth. "You go to work, you do your job, you may answer a phone call at home here and there, but you also, like, want to watch Netflix or fix cars or whatever you do. Like finding a purpose for yourself too."

"Balance," Bisa added. "We all have emotions, interests, things we need to do that nourish our spirit—that make us happy."

The word alone—*happy*—was a trigger for Leo, much in the same way that *abortion* was a trigger word for pro-lifers. It was a concept that didn't truly make sense to him. For him, watching people experience happiness looked like hearing a foreign language sounded. It didn't make sense. It was precisely that for him—a language he didn't understand, a word for an emotion he couldn't understand. And not knowing why was maddening.

Leo started picking at his toenails, a nervous reaction to his discomfort around the concept of happiness. "Oh yeah? What do you do, Bisa? What makes you happy?" he asked her.

Bisa shrugged and stared into the orange embers that were slowly dwindling. "A lot!" She had been through a lot in her thirty-some years: heartbreak, trauma, life. She had been told from a very young age, mostly by her father, that she should always try to be happy about something, even when things were difficult. She was a terrific makeup artist, but she didn't love it, and it didn't make her happy. She had art in her blood, and if she were cut, she would use what bled out as a medium. It was how she thought, but it wasn't always how she acted. Her choices were more logical and rational. Her brave spirit was what had given her the strength to leave Nigeria and leave everything she knew, and everyone who was left, behind. She had thrown herself into the beauty industry because it was the industry that manifested. The soul-crushing beauty world was put on its head when Bisa approached it from another angle. When she applied makeup to herself and others, she chose to see it as a reflection of mental, spiritual and physical health. The reflection in the mirror wasn't who she was—it was art, a mask—but the makeup was a reflection of her self-worth, her pride and how she cared for herself.

"I like art," Bisa said softly.

"What kind?" Oliver asked politely.

"I like to paint."

"Do you have a favorite artist?" Oliver pressed.

"My favorite *painters* are Bruce Onobrakpeya and Francis Bacon."

Nina dipped her head back in surprise, her eyes fluttering. "Bacon! Really? I always found his stuff to be a little dark," she said, smiling with intrigue.

"His later stuff is a little melancholic, but it's such a striking style. His earlier stuff is really raw, with this sort of infant energy. You can really feel emotion when you look at his paintings. What could he have been doing or thinking when he painted is what I always wanted to know."

"I took an art history class once. His stuff was pretty shocking. I was more into Klimt," Nina said lightly.

"Also beautiful stuff. I love all art, though."

"That's what most people don't see," Nina said as she looked up in the sky. "Including me sometimes."

"What?" Bisa asked.

"The beauty in things, all things. Even things that make most people uncomfortable. You see beyond that, the beauty inside it—behind it, even."

Leo waved his hands at her statement. "If I step in dogshit, I'm not gonna see that as beautiful. I'm not gonna clean off my shoe and say, *Damn, how beautiful to experience stepping in shit*," he said sharply.

Avery sighed and narrowed her eyes at Leo. "Why do you have to do that?"

"Do what?" Leo asked, innocently but truthfully.

"Shit all over everything."

"Because I've seen some fucked-up shit. When I got busted for weed a few years ago, I spent some time in jail. That wasn't beautiful. No one in there was beautiful. The bars weren't art. The only sort of…poetry I heard was me telling myself over and over that I was a fucking loser for getting locked up in there in the first place!"

"Come on, Leo," Nina interjected. "You and I know you're greater than that."

"Yeah, you're an asshole!" Avery added flippantly.

Oliver laughed a little under his breath and broke the tension with another question. "What do you like to paint?"

Bisa shook her head and said, "It's been a while since I've picked up a pen or a brush—well, one that wasn't a makeup brush. A long while." She paused and saw the length of time that had passed since she'd last painted something as if she were reading a physical timeline. Her eyes flickered, and she considered how to conclude the conversation. "I have started doing macramé recently! I said I would help a friend make some pieces for a wedding reception, and after about two, I thought, *Hey…this is for me.*"

"Macaroni?" Leo asked, puzzled.

Bisa closed her eyes and waved his comment away, leaving that as her only response.

"So tell us, Leo. What makes you happy?" Nina asked sweetly.

"When I find out, I'll let you know first," Leo said.

"Oh, come on, what do you like to do?"

"Nothing that makes me"—his face puckered like he had smelled a stinky cheese—"happy."

Mitch struck his ankle, ending the life of a thirsty mosquito in a moist blow.

SLAP!

Then another smack on the back of his neck.

WHACK!

Mitch looked around the grounds and could see the swarming clouds of insects looking for another bite. "Can we go inside? I'm being attacked. And why is it still so hot? The sun's down!"

Nina stood and began to gather up things to take inside. "Yes, let's go inside."

"So, what happens now?" Avery asked as she brushed off her feet. "I don't even really know how to do…anything…or what I can do. I mean, how do I even do any of this? Or develop things?"

Mitch nodded and began to follow everyone toward the house. "Yeah, do we just, like, wave our hands really hard, or like, glower intensely? Like, if I snap my fingers, can I like, accidentally start a hurricane?" As Mitch walked alongside Leo, he lightly smacked him across the cheek as repayment for Leo doing the same to him earlier. Leo closed his eyes for a moment and accepted that he had dropped his guard, but he hadn't anticipated Mitch ever retaliating.

"Tonight, let's just get some sleep. Tomorrow let's…" Nina said.

"Tomorrow what?" Bisa asked.

Nina slowed in her tracks and then stood still for a moment. The footsteps of everyone else behind her followed suit. Once she heard them come to a standstill, she twisted just enough that they could see her face. Her words hung on the tip of her tongue. They stood a few steps away, and their faces gleamed at her as if they would combust from anticipation if they had to wait any longer. Nina stared at the coven, figures dimly lit by the lights from the house and silhouetted by the fading fire behind them. The corners of her mouth rose into a smirk, and she stared a moment longer. A warm, delicate breeze puffed through her hair, sending pieces across her lips and cloaking her mouth from sight. She had the attention and the breath of every single one of them. "Let's get witchy."

CHAPTER 9

Leo stood in the doorway to the study. The lamp was on, but the room was empty. Everyone else was preoccupied with their own private rituals: calendula face masks, Instagram, cups of tea. His tongue swished back and forth in his mouth, encouraging the tab of acid he had dropped a few minutes earlier to be absorbed faster, if such a thing were possible. For Leo, casual micro-dosing was as common as having a cup of coffee in the morning. It was the dosage he considered micro that was uncommon. A single tab—sometimes a tab and a half—was micro. Macro started at two and went up to four. Nina had said they were going to delve into their abilities the next morning, but that might as well have been weeks away for his eager, impatient mind. He had a hard time sitting still, so what Nina had said was basically the equivalent of showing an eight-year-old boy all his wrapped Christmas gifts and insisting that he wait to open them until after breakfast the next morning.

If Leo sat too long with himself, his life started to flash before his eyes and he lost himself in thought. Not a lot in his life brought him joy. He was an only child, with few friends, and at the age of twenty-nine had accumulated more painful memories and traumatic incidents than anything else. The present moment seemed like a welcome hiatus, a vacation of white sand and turquoise water after a couple of solid decades of disappointment and struggle. Leo could never seem to illuminate the space around him and erase his shadows. It was his shadows that swallowed him whole. He told himself that he had dealt with his daughter's death and the mistakes of his past, but that was partially why his doses were so high. Life was a little too ordinary without being altered. Ordinary meant he was subject to boredom, which left him with his thoughts, which left him feeling disappointed, without joy, with only his shadows for friends. Under the spell of drugs, he could manage all of that—even avoid it completely. Yet even now, when chance changed his pattern, it wasn't enough.

Leo looked over some of the books in the study and even pulled a few off the shelves to flip through their pages. He glanced through books on all sorts of topics: chakras, oracles, the Magnum Opus, flower remedies. None of it made any sense and most of it seemed like fiction, or ramblings from a psych patient. He swallowed the tab, and as it fell down his throat, he saw a dark crimson object with rough edges on the bookshelf. It was a raw garnet. It wasn't the acid that made the stone so alluring; it was something else. A mesmerizing quality seemed to emanate from within the stone's center. Leo lifted his hand and stretched his fingers toward the garnet. His hand drew near, almost magnetically drawn to the stone. He clasped his fingers around the garnet and clutched it in his palm. His rough skin and the coarse surface of the rock made for a quaveringly satisfying symmetry.

There was something beyond the rough surface, something cosmic and supernatural, something he would usually have cast away as fiction. He could feel beyond the physical surface. He could feel the stone's essence. It was strong—delicious, even. For a moment he felt semiconscious. *Maybe it's the acid. But it can't be...It's too soon.* Before he could think another thought, he had acquiesced to the stone's effects. He was wielding something banal and ornamental that nonetheless had a powerful and mysterious effect, and he was suffused with a spark of stimulation. The feeling spread like poured honey, and there was a dawning cognizance that something stronger had been piqued. *This totally isn't the acid.* Leo slipped the garnet into his pants pocket and with wide eyes, left the house and got into his car. He was charged in a way that he hadn't felt before—subtle, but significant.

With everyone in the house preoccupied, no one seemed to notice Leo slipping out the front door. He put the car in reverse, did a quarter turn and drove out of the property. He normally didn't like to drive while tripping; it was always a little too disorienting. It wasn't that he didn't feel safe—he liked how dangerous it was—it was more that he couldn't actually seem to get where he wanted to go. His foot pressed into the gas pedal as he merged onto 310 North. When he took the exit for I-10 East to New Orleans, he looked out the passenger-side window at the airport. For many years now he had wanted to fly somewhere far away, out of the South. The South was like a glue trap: every time he tried to escape, he got pulled back in and ended up right back where he started. Time would pass, he would get older, and people he knew would come and go, but it was always the same thing: a cyclic pattern that felt inescapable.

He could remember the last time he'd taken a trip, which had been some six, maybe eight, years earlier. It was also the first time he had ever been on a plane. His trip to Colorado hadn't worked out like he'd thought it would. He had booked a one-way ticket to Denver and upon arrival, had nowhere to go and only a few thousand dollars to his name. He had made it work by doing what he needed to do, the things people do when they have to survive, but it was never enough. He had called his parents as a last resort, and they had coughed up enough money for a plane ticket back to Louisiana, a place he knew, with couches he could stay on, drugs he could find.

Fifteen minutes later he pulled onto Burgundy Street and nestled his car into a parking spot on the corner of Burgundy and Conti. The car needed work, like most other things in his life, and a burning, oily smell from under the hood wafted in the hot air as Leo slammed the door shut. The door squeaked, the oil leaked, the left front tire was splitting. *One day I'll get what I really want: a bike.* Leo walked down Burgundy, avoiding the pools of liquor and plastic cups. He could always tell when he was in the Quarter. Without actually having an agenda, he found himself walking into the first bar that caught his attention. It was the glimpse of an empty pool table illuminated in the dim light that enticed him. He ordered a drink and grabbed the pool stick from the top of the table. It didn't really matter what kind of bar it was; it was all the same to him, and he didn't have opinions about bar aesthetics or ambience. Anything was interesting enough when he was on acid.

After a few minutes of hitting the balls around on the table, they suddenly began leaving trails behind them. The eight ball shooting across the table looked like a segmented caterpillar sneaking off into the corner pocket. Days with visual phenomena like this seemed more normal to him than days without them. He collected the balls from the pockets and racked them back up inside the triangle, whose wood grain flowed like sand on the bottom of a shallow stream. It was at this point that he rediscovered his skin, or what he imagined it would feel like to do so. He had been told that this batch of acid was a little stronger than the last. It was true. He was able to see and experience the things that he thought had disappeared because of habitual use. A second passed. A minute. He then decided to keep playing. He had just pulled the stick back to break when a voice caught his attention. He looked up to see a young man in a green polo shirt—*so New Orleans*—with four eyes. Not glasses—literally four eyes when Leo stared at him. These were the visuals he missed when he was sober, the kind that made him feel like he wanted to throw up or take a dump.

"Hey, can we join?" the four-eyed man asked in the type of Louisiana accent that gave every sentence a sense of being curved, rising in the beginning and slowly declining into the finish.

Leo stared at the man and his friend behind him, who was swirling in a pool of geometric patterns. He said nothing. Inside his head, thoughts were flying a mile a minute, but his tongue wasn't moving.

"Hey, ya heard me?" the man asked.

Of course I heard you.

"You playin' with anybody? Wanna play in teams?"

Leo dipped the pool cue down, and the tip smacked the top of the table. He was immediately immersed in sensation. He was certain that his mind was playing tricks on him. He could have sworn he had answered the man, but he couldn't be entirely sure. It was as if he were struggling to string sentences together that made complete sense in his head but not when he said them.

"Hey!" The four-eyed man snapped his fingers a few times in front of Leo's face. "You done?"

"I said no, dude!" Leo wasn't entirely sure he had answered, but he knew he had at least thought it. The pool stick fell from his clammy hands, and he picked up the cue ball and tossed it back and forth in front of the two men. The mesmerizing trailing effect of the ball traveling between his hands was suddenly the most important thing in the bar. "I'm still playing," he said, his voice sharp and uninterested.

"It doesn't look like ya are, and we've been waiting an hour for you to finish so we can play."

Leo lifted his eyes from the streaming haze of the ball dancing on the table and looked into one of the man's four eyes. The man looked different—increasingly different. The longer Leo stared at him, the more his face seemed to change not only shape but personalities, ethnicities. It wasn't long before the young LSU student from Lake Charles became what Barack Obama would look like if Pablo Picasso had painted him. *How could this acid be so strong? I'm so used to it. It's familiar, but different. It all makes sense. What's it all for?*

"I would still be playing if y'all hadn't interrupted me," Leo said, his voice lower than before. Still annoyed. Still amazed.

The friend on the left emerged from the algebraic configuration that pulsed around him. "Man, I don't even like pool," said the man, who looked like David Bowie but with Jimmy Fallon's face. "Come on, let's play darts." David-Jimmy gripped Four Eyes by the shoulder and pulled him toward the dartboard.

"I fuckin' hate Jimmy Fallon," Leo said, his eyes wide and flickering over the man's face. "He's not funny. Why do people think you're funny? Your jokes are weak as fuck." He suddenly looked off into the distance and read an ad posted on a bulletin board that caught his attention for no reason at all, other than the unnecessarily large callback numbers 444-4444. *Dude, what's it all for...for for...for for four four.*

"All right, you're done. Gimme the table," Four Eyes demanded as he nudged Leo out of the way.

Leo stepped away. Inside his head there had been a mild explosion of emotion. From deep within the roomy caverns of his head, he spat out, "How many times do I gotta tell your dumb ass, I'm not done! Get in line, bitch!" *For for for—four four four for.*

Four Eyes stepped closer to the pool table and pushed away the hand of his friend, who was trying to pry him out of what looked to be the beginning of a fight. None of his friends wanted him involved in something like that. Four Eyes had been to jail once after being pulled over after leaving the drive-thru daiquiri shop in Slidell. The cop had arrested him for driving with an open container, which, in Louisiana, could simply mean having a straw in the cup. David-Jimmy hadn't ever been in a fight, but he could run really fast if he needed to.

"Oh, so you wanna be an asshole then, huh?"

"Dude, chill the fuck out," Leo snapped, and he pushed Four Eyes *four four four—four four four four* in the shoulder.

"Watch where you put your hands, faggot," Four Eyes snarled.

Leo clicked his tongue, tossed the cue ball onto the table and grabbed the baggy crotch of his pants. "Watch deez nuts."

Four Eyes grabbed hold of the pool stick, pushed Leo out of the way and motioned for his friend to join him at the table. Leo stepped away as a twinge of rage spilled out of his hands so quickly that he didn't even know there were objects in their path. One hand whirled to a plastic cup half filled with watery Jack and Coke, and the contents sprayed over the table and drenched Four Eyes's face. The plastic cup bounced off his polo shirt and clinked across the floor until it rolled under the pool table. The whole moment lasted only a few seconds, but Leo existed at a different speed. He had a moment to consider the sensations in his hand after he picked up the cup. He looked at the front and back of his hand and brought his other hand to hover above it. It felt like a combination of electricity and magnetism was vibrating from his hands. That was when his attention was drawn back to Four Eyes, who was steamrolling toward him. In the short moments before he had to act, he contemplated what exactly was happening. He knew he was acting up, and he knew the guy was angry, but he was positive he'd turned into a Tesla coil. *Am I really this fucked up right now?*

Leo bolted out of the bar and ran into the street, followed by the two men. The sound of heavy scampering echoed in his ears. He heard them chasing him, but it was a little different from how it would have been if he'd been sober. Every noise was accompanied by a hollow, metallic echo, as if they were running inside a Tibetan singing bowl. The perceptions were illusions, but the chase was real. Leo ducked down a dark side street that seemed to spring out of nowhere. A few long strides into the quiet street, a parked car with a license plate that ended in 4 4 4 sang out to him. He read the license plate in his head. M N X 4 4 4 *four four four four four.*

It was enough of a distraction to stop his legs from running. He didn't realize he had been standing still on the uneven sidewalk, waiting to be caught, until Four Eyes leaped into view and grabbed him by the collar of his oversized T-shirt. Leo snapped back to reality. Four Eyes seemed to lose two of his eyes and now was like everyone else, with only two eyes. For a moment, Leo didn't recognize him, but the smell of cigarettes and cheap beer mixed with the sight of the green polo shirt jogged his memory. Leo's bulging eyes were fixed on the man's face.

"I'm gonna beat your ass!" the man shouted. The friend stood back.

Leo's nerves all but cracked. In fact, they seemed to strengthen. His eyes darted toward the man's fist, which zipped toward Leo's face and crunched with the volume of a car wreck. A string of screams and cries mixed with stuttered panting. Leo was completely unscathed but still tripping on the inside, while the man stood before him clutching his hand, which had been crushed like a recycled soda can. The fingers had folded into a bloody, lumpy stump. It was miraculous: the man had never even made contact with Leo's body, yet his hand was damaged as though he'd tried to punch a moving train. Leo knew he wasn't exactly of sound mind, but he also knew he wasn't mistaken: the man had never touched him. It gave him a sort of arrogant confidence for a hot minute.

"Yeah, that's right, try it again, you brittle-boned motherfucker," Leo snapped as he started to grin. He wasn't sure what was actually real, but he knew he wasn't the one in trouble. With a bullish might, he shoved Four Eyes back into his friend's chest.

The student lost his footing, his legs buckled and he tumbled to his knees. No one knew exactly what had happened, but it was clear who had the upper hand. The friend shuffled his feet and turned to run. Leo was only a few steps behind him and thought the guy was within arm's reach. All he wanted to do was grab him, look him in the face so he could see the fear in his eyes, and then release him and watch him run away in fear. It would be so satisfying, he thought. The man hadn't taken more than a couple of terrified steps before Leo reached toward him and the man's neck flipped backward with a chiropractic snap. Although Leo hadn't made physical contact with him, his head bobbed flaccidly until he crashed to the ground like a marionette without a puppeteer.

Four Eyes knew he was the one being chased now, and it didn't look like it would last very long. Tears welled up and gushed down his face. His friend had just been killed—murdered—and he was most certainly going to be next. He reminded himself that he had known it was a bad idea to go out tonight and that he should have stayed in to study for his marketing quiz. He couldn't help it: he liked to party and he liked to drink, things that were part of his DNA, having grown up in Louisiana. He had always been too loud and overindulgent, and had a short temper to boot. It was something he felt he would never escape. He and Leo had that in common. Four Eyes had never been out of Louisiana and never really had any intention of leaving. He knew that moving three hours away from home was as far as he would ever go. But he would give it all up—the booze, the partying, the desire to stay homegrown…if he could just live through this moment.

Four Eyes tripped and collapsed under a gas streetlight, and Leo caught up and hovered above him. It had to be true. Everything that Nina had told them had to be true. He did have powers, maybe even more than he thought he was capable of. The newest and most fascinating discovery wasn't a power at all. It was the feeling of superiority. Leo was quarrelsome—he always had been, like a skinny Chihuahua that snarls and barks at everything and everyone. Now he felt empowered and justified. He wasn't thinking clearly, and in a matter of seconds, had entire conversations with himself about life and the many awakening possibilities he had witnessed. It was this cloudy perception that led him to test himself before he left the Quarter.

"You gonna try an' hit me again?" Leo shouted, his hands open, fingers trembling.

Four Eyes writhed in pain, unable to speak. Leo stood his ground and watched him struggle. Fearful for his life, the man finally scrambled to his feet, surprised that he was being given a chance to run.

"Yeah, go on. Run…" Leo said as the man began to run away. He lifted his hand, dismissing his cowardice with a wave as if swatting a fly and whispered, "Pussy." Four Eyes plunged to the concrete with the swiftness of a magnetic attraction. Leo snorted and huffed in amazement. He looked all around to make sure no one had seen what had just happened. The street and every window down the block was still empty apart from the two bodies of people he had just killed without ever actually touching them. If that was as true as he believed it was, he needed to get out of there pretty damn quick.

Leo beetled off and made his way back to his car. Nina hadn't told him anything about being able to do something like that, but he couldn't tell anyone, not even her. He barely knew her. What if she got upset? What if she turned him in to the police? She wouldn't do that, though. It might mean exposing herself as a witch and everyone else, too—and she had made it very clear that that information was meant to stay in the dark.

As he made his way out of New Orleans and back toward the house, he tried to collect his thoughts. *Just be cool. Think about what you're gonna say, and be calm about it. Maybe they'll understand. You can't tell them. I'm such a loser. What the fuck. Wait, what even was that? What did I do? What else can I do? I know what I can't do: I can't go back to that bar anymore, not a single time more…four four four—four four four four. Man, shut up with that shit!*

CHAPTER 10

Leo didn't really mind how hot the evening was; that was the least of his problems. He pulled up to the house, parked and walked up to the door. He still hadn't figured out what he was going to say to anyone if they asked. He stepped inside and locked the door behind him. Already he was acting strange. Locking the door wasn't something he was known for doing regularly. He heard voices. Obviously, people were awake. He was still gliding down from the peak of his drug experience, and things weren't exactly perfectly clear. Holding his head down, he made his way around the corner and down the hall toward his room. He was less than a foot away from his door when he heard a voice from behind.

"Leo!" Nina called.

He whipped back around, looked at Nina, lifted his vape to his mouth and sucked in. He nodded to acknowledge her before he blew smoke into the air. It was a hefty amount of smoke, for which he was thankful, because it meant he didn't have to look at her immediately. He felt incredibly guilty, like the time his girlfriend found out he wasn't having sex with her because he was more satisfied masturbating in secret.

"Sup?" Leo said.

"Where did you go?"

"Just out for a drive," he said quickly.

"I had no idea you'd even left. No one knew where you were."

Leo laughed. "This isn't a foster home."

"It's not a bed-and-breakfast either," Nina said as she crossed her arms. She wasn't sure how much control she had over the group members' personal time and what was allowed. It made it difficult for her to enforce anything when she wasn't clear on her own policies.

"Well, we all learned that the first day we were here, didn't we?"

"Look…" Nina stepped closer and lowered her voice. "I'm not trying to be your mom, and I can't tell you where to go and when, but with all of us here—together—for a purpose, it's key that we know you're going to be here in the morning. You don't strike me as someone who likes being told what to do."

"I'm a little anti-authority, yeah," Leo agreed.

"If you want to stay here and be a part of this coven, you are more than welcome to do so. I want you to. We need you to. I know you're an antsy person and you get bored easily, but can you try to understand where I'm coming from? I'm, in a way, responsible for all of you. If you want to go out for a drive, go to the bars, whatever, be my guest. Just try to understand that we work best when we work together." Nina ran her hands through her hair and let out a deep sigh. "I just don't want to wake up one morning and realize your room is cleared out and you're halfway to San Antonio. I want you to be able to talk to me if something's wrong or you're thinking about leaving, and if not me, then someone else here."

"I'm not going anywhere. I have nowhere else to go," Leo said glumly. "I went for a drive, played some pool and that's it."

How would he ever be able to explain that he had accidentally (or intentionally) murdered two people while he was fucked up? He wasn't able to articulate the creepy rush of megalomania he'd felt when he'd heard the crackling pops of breaking bones in the empty street. It was curious that he had felt such a rush to begin with. He didn't know what to make of it or how to identify it. What emotion was it that he'd felt? Even he didn't think he could use the word *happy* to describe how he'd felt when he'd killed two people. That seemed psychotic. It led him to question if that's what happiness was and how he would even know, given that he truly thought he had never experienced it before. He decided to talk to her about that instead.

"Can I ask you something?" Leo asked politely.

"Of course, what is it?" Nina said with the softness of a feather.

"I've never told anyone about this before. I don't even really know how to tell you."

"Try."

"Sometimes, I feel like—ever since I can…" Leo could decide what would make the most sense. He licked his lips, took a drag from his vape and blew it to the side so it wouldn't hit Nina in the face. "This is gonna sound crazy, but I don't know if I've ever been happy. Not like I can't remember the last time I felt it—it's not like it's just been a long time or whatever. I really don't think…I can…*feel* happiness." He looked up at Nina, his face pinched and confused.

Nina said nothing but simply stared at Leo, which encouraged him to keep talking to fill the silence.

"I know the word, and I know other people are happy, but I can do the same thing that makes someone happy and not feel the same way. Even things that would make anyone feel happy. I think there's something wrong with me, because I…I can't feel it."

A spark in Nina's eye signaled to Leo that she knew something he didn't.

"You mean you feel you should be happier than you are?"

Leo threw up his hands and said, "No, dude, like, it feels like, empty. I have some ice cream and I know it's good and I know I like it, but it doesn't make me feel any better. I can laugh and cry, do things I actually like to do like drive, be outside, look at the stars, have my alone time, even be nice to other people, cuz I heard that makes a lot of other people happy, but I don't feel anything. None of it makes me feel anything. I just feel numb. Even—sorry to say this, but even fucking doesn't help. Sure, it feels good, but I'm not, like, happy. Even if it's with someone I like."

Nina had a suspicion about Leo and wanted to furtively delve into the answer.

"Where were you born, Leo?" she asked in a velvety voice.

He stared at her for a moment, wondering if she had heard anything he had said. "What?"

"Where were you born? What city? Where?" Nina pressed.

"I'm from here. Well, not here, but down the bayou a bit, in Golden Meadow. That's where my parents live. What do you wanna know that for?" *Four four four—four four four four. Goddamn it! That's the last time.*

"Were you born in Golden Meadow?"

"Naw, New Orleans. We left when I was just a few months old. My grandma was sick or something, and my parents inherited her house. So they moved to Golden Meadow to deal with it all, and they just ended up staying."

"Altitudo Impedimento."

Leo rolled his eyes and took a long drag from his vape. "Oh God, here we go. What's this now?"

"It means you have a magical altitude handicap."

Leo's eyes widened. "Handicap? So I'm, like, magically retarded?"

"Not retarded, handicapped. It's nothing you did, nothing you could have controlled or fixed. It happens to someone with the"—she made air quotes—"witch gene. It's something to do with the elevation and air pressure and being born below sea level. It can sometimes be a little screwy. It's like baking cookies in high altitudes. The same recipe...it just doesn't come out the same. Same principle, different altitudes."

"I came out wrong? My parents didn't bake me right?"

"It's not their fault," Nina said gently. "They couldn't have known that you had the gene, and even if they had, they might not have had the luxury of moving somewhere else."

"So that's a thing? You're saying that can be like a side effect? Not being able to feel normal human things?"

"Unfortunately, yes. It does happen. But it's something we can work through," Nina said reassuringly.

The curtains of disappointment in Leo's eyes parted just enough for him to have a moment of clarity. There were no tears for what he had just learned, but there was sadness and a revelation. It was something he had always known, but now he had learned a reason for it, an explanation. He chased danger not because he was naturally reckless but because the feeling was the closest substitute for the kind of fulfillment that comes from being genuinely happy. It made complete sense in a way that it never could have before. A part of him deep down had seemed to know something was off. Here proof was, staring him in the face, which was satisfying, but it still didn't make him any happier. What does one do with that kind of information? For a moment he wished he hadn't known the truth. Having an explanation but no cure only made it worse. It was like being born with a terminal illness and not knowing why you were always sick, until you found out and were told nothing could be done to save you.

Nina walked Leo to his room and made sure he didn't need anything else. Warmly caressing his shoulder as a sign of support, she reminded him that they were all there to help him and help each other. She lingered in the doorway for a moment, then said good night and closed the door behind her. Leo lay flat on his bed, his black, low-top canvas shoes hanging over the edge. He kicked them off, one after the other, before closing his eyes. He needed to think. He was too high to be unconscious, so he remained still and stared at the vast blackness on the inside of his eyelids. He started to wish Nina had asked him what else had happened tonight. If she were anywhere near as understanding and calm as she had been with him just now, maybe she wouldn't make a big deal about it. Or perhaps she would know what to do, if there was something to do. He would have told her everything—about the two men, about how he had killed them, about the phone number that he couldn't keep from haunting him. If he did that, he might have to explain a lot more if she asked about it, which she surely would. He would have to confess everything that he was feeling if it was going to be helpful—truly helpful. Could he do that? Could he tell her what he was thinking right now? That, as he was coming down from his high, he knew he had deliberately chosen to murder those young men…and didn't feel that bad about it? Leo didn't know for sure, but he was pretty certain there wasn't an altitude issue that caused him to be without empathy, without any remorse or guilt.

He slid his hand knuckle-deep under the waistband of his underwear and rested it there while he listened to the endless chatter and debate in his head. Eventually, it began to fade, and over time—such exhausting time—he started to feel like his normal—sober—self again. He opened his eyes and found the house to be dead silent except the buzzing insect noises from outside his window. He sat up, looked around the room and thought, *How did I ever get here and what is even going on?* His mood had acclimated back to somewhere between dark humor and sadness. He stripped off all his clothes and sat on the bed feeling extremely vulnerable.

The lightbulb in the little side-table lamp flickered and even made a faint purr while it stabilized. It was time to actually sleep, not just go to bed. He reached over to turn out the light and then slowly retracted his arm. Leo focused on the knob of the lamp. In the quiet of the room and the coolness of the conditioned air he could feel the subtle differences taking place in his body. He could feel the rise in temperature and the electric, dance-like connection he had made with the knob of the lamp. Then...the light switched off.

The coven members were fully awake by half past eight in the morning. Leo was the last to rise after a night of light, troubled sleep in which he dreamed up scenarios of murdering innocent people. It wasn't an alarm clock or any sort of circadian rhythm that woke him up, but a series of thumps at his bedroom door. The first three were shy and respectful, followed by a brief pause and then four more, heavy and urgent.

Thump. Thump. Thump...

THUMP THUMP THUMP THUMP!

"Yeah, what?" Leo bellowed as he slipped his bare feet onto the floor and started to put on his clothes from the previous day.

"You up?" Mitch asked from the other side of the door.

"What do you want?" Leo asked as he pulled his pants up, fearful that the gay would open the door uninvited and see him standing there naked.

"Are you going to eat breakfast? Avery made some eggs and stuff." Mitch leaned with his ear close to the door, listening—spying.

"I don't be eatin' like that in the morning," Leo said. He was a strange eater, with preferences that baffled most people who discovered them. He didn't like eggs, hated cheese on anything and preferred dry cereal straight out of the box with no milk.

"There's also some bacon and potatoes," Mitch said.

"Yeah, I'll be out in a minute."

Mitch stepped away from the door. "Okay. Um, just, like, don't wait too long, because I kind of ate the last of the potatoes, but there's still some on my plate. There's also only like a piece of bacon left too."

"Did you guys eat it all or what?"

"Well, Avery didn't think anyone was going to be up, so she only made enough for herself, but like, if herself was someone with a bigger appetite. It's getting a little cold. Except for the potatoes, I reheated those. But those are like, gone, except for what's on my plate."

Leo swung the door open, surprising Mitch. He stood without a shirt on, and Mitch tried hard not to look at his chest. The only way he thought he could avoid staring was to react in the language that Leo understood best: aggression. Before it was even a thought, Mitch slapped Leo across the face and scurried off down the hallway. Leo restrained an urge to scream or retaliate and finally put on his T-shirt and headed into the kitchen.

When Mitch said there was very little left of the eggs, potatoes and bacon, it was not an exaggeration. However, Mitch had taken a plate from the cupboard and put all the leftover food, including his fried potatoes, onto it for Leo. The plate was ready and partnered with a fork at the breakfast nook. Leo ate like a barbarian, the fork gripped in his fist like he was churning a crank. Fork down, scoop, fork up, food goes in, fork down, scoop, fork up, food goes in. It was the polar opposite of how Bisa ate, slow and refined. She made it look like eating a meal was no different from appreciating a painting on display at a museum. She looked at the plate as a whole, admired each component and then politely gathered her food onto her fork and placed it in her mouth. She wanted to taste the flavors. She wanted to taste how well they worked together or didn't work together, even if it was just a salted bagel with cream cheese.

Leo had finished the food on his plate and was eating Apple Jacks straight out of the box when Avery gasped at whatever she was reading on her phone.

"What?" Nina asked.

Avery kept her eyes glued to the screen as she continued to scroll through the article for additional details. "Oh my God! Two LSU students were beaten to death in the Quarter. Or mutilated, or something."

Leo stared at Avery but kept pulling cereal out of the box.

"What? When?" Nina probed.

"I'm not sure—they think sometime last night between ten and eleven." She paused for a minute as she flicked her finger across the screen to find specifics. "Whoa! Right off Burgundy. Like the Burgundy and Conti area. The police said their roommate said they were planning to go out drinking at Fahey's and be out for a while. The evening bartender said she served the two men but that they left around nine. That's all they know for now, I guess."

Leo tried to act completely normal, although now that he had come down and was sober, he wasn't sure how that was supposed to look. How does a normal person act when they are guilty but trying to hide it? Was he normal? He couldn't tell. What was normal? He couldn't decide on that either, not after the last few days. He kept quiet, thinking, *Fuuuuuuuuuuuuck*.

Nina turned to Leo without suspicion. "You went to the Quarter last night, didn't you? Do you know where that is, Burgundy and Conti? Did you see anything?"

Yup! "Nope." He popped another handful of cereal into his mouth. Two pieces fell to the floor. That's how he thought he should act: impolite. That was normal.

"New Orleans is ridiculous," Nina said. "Every news story is about either a murder or a parade."

"Who you tellin'?" Leo gagged out through the cereal. "I've lived here pretty much my whole life, and we have more murders than tourists and about half as many parades. And that's a lot."

"Are you really that insensitive?" Oliver asked from the other side of the kitchen, where he stood with a cup of coffee, his words running out of his mouth at icy speed.

Leo turned around, sending a trail of Apple Jacks across the floor like dollar bills in a rap video. "No, I'm telling it like it is."

Avery had moved on to another article about the same crime, and her fingers scrambled down her screen, looking for other information. "Well, Leo, you can either complain about the problem or be part of the solution— Oh my God!"

"What is it?" Nina asked, leaning against the kitchen counter and positioned to watch them all.

"One of the students, apparently beaten into the sidewalk, was the youth council president and events leader for that really big church. You know the one with the commercials?"

"What church?" Leo asked.

"You know, the one with the really long commercials with the organ music and the really clean couple…The wife looks like pink lemonade with brown hair. Always look like they're on a permanent honeymoon."

"I have no idea who you're talking about," Leo said honestly.

"Neither do I," Bisa added.

Avery hesitated for a minute and then tried to catch them up as quickly as she could. "They have three or four campuses." No reaction. "They're really into Water Baptism Wednesdays—they're like mini carnivals." Still no response.

Then, "The Whole Truth and True Light?" Nina exclaimed.

"Assembly of God Church," Avery said, finishing the church's full name. "Yes!"

"Who the hell is that?" Leo barked through his last handful of cereal.

"The Bonners," Nina said, having finally understood who they were talking about.

"How do you know who they are?" Bisa asked.

"I watch TV."

"See?!" Avery said. "Those commercials. With the falling rose petals. Didn't you guys see their billboard on your way here from the airport? They are gonna lose their shit, oh my

God, I can't even imagine what kind of nonsense they are going to come up with. I'm sure they will blame another minority group like they did when they tried to add Bible study to lunch periods in public schools." She rolled her eyes.

"Boo hoo, they're hateful Bible-banging rednecks," Leo said darkly.

"Aren't you a redneck?" Bisa said only half jokingly.

"Nope. I'm white trash."

"Is there a difference?"

"Damn right there is."

"What?" Bisa challenged.

Leo pointed the edge of the cereal box at his crotch, cupped his balls and squealed, "Deez nuts! Ha!"

Bisa rolled her eyes, but then, for a reason even she couldn't understand, she smiled. Actually, it was less of a smile and more of a sneer, but it was done in a lighthearted spirit nonetheless.

Leo slammed the cereal box down on the counter and started to walk out of the kitchen. He stopped a few feet from Bisa and crossed his arms. "You know what? I don't like your flip attitude," he said jokingly.

"All right, you guys. Enough," Nina said. "We aren't going to last very long if we keep up like this. We need to start trying to understand each other a little better and, beyond that, start accepting each other and our backgrounds. If that news article and having Trump as president has reminded us of one thing, it's that we *haven't* become more progressive. We've only removed the masks that people have been wearing and pulled the gags out of their mouths that they've kept on tight. And that has shown our true colors, our lack of integrity, humanity and compassion as a species. Those horrors have just been spilling out and spilling out, and it's the worst kind of poison, because it's contagious, it spreads. And it's killing us. *We* are killing us. We are hateful and without empathy, remorse or even the slightest interest in being empathetic or remorseful. Now, if there is one thing I know about greatness, it's that it starts from something small, something humble, and becomes great."

Nina stood motionless by the door to the kitchen like some kind of empowered politician, one who had just watched a moving Beyoncé video. In her knee-length dress with its long cape sleeves the color of crushed berries and her strappy sandals, her hair natural and flowy with the shine of morning dew, she looked like an enchanted version of herself, a woman so devoted to the art of delivery that she moved even herself when she spoke. That feeling came and went for Nina, but everyone else thought it was ever present.

"Everyone, wash your hands," she said. "Clean up your mess and meet me in the great room. It's time to see what everyone can do." Her face was relaxed but authoritative as she glided out of the kitchen and around the corner.

The group began making their way to the great room. Leo was still riding the joke he had made earlier about Bisa's flip attitude—a joke he had been riding specifically because he wanted another excuse to talk to her. He made it a point to walk past her, narrowing his eyes, then shake his head and say, "I still don't like it."

CHAPTER 11

It was only a few minutes past nine thirty, and the temperature was already pushing 90 degrees with the potential to get even hotter as the sun blazed through the cloudless sky. Depending on how well Avery could generate fire, the air conditioner might not be able to keep up. It was about to get hot. One of the few things she had left behind in her travels was her lighter, a butane torch lighter that looked like a chocolate bar. She'd found it at a café in Brooklyn, and although she had never smoked, it was too delicious to pass up. It came in handy when she started smoking, even though she couldn't for the life of her tell you exactly what made her start. It was probably her old boyfriend, the one who smoked a lot of medicinal marijuana for his ulcer or something that didn't seem to make sense to her. Whenever someone would ask why she'd started smoking, she would always say, "When you live with someone who complains all the time about everything, even if you're one hundred percent in love with this person, you will probably end up smoking their pot just so you can tolerate how much they bitch." She meant it with love. The love was gone, and she missed the lighter more than she missed him.

The end of their relationship had initiated the awakening of her spirit. She had become more confident in what she wanted for herself and stopped apologizing for things she had no reason to feel guilty about. One could say she felt lucky to have dodged that bullet, one that would have struck her in the heart. She was so overwhelmed with the psychic vampirism of her boyfriend that she would've had no other option but to stay in the relationship until it killed her. At least that's how she envisioned her future if she hadn't chosen to leave. That's when her traveling began. It suddenly became one of the most important things to her. Her boyfriend would rather watch someone on television experiencing something worthwhile than actually go and do it himself.

Avery had become a manifestor and had many truths she wanted to unearth, many places she wanted to experience and many better ways to spend her time. Things started to fall in line for her as if falling into her lap. Luck. Or manifestation? She didn't know, but she kept a journal about it, a ratty, wide-ruled wireless notebook with a blazing purple cover. She had always loved notebooks, the kinds with actual paper that had perforated edges and cost seventy-nine cents at the drugstore. It felt like a dying relic in the age of the smartphone and tiny supercomputer laptops, but Avery loved it. It gave her an opportunity to explore her thoughts and expand her consciousness, her life, where others just saw a quirky girl writing in a paper notebook. The more she wrote in it, the more divine intervention seemed to be guiding her down a path rich with the reward of fulfillment and satisfaction.

When she arrived in Charlotte from New York City, she filled her notebook up to the very last page and even onto the inside of the back cardboard cover. She told herself that when she filled the notebook, she would burn it with the chocolate bar lighter she'd found on a cracked tile floor in the middle of a breakfast rush. But now the lighter was gone, her boyfriend was gone, her former self was gone and suddenly there she was, another version of Avery that she had only just begun to discover. She was so excited about practicing her powers that it caused her to miss what Nina had been saying for the last couple of minutes.

"There are other witches out there—not many, but some," Nina said. "Some are even in covens like this one. But all of you in this group are exceptionally special, because the Advisory was given a prophecy, foretold by someone named Volustina. She had a moment of enlightenment. She was a sort of…oracle, and what we know is that one night on a blood moon, she had a dream that told her the events of our world and gave her six words. Those words would be the key to the ultimate discovery, one that would benefit all of mankind. This prophecy has been kept mostly as legend, but always with someone watching over it, ever since it came into existence. When that was, we aren't sure. But the words that came to her turned out to be names, the names Avery…Oliver…Leo…Mitchell…and Bisa. Your names. Plus the addition of the one to guide them, Nina. This is why we have come together and why we must work together. We are responsible for three specific and subtle tasks. Our energy completing them will tip the scales in the right direction. We need to complete an act to balance spiritual, mental and emotional energies."

Bisa scratched her head for a few seconds and then raised her hand to talk, something she might not have done the day before.

"You don't need to raise your hand, Bisa. You're free to talk here. Everyone is," Nina reminded her.

"But doesn't everything we do, magically or not, end up having an effect on everyone in those ways anyway?"

"Of course—just like someone without our powers could change the energies by doing something that they think has little significance. But it's *our* energies that affect the balance, like chemistry. Like baking soda and vinegar."

"What are the tasks?" Bisa asked.

Nina crossed her legs and clasped her hands together. "To enter the spirit realm and retrieve or release a spirit." She looked at Oliver and Bisa. "To reverse a strong, influential and negative pattern of thinking." She scanned the rest of the group, briefly stopping at Leo before continuing to scan the group as a whole. "And to reverse the emotional wounds that are otherwise beyond repair. Then there is something extra that one of us can do or all of us can try to do. We can locate the rafkolite*."

That was when Nina, who had been telling a chilling tale of mystery, suddenly lost most of the group. Oliver had been the most receptive to the story, but Leo and Bisa, who had guesstimated their own futures many times, had failed to ever include being part of a prophecy given by someone named Volustina. Mitch, however, was into it; he was the sort of person who kept crystals and stones in his pocket, and rafkolite sounded like something he didn't have but needed to. Avery was the first to break the silence.

"What's that? Sounds like a rock," Avery suggested.

"You're close. A meteorite that hit the earth millions of years ago. It is rumored to do many things, but the one thing for certain is that it will generate a butterfly effect of positive energy when used by the right person or group. That's us, in this case. One or more of us will find it."

"How do we find it?" Leo asked, already very interested. It sounded like a challenge, and challenges were often dangerous. Which meant he was already 100 percent engaged.

"We start by strengthening our abilities first. As we do that, we have a better chance of finding and using the rafkolite."

"You're telling me that between us, the Advisory and whoever else there is, no one can find something, even with all those abilities combined?" Leo asked.

"No one has been able to complete all the necessary steps to find it. Most witches don't even try because it's so complicated. There's more to it than just looking under a rock," Nina said. "There isn't a spell that can help detect its location, and there's not a single witch that can divine where it is. It's beyond that. But it has been confirmed that one of us in this room, at some point in the future, will be able to locate it and use it. I don't know who and I don't know when or even how."

"I bet I could find it," Leo said proudly.

"So, now you're Marco Polo?" Nina joked.

"I've seen enough movies to know there has to be a way," Leo replied.

"Rafkolite is more than just a quarter on the sidewalk. There's only one way to find it."

"So there is a way!" Avery exclaimed.

"The only way is through completing the Union of the Divine Dualities and invoking the *nigrum pullum*…the black pullet."

"Well, fuck, what are we sitting around jerking off for? Let's do that then!" Leo shouted with the tone of someone who had just realized they were holding the keys they had spent ten minutes looking for.

Nina shook her head and said, "None of us are prepared or have the tools to even begin something like that. That could get any of us killed."

"Y'all are a bunch of hoes," Leo said as he spread his legs out and leaned back to take a puff off his vape.

"What's it like?" Bisa asked as she shot a heavy stare at Leo.

"What's what like?" Leo answered with a smirk.

"To be so miserable? Is anything safe from your mocking?" Bisa shook her head as if she already knew the answer to her own question.

The smirk slowly faded from Leo's face before he said with a perfunctory puff, "Nope."

Nina frowned, a mixture of irritation and frustration flooding her face. Whatever her feelings were, they were irrelevant to the greater good at the moment. She was, however, responsible for giving the coven a sense of guidance and assuming the role of leader. It was time, once again, to put her feet into those shoes. The easygoing and approachable tone she'd begun with was transforming into a stern and authoritative one. She lifted her left hand and snapped her fingers.

"We're getting off topic here. We will get to everything we need to when it's time. We start off small—that's how we get to where we need to be. So stop the bickering, put down your vape and let's get to why we're actually here. Your powers."

Everyone adjusted themselves in their seats, turned to Nina and got quiet. Oliver was the most prepared. Mitch had been thinking about how Bisa had called Leo miserable, and his heart sank. He could see it, he could even feel it, and if there was something he wanted to do more than anything else, it was to help him out of it. Perhaps that was the second-most important thing. Ever since Leo had used *jerking off* in a sentence, all he could think about was Leo…jerking off. The fantasy stuck in his head and started to grow, in more ways than one. Before he knew it, Nina was telling them it was time to begin. Avery and Bisa were somewhere between nervous and exhilarated. That's when Nina stood from her chair.

"I'd like to start with some magical sit-ups, starting with the other Transcendents." Nina raised her palms and pointed at Bisa and Oliver. "You two are the ones most in touch with the divine and the gifts that germinate from that. The best way to harness your gifts is to trust your vibes. You have sight beyond the physical senses, and you receive information with this sight. It's how I was able to find all of you. You're a sort of antenna. Listen to your body, feel the clues."

"What does it feel like?" Oliver asked as he rubbed his hands together.

"Gut feelings, tingling up and down the body, particularly the spine, physical reactions. Think of when you first meet someone or when you start something new. Those are times when you can really tune in and figure out the nuances around you. Although we all have access to this type of power, you have a natural gift for it—a way to create magic with your intention. Essentially that's all magic really is: living and acting with intention. Now that all of you have been attuned and have entered this coven, I can teach you how to live with this type of power." Nina broke eye contact with Oliver and Bisa and addressed the others. "We have all been attuned, and you will have these powers for the rest of your life, so pay attention, because everything you learn will only make you a better witch. It will only help create change."

"Where do we start?" Oliver asked with the excitement of someone given keys to a new car.

"Everyone give me something that has some meaning for you—anything. Don't let anyone else see what it is. If you don't have anything on you, grab something from your room and bring it back." There was a flurry of energy as everyone shuffled through their pockets or scurried off to their room to retrieve something. Nina grabbed a small bowl made from a coconut shell and painted cobalt blue on the inside. "Bisa and Oliver, come here. Stand next to me," she ordered.

"You can just call me Ollie," Oliver informed her as he approached Nina's side.

Nina nodded and said, "The vibes we get are as common as breathing, so we usually just overlook them and their significance." She stood behind Oliver—Ollie—and placed her hands on his shoulders. "Close your eyes, Ollie. Open your *third* eye, and see what others do not." She paused for a moment before removing her hands from his shoulders. "What do you see? What do you feel?"

Oliver shook his head. "I don't know. Nothing?"

"Look beyond that nothing. Listen to my voice, then listen for what you hear in the room, listen to what you hear outside. What do you hear going on miles and miles away in the city? The vibes are subtle. They will grow stronger as you become more aware of them." Nina left his side, collected the items from everyone and placed them in the bowl. Ollie looked like he was dreaming. His face was serene but with a hint of concentration. He had never been so focused in his life, yet he wasn't sure what he would be able to achieve by being so. Nina circled back to Ollie. She lifted the bowl to his belly, grabbed hold of his hand and placed the tips of his fingers on the rim of the bowl.

"Keep your eyes closed and choose an object from the bowl," Nina instructed, her voice soft and hypnotic, like the after-ring of a small bell.

Ollie slipped his fingers over the rim and into the bowl. His middle finger snagged on a few items while his thumb and index finger pushed the other objects around. He wanted to choose something based on instinct. He grabbed hold of something and drew his hand up quickly. The rest of the unknown items clinked back into the bowl and settled at the bottom.

"Listen to your body," Nina coached. "Don't try to determine what the object is just by touch. Go deeper. What vibrations do you feel?"

"What kind of magic is this?" Avery asked, curious.

"I'm trying to help him develop his physical intuition. Psychometry," Nina said without taking her eyes off Ollie's face. "What do you feel?"

Oliver's eyelids twitched a little as he fumbled for words. "I'm not sure. I feel, something? Maybe? How do I know I'm not just making it up?"

"That's part of how it works. We receive, but it doesn't come like how we've all been trained to believe it comes. It's something the logical mind will try to find holes in because it's not logical. It functions outside of logic, but it's not any less valid. We can understand something and see the hard truth of something, that's logic, but feeling is beyond logic. What do you feel?" she pressed further.

Ollie's ears moved and his nostrils flared a little. Something was happening. "What if I'm wrong?"

"Then you'll be one step closer to knowing what to trust," Nina said simply.

Ollie let out a gentle sigh but felt a little doubtful. He wasn't just being tested, he was being tested before a group on something that seemed to function outside of rational logic. "I have…I kind of have some pain. Right here." He tapped his forehead with the tip of his finger. "Like a headache. Is that normal?"

"You tell me. Did you have one earlier?" Nina questioned as she began to walk farther from him, leaving him to rely on himself.

"No. It just now started." Other facial tics began to spill out as he tried to make sense of what he was seeing, thinking—feeling. He took one more deep breath and balled up his fists, his thumbs running across the length of his knuckles. Then, he could feel it—he could feel beyond what was in his hand. "I think…it feels like…I have a headache. Also…I see…red. Red, but, it feels…I don't know how it feels. I see clouds or fog—no, smoke. It's smoke." Ollie took a deep breath in through his nose, and on the out breath, he let out a sigh of satisfaction. "I can't believe I'm saying this, but it tastes sweet. I can…kind of taste it."

Nina smiled and started to walk toward Ollie, knowing that she was about to stop the exercise very soon. "What does it taste like? Describe it. Trust your vibes."

Ollie licked his lips, ran his tongue back and forth and then said, "It tastes…cheap, like drugstore candy, but I like it. Why do I like it?" He was confused. Usually the thought of it would repulse him. It was something he'd never choose to eat. But there he was, seeing it, tasting it, and liking the taste. It made no sense. It was remarkable.

Nina walked up next to his side and lifted his closed fist for all of them to see. "Now, open your eyes and see what's in your hand."

Ollie did as instructed, and snapped back to reality. He looked down into his palm to see a tiny piece of raw garnet. "Whose is this?"

"Wait, no one say anything!" Nina broke in quickly. She held up her hand like a stop sign to everyone else and then returned her gaze to Ollie. "Who do you think it belongs to?" Nina took a second glance at the item and realized that it was the garnet stone from the study, the one she had single-handedly placed on the shelf for energetic and decorative purposes. In that moment, she felt a little confused. What energy was he interpreting, and more importantly, who had put that stone in the bowl?

Ollie stared at the floor for a moment and then looked up at Leo. "It's you. It's yours?" he said, but only half confidently. When there wasn't an immediate response, he looked to Nina for verification. "Right? It's his?"

Leo raised his hand high and waved it in the air. "Yeah, I put that in there."

"Do you have a headache?" Ollie asked, realizing that the head pain had subsided now that he had stopped concentrating.

"No, but I smoke. The vape juice I got is strawberry custard."

"So, the red…" Ollie questioned the void.

Nina raised her hands slowly and then spoke. "Could be many things. It could be the color of the rock you picked up on, it could be a color he is connected to." She knew that it could be something else entirely, but it wasn't the time to delve into situations like that. "Good work. That's only the start. And don't worry about it being a little wonky. That'll improve, but you also may be really strong in other areas too. Maybe you're a spiritual clairvoyant." She had a gut feeling that he fit the characteristics of someone with spiritual sight. Once she'd congratulated Ollie on his first exercise, she turned to Leo. "Where did you get this?"

"From that room with all the books," Leo said, pointing toward the study.

"Why did you already have that in your pocket?"

"I don't know. I picked it up the other day and it just felt kinda cool. Like, powerful. So I kept it. People do that, right? They carry stones and shit, right?"

"Yes…usually to draw from the power the stone gives," Nina answered with a vague sense of suspicion. The feeling passed as quickly as it had come, and she decided to continue with the exercises. "Bisa…one of the more controversial gifts for a Transcendent witch is the ability to have an effect on someone's motivations, the power of suggestion and influence."

"Manipulation?" Bisa inquired.

"Encouraged direction," Nina corrected, trying to make the concept seem a little less sinister. "The nature of the witch is what makes it dangerous. Let's say you got into an argument with someone, your emotions got the best of you, and you bent their will to satisfy yourself. That's where we get into trouble— that's where a lot of people have gotten into trouble." She turned her eyes toward Mitch and tilted her head down slightly. She forced her influence upon him in the gentlest way possible. "Mitch, you're going to get up, go to the kitchen and grab me a slice of bread and the box of salt."

Before anyone could even process what was happening, Mitch had fallen under her influence. There wasn't any noticeable difference in the way that he appeared. He still had the same hunched posture, and he didn't look excited or confused or nervous.

"Okay," Mitch responded, and then he stood up and walked toward the kitchen. There was no hesitation. It was as seamless as if it had been his own idea.

"You want anything to drink, Ollie?" Nina asked swiftly.

"I guess, water?" Ollie answered uncertainly.

Nina leaned forward. "Bring Ollie a glass of water. Ice water. A big glass."

"Okay," Mitch said as he rounded the corner into the kitchen.

Underneath the mystery of Nina's strange requests was solid reasoning. The room was quiet except for the faint hum of the air vents and Mitch tinkering around the kitchen. As he poured the water, everyone looked at Nina expectantly, but she said nothing. She could feel their curious minds waiting for some clarity, but she wanted to unveil the surprise at the appropriate time, to make for a more explosive impact. Nina clasped her fingers together, crossed her legs and patiently awaited Mitch's return to the great room. When Mitch came around the corner holding the glass of water and the piece of bread and box of salt on a plate, Nina instructed him to hand Ollie the glass and give the plate to her. She opened the spout on the top of the salt container. With a slow tilt of her hand, she overturned the canister and covered the slice of bread with a thick layer of salt, so much that the bread could no longer be seen. Nina looked up at Mitch and thanked him with a nod.

"Mitch, you realize that you're under my influence," Nina said.

"I am?" Mitch responded, surprised.

"Yes, but you're going to go sit back down now, and then you'll forget that I ever asked you to go to the kitchen, all right?"

"For sure," Mitch said. He turned around, sat back down in his seat and returned to being an active onlooker.

Nina smiled. She looked down at the plate with a mischievous grin. She could have done several things, but she had chosen to have a little fun instead.

Leo snapped his fingers a few times at Mitch. "Hey, Mitch."

Mitch looked over at Leo, puzzled. "What?"

"Do you remember doing that?" Leo asked sharply.

Mitch scrunched his eyebrows together. He gently shook his head, smiled nervously and said, "Uh…doing what?"

"Going to the kitchen, getting the water and salt," Leo said. He expected him to say he did remember. How could he not?

"What?" Mitch said, cocking his head to the side as if Leo were talking straight-up nonsense.

Leo pointed to the glass of water in Ollie's hand and spoke deliberately, his tone condescending. "That. Glass. Do. You. Remember. Getting. That. Glass. Of. Water? Just. Now."

Mitch looked perplexed. Leo was asking about something he clearly had not done. Or so he thought. It seemed like a preposterous question. How could he have gotten up to get water when he was 100 percent certain that he hadn't once left his seat? "Um, I don't, yeah— I don't get it. Like…" Mitch paused for a moment and then continued, raising his hands for emphasis. "No!"

"Oh, what the crap," Leo said excitedly.

While Leo had been questioning Mitch, Nina had been turning Oliver's attention back toward herself with the magnetic pull of her mind. As she looked over the features of

Oliver's face, she remembered a moment in college when she had argued with a professor over her midterm assignment for a class called Thinking and the Visual Arts. Her professor was a handsome man and, apart from the age difference, looked very similar to Ollie. She had conflicted feelings about him. She loved the poetic wisdom he oozed about life and art but loathed his teaching style. Vitus Dicer was his name, or Pompous Ass to most of his students. He had the appearance of being a dynamic mentor with an undeniable fanatical love of his field, but under that, he cared less about his students and more about his own perspectives.

Vitus had a bit of a reputation, one known across campus in every program of study. Even those students who weren't art and design majors knew about his appetite for weak students. Every now and then he would psychotically lash out in front of the entire class, usually during a critique of a student's piece, and would send the student away either in tears or to the registrar's office to drop his class. Those who were still on the class roster and survived every week called the process getting "Diced." Nina had no intention of being Diced. It was bound to happen at some point, though. Where he was rigid and uncompromising, Nina was often imaginative and idealistic.

The final straw that nearly forced her out of class came up when the students were assigned to create a 4D project in the aesthetic of another artist. It wasn't the concept that caused the problem, although she strongly disagreed with the idea of re-creating the work of other artists; it was the events that in her private life that forced her to procrastinate. Being the resourceful and creative spirit that she was, she had changed her piece to something more performative and run it by her professor a few days before it was due.

She never forgot Vitus Dicer's words: "Nina, you have to be flexible and respond to conditions. I don't know what to say about having the last two days of a three-week project be the make-or-break moment. I'd expect you to be putting finishing touches on something, not starting it. But we will see what you come up with."

She didn't exactly get Diced, but it pissed her off. That was the moment when she wished she could have used her power of influence, to Dice Vitus Dicer. Had it not been for that assignment, her grade wouldn't have dropped from an A to a B. But that's how the abuse of power starts, with small manipulations like that. Soon they take over every choice you make. However, looking back on it, she realized that Vitus did have a point. She never procrastinated from that point on, and vowed to practice integrity over self-interest.

Nina had started Ollie's exercise with integrity in mind, but as she prepared for his next task, she realized that her style of thinking had perhaps led her to teach with self-interest, at least about the next exercise. She looked down at the plate of bread and salt and wondered if there was another technique she could've used. Of course there was, but now it was she who had become the uncompromising teacher, albeit seeing her students as equals—cooperative members.

"Bisa…" Nina said in a cloudy voice. "Right now, Ollie is under my influence."

Everyone turned to look at Ollie, whose eyes were fixed on Nina. He was blank-eyed, his face as empty as a dilapidated house for rent. A heaviness in his cheeks seemed to pull down on his jaw and open his mouth ever so slightly. Nina smiled with the magnificence of a waxing crescent moon. "I want you to try to exercise your power of suggestion on Ollie."

Bisa, both surprised and a little worried, looked at Ollie and asked, "How do I do it?"

Nina held her hand out toward Bisa and grabbed hold of her soft fingers. With a tight but gentle pull, Nina brought Bisa in closer toward her body, keeping her eyes on Ollie. "It's easier to start with the eyes. Come close. Try not to overthink it or rationalize it. Breathe. Listen. Do you hear it? Do you hear his mind?"

Bisa bit her lip and shook her head slightly, as if trying to see through a dense fog. "I'm not sure. I hear—static." She was excited now and could feel the rush of adrenaline as her heart beat faster and faster. "I feel it," she said slowly. For a brief few seconds, her mind was flooded with information, a steaming crucible of thoughts and insights.

Nina continued to soothingly guide Bisa through a series of whispers. "Allow your intention to give that energy a purpose, create that purpose, imprint your intention onto that energy. Leave the conscious, ego-driven mind behind, let that higher-frequency energy flow." Nina stepped back a few paces and said, "It's no different from art. Create change with your intention."

"I feel spacey, groggy," Bisa said as she blinked, trying to recover a sense of normality.

"That's natural as you continue to raise your vibration. It's like running water through a clogged and rusty pipe. It just takes some time to clear." Nina crossed her arms and took a second to look at the coven, all of them—mesmerized. "Now, make Ollie take this piece of bread and take a bite."

For a moment, Bisa didn't answer. She stood there, fixed on Ollie, uncertain whether she had complete control or it was just her imagination. Then she spoke with belief. "Are you hungry, Oliver?"

"No," he responded, idle-faced.

"But you are hungry—in fact, you're starving…"

Nina interrupted, "You don't have to speak…Remember, tune in, and communicate. Trust yourself."

Bisa took a deep breath and narrowed her eyes on Oliver as if he were disappearing into the horizon. In the time it takes for a wick to catch fire, she suddenly felt the connection stronger than before, as if it had been turned on full blast. Inside her mind, she focused her intention to provide clear and accurate instructions to Ollie as if they were his own thoughts. Everyone looked back and forth between Ollie and Bisa as though they were watching cars drive up and down the main street of a small town. Then Ollie stood up and casually walked over toward Nina, reached down to the slice of heavily salted bread and picked it up with the support of all his fingers. The bread might as well have been a scoop of ice cream, judging from his lack of hesitation. As he took a bite, salt crystals fell from the bread and onto the plate, and bits of white stuck to the sides of his mouth. He chewed without question and had no reaction to the taste or the act at all. He was on the verge of swallowing when Nina took the slice of bread from him and set it back down on the plate.

"Now release," Nina said.

Bisa dropped her suggestive intent, and suddenly Ollie's urge to eat the bread was gone. He gagged and spit out what was in his mouth into his hand. "Why did I eat that?" he exclaimed.

"That was Bisa, giving her influence a test run—and it worked flawlessly, by the way," Nina said.

"Holy shit! Make him eat something else!" Leo shouted.

Ollie drank the ice water and washed the salty taste in his mouth away. "Oh yeah? I have that power too, you know? Keep it up and I'll make you eat something off the street the next time we're out."

Leo scoffed. "Man, I've been eatin' from these streets since *Cosby* was on TV."

"Ollie, I'm sorry to have put you through that," Nina said. "I wanted everyone to see what exactly Transcendents can do. But now, it's time to see what the rest of you can do. Who's ready?"

Suddenly everyone's hand was in the air.

"All right," Nina said. They were interested, hooked and ready for more. "As much I believe in lecturing, I know that's not everyone's learning style, and when it comes to magic, I think a hands-on approach will help things sink in a little faster—encourage success."

Mitch, who had been playing with a crocheted bracelet, spoke up. "So, this might be a stupid question, or like, super late in the game to be asking something like this, but, like, what *is* magic?"

"We—not just witches, but humans too—all have boundless potential," Nina said. "That doesn't mean that we as a species are ready for that. But we all have that potential. It defies logic, and magic is really the opposite of logic. It's the act of shifting your consciousness to create and encourage change with your intention. Witches do this in ways that throw logic straight out the window. We do the same things that everyone else does, just at a higher vibration. Our abilities are enhanced because our thoughts make it so. We've got more style," she finished with a wink.

"So, it's not really good or bad, it just, like, is," Ollie added, half lost in his own thought.

"Exactly. Think of it like when you break up with someone. The breakup itself isn't really good or bad, it's the people involved and their actions and beliefs and intentions. Intention and belief are powerful things. Fire is inherently an entirely neutral force, but what do we do with that fire?…Do we light a candle so we can see in the dark or do we burn down our ex's house?"

Her comment raised a few eyebrows from the coven and left them debating whether that was just an example.

"As you get further along, try to ask yourself with everything you do—whether it's an incantation for rain or to change someone's mind about something—*what is my intention?*"

As Nina finished, she felt that she wasn't actively engaging the coven, so she switched gears on the spot and introduced the next lesson. She walked over to the counter in the kitchen and retrieved a large, smooth olive-wood bowl of water, its imperfections so perfect that it could only have been handmade. The grain patterns flowed across its surface like swirls of cream in hot coffee. Cupping the bowl with both hands, Nina set it down on the dining room table and leaned down slightly, pressing her palms against the side of the table behind the bowl and causing the table to creak.

"Water is a tool for many things. Understand it, respect it…and you can do wonders with it. I have a better relationship with water than I do with most people I've met. It's healing, emotional and transformative. Going forward, I want you to think about where elements come from, and in what forms. Different water has different personalities and purposes. It's never just water, just as you aren't only one thing. There's stormwater, river water, seawater, brackish water, morning dew, melted snow—"

"All right, Forrest Gump," Leo cut Nina off.

Nina glowered at Leo's smug face, which sported a grin full of teeth. It was more a mask of self-preservation than anything else. It was after Nina failed to continue talking that he stopped smiling and realized that the only one chuckling at his joke was himself.

"Water is the element associated with emotion in tarot. It's responsive, especially to us," Nina said as she waved for Mitch to come closer with her left hand and Leo and Avery to join her with her right hand. "Dr. Masaru Emoto found that human thought, music, words and various environments had an effect on the crystalline structure of water. Speaking positive affirmations or playing classical music changed its molecular structure. Now imagine what we can do."

Leo leaned against the southern wall, where the dining area connected to the great room, watching from afar. Avery and Mitch followed Nina's motion to join her by her side over the bowl, but Leo remained distant and alert. He took a deep suck from his vape and blew it to the side, away from everyone at the table. He did have manners sometimes, when he wanted to.

"We can communicate with it. Mitch, reach into the bowl and touch the bottom."

Mitch had lifted his hand and extended his left index finger when Nina held out her hand to stop him. She smiled, looked deep into the cosmos of his eyes and gave him one further bit of instruction. "Without getting wet."

Mitch never could have predicted that he would be here at this very moment, being put on the spot to perform what he believed was an impossible task…that is, if he were to apply logic. Mitch dashed through his memory to try to find what Nina had said earlier, about functioning outside of logic. He struggled with the realization that he was turning out to be more logical than he'd thought he was. No one had ever called him logical in his entire life. How could he believe in the esoteric art of tarot but doubt other kinds of magic beyond the tarot that also defied logic? It was a conundrum. The water was five inches deep, but the bottom of the bowl might as well have been a cavernous ocean. Mitch didn't usually admit defeat. One often isn't when one marches to the beat of one's own crochet-covered drum, so he decided to put his ego aside and try his best to be free of logic. He dipped his finger into the bowl with the swiftness of a lightning bolt and of course, failed at not getting wet.

It wasn't the immediate failed attempt at the task that bothered Mitch, but rather the callous snicker from across the room. Mitch sighed, dropped his shoulders and stared Leo down like a child at a new stepparent.

"You suuuuuuuuuuuuuuuck," Leo hissed out in a wheezy whisper. A tight-lipped smile then followed and was finished with a wink. Mitch was irritated at first, but then the feeling faded as he was distracted by how adorable Leo was when he winked. It inspired a few quick fantasies of Leo pulling him in close, smiling that conceited smile and winking at him only inches away from his face before he closed the gap between them with a soft kiss with the edges of his heterosexual lips.

"Ignore him. Concentrate. Remember: focus, release logic," Nina said to Mitch as though she were a kind of spiritual cheerleader.

Mitch had been trying to ignore Leo—they seemed so different—but it wasn't easy to dismiss him when the very sight of him provoked sexual fantasies. If he closed his eyes, it made it worse. If only he'd realized that beforehand. Now he had to ignore his fantasies and an erection while trying to complete an impossible task in front of a group of strangers. It felt like a nightmare. When he opened his eyes, he found that he was suddenly more aware than he had been, more focused. He cracked his knuckles, breathed in deeply and looked through the water into the bowl. He released his fist over the bowl and spread all five fingers as far as they would stretch. Then he slowly pulled them back into a fist except for his index finger. It was almost as regimented as a gymnastics routine, and just as precise.

He began to lower his finger, but in those few seconds before it reached the surface of the water, he suddenly understood what Nina had meant. He recognized his logical mind immediately taking control, like the FBI arriving at a state police investigation. But the state police knew more of the subtleties than the FBI, who were trying to rationalize the crime and judge the cops. Two things made sense to him: he watched too many crime shows and he needed to let his psychic awareness take the lead. That voice he had listened to in the past but ignored even more had ideas that came in pieces and eventually unearthed themselves as truth. Mitch knew what Nina had meant when he thought back to a previous boyfriend. He had known Mitchell wasn't right for him, and not just because they shared the same name. It was a pressing awareness, a voice that told him day after day that the relationship he longed for was not going to be with Mitchell. He later realized that the voice had been telling him the plain truth the entire time. Sadly, the relationship ended with Mitchell leaving town along with Mitch's MacBook Pro and three hundred dollars he'd had in his dresser drawer for a Tori Amos concert he wanted to attend. That had to happen for Mitch to finally get the message that Mitchell was not the love of his life. Mitch learned a few lessons that revelatory day: never date off an app again, don't trust someone just because you think they're hot and start listening to that voice in your head—you're not schizophrenic.

Mitch set logic aside, stopped thinking and only remained aware. A tingle in the tip of his finger intensified as he moved closer to the water's surface. Like a needle pushing through a pincushion, his finger entered the bowl. The water parted around the circumference of his finger, sending pulsating ripples out toward the edge. His finger, like the center of a tornado, touched down to the bottom of the bowl, the water holding the cylindrical shape around it. He did it: his finger was dry, the water moved. It looked like the scene at the end of the *Little Mermaid* where Ariel is on the ocean floor surrounded by a whirlpool of ocean water and is about to be impaled by Ursula. It snapped into his memory so fast that he blurted out a quote from Ursula with a slight alteration.

"So much…for true logic," Mitch said in a raspy voice before laughing wickedly.

No one got it. When the point of reference for his joke failed, the water swooshed back and soaked his hand like a water balloon popping on impact.

Leo had moved right up to the edge of the table, and saw everything unfold right before his eyes. Things were starting to get real. Nina wrapped up the experiment with a few extra pointers, suggestions and techniques that would help all of them harness their power. It was a stepping-stone toward other things. They now had the opportunity to take what they had learned and apply it in ways of their own. Water, like all the elements, could be used for divination, spells, potions and amulets. The world in which they could be used seemed endless. The coven members had the same sort of enthusiasm a young cook has when he begins to learn how versatile a single ingredient can be. Avery was the most intrigued by the idea. She and Leo were probably the closest to being kitchen witches. What kinds of magic would they cook up? she wondered. But there was no time for that. Fire was next.

Nina stood over the fireplace in the great room, holding a single white pillar candle. She kneeled down and set the candle in the empty fireplace.

"Fire is a life force and Primordials have control over that force. It's like speaking a language, and some witches will be better able to grasp and speak the language than others. Take off your shoes and socks for this. It will help keep you grounded as you learn," Nina instructed, fanning her face as she looked over at the thermostat. *How the hell is it 76 degrees in here? Good Lord, this is gonna be hot.*

Avery, Leo and Mitch removed their shoes and socks.

"I would have used some firewood, but I think it's best to start small, especially when you don't really know how your body will react," Nina said. "Instead, I want you to focus on trying to light this candle. Leo, we already know that you can do this, so, I guess, put your socks back on."

"Oh man, come on!" Leo shouted childishly.

"Avery, I have a feeling that you'll be good at this," Nina said. "You go first."

Avery pressed her fingers to her forehead and pulled back thin strands of her hair that were starting to stick to her skin. She was from the Midwest, but no matter how much she traveled, she would never get used to humidity as inescapable as student loan debt. The humidity in Louisiana loved that about her. The more she tried to hide in the air-conditioning, the more it wanted to find her. *Peekaboo, Avery...I found ya...You might go an' hide in the air-conditioning and do like dat der, but I'll always find ya. If yuh buy groceries, I gonna git ya. I always gonna find ya...I'm like yur Wisconsin accent, ain't goin' nowhere. I'm gonna find ya at Christmas when ya goin' 'round wit ya mama 'n'em, the swamp, ya bathroom, in front uh the air vent. I'm gonna git ya and there ain't nothin' ya can do, except be hot 'n' sticky.* At least, that's what Avery thought as she anthropomorphized the humidity, and for some reason with a thick Nawlins accent. She might have made that part up simply for regional appropriateness. Or maybe now that she was attuned, she wasn't really sure if she had made up the personification or it actually...*was real.* Avery shook her head and thought, *Don't be silly. Humidity doesn't speak to you. Just because you can set things on fire (apparently) doesn't mean that everything crazy is suddenly a thing.*

Nina directed her attention to the wick with a sharp point of her finger. "That candle, in the fireplace, light the w—"

Before Nina could finish her instructions, a spark of orange fire crackled from the candle and fizzled softly as it steadied on the wick. Avery had barely finished a thought about how she was going to light it when the candle lit up like a Fourth of July sparkler.

"Unbelievable! How did you do that so quickly?" Nina asked, her breath puffing out in laughs of surprise.

"I don't know, I just did it," Avery said, shining with pride, but in a nice way. "I just listened to what you said before when you were talking to Mitch and I thought…I just *barely* began to think about how I was going to light the candle, and then I lit the candle."

Leo puffed on his vape and shook his head slowly in approval, eyelids half closed. "Now, that's hot," he said, as if it was a twisted kind of turn-on, like when people in the South see bread pudding on a menu, or an dated chef puts a superfluous sprig of mint on a dessert just because it's dessert.

"All right, try again," Nina said as she rushed over to the candle to blow it out. "But send your intention out through something other than your mind. Use your body."

Avery lifted her hand, and with the snap of her fingers, the candle blazed to life with another burst of sparks just like the string of Christmas lights a few years ago—the ones that had fizzled out shortly after she plugged them in to test them. Nina blew out the candle and moved it to a side table, and Avery tried again, this time with her back turned. She stared out the windows along the wall of the back patio, the eastern sun blazing in, reflecting off the floor and illuminating her face. Two fires set and hardly any practice. She was a natural firestarter and on a roll—on fire. Even the humidity couldn't bring her down now (but she could still feel it, tapping her on the cheek and saying, *I gonna git ya*). Avery lifted her chin up high, proud and confident, and when her eyes closed, her mind found the candle behind her as if she could see it on the inside of her eyelids, clear as day. There was a pop and a hiss like the sound of a soda bottle being opened, the candle set fire once again, and Avery basked in the indirect illumination from the floor.

"Extraordinary, Avery! Really!" Nina said, overwhelmed with how easily she had used fire. With open arms, she walked to Avery, caressed her shoulders and stood behind her, her cheek next to Avery's ear. "Now, grow the flame, control it, tell it where to go, tell it what to do…" Nina slyly turned her eyes toward Avery and back to the candle and said in good humor, "Make it your bitch."

Avery popped out in laughter and then tried to refocus herself. She felt a new sense of self, guided, one that marveled at her talent. She was as excited as the flame was hot. Avery brought her hands toward her sternum, her palms facing each other but not touching. It came as easily as a formed thought. Some matches had a harder time setting fires compared with Avery's firecrackers-on-wax show. With a simple idea, she had manifested the connection to the flame. She could feel the heat between her hands, but it didn't hurt. When she thought it was right, she pulled her hands apart as if holding a balloon that was being inflated. The flame grew larger, brighter, taller.

"Let it talk to you, you're in control," Nina guided, awed by Avery's effortless talent.

Avery grew the flame to a relatively safe size before Nina started to notice she was essentially watching a Roman candle, but it was so beautiful that she didn't mind. Shards of dazzling flames flickered off into the air. It was resplendent. Then with a sudden clap, Avery extinguished the candle to a thin wisp of gray smoke attached to an ember-tipped wick. Ollie and Bisa clapped, excited and proud. Avery covered her mouth with her hand to hide her smile. She took a few steps closer to the candle until she was directly in front of it. She waved her hand over the candle, and the wick relighted. As a child would stick their hand over a socket and plug something in over it, Avery dipped the tips of her fingers into the flame.

"Ahhh!" Avery shrieked as she whipped her hand away from the fire and fanned it. "It burned me!"

"What did you think was gonna happen?" Leo cracked.

"Oh my God, that hurt really, really bad. Oh my God. I told myself that was a bad idea. I said, *Don't touch the fire, it's hot, you're gonna get burned…*but I could *feel* the heat over there on my hands. It was like I was holding fire, but it didn't burn me—like, it didn't hurt."

"Direct contact is different," Nina said. "Just because you understand or control the fire, it doesn't mean it's any less dangerous. You can still get burned no matter how strong you are." There was a delicate sigh of woe and then she continued, "Look at all those women during the witch hunts and the women before them, burned as witches, burned for being women, burned so that ignorant people could see the light of the fire on each other's faces. Go get some ice, Firestarter."

Mitch waved his hands in the air. "Um, actually ice is, like, not what you're supposed to use on a burn—it can, like, damage the tissue or whatever—so you're just supposed to, like, use cool water, like not ice cold or ice, or anything that cold. A nurse told me that once."

Avery didn't care about Mitch's advice; she wanted instant relief. "I'm getting ice," she said as she left for the kitchen.

Bisa was interested and wanted to see more, so she was the first to push forward with the ability training exercises.

"You said Primordials had a connection to animals, right?" Bisa asked.

"They do—it's one of their natural gifts," Nina said.

"I get to do this, right?" Leo said. "It's me this time. I'm takin' my socks back off."

"Yes, Leo. It's finally your turn. Everyone, please." Nina mockingly raised her voice. "Everyone! It's Leo's turn! He's going to perform an exercise for us! Please don't miss this magnificence!"

Leo bowed his head up and down like a gangsta accepting an award for song of the year. "All right, so what am I gonna do? I'm ready. Wait—hold on." He took a quick puff of his vape and blew it back and forth until his breath was clear. "All right, now I'm ready."

"Primordials are the Doctor Doolittles of the witch world," Nina said. "So, let's work with that."

"I'm no Denzel Washington, but I can try," Leo said.

"That was Eddie Murphy. We don't all look the same. Christ," Bisa said disdainfully.

Leo nodded. "You right."

Nina chose to pick her battles with Leo, banking on the notion that perhaps one day, preferably sooner rather than later, he would stop being so…Leo. "A lot of people in the past have found out about this power at random, being outdoors. This skill isn't as easy as the other ones, though. It's like trying to speak French when you speak Spanish. It's similar but still very different. Sometimes if people have established a familiar, or spirit animal—"

"Those are real?" Mitch asked.

Nina turned her head toward Mitch. "Oh yeah, they're real. Don't let them hear you say that or you'll wake up one day with the worst case of spirit animal death syndrome."

"Oh my God! Can we talk about your bedside manner? What the hell is that? Can they like, kill us?"

"No, I'm just kidding. But not about the spirit animals. They're a thing." Nina hadn't finished her thought before she was interrupted, but at the moment, it wasn't necessary. What was important was for everyone to start believing in themselves and their gifts, and that meant they needed to practice. "Let's go outside for this one."

"Really? It's so hot," Mitch said.

"If Avery keeps it up, it'll be hotter in here than all of Louisiana. Come on now," Nina said as she herded them toward the back patio doors. The far east wall of the great room was made up mostly of three arched, nearly floor-to-ceiling windows flanking windowpaned French doors. Nina twisted the handles on both doors and pushed out to the back patio. A dense rush of sultry air slapped her in the face. She didn't think she would ever get used to how hot it was, even in September. She paused before walking out onto the patio. The rest of the coven followed and were met with the same scorching slap.

"We should get some plants for the patio. It could be really nice," Ollie said.

"We can take a trip into town tomorrow and pick up a few things," Nina said pleasantly, nodding. It made sense. Ollie like gardening, and perhaps they could use it to their advantage and grow some things for magical purposes.

"Whew boy!" Leo said as he fanned his face with his rough hands.

"You guys already know the power you have, and new thoughts lead to new beliefs, which lead to new experiences. That's how we can constantly grow stronger—as long as you're focused. Where we put our focus is where consciousness goes, and there are realms beyond this one that we can access." Nina took a deep breath and exhaled. "Leo, I want you to focus on developing your connection to the animal kingdom."

"What should I do? Whistle for a wild boar? Call for them gators?" Leo said jokingly.

"There aren't gators out here," Mitch said.

"There are too! Where do you think you are, dude? This is all swampland. It probably shouldn't have even been a city! There's gators all over the place. There's probably some way out back in those weeds back there."

"Why don't you go back there and find out?" Bisa suggested.

"Naw, I'm good. That's how people avoid court fees down here—send their partners out into the swamp with a fistful of marshmallows. That's a Cajun divorce right there."

"Marshmallows?" Nina asked.

"Everybody knows gators like marshmallows. Toss one of those in some water, some still-lookin' water you think is empty, and those things come rushin' out to get it. It's like SeaWorld."

"Really? You'd protect me, though, right?" Mitch probed.

"Pfff. A gator bites down on you, there's nothin' I can do about it except wave goodbye and call your folks before I go through your shit."

"Leo, focus," Nina reminded him.

"All right, well, what do I do?"

"You've heard me give instructions over and over. It's the same thing, just with a different outcome. Apply what you know."

Leo frowned with irritation, crossed his arms in front of his chest and looked around for help. There was none. Each person stared back at him. Leo looked out toward the tall grass and weeds at the far end of the lot and then up into the sky. He tried to listen for any familiar sounds, but all he could hear were the cicadas buzzing in hypnotic, rhythmic patterns. That would have to do. He wasn't entirely thrilled about calling a bunch of bugs, but he had to start somewhere.

"All right," Leo said as he uncrossed his arms. He walked a few steps away from them and held out his right palm. His eyes became engrossed in the tiny lines of his palm, which looked like dehydrated desert mud. Listening carefully to the sounds of the cicadas, he tried to focus on their song. At first, it was nothing but a pulsing buzz, slowly winding down to silence. Then, as if by pure chance, his mind shifted from thinking about calling them to actually calling them. It felt involuntary, but with purpose. If there was such a thing, he couldn't articulate what he was feeling, and he sure couldn't understand it. It made sense beyond the language of words. There was a partnership between his brain, his thoughts, his intention, his energy, his hand and the natural world. His intention was converted to energy and translated to that of the cicadas with a slight trace of command. The buzzing stopped, and although Leo looked out into the sky, he saw nothing.

"What did he do? Did he do it?" Avery asked.

Nina shook her head. "No, not yet. He's doing it now," she said with a proud smile.

The silence in the air was filled with a heavy whirring, and a few cicadas clumsily landed in Leo's palm. He looked down at his hand with surprise, almost as if he hadn't expected it to happen. Fluttering around like a trio of wind instruments, the cicadas flapped their wings in the sunlight. Leo could feel their beady red eyes looking at him as if they were awaiting further instructions. He was in control. He turned around to face the coven and walked closer with his palm outstretched, like a cat offering up the gift of a freshly caught mouse. Leo's eyes stared sightlessly at the insects in his hand, as if he were in a trance of his own doing. If he kept his eyes completely frozen in space, he could see their auras—faint at first, like heat rising from a sun-beaten highway, then in vibrating tones of kaleidoscopic color. He assumed that it was just what happened when you did this sort of magic, so he said nothing, but simply marveled at how…good…he felt, how empowered he felt. It was the feeling he had when he drove over the bridge at eighty-five miles an hour, or when he climbed out onto the edge of a building. It was a rush that was all too familiar, but stronger. He wouldn't go so far as to say that it made him feel happy, but he assumed it was pretty damn close.

"Dude, look, I can make 'em dance!" Leo said, chuckling.

The insects crawled clockwise, stopping at quarter intervals to flap their wings in unison, spin and then move counterclockwise again. He pushed it a step further without intention or reason, and raised his left hand a foot above his right palm, which was holding the insects. They stopped moving, straightened up and then one by one flew up toward his left hand in a soothing spiral motion. When the first cicada reached the top hand, it delicately changed course and sailed back down in the same fashion. They continued flying in their figure-eight pattern flawlessly as if rehearsed and performed night after night, until Leo instructed them to meet in the center. There they hovered between his hands, and as Leo pulled his left hand away, the insects flew away into the trees.

"I'll be here all day," Leo said, grinning.

"Can you do it again, though, or was that just beginner's luck?" Bisa teased.

"Is this more of your flip attitude?" Leo said tauntingly.

"Yeah! I have to meet my quota of snarky comments so I can get my autographed headshot of Denzel Washington. Or was it Eddie Murphy? I'll have to check the basic black people contest rules."

"Hell yeah, I can do it again. That was nothin'."

"How do you feel?" Nina asked.

"I don't get it. What do you mean?" Leo asked.

"Summoning and controlling is pretty strong magic. It's exhausting on the body. Do you feel sick, or fatigued?"

"No," Leo answered.

"Pay attention to that. Everyone pay attention to that. Our powers are just like every other part of our body. We'll collapse if we run too far, we'll throw up if we eat too much. Pay attention to the clues your body is giving you. We are so conditioned to ignore the most important thing we have: our bodies. Be mindful of your body, your insides, yourself as a whole. What you feel is more important than what you judge with your eyes or your brain as a witch. Your brain functions on ego and logic, but what you feel has truth to it."

Leo, still high from the excitement of his summoning experiment, rubbed his hands together. "I feel peachy," he said. "Lemme try again. I'm not finished."

Nina raised her eyebrows and looked over her shoulder at the house, where she secretly wanted to be because it was so damn hot. "Oh, you're not?"

Leo shook his head. His floppy hair swung back and forth across his forehead and glistened in the hot Louisiana sun as though each strand had been dipped in gold leaf. "Nope!" He dropped his focus to the ground, holding his fists out from his chest as though gripping a steering wheel. He concentrated on the sounds in the environment but heard nothing. Then it came, all at once, an idea that was very out of the box for Leo. Staying within the realm of flying creatures, he aimed to reach for something else, something with wings. He fell to his knees, stretched his arms above his head, and slowly opened his fists, fingers extending toward the open sky. His focus consumed him and drowned out everything around him—all sounds, all stimulus, the heat on his skin, and for a moment even the task at hand. It was like he had been dropped into a sensory deprivation tank and drowned in it. Slowly, Leo's intention gained momentum and repeated in his head like a mysterious mantra. He could feel—them.

Nina tore her eyes away from Leo and shifted her sight toward the sky. She became hazily aware that a few birds were circling above where he was kneeling. Nina shielded her eyes from the sun and stretched her vision as far as she could. They looked like some kind of crow or blackbird. As they circled, they seemed to also be diving downward. Her jaw dropped as the few birds turned into more than a few. Blackbirds were coming from the nearby trees, from behind clouds, and from places that seemed to have no origin. The sounds of the cicadas were drowned out by the squawking of the birds orbiting Leo. The mass of birds loosely formed a halo in the sky and continued to grow in size, all the while getting louder. Dozens at first, then hundreds, all cawing and cackling in some kind of grotesque and vexing chorus. Goose bumps ran down Nina's body, despite the harsh heat. She hadn't expected to see such a sight, or such a display of power from someone so new.

As the birds drew closer to the ground, Leo's internal temperature rose. The lower the birds became, the more his vital signs fell out of balance. Beads of sweat began to collect around his hairline and fall to the ground, and his once calm and regular breathing suddenly ceased. Leo's body trembled as the tight cluster of birds—a mixture of fish crows, purple finches and turkey vultures—obstructed the sunlight that had bathed him only a few moments earlier.

Concern fell across Nina's face, her eyes wide and her brows shrunken. For a moment she thought she wanted to see what would happen if she allowed Leo to continue summoning the birds, but it seemed to go against her better judgment. What good was her education if she couldn't determine when she was in danger? However, Leo was new to all of this, and she was a bit more seasoned than he was. Yet he still exhibited a magical potency that was beyond what she'd thought he'd be able to achieve. She had gessoed all of them so that magical thinking would stick to their consciousness, but she had never expected such a display of artistic talent from any of them—especially Leo.

A single crow dived out from the swarm in the sky with the swiftness of a propelled dart. The bird winged by Nina, scratching her arm with either the sharpness of a feather or its claw, she couldn't tell. The tiny cut turned bright red as blood rose to the surface of her split skin. It startled her and sent a shiver of terror down her spine, but it wasn't entirely unexpected. The sense of danger rose when two more birds dived down and struck Avery, one in the leg and one across her scalp, pulling a few chunks of hair away as it continued in chaotic flight.

"Leo, stop!" Nina shouted as she pushed the coven members behind her and stepped back toward the house. Leo didn't respond, and she couldn't determine whether he was deliberately ignoring her or was so consumed by the power of his magic that he wasn't able to stop. She shouted again, her voice freckled with fear. "Leo! Enough!" Again, Leo remained stationary, his knees sinking to the ground, his fingers stretched out toward the cone of birds only a few feet away. "Everyone, get inside!" Nina shouted. She didn't have to say it twice; all of them were already halfway to the door by the time she spoke.

Nina scurried up to Leo and stood in front of him. His eyes looked completely normal, as if he had been watching a really pretty sunset and nothing more. She reached down and slipped a hand onto each cheek, her fingers scissoring his small ears. Would she be able to stop or distract him? She had to. With a little faith in herself and using the talents she knew she had, she could stop him. Then she heard the divine chatter within Leo's head. It wasn't like a normal voice or a spiritual presence. It was almost electric—like listening to a ubiquitous collection of failed radio transmissions that were nonetheless in harmony with one another. It was like a mysterious broadcast of hisses, clicks and high-pitched whistles.

She had to act, and she had to do it now. Nina closed her eyes and streamed her influence through her fingers and into Leo's mind. Her fingers were hotter than Louisiana ever could be, so hot that she thought for a moment she might leave a burn scar across his face. Yet she continued, past the ocean of noise, until she reached a radio silence. That was it, that was where he could be reached and the flow of his intention could be disrupted. She sank her psychic teeth into the void and hooked herself into Leo's mind.

"*Ad praesens*," Nina said aloud. It was a phrase she'd heard in the Somnium plane after she'd lost her focus and fallen too deep into consciousness. Thanks to Rosemary, the eldest member of the Advisory, she had returned to the present.

Nina opened her eyes and heard the commotion inside Leo's head break and return to silence. She removed her hands as Leo shifted his eyes from the absence of space to Nina's concerned face. The funnel of birds sank back into the sky, like a swirling tornado inside a stirred cup of tea. Nina looked up into the sky and saw the circling horde of birds still revolving around them.

"Holy shit!" Leo said as he noticed the birds and how the sunlight had grown faint because of them. "It worked," he said, sounding surprised and marveling at the ring of birds in flight. "I didn't think it would work like *that*, though."

Nina looked into his amber-green eyes and realized that he might have been completely in control and deliberately ignoring her calls earlier. Normally that would mean a serious discussion and probably some sort of consequence, but then Leo spoke again.

"Why are they still there? Why haven't they flown away?" he asked.

It was then that Nina realized he hadn't been fully in control of what he had just done. It was like a single spark that started a forest fire: whatever he'd had control over had grown into something much bigger than he was able to manage. She held her tongue and tried to collect her thoughts. Nina slowly raised her head to look at the sky and saw the birds tighten up into a ring as if waiting for a command. "Come on, let's go inside," she said as she pulled Leo up from his knees. Her hand slid up his arm to his shoulder, her eyes remaining on the birds all the while. They walked toward the house, and the birds grew louder and angrier sounding. As they entered the house and pushed their way past the rest of the coven, who had been watching with their faces practically pressed to the glass, the birds suddenly stopped squawking. Nina shut the patio door, locked it and stared out into the backyard. The birds were out of sight, but she knew they weren't gone. Something was wrong.

"What the *fuck* was that?" Mitch shouted.

Leo turned around and looked him directly in the eye, a cheeky grin on his face. He nodded arrogantly and murmured, "You know what that was? Deez nuts," and finished with a wink. Mitch couldn't figure out why Leo kept saying that. It was almost as if he wanted to put the idea of his nuts into Mitch's head.

"Quiet," Nina shouted. She looked over at Avery. "You okay?"

Avery nodded and said, "I'm fine," as she caressed the scratch on her leg.

"That was better than anything I've ever seen while trippin'!" Leo exclaimed with juvenile delight.

"I just knew that was going to happen," Avery said, full of tension.

"Man"—Leo shook his head and waved a palmful of annoyance toward her—"you did not."

Nina looked back outside and peered up at the sky, which was mostly overcast, a startling difference from a few minutes earlier when there had been only a few puffy clouds.

Leo continued to test Avery while blatantly mocking her. "What about this?" He stared at her and pointed to the closest candle. It flickered to life as a tiny flame erupted from the wick so effortlessly that it only fueled Leo's arrogance. Even he hadn't been sure he would be able to light the candle, but there he was, standing beside it and basking in the glory of his own accomplishments. "You smell that comin'? Abracadabra, bitch!"

Nina couldn't be concerned with the banter happening behind her; there were other things to worry about. Right then came a muffled clunk from the other end of the house. Everyone fell silent and listened.

"Did you hear something?" Ollie asked as he whipped his head around toward the source of the noise. "What was that?"

Leo wasn't concerned, still smiling over his ability to create fire.

Bisa shook her head and whispered, "I don't know, but I heard it too."

THUD!

Another strange noise pounded from somewhere in the house. Two more followed, this time from the study.

THUD! THUMP!

They stood in the quiet of the room, looking around at one another for answers. The mood shifted instantly after the third mysterious noise, and with it came a dark buzz of uneasiness, like a nest of angry wasps slowly approaching.

"Well, are we gonna check it out or what?" Ollie said aloud.

Nina held out her hand to stop everyone from moving. "Stay here," she said.

A moment passed. Then a few more. Total silence. Ollie took it upon himself to investigate. He didn't like waiting around. He was like a cat, only cleaner, curious, but not without caution. Ollie walked the length of the great room and entered the foyer. He stood there for a moment, looking back and forth down the hallway for clues.

"Anything?" Bisa asked quietly.

Ollie didn't want to answer just yet. He was sure he could find out the source of the noise. His mind started to wonder. What *was* making that noise? Now that his whole world had turned upside down, it could be any number of things. A ghost. A slimy goblin, maybe? A wolf with glistening, sharp fangs and crawling skin that made its fur look like the tide. Ollie poked his head into the study. Nothing there. What would he have done if something had been there? he wondered. He hadn't thought that far in advance, but he was certain that he would've reacted with bravery rather than cowardice, although he hadn't ever encountered something as supernatural as he was imagining.

Just how dangerous was a ghost? Was a goblin agile enough to sprint past him and slice his throat with its fingernail? If there had been a growling wolf, with cheese-yellow teeth and a thirst for his flesh, would he have run or would he have done something like shut the door and hope for the best?

He could easily have been walking toward certain death armed only with a sense of curiosity, which surely wouldn't have helped him survive. He hadn't ever even been in a fight, not even in elementary school. There was that one time during recess with Daniel Dustwood in fifth grade. The details of the encounter escaped him, but he remembered that Daniel threw a punch and Ollie caught it. Dan threw a second punch and Ollie caught that one too, and with the odds in his favor, he shoved Daniel away. The little bully in the making, shorter than Ollie but with more pride than both of them put together, fell back and tripped over his own feet, causing a roar of laughter from all the onlooking children. Ollie had walked away from that encounter, but it was hardly the type of situation he could use to judge how he would react as an adult. A scuffle during recess is hardly life threatening, and anything could have been making those noises. He couldn't walk away from it now, not when everyone had watched him actively seek out the danger with such valiance. Lucky for him, there wasn't a threat in sight.

"There's nothing here," he said happily. He began to saunter back toward the group, looking back every few steps to make sure nothing was following him, like a set of punches he could grab. In the middle of the great room he turned back one final time. No one. Nothing.

The patio door crashed open, and glass shards spilled out onto the floor and over Nina's feet. After the pieces settled, Nina opened her eyes, which had reflexively shut as the glass broke, and saw a large crow flopping around in the pile of glass. It was barely alive but still able to flap its blood-soaked feathers enough to spray blood across the floor like speckles on a robin's egg. Before anyone could react to the dying bird, there was another series of bumps.

THUD! THUD! WHACK! CRACK! CRUNCH!

One by one, then many at a time, birds of all shapes and sizes began to fly directly into the sides of the house as though pulled by a magnet. The sound was deafening, like the thunderous rattling of hail during a storm, the kind that dented hoods of cars and shattered windows. The group closed the gap between them, and Nina covered them with her arms, forcing them into a safe bundle.

"Leo! Stop!" Nina shouted.

For the first time since he had summoned the birds outside, Leo looked panicked.

"I'm not doing it!" he called back.

Another bird flew in and knocked over the candle Leo had lit only moments earlier. The wax sloshed onto the floor, a fire still burning from it. Leo was unable to speak, stunned by how awry his spell had gone. *Was it a spell?* he wondered.

Avery released herself from the group and stood up tall. She remembered a snippet from the book she had borrowed from the study. Ironically, she couldn't remember the title, but she could recall parts of the actual text. The instructions weren't very clear, and the purpose of the incantation wasn't exactly plain as day either, but she had to try something. She could feel the familiar twinge of *this is right* in her chest. She hesitated slightly because she had no idea how to pronounce what she had read, and even though she knew it was going to work, she didn't know exactly what it would do.

She stretched her arms out, swung them sharply and shyly called out, "*Incendere!*" She remembered reading that it was used as a defense, but she couldn't remember by whom, or from what. It didn't matter, right up until she said it. Then she worried.

All the noise stopped instantly. Avery stood at the patio door with her palms facing the backyard. She didn't know how this part worked. Did she have to do it at all? Would she have to hold her arms there for a certain length of time? Those pieces hadn't been covered in the book—or if they were, she had skimmed over them.

The noise resumed, but this time it was the result of birds falling from the sky, not flying into the house. Avery watched in amazement but also with a little sadness as the swarm of birds plummeted from the air and landed on the grass in droves, like the frogs in that movie *Magnolia* that she had never understood. The sound, like a sack of wet clothes against concrete, made her stomach turn. The backyard was littered with birds, but before Avery could question what the spell actually did, they caught fire all at once. It was the type of flame that one usually associated with a lit cigarette—swirls of bright vermilion and charcoal black, like a lit jack-o'-lantern. The flames were hardly flames at all but were more of a sneaking wave of flaky embers that cascaded over the birds. The yard became still as the fire swallowed all signs of life. Avery could feel the heat on her skin, even from inside the house. It reminded her of when she'd gone to a concert just outside Madison where she could feel the pyrotechnics on stage even from her cheap sixty-five-dollar seat.

Avery drew in a deep, weepy breath. The reality of what had just happened struck her hard, and for a few moments, she slipped back and forth between wanting to cry and wanting to scream at the sheer wonder of it all. She could hear the gasps and the wheezy panting of the coven behind her, and she didn't know what to say or exactly what expression was on her face. Finally, she let her body decide what to do next and lowered her arms to her side. She felt Nina's hand on her wrist and turned to face them.

"How did you do that?" Nina asked.

"I don't know," Avery said calmly. "I mean, it was in a book I was reading from the study. I wasn't really sure what it was going to do, or how it was going to work, but I just did it. I just reacted."

"Well, goddamn, Avery!" Leo said, slightly jealous.

Avery looked down at the ground and saw the two birds that had made it into the house. Their bodies were singed and cooked. It brought the idea of four and twenty blackbirds baked in a pie to her mind, and she winced, cringing at the grotesqueness of the nursery rhyme. There was no pie, only burnt flesh mixed with the nauseating smell of barbecued feathers.

"Oh my God, that's awful," she said as she covered her mouth with her hand.

Bisa followed suit and blocked her nose from the stench. Avery's eyes began to well up with tears, and she turned back to the sea of dead birds in the yard.

They took some time to recover from the shock of what had happened before Nina instructed Avery to go sit down for a while. Nina, along with Ollie, Mitch and Bisa, first cleaned up the mess on the floor and then moved outside to collect all the dead birds. Leo finagled his way onto the roof and kicked down the ones that had stuck.

As the group piled the birds into a ridiculously large mound, making sure to pick up the legs and wings that had burned off, Avery found her way to the bathroom. She feverishly pumped soap into her hands as if she would be able to wash off the experience. After she lathered and scrubbed her hands and up past her wrists, she looked at herself in the mirror. Her hands were clean, but her conscience was not. The smell of roasted bird flesh still hung heavy in the air, reminding her of what she'd done.

Avery whimpered for a few minutes while she stared at herself in the mirror, contemplating her choices. Was she overreacting? Was this how magic worked? Were there bound to be casualties for the greater good? She didn't have the answers to any of the questions running through her mind. She cupped a handful of water from the faucet and splashed it across her face. She then became at peace with her decision, wiped her face dry and headed out into the backyard.

The coven members stood by the pile of bodies. All they needed to do now was burn it—really burn it this time, to ashes.

Avery opened the patio door, minding the tiny shards of glass that fell from the broken windowpane. She walked with purpose out toward the group. Halfway between the house and the mound of bodies, Avery stopped. She was going to finish what she had started. After all, it was her mess to clean up. She was more in tune with her body, more than she had been two days ago. She held her breath for a few seconds, and as she exhaled lightly, the pile ignited from the bottom and fire spun up toward the top. The stench intensified, but the light was brighter still.

Everyone turned around to see Avery standing motionless and without sentiment. Nina made her way toward her, the bonfire billowing pungent, black smoke behind her.

"That was a good thing you did," Nina reminded her.

"Killing hundreds of animals?" Avery asked.

"We had no way of knowing what was going to happen. Or what could have happened if you hadn't stopped it. I hate to say it, but I wasn't prepared for that. So for that, I apologize. Creative witches work intuitively. You acted on instinct. When you're in the frequency of instinct or creativity, creativity shows up. Think of it like creative problem solving through new solutions. Look, these things will happen. That's why we need to learn together. Magic is…an expression of something that can't be expressed, it's a language without a language, and that's why it's so powerful, because it *is* expressed through us—like emotions. And when we're acting on impulse, or in a crisis, it's just as audacious."

Avery nodded a few times in agreement and looked down at the ground, then out into plumes of smoke. "Yeah." She paused, her face speculative. "I don't actually know what *audacious* means." She rolled her eyes over toward Nina.

Nina's face was engulfed in a contagious smile, and she laughed.

"So?" Avery stuck out her neck and glared at Nina, a small grin slapped across her mouth. "What does it mean?"

"Look it up," Nina suggested sincerely.

The mood lightened ever so slightly, enough to allow Avery to poke fun at herself.

Avery grinned, let out a humble chuckle and said, "Watch it be on the news tomorrow." She held up her hands to exemplify an imaginary headline. "'Midwestern Woman Kills Entire Species of Wildlife, Claims Extinction Was Accidental.'"

"You'll never be able to go to a zoo ever again!" Nina joked.

Avery chuckled. "Watch me end up volunteering there or something. Or like, getting married at the zoo. Wouldn't that be something? Right as I say *I do*, every animal in the entire zoo just drops dead."

"People would think you're a witch!" Nina said with a soft laugh.

"Hey, I'll take it, I've been called worse things. Usually, those things rhyme with *witch*…and then people usually shout, *I never wanna see you again!*" There was another small pause. "Not really…but sometimes."

CHAPTER 12

Edie liked rules, clean things and Christianity. Of course, there were other things, like key lime pie and Spinning class, but those didn't fit into her holy trinity. She and her husband, Joshua Bonner, were the co-founders and co-pastors of their only child—the Whole Truth and True Light Assembly of God Church or, to the general population outside of their devoted followers, the church with the commercials. Edie was exceptionally proud of that marketing strategy, so much that she arranged to have a commercial air during the Sunday worship service so that the sermon included a show-and-tell of her latest project.

When Edie was a child, she wanted to be an actress, but only in Christian films. So when the church's budget could accommodate a commercial, she jumped at it. The segment was kind of like acting, only the Bonners weren't acting. It gave her a chance to show just how passionate (and delusional) she was about her faith. She respected punctuality and delivered her lines clearly and succinctly, to fit within the restraints of their airtime.

It was two in the afternoon—well, eight minutes past, and that was three minutes too long, according to Edie. When the reporter from Channel 4 News told Edie and her husband that they would take up only five minutes of their time, she expected five minutes and not one second more. Edie looked at her Breguet watch, so accessorized with bright sapphires, garnets, rubies and tourmalines that one almost needed a map to find the actual clock face. She let out an impatient puff of air as she delicately tapped it three times.

"Look, I appreciate y'all comin' out to talk to us about the hideous tragedy of our youth council president, but you said this would take only five minutes of our time, and here we are, still talking at eight minutes." Edie brushed a piece of her shiny honey-brown hair out of her face and back into place among the other large, voluptuous curls. *I am lovin' this part down the middle.* She had been blessed with her mother's hair, thick like peanut butter. If, heaven help her, she styled it without some anti-frizz oil, her hair was a great place to hide her purse. Though she was only forty-five, she had very few wrinkles apart from the inescapable crow's-feet that she had noticed on her mother right up until the day she died, *Lord bless her soul.*

Big was popular in the South, and Edie's hair was the biggest thing about her, aside from her personality. She wasn't exactly what people would call fat; she was more along the lines of a woman who exercised on a regular basis but still ate pecan pie like it was going to save her soul. And what a soul it was: one that she saw every morning in the mirror, in her motivated pasture-green eyes and on her unusually moony face. "But..." Edie began brightly before she lowered her voice, "I'm not tryin' to stay here all day, so thank y'all for comin', but now y'all need to go."

The reporter, a needy man with flinty eyes in a sad button-up, pressed for more time. "Please, Mrs. Bonner, just a few more questions!" he exclaimed—almost demanded—as he reached his hand out, sweaty from holding a microphone in the sun.

This man has crossed a line, she thought as she smiled, sweet as a glass of sweet tea. There was a timelessness about her—or rather, the sense of being stuck in time. Perhaps it came from her French manicure, her hairstyle or classic southern wardrobe. Regardless of how timeless she considered herself, she had no time left for this eager man. "All right. That's not gonna work for me. I'm done," she said, and then inhaled deeply and turned on her heel. The clickity-clack of her white stilettos echoed in the foyer of the church as she bigheadedly walked away. *Click, clack, click, clack, click, clack.* The interviewer was left with the scent of her perfume, a fervent citrus smell that, when mixed with her sweat, made it seem as though she had showered in lemon-scented floor cleaner. Which Edie didn't think was half bad; after all, cleanliness was next to godliness. However, there wasn't enough perfume or cleaner in the whole God-loving nation to cover up her shade when she threw it. She was a master of making everything she said seem harmless and like it had come from a place of holiness, even when it didn't. It was precisely that characteristic that made her so disliked by many but worshipped by so many more.

Edie entered the office of the church and adjusted the ties of her flowy, necktie blouse in goddess blue and pressed her fingers along the pocket seams of her white ankle pants. She basked in the comfort of being unapologetically southern for a moment before she addressed her husband, who was sitting at his desk.

"Joshua, I'm fixin' to write a letter about those reporters. You agree to voice your thoughts one time and they expect you to bend to their every whim like my time isn't precious. I already feel a headache comin' on, and he was only aiming to make it worse. That man had absolutely no boundaries, just didn't know when to quit! It was like a hog in a kitchen full of pecan pie."

"I've seen you around pecan pie, especially when Ms. Boudreaux brings it to Water Baptism Wednesday," Joshua said slowly and courteously in his customary, long-winded manner.

There was a pause as Edie realized he was right, but she refused to let the comment pass. "That's different."

Joshua returned her retort with a shake of his head and a smile that they both knew meant *Bless your heart.* Joshua Bonner was a tall man, always in a button-up shirt and a blazer. His lustrous, short, caramel-colored hair was seasoned with patches of gray around his temples and seemed to plume out from a razor-sharp widow's peak. His eyes, although so dark brown they almost looked black, were filled with splendor. He was a handsome man, with a meticulously groomed beard, shapely muscles and skin that was moisturized with expensive skin-care products. He had just celebrated his fortieth birthday but had the energy of a man ten years younger. His smile was as wide as Texas, and where Edie's tongue was quick and direct, his was slow. Listening to him speak was like watching a fly try to crawl out of a puddle of molasses. It tested people's patience often, but Edie had grown accustomed to it. It allowed her to speak first, and she would never complain about having to do that.

"That reminds me," Edie said. "I rescheduled the meeting for the West Bank Women Warriors' Faith Walk for Christ because I moved up our meeting with that man with the strange last name—sounded like a monument in Mexico?"

"De La Fuente," Joshua spilled out sluggishly.

"That's the one! He was sweet as pie on the phone, and we got to talkin' about all sorts of things. How he was a true believer in our mission, loved how infectious our faith was…"

"Now, Edie, you know how disappointed those women are gonna be," Josh interrupted. "They were really looking forward to it. I know for a fact that Bethany Bordelon went out and bought a new outfit just for the event."

"I know she did. I ran through the directory, personally talked to each and every person who signed up, and explained the situation, rescheduled everyone to next week and even managed to persuade Ms. Boudreaux to bring a few of her pies along with her." Edie touched her upper lip with the tip of her tongue.

"Well, butter my butt and call me a biscuit—look at you go! You make me so proud to be your husband," Josh said.

Edie fluttered her eyelashes a few times, and pressed her lips together so much that her soft-core pink lipstick practically disappeared. "I do?"

"You do," Josh declared.

"But you haven't even heard the best part yet!" Edie said as she plopped herself into the chair. She cleared her throat and prepared to deliver the exciting news to her devout husband. She held her next breath deep inside her chest for a moment, exhaled and then sniffed the air a few times—three, to be exact. "What's that smell?"

"It's the new carpet. It was laid down really early this morning. Remember?"

Edie looked down at the ground, over her hidden belly rolls, and lifted her DKNY heels off the floor. "Now look at that! That's just precious, isn't it? I'm glad we agreed on the Crème Brûlée over the Sands of Time—it makes the room so much bigger! That sandy color would've just looked dirty, don't ya think?" Edie chuckled and looked back at her husband. "That smell, though. Is it gonna go away? Is that normal? It's so strong, my God, it's makin' my headache worse!" Edie touched the center of her forehead with her middle finger. "It's all right. I'll take something. I'm sure there's some Advil around here somewhere. Next time we'll just make sure to open a window so we don't pass out from the smell or anything. Anyway, let me tell you the exciting news!"

"All right, now!" Josh said as he put down his pen and leaned forward over his desk in anticipation.

"The reason why I moved up this appointment with Mr. De La Fuente is that…you're just gonna fall over, I can tell," Edie said, putting her hands together over her mouth as if in prayer. "He has something for us. A gift, a true gift from God!" She leaned in over the desk, her mouth hung open, her eyes fixed on Joshua. "This man was brought to us. He saw us on television when we were picketing that homosexual's funeral in Thibodaux, and he said he had to meet us. At first, I was a little skeptical, him being Mexican and all, but then I thought, *Edie, Carlos, the janitor at our Houma campus, is an amazing janitor. He set a good example for you, now, you give this man a chance and hear what he has to say.* It was like the Lord was speaking right to me and so I did, I listened. He went on and on quoting, well, basically quoting everything we stand for. How he believes in our mission to stamp out Satan's minions on this earth—all the shameful, disgraceful people who have turned from God and aim to send this country and all that we stand for straight to the depths of hell with their sin, perversion and homosexual rapings!" Edie nodded, and her dangling pearl earrings bobbed from her earlobes. "I said, 'Amen.'"

"Amen!" Josh repeated.

"Amen. Mmm-hmm. And then, he said we deserved a gift, something that he felt we deserved and would use to carry out God's justice." Edie licked her top lip with her tongue again.

Joshua had an idea of what she was about to say, but it was too outrageous, it was too unbelievable for it to be that. His smile began to fade, and all sound abandoned the room. He had been waiting his entire life for this moment. He had questioned his faith at times, and those days were over now, but was it all to lead him to this moment? To give him the ultimate gift he had always heard of as a child? "It's not…it's not what I think it is…is it?"

Edie's hands instinctively fell into prayer position only for a brief moment, and then she reached over to grab her husband's hand. She was on the verge of tears—tears of joy. She pulled her left hand back and dabbed under her eye with her index finger, collecting the tiny wells of joy that had begun to pool. She had been waiting to tell him the news all day, and now the moment was upon her and the excitement only made her headache throb harder. As she gripped Josh's hands more tightly, she remembered when he had proposed to her, another moment when they were holding each other tight and fighting back happy tears. It was after she sniffed, sucking back the emotions in her head, that she nodded.

"He has the *lunastaterum**," Edie whispered.

"No…" Josh uttered, his emotions teetering between "Lord help us" and "Hallelujah."

Edie nodded again, this time with a wicked smile, her fingers lined with tiny rivers of mascara and tears blended together. "Yes! Your father's family was right! It *does* exist!

He described it the same way you did. It's real! And he's giving it to us!"

The air-conditioning kicked on, and cool air began to flow from the vents. Josh and Edie's coos carried out into the hall of the church. But it was more than a church. It was a safe haven, it was America, and now they would be able to defend it with the tool they had secretly thought was only legend, even though heaps of meticulously preserved records in the Bonner family library documented in detail the history of witches and the lunastaterum.

"This is going to change everything, Joshua," Edie said, half out of breath from the mere thought of possessing the lunastaterum. "Everything we've fought for, everything we've built, the devoted followers we've led to the light—all of that has shown God that we are worthy to have such a gift. He trusts us. We built this facility, remember? Thanks to our words, our sermons and our values, our faithful members provided us with the funding to purchase this place, all 42,781 square feet of it. Now it's our flagship campus! Then came the campus in Houma and we're talkin' 'bout another in Baton Rouge!" Edie released her hands from Josh and stood up from her seat. "We are a powerful, powerful force, Joshua. Now, I reckon he'll be here any minute now, so let's finish up in here and head out front. I want to be there waitin' for him when he arrives."

The church was empty apart from the Bonners. Even the custodian was gone for the day. Edie entered the stretch of hallway that ran between the front door and the nave. It boasted high ceilings, walls of backlit, paneled, reclaimed wood and a high-gloss hardwood floor. The light that poured in from the front windows and the endless skylights gleamed off the surface and gave a whole new meaning to the term *holy light*.

Which is just what Edie had wanted when she'd given the architect her design ideas. She knew what she wanted, and she wanted resplendence. She wanted other things too, something that put them at the forefront of modern Christianity while still leaving a whole lot of room for tradition. That's why she insisted on having a coffee nook with an espresso machine, a nursery, three large classrooms, a wing for the youth group and a set of prayer cabinets for those who wished to pray in private.

Edie clutched her husband's arm as they strolled down the hallway. She looked through the double doors into the nave, her most favorite part of the entire building. Rows upon rows of seats filled the length of the room straight up to the chancel around the altar, where professional stage lighting illuminated a gray stone wall with a large silver cross hung in the center. The room was just darling, covered in okra-green carpet all the way from the doors to the surplus of peace lilies that lined the stage. The carpet, the kind one would expect in an insurance or dental office, had been offered to them at a discounted price from devoted members Mr. and Mrs. Arbuckle over at Crescent Carpet Collection; it pays to be in the pulpit, especially the antique wooden one with carvings of muscadine grapes the Bonners stood behind.

Light poured in through six large, floor-to-ceiling windows lined with doily-style drapes that reached toward the upper tier. Two gargantuan American flags filled the space on either side of the chancel that almost stole the show during the worship service. They shouted patriotically *We're Americans here*, which is why flat-screen TVs were fixed to the wall right beside them, supposedly for the people who couldn't see very well. What kind of America doesn't have a TV? Not one that the Bonners wanted to live in. It did make sense for them to have visual aids when people started having to stand along the far back wall because there weren't any available seats left.

Edie hadn't cared about the seating capacity at the time of design; she cared about the service quality. It was hard to tell what her core beliefs were as she admired her room of worship; being on stage delivering a service often made her feel like a musician giving a concert, and with that came the feeling of celebrity. Joined to that was power. She loved her place in the community, she loved her position, she loved that she had managed to get her book *Pray First: Living the Whole Truth Through True Light* in the Christian row at Barnes & Noble, but above all else, she loved what it all gave her—influence.

"Do you want me to grab you something for your headache?" Joshua asked, gently stroking the back of her head.

She didn't answer. In fact, she had stopped moving. Her buttermilk cheeks dimpled as she opened her mouth for a wide smile.

"What's that? Is that yours?" Joshua asked, slightly confused as they stared at a square box on the floor. It was larger than some of Edie's jewelry boxes, but made of pearlized obsidian with a small latch crafted from moonstone on the front.

"It is now," Edie said, her heart full of pleasure as she click-clacked toward the box on the floor.

"Is that it? Where's Mr. De La Fuente?" Joshua asked as he scurried toward the box to get a closer look.

Edie shook her head, picked up the smooth box from the floor and held it between her hands. "His presence is no longer necessary. The gift has been given to us. He served his purpose, and he delivered to us the true gift from God." Her excitement was pounding like the headache she was ignoring, yet she remained entirely calm on the outside. The box felt like a birthright, an inheritance that would finally allow her to live out her dreams and the ambitions that she believed in so much.

Joshua, although intrigued by the box, was still concerned with how it had gotten there. "How did he get in? Why didn't he come find us? Who just leaves a gift in the middle of the floor like that?" He shook his head, completely disappointed. "He must not be from around here."

"Don't you understand, Joshua?" Edie exclaimed. "Inside this box is what your parents have told you about your entire life, what your family has been aware of and searching for!"

"Here, let me take a look at this," Josh said as he grasped the box from his wife's hands. He couldn't hear anything rattle when he moved the box. It was heavy like a chunk of raw marble. His thumb slid over toward the moonstone clasp, and with a heavy swing of his thumb he unfastened it. The hook-shaped latch swung upright to its unlocked position with a glass-like snap that echoed into the abyss of the hallway. He hesitated—the box was unlocked, yet the lid remained closed. If it truly was what Edie claimed it was, and he had no reason to believe it wasn't, it would be a phenomenal moment for their future—and all those who followed (and didn't follow) them. His delay in revealing the contents of the box wasn't based on fear like so many other things that are merely different; rather, it came from a place of knowledge.

The awareness of the lunastaterum had been drilled into him ever since he was a young boy, as a device that could seek out Satan's minions—his witches. While other children were being bludgeoned with Sunday school information, Joshua was pulled aside for private lessons with his parents. Sometimes his uncle was present for the lessons, and occasionally his grandfather was too. His education consisted of the standard curriculum of Christian knowledge and teachings of the Bible, but he was also tutored in the covert and mysterious compositions of his ancestor Samuel Wigglesworth.

Samuel was a frail-looking merchant who awoke one day with knowledge and answers to questions he hadn't been asked yet. Over the next few months, his interest in trading faded and his time was replaced with hours locked in prayer expressing mysterious mantras. It was an unusually warm day in late February 1686 when he felt compelled to enter a modest church with no more than forty seats to speak with the minister. They exchanged dialogue about good and evil and discussed in great detail the presence of Satan. The minister, who had been studying texts from a range of sources outside the Christian library, had determined that there was indeed a prophet. It was then that Samuel learned of the minister's search for what the texts referred to as the Pure Redeemer. Right then, Samuel claimed the title and identified himself as the one the minister had been searching for.

The minister examined Samuel with every manner of question in his arsenal. The Pure Redeemer couldn't be just anyone, and the minister was going to make certain the chosen one was without fault. Samuel passed every test and answered every question with the effortless candor only one with divine knowledge can have. Samuel knew the truth about Yesun and Changshi, he was aware of the powerful slaves of Satan walking the earth and the dangers of their witchcraft, and above all else, Samuel identified the object that was loosely referred to in the minister's texts. Samuel described the lunastaterum with stunning accuracy and painted its actuality in specific detail. The minister only knew of the tool, whereas Samuel understood its mechanics—he demystified it. It wasn't just a tool to locate witches, it was a device that monitored the earth's gravitational pull and lunar rhythm and indicated the direction of the closest witch, like a compass.

Minister Arthur Bonner dropped to his knees on the weathered floor and acknowledged Samuel as the Pure Redeemer that had been prophesied to arrive. That very afternoon Arthur declared February 19 as the first Sacred Day in the Redeemer Allegiance—the origin of the witch hunters.

Joshua reflected on how much things would change if the lunastaterum were inside the dark and mysterious box. It would be the validation of everything the Allegiance believed in and would allow them to single-handedly carry out the mission set by his ancestors: to eradicate sin. What does a mystical weapon used to find witches look like to a young and impressionable boy? Joshua knew that it was round and turned white when it detected witchcraft. He had always imagined it was too large to hold in your palm, despite being told it was something he could comfortably do. He drew what he imagined it looked like with crayons in the privacy of his bedroom—an orb larger than a bowling ball and too heavy to hold, one that emitted a white light in the direction of danger so brightly that you could barely see the hand that was holding it. Children already see the world much larger than it really is, and Joshua was from Texas, where everything was always bigger. It made for a rather anticlimactic discovery when just the box itself could be held in his hand.

Joshua switched the position of his hands so that one hand was free to grab hold of the lid. He broke the seam of the box and opened the lid. There it was, plain as the moon in the night sky: the lunastaterum. The small bowl no wider than a few inches was secured in a hollow of the box and showcased by the surrounding black silk that lined the inside. The interior was pearlescent like that of an abalone shell, trimmed in gold around the rim with a tessellated malachite exterior. The right third of the bowl was not the same solid material as the rest of the bowl, but rather an assembly of fine golden threads that intertwined to create intricate patterns. It was like a stylized version of the spiderweb in the backyard of their home, where a web linked banana leaves to the trunk of the tree. Joshua stepped into the light that poured in from the skylight, and the light shimmered over the iridescent bowl.

"Lord have mercy…that's just the most precious thing I have ever seen in my entire life," Edie said as she brought both of her hands to her chest. Her face began to twist in fury as her mind wandered with possibilities. Suddenly the cavity of the bowl started to pool up with something more substantial than smoke and more yielding than rubber. A milky white matter with a glittery essence filled the bowl yet didn't spill out the holes formed by the web-like strings. The contents remained inside the interior.

"Hold the box," Joshua said to Edie as he placed it back into her hands. He plucked the lunastaterum from the box with the thumb and index finger of both hands. In one quick movement, he slipped it into his palm so the bottom of the bowl made direct contact with his hand. He remembered everything—all that he thought could just be superstition, legend or pure fiction. "If you hold it in your hands, you should be able to visualize the witch it's detecting and it should direct you where to go," Joshua said as he stared into the milky liquid and waited for something, anything, to happen. Then he saw it—him. A young man, tall hair, slender with bright blue eyes. He removed his palm from the bottom and turned to Edie. "It worked. I can see one." At that moment, a black orb with a point, like an ice cream cone, appeared in the liquid and swung to the right, bobbed back and forth and then settled in one direction.

"We are going to send them all to hell in a handbasket," Edie said. She ran through her Rolodex of sinners who made her sick: homosexuals; Catholics, a.k.a. mystic perverts; Jews; anyone from a Muslim country; African Americans (which is why Edie had persuaded a local bookstore to create a section called "Black Authors"); people who didn't like sweet tea or fried things; people who supported the removal of the Jefferson Davis statue in New Orleans; pro-choicers; redheads with curly hair; women with tattoos; women who didn't wear makeup; women who wore too much makeup; men who wore makeup; Indian food; and people who wore orange. To Edie, the lunastaterum was a loaded weapon. There was a whole new line of work to do in the name of the Lord, and her ambition was fueled by cruelty. The lunastaterum provided her with a way of justice that she could serve in secret, and she immediately felt a peculiar fondness for the object—a reverence, even. The Bonners were a force to be reckoned with, even their antiquated, bigoted and ignorant values—and they had survived by attracting large numbers of loyal followers and hefty monetary donations through the years. The addition of the lunastaterum would only serve to make their ministry more interesting.

CHAPTER 13

The pile of birds was nothing but ash when the sun rose the next morning. The air wasn't foul, but it wasn't exactly as fresh as sliced fruit. The magnolia tree in the backyard had popped out a few more blossoms, and their perfume wafted over the cinders on the warm breeze. The weather in Louisiana was often unpredictable, and the clearest skies could attract storm clouds just as fast as any spell, especially during hurricane season. It was with this in mind that Ollie and Nina made an early trip to the garden store to pick up some new plants for the back porch. It was Ollie's newest hobby. His green thumb was dying to plant a few seeds and wait for growth. They brought home a jungle of star jasmine, dragon trees, creeping fig, and herbs such as lavender, sage, thyme and rosemary. The larger additions like the monstera plant, birds of paradise and Kimberly ferns filled out the space and instantly transformed the back patio into a tranquil and welcoming retreat.

If only there were a way to do something about the nasty heat. Nina watched Ollie smile as he introduced himself to the plants, tickling them and chatting with each one individually before moving on to the next. He was graceful and genuine about it. Ollie took a moment to head to his room and moments later came back with a small ziplock bag filled with smaller yellow bags, each labeled with a name in green ink.

"What's all that?" Nina asked.

"Seeds I want to plant," he answered innocently.

"You just carry seeds around with you wherever you travel?" Nina said with a smile.

"Yeah," he answered simply. "These might be useful for something." He shook out the contents of the bag and sifted through the tiny sacks, each labeled with their common and scientific name. Wormwood, water hemlock, deadly nightshade, wolfsbane, black henbane and starlight dancer.

"Poisoning someone being at the top of that list!" Nina said as she picked through the packets, reading the words *deadly, poisonous* and *highly toxic.*

"Not all of them are deadly. There was a book in the study that listed a few of these plants as among those used for magical purposes, and I thought they could come in handy."

"Please be careful," Nina stressed. "Let's get a separate stand for you to sow these, so we know what's what. I don't want anyone to stop to smell the flowers and end up in a hallucinogenic coma. I mean, my college days are done, but I'm not the only one living here!" She winked.

Despite the sweltering sun Ollie gave the small garden in the backyard a slight overhaul and planted morning glories, purple pansies, pink snapdragons, red fuchsia and a healthy amount of lavender. With some effort the flower garden would be a lovely place to relax and read a book, if you could stomach the heat and humidity.

Avery also had some work cut out for her as she began to fix up the apiary in the backyard. The hive was next to a couple of large trees that blocked the wind and rain. It needed a light cleaning, and Avery got to work just after ordering ten thousand bees. Strangely enough, she found, bees could be delivered through the postal service. Using a green scrubbie from the kitchen, she scoured a layer of dirt and debris from the lid that covered the hive. Once it was spotless, she returned it to the hive and placed a heavy rock from the garden on top to secure it. Avery volunteered at a science museum back in Wisconsin and had dreamed of having a hive of her very own if she could ever settle down in one location. It looked like that time was finally upon her. A gust of conversation erupted between Avery and Ollie as they worked.

Bisa was quietly starting a macramé project in the great room, taking a moment to look outside and watch Ollie and Avery working under the hot sun. Mitch shuffled through the kitchen, grabbed a bag of stick pretzels and headed back to his room. He settled onto the bed and shoved a handful of pretzels into his mouth with one hand and retrieved his tarot cards from the nightstand with the other. The sounds of the card shuffling and crunching were soon drowned out by the sound of an engine being revved outside his window. Again, there was the rising and falling of a roaring engine. Mitch closed his eyes and tried to concentrate, but the sharp mechanical noise pierced his ears. The engine screamed and screamed again like someone was deliberately trying to distract him.

"Seriously?" Mitch shouted as he slapped the deck of cards down onto the bed. A few cards slid off to the side as he uncrossed his legs and stood up. Pretzel crumbs flew off his lap and sprinkled the floor. His feet thumped sullenly across the floor as though he were a child told to go to his room. The art of divination, as Mitch liked to refer to it before he found out he was a witch, required concentration, and there was no way he could focus with that obnoxious vroom-vrooming. He arrived at the window and peered outside, his nose almost up against the glass. It was Leo—*of course it was Leo*—sitting atop a Suzuki sports bike. It could have been a motorcycle, if that's what they called it, but Mitch didn't know one thing about bikes—or cars, for that matter. It was a good thing he didn't have one, because he couldn't change a tire or jump a battery. He didn't need to know any of those things. All he knew was that it was loud and annoying and Leo's unrelenting revving was infuriating. It sounded like an angry growling cat mixed with a chain saw.

He watched Leo's wrist move back and forth, and pondered why people do that in the first place. *Do they like the sound it makes? Is it necessary? Of course it's not. They just want everyone to know they have a bike and they're on it.* There was some slight PTSD oozing out. He was reminded of an old neighbor who left for work very early in the morning and arrived home late every night on a bike that was eerily similar to the one outside his window now. Mitch almost failed to notice that Leo wasn't alone. A stockpot of a man with a bald, sweaty head and used-to-be-white flip-flops stood alongside Leo's car, a set of keys swinging from his hand. Leo shut off the bike and swung his legs around to one side. *Oh, now you turn off the bike.*

The two exchanged a few indecipherable chunks of dialogue before Mitch remembered who he was, and what he was, or might be, capable of. He slipped his fingers around both ears and placed all of his focus on his sense of hearing. Nothing. He closed his eyes and tried again. A moment passed, and then suddenly there was something, like hearing voices while underwater. Then came words. They gushed into his ears messily, soft at first, muddled and wet, like each one had been slathered in honey before being spoken. Mitch pulled his hands away from his ears and opened his eyes. The instant his eyes made contact with the two outside, he heard it.

"She's all yours," the man said. Mitch always hated when people decided vehicles were intrinsically female. It seemed like another way to control women and treat them like objects and not actually be up front about it. If he ever had a car and had to name it, it would have a masculine name. Not because he wanted to ride it—it wasn't a sexual thing, although it may have been a gay thing. He doubted any straight man he had ever known would willingly choose to ride good ol' Dale instead of Bettie. That needed to change, he thought. *I can balance that out.*

Leo handed the man a crumpled roll of bills and watched the man count it with his chubby fingers. Satisfied, the man smiled and tapped the wad of cash to his forehead in gratitude.

"Let me know if you have any problems or anything," Leo said. "I took pretty good care of her." *Ugh, again. Why is it a girl?*

The man saluted him with a couple of fingers and opened the car door. "All right now!" He started the engine and drove away.

The car wasn't something that Leo loved. It didn't give him as much of a rush as the bike did. He had ridden one only once in his life and had almost bought one, but his ex-girlfriend said it was a stupid idea, so he never did. Things were different now. He could do what he wanted, when he wanted, and if he had to drop a few hundred dollars to do it, then he would. He had already dropped a little acid immediately after waking up; what was dropping a few hundred dollars more? He hadn't showered or even brushed his teeth, but goddamn, that bike made him look better than if he had. He adored being exposed to the wind when he rode, being able to look down and see the ground speeding directly underneath his feet like a riptide.

The air felt like a blow dryer against his skin as he sped out onto the highway in a T-shirt, jeans a couple sizes too big, frayed Vans and no helmet. He accelerated ten miles over the speed limit, then fifteen. The roads in Louisiana were always filled with drivers who couldn't drive and did things that would normally get you either arrested or killed in other states. People would dart across two lanes to cut you off when there was an empty street behind you (yet they were always slow when it came to everything else). Some threw their car into reverse at the top of an on-ramp. People were ridiculous. It became more of a game to try to zip through the mass of cars, like a mouse making its way through a maze.

He stopped at the grocery store and picked up some ingredients for dinner. It was Monday, and in Louisiana that meant it was a good day for red beans and rice. Leo could cook a few things, and even a few things pretty well if he wanted to. Red beans was one of them. The dish was one of the few things his mom had passed down to him that he liked, something that had nothing to do with the religion she also tried to pass down. It was a good recipe, and although it had changed over the years and he had tweaked it here and there, it was still his mother's.

CHAPTER 14

While Bisa was wrapped up in her cotton knots, she had a sudden thought: *what am I going to do tonight?* She felt a creeping and primal urge to enjoy herself. Perhaps it was the incense Nina was burning in the study, which smelled of cinnamon and sandalwood, or maybe it was the budding powers manifesting in her body. The one thing that Bisa knew for certain was that it felt slightly inappropriate. She hadn't been romantic or intimate with anyone in such a long time that she couldn't even remember when the last encounter had actually happened. It had always been…unimportant to her.

Bisa set aside the yarn and rose abruptly to her feet. She could feel the seed of an idea, the excitement of exercising her power. *What exactly am I capable of?* There were so many gray areas in magic. Witches shared certain abilities, like infusing potions, amulets and other talismans with intention. All witches could do that with a little practice, *so why aren't I practicing?* Eagerness gripped her where only moments ago there had been complete composure. *This is a gift,* she reminded herself as she found herself walking toward the study, toward the mysterious incense. When she rounded the corner to the room, the incense fizzled out in a woodsy wisp of smoke. The vast selection of books was upon her. She hadn't considered that she could browse them at any given time. If she could teach herself how to apply makeup to aging skin, she could certainly educate herself on magical teachings.

She walked along the bookcases, reading as many titles as she could before circling back. On the bottom left shelf closest to the door, a book so light purple it almost looked gray fell flat and lay horizontal. Bisa walked toward the book and retrieved it from the shelf. *Transmogrification of Love and Lust*. Bisa raised her eyebrows at the title before she flipped through the first few pages. There was no publisher and no copyright. She reached the table of contents and browsed the chapter headings. Chapter 1: "Magical Timing and the Moon"; chapter 2: "Oils"; chapter 5: "Foods"; chapter 6: "Compendium of Carnal Criterions"; chapter 9: "Potions and Tinctures." There were thirteen chapters total, and Bisa was instantly intrigued by each and every one of them. The book read like art—no, poetry. It spoke to her and was easily understood, and for Bisa, all things quickly understood led to inspired improvements and artistic originalities.

Bisa began to pick through the information, filled with enthusiasm and excitement as she studied segments from all the chapters. She loved learning new things, and this was like being back in school. It was different from anything she had ever learned in the past, more diverse than any art class she had ever taken. The skills and techniques in this book outlined a whole new way of living—as though she could be Julia Child, Frida Kahlo and Billie Holiday all rolled into one enchanting package. It wasn't just *cast a spell and be done with it*; there were subtleties to consider. The time of day, week and year could sway your magic. A new moon was more suited for fostering beginnings, whereas the full moon was more useful for amplifying fulfillment and awareness. If one considered using the natural world to their advantage, their spells could prove to be stronger, more efficient. Magic was immediate, even if the expected or intended result wasn't. During the two hours Bisa took notes from the book, she also decided on what kind of art she would make—what kind of spell. Taking little pieces from several parts of the book, she wrote down a poem, an affirmation, that she could also use as an incantation.

Let my beauty be felt throughout this night, let my aura shimmer and glisten bright.

I am lust and beauty, I am art, charming the desires of the heart.

People, men and the heteroflexible, twist their cravings, make them susceptible.

Bring me joy, bring me pleasure, stop what they are doing, until the light of day, let them still be pursuing.

A dash of grapefruit, honey and love to taste, bring me passion and lust, interlaced.

It wasn't going to win the Pulitzer Prize, but it certainly gave Bisa a sense of achievement. When the kitchen was as clear as her evening schedule, she glided in and started to pull out everything she would need for her potion, or milkshake: vanilla ice cream, milk, honey, grapefruit, orange, salt, cinnamon, vanilla extract and dried mint. Thank God for Nina and her thorough grocery shopping. Everything she needed and more was at her fingertips. After neatly arranging everything on the counter in a small cluster, Bisa wrote out the recipe along with her notes.

> 3 scoops of vanilla ice cream (can substitute any flavor—I like vanilla)
> 1 cup milk
> ½ cup sugar (linked to Venus and love)
> ¼ teaspoon ground cinnamon (*strong* aphrodisiac)
> 1 tablespoon honey
> ¼ teaspoon salt (to balance the sweetness)

> Zest of ½ grapefruit (to appear younger)
> Zest of ½ orange (stimulates blood flow and sexual appetite)
> ¼ teaspoon dried mint (awakens sexual organs and desire; named after a Greek nymph!)
> 1 tablespoon vanilla extract (boosts arousal in *men and women*)
> Mix the sugar with the cinnamon. Combine the milk, cinnamon-sugar mixture, honey and salt in a pot. Bring just to a simmer. Remove from heat, add zests, stir to combine, cover and let sit 10 minutes to infuse flavors. Cool completely. Add the vanilla and dried mint, stir to combine. In a blender, add ice cream and pour the milk mixture over it. Blend and serve.

Bisa was very methodical when it came to preparing her food, and executed it with an artistic temperament. She remembered Nina saying, *Trust your vibes—focus your intention and will your goal into being.* She had to apply what she already knew—art and technique. With that under her belt, a choreographed series of instructions formed in her head, layer upon layer, with magical vibrations added to each step, as though she were a chef building flavor in a soup. She hadn't taken into consideration the influences of the lunar cycle, or the time of day, but she could work on that later—she hoped. As she jotted the spell for the love potion—milkshake—down on a scrap piece of paper, she thought more about what the potion was actually for. Ironically, its purpose was the last thing she thought about. She paused for a moment, thought about what she was doing and translated her actions into something she could understand—art. If she was going to make art about love, she needed to understand what she was going to paint if she expected to express that. Without a clear intention, she might not successfully make the art achieve that intention. It had to mean something—anything, but something. There was art in everything Bisa did, whether it was applying a full face of makeup or the way she set the table. This couldn't be any different.

She closed her eyes and concentrated on the vibe she wanted to bring into her life through the milkshake. She wanted to be desired, to drip with sensuality and be simply irresistible, craved…but only by those she found…acceptable, people she was attracted to, although no one specific. The book made it very clear throughout several chapters that manipulating the will of a specific person had its drawbacks and even consequences. She paid little attention to that, though, because she wasn't interested in the love of one person. She wanted love in general. Not even love, but affection—adoration. She didn't think she had a type. Either she was attracted to someone or she wasn't, with a range as wide as the color spectrum. She hadn't considered where she was, either. What kind of people would she find attractive in Louisiana? Only time would tell.

With her intention set, she began the instructions for the ritual she had designed. She held her hand over each ingredient, pausing to infuse her intention into each one. If this had been anyone else, it might have just been simple new-agey words, but she could feel it, she could see it. It wasn't just a visualization happening inside her mind; she could feel the magnetic flow of energy under her hands, infusing the ingredients with her thoughts. After all the ingredients had been charged and programmed, she got to work on the recipe. While the milkshake whirred in the blender, she cleaned up her mess, put everything back in its place and folded the recipe up to fit nicely in her front pocket. No one would ever know.

She poured the creamy milkshake into a tall, slender glass, one that looked more like a bud vase, an artful choice from which to drink the potion. In a fast jerk of her wrist she dumped the trivial amount of milkshake left in the blender into the sink and washed it down with hot water.

Nina entered the room unexpectedly. "I smell citrus! What are you up to in here?" she said.

"Milkshake for one! Felt like a treat."

"Well, you certainly deserve it. Everyone else is doing their own thing, or maybe they're just pretending to be busy so they don't have to hang out with someone old. What are you up to? You wanna go get a drink? Catch a movie? Hide from the heat?"

Bisa swallowed a thick mouthful of her love potion, and her tongue licked the creamy whiteness that clung to her lips. "Any other time, I would say yes, but I kind of just want some alone time tonight."

"All right—I won't push it. I'm sure I can entertain myself. Maybe I'll try to give Mitch some competition in the crochet department, or have a spa day. I have a neti pot in the bathroom I've been wanting to try!"

Bisa gulped a few more times and tipped the glass to get every final drop. "I'm really not trying to avoid you."

Nina narrowed her eyes, having picked up on something strange in Bisa's energy. She didn't mean to pry; sometimes psychic awareness was utterly involuntary. "Everything okay?"

Bisa adjusted the topknot of dreads on her head and said casually, "Yeah, everything's good!"

Nina delayed saying anything as she picked up on some frivolous vibes. "All right. Another time then." She looked down at the empty glass, smiled and started to walk out of the kitchen. "Have fun tonight!" Right before she turned the corner, she said one final thing. "Make good choices!"

Then it happened. The dizzying rush of the potion radiated from Bisa's stomach and charged up and down her body. Bisa could feel the magnetism, like electricity, all over her face. She rushed to the bathroom and found the mirror. Her face was beautiful and alert, and although her eyes were approachable and empathetic, this was the powerful and seductive face of a commanding femme fatale, the eyes intense and entrancing, the lips ravishingly pulsing. She was so startled by the sight of herself that she lost her breath. On the outside, there was little to no difference physically, but emotionally, energetically—magically, everything was different.

There were fundamental truths that Bisa had been unaware of when she cast the spell and drank her milkshake. She had tapped into the sexual energy that is tied with the creative energy of the universe. All life and forms of energy were forms or by-products of sexual energy, creative energy—in short, a means of manifestation. Not only did Bisa manage to boost her sex appeal, but she also broke out of the confines of her emotions around sexuality. Sex wasn't something that made her feel safe. It wasn't something she sought out. It was linked with pain and trauma instead of discovery, pleasure and creation. The sex she'd had in the past had been forced, cruel and far from shared and consensual. Why would anyone want to experience the very act that they associated with pain?

She wasn't the same person she had been all those years ago, and the creative process of her sexuality had taken a new form with a new energy. There was an urge to heal. Although her body and spirit knew this, her mind and emotions did not. As beautiful as she made herself every single day, her sexuality was repressed. The milkshake was a skeleton key to a sexual prison cell, and that repressed energy was just dying for the gate to be unlocked. Sex didn't have to be unhealthy and toxic, it could be healing, and the spell allowed her to embrace the option to evolve beyond the resistance.

The awakening of sexual strength brought a certain amount of satisfaction. She felt empowered, alive and free from the cells of her past. She washed her face, moisturized and brushed a layer of fresh makeup over her enigmatic eyes. Bisa smiled with a gleefulness she only seldom saw in the mirror. Who was this Bisa? How could she determine what was real and what was the glamor of magic? How honest can a person be when wearing a mask? Or was it the application of the mask that captured one's essence? Was this who she truly was or was this new energy just a performance for the duration of the spell? A thought rushed to the front of her mind: she had to return to her spirit, where her life was being lived. It was a feeling of timelessness that she experienced—understood—as thoughts of sex, love and life ran through her mind. That timelessness encouraged her to discontinue the relationship she had with the feelings of being stuck.

She got a Lyft from the house and set her destination for a hotel bar that she had never heard of but had been highly recommended by a couple of websites that listed must-visit cocktail bars. When she stepped out of the car and placed her foot onto the still-hot pavement, she took a deep breath of the evening air. On the exhale, she noticed two men standing by the entrance, gazing at her in spellbound silence. Was it already working? Or was it that she looked so different from everyone else they'd seen? The car pulled away, and Bisa promenaded toward the entrance to the bar, her presence as hot as the flame in the hanging glass lantern above the doors. She passed through the doors and looked over the dimly lit space. It had once been a church, but had been turned into a guesthouse and bar. Stairs before her led to the rooms, and the parlor with its lofty ceiling, drapery, marble fireplaces and outright opulence was to her left.

Bisa strolled down the narrow hallway painted a rusty orange and adorned with mid-eighteenth-century candle sconces with iron bars acting as shelves for plants with dangling, leafy tendrils. Her heels snapped against the old wooden floor as she made her way, luxuriantly, toward the bar. Had there been soft music, the conversation and chatter would have reduced it to a thumping, muffled beat. After doing a quick lap through the open courtyard, passing the illuminated potted palms and magnolia trees and the diverse crowd exchanging conversation over crafted cocktails and shareable plates, she stopped at the door to enjoy the ambience. The smell of aperitivos and tomato-braised mushrooms floated across the patio.

Bisa was getting attention for simply standing still. Men adjusted themselves in their seats to get a better look at her, and women pretended to roll their eyes so they could secretly get another eyeful. In a hot minute, Bisa was encircled by strangers. People led their partners step by step toward her, like awkward teenagers slow dancing for the first time. *It's working. My milkshake is working,* she thought. A waiter on the patio suddenly turned his head toward Bisa, as if he'd heard the screeching tires of a car accident, and his eyes landed upon her face. Ironically enough, an accident was about to happen. With his focus led astray, his leg jammed into a recently vacated table and knocked it off balance, sending a wave of dirty plates, silverware, empty glasses, ice and a white pillar candle hurtling and flooding onto the damp brick floor.

There was no doubt about it: Bisa was queen of the night. She was emerging from the depths of her confines with the oomph of a harmonious Siren. As the ring of people slowly closed in, Bisa sneaked through them and made her way inside. Her powers were beyond the range of what she had believed she was capable of, beyond what she understood a Transcendent to be. There was an empty seat at the bar and she took it, her face bathed in tones of amber from the flickering candles. Conversations began to fade out at a slow and steady pace as people, both men and women, began to notice her. Her magnetism had the strength of freshly baked chocolate chip cookies wafting through the air, with the promise of a serious sugar addiction that left you wanting and craving more. She wasn't a big drinker, but tonight there was reason to drink. She was going to celebrate herself, celebrate her spirit.

When she looked up from the cocktail menu, she caught the well-groomed bartender smiling back at her. *What is it about her?* the man thought. *I can't even describe her, she's too gorgeous. Everything about her makes me question if I'm really gay!* Bisa chuckled as her eyes caught a couple of beads of sweat forming on the man's temple and slowly falling down his face. *She's making me sweat. I've never felt this way about anyone.* Her eyes dropped back to the menu. She hadn't had much experience with liquor, having never really acquired the taste for the harsh burn it left on her throat, but she knew exactly what she was going to order.

The bartender clumsily approached. "Good evening; what can I get you?" he asked sweetly.

Bisa looked up with a smile and said confidently, "Season of the Witch."

The bartender could barely concentrate. It was as if someone had put his brain into a shaker, tossed it around with some ice and poured it back into his head. By the time he finally started to make her cocktail, Bisa had already greeted three men and a woman who had inexplicably introduced themselves one at a time. Boring introductions paired with sloppy deliveries of romantic pickup lines poured in. Each person had unique qualities that were attractive in their own way: the bartender with the buzzed hair, gold-bar-shaped jawline and sweating temples; the woman who declared age was nothing but a number with her layered auburn locks in natural waves, green eyeshadow and geranium-tinted lip; the tall man who spoke so prudently that the inflections of his native accent were smoothed to the point of there hardly being an accent of any kind; and the shorter man with perfectly symmetrical eyes with colors that, depending on where he stood, seemed to change from blue to green to somewhere in between.

Tension rose as everyone tried to pay for Bisa's cocktail, which the bartender had already given to her on the house. Bisa raised the glass to her smirking lips. She had never been a whiskey fan, but the cocktail was mild with a palatable sweetness similar to vanilla and sautéed butter. The vulturine bar patrons nearby faded to the background as she savored the introductory notes of plum bitters, newly picked rosemary and fresh citrus, and then the lingering notes of Strega and a hint of black tea at the finish.

Bisa set the drink down on the counter and angled herself to face the group.

"Do you like it?" the shorter man asked.

"My drink?" Bisa replied quickly. "Too early to tell. Suited for someone like me, though. If I had to answer, I would say it's dangerously close to being exactly what I wanted. Why? Are you tryin' to figure out what I like?"

The taller man interrupted. "Where did you go to high school? I went to Brother Martin."

The redheaded woman pushed in front of both men. "You're not from here, are you?"

Bisa resisted the urge to try to exercise her power of influence, because the desire to see how well her spell worked was far greater. "Why, what is everyone saying about me?"

The tall man answered, "That you're beautiful. I don't always like to listen to rumors, though, so I wanted to see for myself."

The short man interjected, "What do you do?"

Bisa took a small sip from her cocktail. "I'm a witch!"

"Well, that explains it! You put a spell on me!" the tall man joked.

"Do you all know each other?" Bisa asked.

The woman responded first. "We do now. I'm staying here. I have one of the rooms upstairs. I just met these two fools tonight when I overheard them talking about how they just had to talk to you. I barged in and said, *I'm pretty sure she is totally not interested in you guys. You are not her type.*"

"Well, I wouldn't assume too much about what my type is. I don't really have one."

"All women like tall men, right?" the taller one said.

"I'm willing to bet she's interested in more than just someone's height. Like age, it's just a number," the woman said seductively.

The short man reached up to touch her dreadlock knot. "You have some wild hair, but how do you wash it?"

Bisa crossed her legs, smiled and shook her head. "I told myself I would kill the very next person who said something like that to me, but you're ridiculously handsome, so I'll let it slide once."

"See, I knew I was her type," the short man said.

"I don't have a type, not tonight," Bisa said before sipping the rest of her cocktail. The ice cubes clinked around the bottom of the glass as she set it down. "Although, that's not entirely true. I do have a type. Slaves. I don't care where you went to high school or how old you are, I care about having my every need and want met without any hesitation. So, let's all go upstairs to her room and you can all do exactly what I want, when I want it and where I want it."

CHAPTER 15

Leo didn't plan to give the red beans an overnight soak like he had been taught. He'd heard that soaking the beans helped reduce farting, a theory that raced through his mind as he arched his right leg and expelled a warm, rancid, bubbling-wet fart. It was the kind of fart that had bellowed in his bowels, begging to be released, the kind where he knew how rotten it would smell, the kind that left his butt cheeks a little sweaty as it blasted out. He would be lying if he said he didn't take a big whiff each time he farted. And he had to admit he liked it—just a little bit.

He waved his hand over his butt and then started to organize the ingredients for dinner. Leo was not the most refined member of the coven, but he did know how to make a legit batch of red beans and rice. He made it from scratch and didn't cheat by using a seasoning mix by Zatarain's or dumping the contents of a boxed meal into a pot. He blended his own seasonings, cut his own vegetables for trinity and sliced the Cajun sausage himself. The only thing he didn't do was make his own sausage. It wasn't because he didn't want to, but because it was expensive and time-consuming, and red beans was meant to be a quick and cheap meal, like his mama said it should be.

Mama Sullivan's Red Beans and Rice

1 tsp. basil

½ tsp. rosemary

½ tsp. sage

½ tsp. thyme

½ tsp. onion powder

½ tsp. paprika

¼ tsp. cayenne pepper

¼ tsp. crushed red chili flakes

½ tsp. black pepper

3 bay leaves

2 tsp. salt

4 garlic cloves, ground to a paste with 1 tsp. oil

1 onion, chopped

2 celery stalks, chopped

1 green bell pepper, chopped

1 lb. spicy andouille sausage, sliced ½ inch thick

1 lb. dried red beans

Italian parsley

Place dried beans in a pot. Add enough water to cover beans by 2 inches. Cover and bring to a boil. Remove from the heat and let the beans rest for 1 whole hour. Stir in 1½ teaspoons of salt and bring back to a boil. Uncover, reduce heat, and simmer until beans are tender and creamy. Check the beans after 1 hour and add more water if needed.

Brown the sausage in some oil until lightly browned and crispy. Remove and set aside. Add the onion, celery and bell pepper to the pan and sauté a few minutes, until soft. Add the beans and all spices and herbs to the pot along with enough chicken broth to cover by about 2 inches. Bring to a boil and cook for about 15 minutes. Reduce the heat to medium-low and simmer for about an hour, until the beans have started to soften but aren't fully cooked. Add the sausage to the pot and cook until the beans are completely soft. Add more water or broth if needed. Taste and adjust salt and seasonings. Serve over rice with chopped parsley and Crystal hot sauce.

For someone who cared more about whether his bike had gas than whether he had clean clothes, the meal was exceptional. Perhaps it was all that time working in restaurants, or maybe it was just a natural talent he had. It was almost as if he actually cared about something. Leo served everyone their portion, garnished with parsley and a fork. He grabbed his fork and began to eat before anyone else even had a chance to thank him for the meal. Then something strange happened. He felt he was a little too old to have this sort of thing happen at random. *I'm not fifteen, what the fuck*, he thought. He could hide it—luckily that was very easy under the table—but there was no denying it: he had an erection. The pressure in his pants wasn't the only thing that took him by surprise. It was the subtle sensation he felt in his chest, one that he associated with being sexually aroused. His heart beat like he was in the middle of intercourse, but there was nothing but a group of witches he felt no attraction to sitting down to a meal of red beans and rice.

Bisa looked around the hotel room, which exceeded her expectations: expensive linens, a large canopied bed, a limestone claw-foot tub and a bathroom decked out in lavish marble made for a dramatic contrast. The redhead turned on the light and dimmed the intensity to a lightning bug glow, and then lit a candle on a side table under an abstract painting of what looked to be a religious figure. It was a renovated Catholic church, after all. When the candle flared to life, the woman turned around and removed her shirt. She stood next to the light of the candle in her pants and a pine-colored bra with double spaghetti straps. The two men were more interested in Bisa, who stood fully clothed near the door.

The room was chilly and exceptionally quiet, especially for being above the bar, but it wasn't the nippy air that prevented Bisa from entering and removing her clothes; it was her past. It had been a long time since she had had any sexual activity that she hadn't given to herself, and even that took some courage and time to actually get used to. Even then, she still couldn't find the kind of physical touch that she enjoyed or felt comfortable with. She struggled through it a handful of times but could never truly detach from the nightmarish memories that flashed through her head. There was a frigidness to her sexuality, and it only made the room that much colder.

Bisa was turned on—no, triggered. Her body tightened as though bound with string. She was short of breath, slightly dizzy and hot. She felt it all at once and recognized the all-too-familiar symptoms. In some situations, she had convinced herself that she was unsafe and should flee even though she was in good hands and should stay, and other times she instantly felt disgusting, dirty and putrescent, someone no one would or should want. But the milkshake had no plans to stop what she had put in motion. *Be careful what you wish for*, she thought. What did she want? Was it this?

The woman removed her pants and walked over to the two men, who were waiting for Bisa to make a move. Bisa couldn't just tell them what she had told her gynecologist: *I don't really like sex; it doesn't really appeal to me anymore.* She had made it very clear only a few moments ago that she had a strong sexual appetite, but now she was giving off a very different signal in the dim light of the room. Everyone took another step toward her and Bisa closed her eyes. She opened her clenched fists, placed one hand over her belly, took a deep breath in through her nose and held it for a few seconds before she exhaled. She pushed her breath out as far as she could and felt her hand fall as her lungs deflated. A lot hung in the air as she exhaled her panic, anxiety and tension. Bisa opened her eyes and was happy to see the same strangers she had met in the bar, and not the three men who polluted her mind, the ones she expected to see, the ones she remembered clearly.

The tall man placed his hand softly on her elbow, but his unexpectedly smooth skin sent a shock through her body and it all came racing back in the matter of a second: the pain, the trauma, the feeling of being stuck in a perpetual state of crisis. The trick she usually used to soothe herself hadn't worked, and she could smell, taste, hear, see and feel the past. The pressure against her face and from behind, the stench of men covered in ruthlessness and power, the tang of sweat ribboned with blood, the screams—everyone's screams. Bisa's lip began to quiver as she started to lose what little control she had.

The shorter man was the first to notice. "You look really uncomfortable. What can we do?"

"I need…I think…" Bisa stuttered, trying to find the words to explain how she felt and what she wanted. The truth was that at that moment, even she wasn't entirely certain. She was conflicted between wanting sexual contact and wanting to run from it.

The redheaded woman gently pushed the man's hand away from Bisa's elbow to give her some space. "Hey. We're all here for you, and nothing is going to happen that you don't want to happen. You're in control here. And you won't hear one complaint from me if you boss me around—or over any of us, for that matter."

Bisa's mind flooded with noise as if someone had poured it in from a pitcher. The crown of her head felt hot, as though it were melting over her scalp and down the sides of her head. Bisa closed her eyes once again and listened to the voice that she heard as if it were her own. *Desire isn't wrong...That feeling of desire comes from the lack of it in great quantity. Desire is your future self, the need for expansion, to break out of this old paradigm you're trapped in. Feel the rhythm of your body. Be present and use this opportunity to begin anew. Where we put our focus, consciousness goes, and a shift in consciousness is evolution. You are in control. Connect. Explore. Heal.*

As quickly as the voice materialized, it vanished, along with the heat.

The woman grabbed her phone from her purse. "Maybe a little music?" She poked at her phone until she found something she thought was appropriate. She clicked Play and placed the phone on the table next to the bed. "By Your Side" by Warpaint started to fill the room, ironically a song that used to play over the stereo system at Warpaint, where she used to work. But she wasn't concerned with the past, she was only focused on the present moment. She reached up and ran her hand along the blood-red canopy that hung over the unmade bed and then walked over toward Bisa. The woman reached out and grabbed Bisa's hands. Walking backward toward the bed, she led Bisa through the path of the two men. Bisa wanted to be in complete control…and she was.

The woman lifted her hands to Bisa's hips and ran her fingers slowly in tiny circles, tussling the fabric of her clothes and tickling her skin underneath. Bisa smiled, closed her eyes and allowed the woman to raise her hands up the sides of her body. The two men quietly undressed behind Bisa. The short one stepped behind the redheaded woman and slipped his fingers under the waistband of her matching pine-green underwear. He rubbed his fingers back and forth as if to loosen the clothing from her body and then tugged the underwear respectfully, bit by bit, as if unwrapping a gift that was wrapped in paper you wanted to save. The woman lifted each foot to allow the underwear to escape. The man lifted her underwear to his nose and sniffed the twisted silk, still warm from her body.

The tall one was now behind Bisa, and she could feel his hardness against the small of her back. He remained there, pressed in close, as if waiting to be told what to do next. His head cocked toward her neck, and his breath was hot with the scent of whiskey and ginger. The redhead removed her hands from Bisa and reached around her own back to undo her bra. Bisa opened her eyes and looked at the two petite breasts framed by the woman's red hair.

Bisa opened her mouth to speak. "I haven't done this in a long time. And I've never done this before."

The woman smiled and moved in closer, grabbing the edges of Bisa's clothing. "Done what? A foursome?"

Bisa laughed. "That too. But I mean, I've never been with a woman."

"Neither have I," the woman whispered devilishly.

As a group, the two men and the woman began to undress Bisa slowly, politely, but with complete concentration. They removed her shoes, her dress and then her bra. Bisa felt the cold air against her breasts as they hung freely in the candlelit room. The taller man, with hands like fire, pushed his fingers on either side of her waist and with a steady drag removed her underwear and let it fall past her knees, where it rested in a tangled mess around her ankles.

Bisa felt the strength of her own life force and then, as if beyond her control, her power of influence unfolded itself onto the group. Each of them encircled Bisa and guided her toward the bedsheets, with the beauty of a choreographed dance. They placed her on the bed, and the cold, crisp sheets drew the heat from her body as she slipped farther onto the mattress. The strangers hoisted themselves onto the bed and encompassed Bisa's naked body. It began with a wet kiss and day-old whiskers rubbing the side of her face. The sound of the whiskers against her soft cheek sounded like the crackling of an old vinyl record. A set of milky-white hands emerged from her closed knees and parted her thighs. Long red hair that smelled of oranges then followed. A warm tongue ran along the curves of Bisa's inner ear. She heard every movement as she felt it simultaneously, like ambient movement into a microphone. It reminded her of putting a conch shell to her ear as a child and listening to the sounds of the world around her reverberate inside the hollow space.

The room was warm now, and they existed in a single knotted constellation of naked bodies upon the bed. *I'm in control.* Bisa gave in to the pleasure between her legs, cupped around the bottom of her breast, against her lips and inside her mouth. A few deep breaths soon evolved into moans and sighs ripe with pleasure. She reached down between her thighs and felt the pressure of the woman's tongue on her finger as it pushed against the folds of her body. One man hovered over her head, covering her breast with his mouth, the taller man kissing the length of her neck, a hand firmly massaging the back of her head. The bed creaked under the repetition of their momenta. Then it shifted, as Bisa willed it. The woman rose from below and extended her tongue up the length of her stomach, leaving a moist trail behind as the two men kissed each other over Bisa's body. It continued in a song of whispers and quivers, pleasure building upon pleasure, heightened with every kiss, every touch and every entrance. Pressure climbing and expanding to every end of her body and part of her mind. Their sweat dropped onto her chest and mixed with her own as their bodies pressed more tightly against one another. She squeezed and pulled them closer, farther inside—it was her desire. There was no embarrassment, no shame, no disgust—only guilt-free pleasure.

Bisa explored her body, their bodies, their insides, with her hands, fingers, tongue, lips and eyes. There was a newfound strength in her vulnerability. Minutes lasted hours in this vulnerable space, and she melted into them with eagerness. The only pain was the kind she gave to herself when she bit her lip. It took some time, but soon the flicks of their fingers and the licks from their tongues freed her from control and judgment. She tasted herself, a flavor of milk and honey, and in one long-winded moan, everyone climaxed simultaneously, an eruption of extremes amongst a quartet of whimpers and groans.

Bisa opened her eyes and found she was on the ground in a land without light but with more stars than one could see from even the most remote parts of Earth. It was blacker than the darkest midnight, with only the illumination of the infinite stars. There was no moon, and the air was temperate and still. She turned her head and saw a patch of prairie grass swaying ever so gently in the still air. Bisa closed her eyes. When she opened them once again, she was back in the hotel room watching the ceiling fan spin. Slowly her breath returned to normal as they rested, tangled up together upon the bed. The sex, although still slightly uncomfortable mentally, was not what concerned her. Had that been a vision? Was it real? Where was it?

No one spoke. As the playlist finished with "Mile High" by James Blake, everyone, apart from Bisa, fell asleep. She sat up on the bed, covered her breasts with part of the sheet that was free and looked back at the group. She slipped off the bed, gathered her clothes, dressed and left the room without so much as a look backward. *What even just happened?*

CHAPTER 16

The Bonners unlocked the front door to the church and headed to their office. In Edie's left hand she held a small glass bottle sealed with a piece of cork. Inside the bottle was a watery fluid, black like the depths of her soul. In her other hand, she held a bunch of papers, a sort of collection of résumés for the position they had advertised on the down-low. Josh had arranged the interviews and the timetables for their interrogations, but Edie was the one who approved it all. The potion in her hand was a gift from Mr. De La Fuente, a tool to help choose the operatives who would carry out their plans. They couldn't risk doing it themselves. That wasn't what they were good at. They were good at leading, persuading and controlling.

Edie filled a pitcher with ice and then poured in some sweet tea. In a separate glass, she poured a small amount of tea, spilled the potion into the glass and watched the swirls of black liquid become translucent—undetectable. The final step for the potion, as instructed by Mr. De La Fuente, was to add a droplet of saliva. This would activate the potion's true purpose. The potion added to a liquid on its own would reveal the deepest secrets, truths and hidden urges of whoever drank it. If another person added saliva before someone drank it, whoever sipped the cocktail would furthermore obey any command given by that person.

The Bonners had been told it wouldn't work on witches, so it was best to use it to gather up people who would back their cause. It seemed like witchcraft, but they thought the power of God might not be enough and they would have to fight dirty, even if it meant using methods that were questionable to their own faith. If they wanted to truly overcome evil, they had to fight fire with fire. Their grasp of how magic worked was weak, which made the potion's potency a little weak, less precise and slightly unstable. It was like someone who can't carry a tune learning to sing: they would still be able to sing a song, but they'd always be a little off-key.

Edie and Joshua rolled their tongues a few times and built up some spit. Working quickly, they both dropped a dribble of saliva into the glass and swirled it around with a silver spoon. Edie poured the potion, now fully activated, into the pitcher with the sweet tea. It looked just as it should: like a large, glistening pitcher of southern hospitality. She had made the tea herself, with a full cup of sugar and a little pinch of baking soda to offset the bitterness. It was a trick her mother had taught her, Lord bless her sweet soul and that recipe for sweet tea.

They needed to find people who were just as dark as they were, people so full of hate and ignorance that it was how they lived their life. Being hateful wasn't enough; they needed to find the ones whose thoughts were so vile that they could only think them and never say them out loud.

A few minutes later, the chairs they had set outside the office were full of the potential candidates. There were eight in total, all members of their church, spanning across all campuses, and not a single one of them was a decent person. Joshua had a talent for writing, and it was that very talent that drew the insufferables to them after they read his inviting job description. Edie was going to begin with whoever's name was on top of the stack, but a sudden impulse caused her to flip through the applicants and choose the order of interviews according to whether she liked their name. Joshua twisted the squeaky doorknob and opened the door. With a tray of glasses filled with sweet tea, he made his way down the line of applicants, making sure each person had a glass.

Edie and Joshua sat next to each other behind the desk, directly opposite the applicant. The first question was to make sure the applicant had had a sip of the tainted tea. If, like Maribelle Larson, the first applicant, they hadn't tasted it yet, Edie had to guilt them into it by insulting their manners and saying that her late mother would be horribly offended if they didn't so much as give it a little taste. It worked. Edie always got her way. The interviews were short—an average of around seven minutes per person. Edie could tell within the first minute or two if someone was going to work out. If the applicant proved to be someone they didn't want on their team, she could at least have a little fun with them before they let them go. After all, they were being forced to reveal their secrets against their will.

To Maribelle, "Do you listen to Michael Jackson's music?"

To Travis Dupre, "What race would you accept if you could change their skin color?"

To Waylon Martin, "In one sentence, how would you explain Obama's presidency?"

To Beau Walker, "It's a very simple question: either you wear white sheets or you don't."

To Gary Tipp, "Would you rather be black or Oriental?"

To Tammy Armstrong, "When Darla Beasley's dog dug a hole in your yard, how did you decide which gun to use?"

To Wade Shellnutt, "When was the last time you had sex with your wife?"

Edie had had her suspicions about Wade for years, but she had kept them to herself, until now. After Wade left the room, she turned to Joshua and shook her head. "I knew it. He looked like a homosexual. What kind of man doesn't have sex with his wife for three years? She told me herself in confidence after prayer circle on Friday. That poor woman. Someone should tell her…that's not right." Edie was lost in thought for a minute. She felt embarrassed for Wade's wife, but only for a moment.

The Bonners interviewed their final applicant, Stan Gurin, a man made mostly of muscle, clean-shaven, with skin so tight, it was red, and a voice on the cusp of being fully American but not without Russian accents. His hair was buzzed short, but his receding hairline couldn't be hidden no matter how short his hair was. They knew they had someone special on their hands the moment he mentioned how powerful their last sermon about evil was.

It was an accident that Stan had even heard the sermon in the first place. He was a driver for Amazon and happened to be delivering a package the day of the sermon. It was his last stop, and he had planned to return to headquarters to finish his shift, but the Bonners' hypnotizing words lured him in, and he stayed to listen. He wasn't a religious person, had never been to church and could bench more than Edie's watch cost. Given that résumé, he didn't seem like a solid choice. Yet Stan considered himself their best choice. In his eyes he was an activist who had been seeking out those he believed were most toxic to the world, specifically minorities and homosexuals. It wasn't his day job, or one at which he moonlighted; it was more an everlasting hobby that he enjoyed every once in a while, like meditation. The urge came at random, but it always came, the craving to go on what he called safari. A great deal of time had passed since his last expedition—not by choice, mind you, but because he had to be careful. A hobby like that was bound to get you into trouble sooner or later if you weren't careful, and that's exactly what he was: not careful.

He had secured the job as a delivery driver only a couple of months earlier, right out of prison. When Edie found out about his prison time, she was intrigued instead of apprehensive. She pushed for details, and with the advantage and support of the potion running through his veins, she was sure to get them. Stan said it proudly: he'd done time for involuntary manslaughter. The victim—no, target—was a young college kid, black and effeminate enough to set Stan's blood on fire. Both were at the same bar, a shithole of a dive with watered-down drinks and a single-stall bathroom door that didn't lock. The fact that Stan was the size of a mutant gorilla shouldn't suggest that he had a bladder that size. He always had to pee, and vodka ran right through him. It was after vodka soda number two that he headed to the bathroom. He pushed on the wooden door, and it swung open effortlessly. There was a pop as the lock malfunctioned and unlocked, but he didn't hear it over the Eagles blasting out of the speakers, the nicest thing in the place.

There Stan stood, in the doorway, facing an underage college student taking a piss. The kid turned, laughed nervously and said the lock was broken, but that's not what Stan heard. In fact, Stan hadn't understood a single word the kid said. He assumed the guy had left the door unlatched, that he wanted someone to walk in and look at his dick. It made sense. What else would he want want? He didn't really remember what happened next. It was as if he had been possessed by a demon, and when he came to, he was covered in blood. Stan had been possessed, but not by a demon—by rage. He had punched the kid in the face. There was a stiff and heavy slap, like a raw steak falling to the floor, followed by the wet, crunchy sound of bones collapsing under pressure. All of which Stan missed in the haze of his rage.

When Stan punched someone, they didn't get back up. The force of a single blow shattered the kid's facial bones and caused a subdural hematoma—at least that's what the report said when they read it in court. He pleaded guilty, with pleasure, and was sentenced to six years in prison but suspended to two, which included his time in county jail. No more, no less. Incarceration was incredibly brief, so short that he couldn't even reach his personal deadlift goal of 820 pounds. There are people who take pride in their crimes as boastfully as those who take pride in their art, and Stan was one of those people. It would slip out in conversations during his twelve-month, court-ordered anger management courses and community service. Perhaps it was the drug and alcohol testing that encouraged him to apply for the job at Amazon. It was at the drug testing center that he saw an ad for a delivery driver on a bulletin board. It was meant to be.

"You're in," Edie said proudly. "You're hired. We would like to invite you to become part of our team. What do you say, Stanislav?"

"Stan. Just call me Stan. Most people call me Bowie, though."

Josh smiled as he thought of the short period in his life when he had explored David Bowie. "After the singer?"

Stan shook his head, reached around to his back and pulled out a shiny, long, sharp-as-hell Bowie knife. "After this."

The knife glistened in the sunlight that beamed in from the window, a holy sight. The Bonners never asked what the knife was for. They didn't have to; they knew. What they didn't know was how many sinners it had been used on. The number was irrelevant, because Stan was now under their control. Whatever the request, he would be sure to obey.

"Now—Stan, is it?" Edie said as she tapped her fingertips together three times, her manicured nails clicking together. "We here at the Whole Truth and True Light care about values, we care about the lives of true Americans, we believe in the messages we receive from God, and it is our duty, as leaders of this community—leaders who represent the real America—to set right the wrongs of this world…starting with those who want to change the traditions that make us who we are. Ain't that right, hon?"

Joshua smiled and nodded. "That is absolutely right. I couldn't have said it better myself. I could try, but I couldn't do it," he said with a wink.

"Oh, stop now."

"It's the pure truth."

"Is it?" Edie said, even though she knew it was.

"Anyhow, what my wife here is making perfectly clear here is that those who think they are moving us into the future are filled with sin. They are confused, and they have lost sight of what is truly important."

Edie raised her hands to the air. "Amen!"

"Change isn't good, change is just that…change. Now, we aren't talkin' about the kind of change like technology or switching to a diet low in sugar, no—we are talkin' about the kind of change that upsets the balance of what makes us human, what makes us proud to be alive, proud to be children of God, proud to be on this earth walkin' under his light, proud to be a citizen of the greatest country on this whole planet!"

Edie clapped her hands together in agreement. "Praise his grace!"

"There is true evil out there," Joshua said, his voice deep and gloomy.

"And what we are about to tell you must not—will not—ever leave your lips," Edie said. "There is a dark force spreading through the world, changing the minds of people who aren't as strong, who don't have the light, who are unfortunate enough to not know any different. We all know we are the most superior, it's just common knowledge, and people want to talk about making things equal…We aren't equal, we never have been. It is all throughout history and history is truth. I'm not just talkin' about the homosexuals, the atheists, the…the…the…all the rest, I'm talking about the darkness."

"What's darkness?" Stan inquired, one eyebrow raised. "Please, tell me. Let me help you. I can help you."

Edie turned toward her husband and touched his arm. "Should you tell him or should I?"

"Go on, now."

Edie smiled, let out a sigh of exhilaration and leaned toward Stan. "I'm talking about the power of the devil. The minions of Satan. Witches. It's not a myth, it's not hocus-pocus. Witches are real."

Joshua adjusted his belt a few times. "The era of Satan is upon us…the witching hour is here. They will do everything they can to bring about hell on earth and call that the future. That's not the future I want. That is a godless life. We can find them. We know who they are. You will do what you're best at. That's all we ask of you."

"You're going to kill the witches," Edie said. "Every single one we find. You follow our orders and report back to us."

Stan put the knife away and nodded. "I will. You know, some people call you and your church crazy, from what I hear."

Joshua sat up in his chair ready for some heavy words, but Edie held him back with a light shove of her arm.

"What we stand for…what we are…the future…the light…that's not crazy…that's family."

Joshua closed his fist and raised it in a hallelujah fashion. "What does family do?"

"We stick together. We fight for one another. For what's right. For our future," Edie said fiercely.

That's when Ben, the custodian, lightly pushed open the office door. He stood five foot ten if he didn't slouch, a proud and simple-minded hillbilly from Coalgate, Oklahoma, with an accent thicker than the humidity. Everything about him was a caricature of what someone would think of when they heard the word *hillbilly*. Balding with a horizontal patch of wispy raisin-black hair, a few black teeth and impossibly skinny. A chatterbox, if he was given the chance, one with a rambling mind that often told stories beginning with *now, my daddy*…and ended with *well, anyway.*

Edie belatedly took knowledge of Ben standing in the doorway. She looked at her watch and suddenly realized that he might have heard everything they had said. She tried to keep her face clear of suspicious tics and full of a carefree glow.

"Ben!" Edie shrieked, her mouth wide open with a larger-than-life, jubilant grin. "Sweetheart, what on earth are you doin' here? I thought you'd be long gone by now."

Ben took a few steps into the office. He stood proud, knowing full well his shoes had more holes than a honeycomb, his sleeveless T-shirt was unwashed and he had lost most of his teeth to a former meth problem. (That was before he found God at the church. Now he brushed the few teeth he had and only thought about meth.) "I don't want to be interruptin' nuthin', I just came to let you know I sealed up that leak in your window right there earlier today with that uh, uh, expanding foam or whatnot, that stuff I showed you in the maintenance closet. Well…eh-eh-eh anyway, that stuff is real cool, filled up the gaps in the window jambs, so that should help keep all that cool air in here for you. You shouldn't be feelin' any of that hot air no more."

"Ben! I told you to take your sweet time with that. Ugh, that's what we love about you, you're so dedicated. Thank you," Edie said, still grinning outrageously.

Ben stood there with the tenacity of a bellboy waiting for a decent tip. There was silence, so much silence. Ben adjusted the tattered baseball hat with the word *Oklahoma* across the front and fluttered his jaw a few times.

"Was there somethin' else, Ben?" Joshua asked.

"I don't mean to listen—you know I'm not like that. You know, my daddy…he had a farm, and he lived with three sisters, way up in…uh, uh, what was it…I forget, somewhere in Mississippi, and he always said he listened to what his older sisters would do after he went to bed, and he said I shouldn't be like that cuz, well, people don't like covert listeners, and I'm not, well, eh-eh-eh anyway, I wanna help y'all."

More silence. Edie collapsed her chest onto her arms, waving her head back and forth in a sort of acted confusion. "I don't understand," she said—although she did understand. It was the only thing she could think to say while she thought of what to say next.

"Well, now, I heard y'all talkin' about the power of evil and whatnot, and about them witches. Now, back in Oklahoma, we lived next to a farm, and one day the man that owned that farm just straight up and died, and we all thought it was his wife. She was one of those witchy women. You know, when she got mad, clouds would show up in the sky and everything. Anyway, I believe you. I wanna help."

Stan looked at the Bonners, his hand reaching for the knife. "What do you want me to do?"

Joshua reached out in panic. "No, no! Not that!"

Edie gasped, one hand on her heart and one hand outstretched toward Stan. "Oh, good Lord no! Not in here. Never in here," she said with a nervous giggle. "This is all new, fresh carpet!"

Joshua shook his head. "Edie!"

"Well, it is!" Edie then lowered her voice to a light whisper. "They wouldn't give us a deal like that twice now, come on." She turned her head and politely brushed her hair with her hand. She was all smiles. "What I mean is, that's not necessary. That's not what we want. Ben is not just our maintenance janitor, he's a member of this church and he's a friend. Joshua, honey—get him some sweet tea."

"Naw, ma'am, I'm all right. I really shouldn't. Sugar is bad for my teeth," Ben said courteously.

"Darlin', *meth* is bad for your teeth. Drink the tea; what good is a tall, frosty glass of sweet tea if no one is going to drink it?" Joshua handed Edie a glass of potion-licked tea. "Drink the tea," Edie said quickly and without compromise.

Ben accepted the tea and took a polite sip. The liquid rolled over his tongue a few times and he smacked his lips. "What's that flavor I taste? Is that, uh, orange?"

Edie smiled. "No, dear, that's lemon! Fresh from Mr. Albertson's front yard! Can't you tell? It has that kind of West Bank flavor to it."

"Really?" There was a long pause as Ben reflected on the flavor like he had never tasted it before. "Wow!" He smacked his lips again.

Delight spurred Edie, and the uncertainty of what Ben would say next was unbearable—he was under her spell now. "You were sayin'?"

"Oh, right! I wanna help. Whatever I can. I don't wanna be tootin' my own horn or nothin', but y'all remember I was one of the very first members at this church, way way back when y'all called it Angels of Faith?"

Joshua frowned a little, just enough to squish his brow. That was the name he had chosen, but Edie had felt that it wasn't quite right. She had wanted something ambitious, something that shouted loud and clear what it was they stood for. It was only after they rebranded and became the Whole Truth and True Light Assembly of God Church that they really started to make a name for themselves.

"That's right!" Edie said.

"Remember, I helped you pick out the sign and install it in the front yard! I'm a loyal and dedicated member of this family, and I want to be of service. I don't just mean moppin' the floors neither. I mean, really be of service. Whatever you need. Whatever y'all are lookin' for, I'm your guy! Me and this guy!"

The Bonners had him in their pocket. There was nothing he wouldn't do.

"Ben, I would love for you to be our second in command. You're right. You deserve this," Edie said. "Doesn't he, Joshua? Isn't he just perfect?"

"The most perfect."

"Y'all aren't gonna regret this! I'll do whatever you want. I'll kill niggers, steal their children, whatever you want!"

"Slow down," Joshua said calmly. "You'll do what we ask of you. Let's start there."

"Sure thing, boss. One thing, though. Can I get a cool name like Stan? I heard him say people call him Bowie after his pretty knife."

The Bonners looked at each other for backup. Neither of them had planned for any requests, but who were they to deny Ben such a simple pleasure? Let him have his merry little moniker.

"What should we call you?" Joshua asked.

"Buckshot! Now, my daddy, he taught me how to shoot a gun, and when I was eight or so, he took me out to the field and handed me his shotgun. Man, that thing was heavy. Wow! Eh-eh-eh anyway, I thought I had it under control, but I was real young, you see, so I slipped and lost control, lost my grip on the gun and dropped it. Blew off part of my right foot right there! After that, he always called me Buckshot. He was kind of an asshole about it, but…"

"Language, Ben," Edie said softly.

"Sorry, sorry! Eh-eh-eh anyway. Call me Buckshot."

"Welcome to the family, Buckshot! I hope you two like road trips. The first one we need to bring to light is just outside Mobile, Alabama. Let's burn the witch."

CHAPTER 17

Over the next few days, the coven members tried their very best to coexist in the same space. It was similar to being in a dorm where one had no choice but to live with a complete stranger. Although most of them had never lived in a dorm, they had all shared an apartment or living space with a roommate at one point or another. Just because they were all part of the same coven didn't mean they wanted to live with each other. It wasn't like any of them had asked for anything that was now part of their normal everyday life. No one had signed up for roommates, magic, or the task of trying to encourage global balance. Yet there they were, all in agreement to try to make it work for one reason or another. The problem was that what worked for one person didn't necessarily work for everyone else. The coven was not without differences, and when people live together in a small space, things are bound to get a little uncomfortable. It was beyond Leo smacking Mitch across the cheek whenever he passed, beyond Mitch spiking Leo's coffee with fish sauce in retaliation.

One evening a wild storm rolled in and seemed destined to last a long time. A flood warning was in effect, and the grass in the backyard was drowning in pools of rainwater. Thunder crashed, and lightning spilled into the great room where they had all congregated after a quiet dinner during which none of them were interested in speaking to one another. Nina was in the kitchen cleaning up. Avery had picked up a small leather-bound book from a small shop in New Orleans and consecrated it for use as her grimoire, a journal to document all of her magical education. She sat next to Ollie, scribbling journal entries and spells that she had been collecting over the past few days. Between them was a bowl of popcorn. Bisa was humming to herself as she read from a magazine, Mitch was watching fail videos on his phone, and Leo was skimming through Instagram on his phone when he suddenly felt the need to dig nail clippers out of his pocket and trim his toenails. Witch or not, annoying is still annoying, and their nerves were all on edge. It was the little things everyone did that managed to irritate the hell out of people. The more each of them felt irritated by the others, the more they wanted to do whatever irritated someone else. Sure, any one of them could have stood up and walked to another part of the house, but…why should they have to? They were just as entitled to sit in the room and do whatever they wanted, whenever they wanted.

Snap!...Snap!...Snap!

Leo clipped along the top of his big toe, careful to keep the toenail in a single piece. Everyone looked up from what they were doing to see him grooming his feet. They all just listened and watched.

Snap...Snip!

He clipped the last connecting part of the toenail and was pleased to be holding one single piece of toenail in the shape of the Crescent City. *What is he going to do with that?* Avery thought. *If he puts it on the table, I'm outta here*. Leo analyzed the tiny nail and spun it around in circles between his thumb and index finger before tossing it into his mouth.

Bisa's mouth dropped open in horror. "Did you just *eat* your toenail?"

Leo looked up at her with icy, emotionless, matter-of-fact eyes. "Yup." He lowered his head back to his foot and continued clipping the other nails.

"That's gross. Who does that?" Avery whispered before continuing to scribble in her grimoire with her left hand while keeping her right hand in the popcorn. Every time she reached in, her finger would brush the entire bowl of popcorn, like a gust of wind over a dusty floor. Then she would peek at the pieces as she made another sweep around the bowl. It was like she was panning for gold, hoping that something great would be unearthed as she brushed through the top layer. It didn't stop there. She dug her fingers into the side of the bowl and retrieved a single piece of popcorn, examined it, dropped it and started the whole process again until she found a piece that was satisfactory. Only then would she toss it into her mouth.

It drove Ollie crazy. *Maybe I can force her to just eat the damn popcorn*, he thought. But then he realized that it might be unethical to force her to change the way she ate a snack. And then, only a few seconds later, he wondered what his annoying habit was and if it was annoying anyone else. He certainly wasn't cursed with the annoying kind of laugh that Mitch had, the kind that explodes without warning at an ear-splitting level.

Ollie continued to pick the skin from around his thumb, if one could call it that. He had broken blood so many times that his thumb was mostly scar tissue. It helped him think. Someone had once asked why he did it, and his answer was simply that it felt good. Perhaps he was picking now out of anxiety as Avery continued to rustle the popcorn to pluck a single kernel out like she was a princess. When she noticed him staring at her, clearly irritated, she looked down at his scabbed thumb and the flakes of skin that had fallen onto his lap. She then burrowed her hand into the popcorn bowl and churned her wrist around with the violence of the crashing storm outside.

Bisa hummed louder and louder as she tried to drown out the snapping of Leo's toenails being clipped across the room. Every once in a while her eyes would dart up to look at Leo and find him staring right back at her, as annoyed by her humming as she was by his toenails.

Thunder roared and cut through the sound of the heavy rain.

"My God, does it ever stop raining?" Mitch said as he held his hand over his rapidly beating heart.

Avery nodded, but never looked up from her grimoire. "There's a flood warning, so it's probably going to just keep raining for a while."

Snip!

"It's hurricane season—it's always raining," Leo said as he started to clip the toenails on the other foot. "Why don't you try to stop it? You're pretty good at fire. Why don't you try somethin' new?"

Avery closed the leather cover of her grimoire, smiled acrimoniously and then walked over to the back door. She stood next to the patio door, removed her shoes and socks, and took the phone out of her pocket. Avery opened the door to the backyard, and a wet gust of wind slammed against her. The rest of the coven stood up and scurried to the patio door behind her. Avery stepped out onto the back patio and walked past the plants and into the yard, her toes disappearing into the standing water that collected faster than it could be absorbed into the ground. Rain pelted her body, slapping her from all angles. She closed her eyes. *I'm a Primordial...one of the Elemental witches...I can do this*, she said. The sky above was an angry mix of gray and charcoal, and bullets of rain showered down all around her. She felt it…the power of her concentration, just like she had with the candle in the great room. If she could create fire, surely she could help lessen the amount of rain. But the rain kept falling, and if anything, it was coming down harder than it had been before she stepped outside. Nina watched her from the kitchen window, wondering, hoping. Avery opened her eyes and saw only more rain. She opened her palms and outstretched her fingers at her sides. She had seen that happen in movies so many times, surely there was a reason for it. Still nothing. The storm raged on, determined to wash her away.

Leo's jowls were shaking with excitement. He just knew he could do it if he tried. In the time it took him to swallow a toenail, he took off his T-shirt, a psychedelic mix of colors with a giant skull on the front, and dropped it on the floor. Mitch noticed that instantly and kept noticing it until Leo undid his pants. Then he ignored Avery completely. Leo slipped off his pants and walked out onto the patio in his saggy, seafoam-green boxers. The water rose to the bottom of his ankles as he walked farther out into the yard. He approached Avery but said nothing, and instead walked right past her. He took a single look back to make sure she saw him, and then continued a few steps more, his shaggy hair plastered to his face, his skin tightening under the coolness of the rain. He knelt down slowly, letting his kneecaps sink into the soft ground. He raised his arms above his head, one at a time, in a calm, organized and choreographed manner. His torso rose up and down with his breath, his underwear constricted against his body under the heavy rain and he closed his eyes. His eyelids, which held the picture of a sky's clouds dissolving into nothing, fluttered but remained watertight. Suddenly the hairs on his arm started to rise, despite being saturated from the storm. He felt a tingling sensation all over his body. The air seemed to stop, and the sound of the rain was replaced with a clicking noise, a buzzing like a fluorescent light after it's been switched on.

Lightning struck, fast and hard. Nina watched the jagged bright bolt fork just above Leo's head and collide with his hands. Water, dirt and grass blasted up from the ground around his knees as the lightning's momentum and kinetic energy raced straight through his body and into the ground. Nina ran out of the kitchen, dish soap trailing after her on the way to the patio door. She pushed Mitch and Bisa out of the way and stood in the doorway. The rain slowed to a dribble for only a few moments before it stopped completely. There Leo was, kneeling in the yard, completely unharmed. He stood up with a look of otherworldly bewilderment, his face stoic and void of all emotion but surprise. When he turned around, Avery ran up to him.

"Leo! Oh my God! Are you all right?" she shouted, and turned back to the house. "Nina!"

Leo smiled. "That's how you do it, buttercup." He walked past her and back toward the house. Under his breath he muttered, "Primordial…psssh." He smiled and hopped into the air as he pumped his fist. "Goddamn, did y'all see that shit? What the fuck! Lightnin' struck me and I stopped that rain like a motherfuckin' G, dude."

CHAPTER 18

The mileage on Bowie's white 1996 Dodge Dakota was evidenced in the cosmetics of both the interior and exterior. The slightly dented truck had no air-conditioning, some chipped paint in the bed and a graveyard of old soda bottles and fast-food wrappers on the floor, mostly McDonald's cheeseburgers, with a few from Rally's mixed in. Buckshot threw a stained gray backpack into the back of the truck and then hopped into the passenger seat.

It was only a couple of hours to Mobile from New Orleans, but a trip without air-conditioning with a sour-smelling, chatterbox hillbilly in the passenger seat made prison seem like summer camp. After the first half hour, Bowie realized that not responding to any of Buckshot's questions wasn't going to get him a quiet ride. Eventually he just gave up. *Do you like catfish? You know, my daddy, he grew up on a Limousin cattle farm...Now my sister, she's real hot...I don't really drink no more, and when I quit, I started eatin' lots of nuts because I was orally fixated, but now I can't eat nuts neither because of my teeth. Do you like nuts? I ain't never been out of the country to anywhere like Russia or nothing. I reckon it's real cold there, huh? Man, this truck is just perfect for muddin'. You ever go muddin'? I wasn't raised in a barn or nothin', but I kinda like the way that horse feed smells—it's like granola, but I can't eat that because of my teeth. Man, it's hot. I think I soaked my underwear plum through. Wow...are you savin' the rest of this burger or can I finish it?*

It was endless. The more Buckshot talked, the more Bowie wanted to drive right back to prison and lock himself in a cell. He wasn't a big drinker either, but if there ever was a time that he wanted a couple of fingers of vodka, it was during that two-hour drive to Mobile. After about an hour and a half, Buckshot ran out of steam and the conversation died. It was more than a blessing, because if it had gone on any longer, Bowie might have just added an extra kill to his list, witch or not.

"Look! Look, Bowie! It's workin'!" Buckshot shouted with a murderous, black-toothed grin. The lunastaterum began to fill with the same milky fluid that Edie had seen the moment she handled it. It was activated, which meant they were getting closer to the witch. Before they left, Edie had commanded them to take extra good care of the device and to use it, protect it and return it to them. It was on loan for the duration of their "safari." They, of course, naturally obeyed her, as neither of them had any choice, being under the spell of the potion.

"What do you see?" Bowie asked as he kept his hands on the wheel and eyes on the road. The sun had just begun to set on the horizon.

"Nothin' yet, just like, uh, uh, a marker sort of thing."

"That's the direction we need to go. Let's just keep following that."

Driving into Mobile, they made their way down Government Street. Bowie drove slowly, like someone from out of town would, only he wasn't lost—he was hunting. Buckshot adjusted his hands so that his skin made contact with the bottom of the lunastaterum. Right at that moment, a vision flashed before his eyes. It was unlike anything he had ever experienced before, but not totally dissimilar to the painful fever dreams he had suffered during his meth withdrawal, without the vomiting, diarrhea and clammy skin.

"Holy shit!" Buckshot shouted. "I can see it."

"See what?" Bowie questioned.

"It! Him! The goddamn witch! Good Lord, I can't believe this thing…wow!"

Bowie slapped his palms on the steering wheel in annoyance. "Where? Tell me where!"

"He's real close. I can, uh, like, I can feel it." Buckshot licked his lips and focused on the visions that had been superimposed over his actual sight. "Up there, take a right. Down the block a bit."

Bowie pressed on the gas pedal just enough to increase their speed but not to raise suspicion. He hooked a right onto the next street and drove slowly down the road.

"Stop. Pull over here," Buckshot said as the vision slowly disappeared.

Bowie pulled over to the side of the road and parked. "Where is he? Is he in…there?" he said as he pointed to a bar called Daddy Rainbow on the corner. It was a small building, with a brick exterior and blackened windows, just a couple of blocks down from busy Government Street. The strong pulse of unfamiliar pop songs with intense female vocals spilled out onto the street as a couple of drag performers left the bar.

"I think. Yes," Buckshot said regretfully. "Well, I ain't goin' in there. That's just ridiculous, now."

"We won't have to. We wait," Bowie said as he turned off the engine. His mind filled with hate and his heart with excitement. He had finally found his purpose in life. The past was the past, and it had all been leading him to where he was now, doing God's work. No matter how long they had to wait, it would be worth it in the end. Nothing could stop him from carrying out the work he had promised the Bonners he would do.

After twenty minutes of waiting, Buckshot plucked out a ziplock bag of beef jerky from his front pocket. The jerky was soft and supple from being tucked away in his pocket for the drive to Mobile. He shook the bag a few times to loosen the cluster and then plucked out the biggest slice he could find. He lazily zipped the bag back up, leaving the final inch of it unzipped, and stuffed it back into his pocket.

"I don't normally eat this stuff on account of my teeth and whatnot, but Ms. Boudreaux makes two really good things: pie and beef jerky. She brought some to share at the last Water Baptism Wednesday, and I told her I just had to suffer because I couldn't pass it up, it just looked and smelled so good. Now, my daddy, like I said, he lived on a cattle farm, so my mawmaw used to make jerky all the time with all kinds of spices and stuff I'd never heard of, and—" Buckshot stopped talking without warning. Bowie let out a sigh of relief but soon realized that the sudden silence wasn't deliberate. Something was happening. "That's him, right there," Buckshot said, a crooked finger pointed toward the figure leaving the bar.

"Him?" Bowie tapped the windshield as if he were looking at a picture on a bulletin board.

"Yeah, that niglet! That's who I saw! Look, see for yourself, Sputnik!" Buckshot handed Bowie the lunastaterum and swallowed a large portion of the jerky. He continued to chew the other portion of the jerky with his mouth open to alleviate the pressure on his sensitive teeth. The jerky squished and squashed as it mixed with his saliva, sputtering tiny droplets of juice every few chews. He was so excited that he hardly chewed the rest, which wasn't that uncommon. When your teeth are in as bad of shape as his were, you try to chew less and less and swallow sooner rather than later.

Bowie gently rubbed the bottom of the lunastaterum and saw nothing. "It's not working."

Buckshot rolled his eyes. "That's right, 'member Edie said the image would disappear when you were close enough? Maybe wait a minute, wait until he walks farther down the road a bit."

The two watched and waited as the young man walked down the block. Then, right as he reached the next cross street, the image of the man's face flashed in front of Bowie's eyes. "Ben…"

"Buckshot, 'member?"

"Buckshot…you can't fuck this up. There is no fucking around. Get out of the car."

"What? Why?"

"Get out of the car, flag him down and tell him you're lost. Do what you're good at and talk him stupid," Bowie said as he started the truck.

"Well, then what?"

"Then I'll handle the rest. Just don't fuck this up," Bowie said as he plotted out the stalk, distract and ambush technique he wanted to use.

Buckshot tapped the hood of the truck twice and then jetted off down the street, Bowie following slowly in the truck.

When Buckshot was within hearing distance, he raised his hands in the air, waved them back and forth and scurried closer to the young man. "Excuse me! Excuse me, sir!"

The young man turned around. He appeared to be in his mid-twenties, with a buzzed head and a pretty face. All those details were irrelevant, however; he had to remind himself that this wasn't just an ordinary black guy; this guy was a witch, a true demon, the enemy of God and his good friends the Bonners. For half a second, the fact that he was black wasn't even an issue. It was worse that he was in cahoots with the devil. He wouldn't mess this up now. He couldn't.

"I'm real sorry to bother you, but I don't have the slightest clue where the hell I am. I'm stayin' at a little motel not too far from here, I think, I'm not too sure. I'm not very good with directions and whatnot, so could you tell me which direction is north?"

The young man grimaced. He hated being hassled by people he didn't know, especially when he was a little drunk off the stiff Amaretto sours he got for free at the bar. He also wasn't entirely sure which direction was north, but being from the South, he knew it would be polite to try to help, even when he didn't want to. "Well, I think it's that way, but I mean, I grew up in New Orleans, and our directions are only upriver, downriver, lakeside or riverside. Here everything is pretty much west of the river. So…maybe just tell me where you're staying." The young man pulled a pack of cigarettes from his pocket and immediately regretted it. *This guy is totally going to want to bum a cigarette. Why the hell do I always do this to myself?*

"It's a small, rinky-dink little motel, just off, uh, what's that street now, uh, uh, Government Street."

The young man lit his cigarette and blew smoke into the air. "Oh! Well, that's easy, that's just up that way. You see this park here? It's just right past that a bit. What's the name of the motel?"

"Say, can I have one of those cigarettes?" Buckshot asked nervously as he tried his hardest to make conversation.

Bowie had pulled up alongside them and parked the truck. The street was empty, except for a couple walking through the park and the walking traffic on Government Street a short ways away. They would have to be quick about it. Bowie turned off the truck and proceeded toward the sidewalk, never making eye contact or acknowledging Buckshot or the young man. He was on safari, something he was good at. Bowie was a natural-born predator, and he always got his prey.

The young man reluctantly pulled a cigarette out of his pack, which left him with one sad cigarette. "Here," he said as he pointed the cigarette at Buckshot.

"Aw, thank you. I've been tryin' to quit, but hell, it's the hardest thing I've ever done, and I just can't seem to kick the damn things for good. So uh, yeah, the name of the motel—"

"Hey, can I bum a cigarette?" Bowie asked.

"Man, I only got the one—" the young man started. But before he could finish telling Bowie no, he was stopped midsentence by a crushing blow from Bowie's fist. The young man dropped to the ground as though a bullet had been shot straight through his forehead. He let out a few curdled, choking noises, then fell silent.

"Holy shit!" Buckshot shouted. "That was like a mountain lion or a rattlesnake or something!"

"Shut your mouth!" Bowie whispered loudly. "Do you want people to see us? Hurry up, grab his legs, put him in the back of the truck!"

"Right!" Buckshot grabbed hold of the young man's feet, and together they hoisted him up off the sidewalk and tossed him into the back of the truck. Bowie tossed a few oily towels and a tarp over the guy to conceal him. He looked around to survey the area. No one was watching. No one had heard. They had done it.

"Get in the truck. Go!" Bowie ordered as he darted toward the driver's-side door.

At an inconspicuous speed, they pulled out onto the road and began driving away from all the main roads. Buckshot picked between his teeth and dislodged a piece of jerky. For a quick moment, he could taste the spicy flavor all over again. It was almost as good as it had been when he had eaten it the first time. The exhilaration of their kidnapping only made everything suddenly taste that much more exciting, like he could taste for the very first time in his life, really taste. His teeth weren't bothering him like they usually did after biting and chewing tough or hard foods. Maybe he was experiencing things on a whole new level. *Is this what life is supposed to feel like?* he wondered to himself. He hadn't felt this exhilarated in a very long time. It was how he felt when he played with his dog Eddie (named after Eddie Cochran), God rest his soul, or when he was having sex with Theresa, who lived in a seedy motel off Earhart Expressway. The dog was dead, and he hadn't had sex with Theresa since last March when she met a train yard manager at the Rattlesnake Rodeo and moved to Virginia. He felt alive for the first time in a long time.

Buckshot sat in the passenger seat, breathing heavily, every so often looking back to make sure their victim was still knocked out. He was slightly curious to know how murder would make him feel. Would it feel just like meth? Would that kill hit the pleasure receptors in the same way the drugs did? Would he then have to eventually wean himself off of that too? No jerky, dog or sex in the world could top how meth felt. He missed that feeling. Maybe this could be his new addiction, only he could keep his teeth.

"I can't believe how he went down with just a single punch!" he said. "It didn't sound like I thought it would. I mean, I've been in fights and whatnot, but a punch that hard, you expect to hear the kind of smack like in the movies. Whack!" Buckshot slapped the dashboard with his dirty palm. A cloud of debris and dust plumed up around his hand. "Where are we gonna do it?"

"Somewhere quiet. I'll find a place," Bowie said mysteriously, his mind active and alert like a crocodile along the bank of a river. He drove out of the city until he hit a stretch of road that looked rural enough to take care of what they needed to take care of. He took out his phone, checked the maps app and found the perfect spot. It was only a couple miles away off Old Mill Road. He took the next right and made his way up past the last few houses before the road was completely unpopulated. To the right was another road where the pavement turned into gravel, and high, unkept grass grew along either side. He turned there and followed the road into the forest. When it began to narrow, he slowed down almost to a stop. The dust from the gravel road rose around them and clouded the air illuminated by the headlights. He shifted the truck into park and left it running. Ahead of them was a small set of wooden posts and a thin wire holding a rusty metal sign, too worn to read. It didn't matter; the land was theirs for the evening. They parked and hauled the young man out of the truck and dragged him into the beams of the headlights.

The young man slowly opened his eyes. He was lying on his side, and the sounds of voices and laughter faded in from silence. Straight ahead was grass—no, weeds, so many weeds, and dead grass. The grass was as dry and dead as the landmarks they surrounded. Were those rock formations? They were gravestones, old ones, small and abandoned—forgotten. He tilted his head just enough to look up, then shifted his head back down to rest. He was surrounded by nothing and no one but the blackness of the night sky and whoever the voices belonged to. Pain surged back into his face where he had been punched. His nose was broken, clogged with blood and mucus, and each breath in had to be taken through his mouth. Trails of sweaty blood slithered across his lips and onto the rocky ground. The voices were laughing, but why did they seem so familiar? Then it struck him. The last thing he remembered was the man asking for directions. It was his accent. What was happening? Where was he? He shifted his arm from underneath his chest and coughed.

"He's awake! Bowie! Look! He's movin'!" Buckshot said, his voice nightmarishly cold. "Hold on now, I wanna get this on video so we can show 'em later! Right here, on the hood." There was a beep as someone hit Record on their phone.

Suddenly he heard footsteps coming toward him. The light that beamed from the headlights and highlighted the gravel road darkened as the figure moved closer. A set of hands grabbed hold of his arm and flipped him over to his back. Bowie smiled murderously right before he launched a fist at the young man's face. Again. Again. The young man's head flipped back and forth like a floating fish bobber after the first few bites from a fish. Buckshot yipped in the background, rife with pure joy, like a manic addict. In his frenzy, possessed with madness, he rushed over to Bowie's side and landed a kick in the young man's side, reeled his leg back and kicked again.

Buckshot's mouth began to tremble and shake as he collected a sticky pool of spit. Careful not to use too much tongue pressure—he didn't want to cause any more pain to his teeth—he spat on the young man's face.

"How we gonna do it?" Buckshot asked.

Bowie unsheathed his knife. "He's just going to have to wait and see for himself."

The young man made a garbled noise that was supposed to be a plea for his life. Words couldn't be said. He felt pain and fear, but he also felt strength. He just needed to use it. Only there was so much fear. He was surrounded by so much hate. *Is this it for me?* the young man thought in a flash. He thought of his life, his ex-boyfriend and his mother. *I'm sorry for everything. I want my mom. Why did I move to Alabama? I miss Jared. Why is this happening to me? There are so many things I want to do…I'm too young to die.*

Buckshot ran to the back of the truck and pushed around the dirty towels until he found his backpack. He fiddled with the zippers of the bag as he ran back to Bowie's side.

"Take down his pants! Flip him over!" Buckshot ordered, his words dangerously hot like acid.

Bowie turned around, somewhat offended that he was being given orders but also stunned and a little proud. He happily obliged. In what seemed like flipping a burger on a grill, he tossed the young man back onto his stomach. Bowie dug his hands into the back of his pants and pulled them down past his butt to his thighs.

Buckshot slinked in between Bowie and the young man, reached into his bag and pulled out a can of expanding foam, the very same one he had used to fix the draft in the office at church. He had known it would come in handy again sooner or later, but he had never expected to make use of it like this. Buckshot gave it a shake, attached the applicator hose to the end of the can and inserted it into the young man's backside. He pressed the nozzle and injected the foam with the unthinkable enthusiasm of a young boy with a video game controller, mashing buttons out of sheer gusto. Buckshot felt a muted version of what he was looking for—that rush. He pushed on the nozzle a second time, filling and filling until an overflow of foam began to shoot back out.

"Seal that back door right up! Nice and tight!" Buckshot said through a series of gut-tickling laughs. He wasn't finished. The more he watched the young man suffer, the stronger the rush. He hadn't known he could feel like this again. All without puppies, all without Theresa. Without missing a beat, Buckshot dipped his hand back into his backpack and pulled out a half-empty plastic water bottle. He frantically dumped out the water (or was it vodka?), undid his pants and pissed into the bottle.

Bowie flipped the young man back over and positioned his leg so his foot was flush with the ground. He reached the knife back and speared it through the top of the young man's foot, securing him to the ground. The young man screamed like he had never screamed before. Through the blood and through the pain, his voice echoed out into the blackness of the forgotten cemetery.

"You like dick so much, faggot, why don't you drink my piss!" Buckshot said as he began to shake piss out of the bottle and over the young man's body. "Drink it!" he repeated, stepping in closer toward the young man's mouth and pouring it out.

The young man reached up to shield his face, and the urine made a U-turn in midair and sprayed Buckshot in the face. It didn't make any sense and it defied all logic, but the young man knew he had made it happen. Somewhere between logic and fantasy, he understood the language of liquid and manipulated the direction in which it flew.

"You fuckin' dirty witch!" Buckshot screamed through his rotten teeth.

"Stop!" Bowie ordered. "Get the lighter fluid."

Buckshot spat the piss out of his mouth, wiped his lips with his mangy arms and then retrieved the lighter fluid and matches from the back of the truck.

The young man was shivering now, his swollen eye focused on the figure holding the lighter fluid and a pack of matches. Then he was wet. Everywhere. Then he was ablaze, hot and engulfed in bright, roaring flames. A few agonizing moments later, he was gone.

CHAPTER 19

The rain had stopped because Leo had willed it to. The next morning the ground was still sodden, but the sun was trying its best to dry out the land. The mail came unexpectedly early, and a small box with another large buzzing box arrived, both with Avery's name on them. It was a soft sound, but a significant one, and the buzz jolted her awake like a pot of coffee. Her bees and her protective clothing had finally arrived. Beekeeping wasn't just a hobby anymore; it had taken on an entirely new meaning with the knowledge that Nina had instilled in them. The bees were about balance, encouraging it, maintaining it, spreading it. Avery brought the box to the backyard, unpacked the white pullover jacket with detachable hat and veil and then got to work setting up the hive.

Nina had given the Primordials a little homework. They were to practice divination using the elements. Mitch was excited because he already loved divination, and attempting it with a medium besides tarot was fascinating. After a very long meeting with the coven about discipline and using their powers responsibly rather than to satiate their personal desires and wishes, Leo immediately wanted to do the exact opposite. His life had changed rapidly, and given what he was capable of, the last thing he wanted was to hear about how to resist the urge to use power to reward himself. What he didn't fully comprehend was that everyone else in the coven had had their world turned upside down, too. They were subject to the same rules, which were created not to punish them, but to protect them and others. Leo didn't care about that. He liked danger, not rules. He cared about himself because that was the only person he could rely on. Ironically, he didn't actually care for himself. How could he when he lived an unhappy life?

Leo sat down with Mitch and Avery, the other Primordials in the house, to exercise their skill with divination using an element of their choice. Avery and Leo chose fire, and Mitch decided to experiment with water divination. Before they began, Avery grabbed the book she had borrowed from the study, *The Secrets of Magic and Other Curious Practices*. She read a few segments from the chapter about divination and summarized the various modalities. She had developed the habit of reading from the book every morning before breakfast, but reading to others was a rewarding experience. For a moment, she felt like a teacher and wondered if that was how Nina felt. It was empowering for her to describe the types of pyromancy with such enthusiasm, and she wanted Mitch and Leo to be as impassioned as she was. Leo's faint smile hinted more toward mocking than excited. Mitch, however, was already geared up, ready to go, and Avery's zestful attitude was infectious. After Avery finished reading, Mitch was a mess of hand gestures and comments.

"I wanna try using plants! I'm so used to practicing this with tarot, but I kind of wanna be pushed outta the nest with it and learn some new things," Mitch said as he stood up. "Hold on, I've actually been working on something to help with this kind of thing. I wanna try it out." He darted off to his bedroom and returned to unveil a white-and-violet-colored crocheted hat. He placed it on his head and pulled on the edges to ensure a tight fit. Hanging from the front of the hat was a single strand of silver chain connected to a piece of raw blue kyanite.

"Okay, I'm ready!" Mitch said.

"You're so cute," Avery said. "I love the stone. It brings a lot of joy to your face."

"Thanks! It's kyanite, for boosting my psychic awareness and intuitive abilities!" Mitch said proudly.

Leo sat in silence, the familiar petty smile on his face once more.

Avery saw the sarcasm on Leo's face and decided that charging headfirst into the tests would be best. She placed an empty, shallow flowerpot in the fireplace. Inside it, she placed a few small pieces of wood. They sat in silence for a full minute before Avery reached over the flowerpot and set fire to the wood. It was getting easier, and happening more quickly.

She cleared some space between her and the fireplace and poured some salt into her hand. With a short and graceless toss of her wrist, Avery threw the salt into the fire. Her skin tightened as she held her breath and watched the salt fizzle and spark inside the flames. She felt an unexpected quickening of her heartbeat, followed by a tingling behind her eyes. Where everyone else saw just fire, she saw faces. Her jaw dropped open, as though she were about to say something, but she remained silent. The faces again, a mouth here, a forehead there, dancing between the flickers of the flames. In a combustion of yellow sparks, the faces were replaced with a clear image of her own self, surrounded by a raging ring of fire.

As quickly as it appeared, it vanished. When Mitch asked what she had seen, she wasn't sure how to describe it. Avery figured that like with everything else, better results would come with practice.

Mitch took his turn and tossed a fresh collection of leaves and stems into the fire but saw nothing. Disappointed, he turned to Avery for guidance. Of course it was possible that he wasn't adept at pyromancy or divination at all, although if that were the case, he would be enraged. He was the one with the most interest; he was the one who had practiced tarot before any of them had ever met.

Leo rounded out the experience with a slight variation in technique by interpreting the smoke rather than the flames. Ordinarily he would have said something like pyromancy was nothing but a bunch of bullshit, but he'd made the rain stop, and he'd started a fire, so maybe there was something to all of his mumbo jumbo. It would've been ridiculously sweet if it had turned out to be just a bunch of crap, because that was the kind of humiliation he lived for. Except that it wasn't nonsense. Instead he uncovered the secrets of the fire through the whispers that lived in the smoke, the gossip of the extinguished flames. He clapped his hands, and at the precise moment his hands met, the fire was snuffed out. The lit embers gave life to plumes of curling smoke that flowed like sheets in the wind. It wasn't what Leo saw that stunned him, but what he heard. As the smoke rose higher, a deep, rich voice emerged from between the columns of gray and white. Leo heard the smoke speak. He unhurriedly straightened his back and was about to speak when he heard the voice again, stronger this time, sounding more depraved and tempting.

"Maji..." the voice said. "Seek Maji...live beyond joy... renewed...transformed...and with command..." The voice was drowned out by a hollow cacophony of whispers and unintelligible murmurs. Suddenly, it ended with the sharpness of a door cutting off light from another room.

Leo was still listening attentively to the silence, waiting for another string of messages, but there were none. His stupefied face turned dour.

"Did you see anything? Or feel anything?" Avery asked.

"I didn't," Mitch cut in. "I tried, but there was a whole lot of just smoke."

Leo was slightly exasperated. He had been excited to hear something no one else could hear, only to have it fade away before he could make sense of it. Then he realized the magnitude of the experience. He alone had been able to hear the voice, the mysterious and profound voice that swayed in between the layers of smoke with a slightly ominous sense of intrigue.

"Nope!" Leo answered quickly. "Maybe next time." He stood up and headed to his room.

He had fooled Mitch, but he couldn't fool Avery. As she watched Leo stand and walk away, she couldn't help but remind herself that his answer didn't have the honest scent of oakmoss; his answer didn't smell like the truth. Although she couldn't exactly smell a lie, she certainly could detect when something wasn't exactly true. It was a gift that would come in handy, especially if people didn't know of it—or, better yet, forgot about it. Attacking Leo for not being fully honest seemed superfluous. Why would she waste her time trying to work with someone who wasn't as interested as Mitch was? Avery had a higher regard for Mitch, and choosing to practice with him over Leo was potentially more rewarding. Ultimately, she let the moment pass.

Leo puffed away on his vape and pulled out his phone to do a search for the word the voice had spoken. He wasn't the greatest speller in the world, but he could sound out most words, with above-average success. *Magee. Magie. Maggie (no, that's a name). Magey. Majee.* That's when the internet corrected him and provided the name of a hoodoo shop in New

Orleans—Maji. He repeated the name silently to himself, his lips quivering with the word over and over, *Maji, Maji, Maji.* He didn't know what it meant, and part of him didn't actually care to know. He took one last puff of his vape and savored the delectable satisfaction of solving a puzzle. He made his way out the front door and hopped on his bike to see what was waiting for him at Maji.

Leo spent his time on the way to the shop in total bewilderment. Just when he thought he had discovered the center of this new world, he found more layers, and layers beneath those. The small discoveries and visceral demonstrations of power had proved to provide more of a high than the acid he swallowed almost daily. He wouldn't go so far as to say it filled the holes in his heart, or describe it as being happy, but it was certainly entertaining.

His bike roared to a stop at the corner of Dauphine and Louisa. The corner was unexpectedly quiet but intolerably hot. Droplets of sweat began to form around Leo's hairline now that he was no longer riding through the wind. Between a blinding pink house and a crumbling beige building for rent was the hoodoo shop. A wooden sign with *MAJI* carved into it hung above the door. Leo was usually pretty quick to judge most things, and this was no different. The sign alone—rustic, wood that had a story to tell—made him think that perhaps what he had heard was wrong. Maybe he had made the whole thing up in his head. It seemed to make the most sense, though: a witch heard a voice that directed him to a hoodoo shop. It couldn't be just coincidence. A large window to the left of the door was filled with exotic statues, sequined bottles, and candles, all showcased against a sheer, white flax curtain just translucent enough to fill the shop with light but too opaque to allow passersby to see inside.

Leo turned the handle on the door, and a whip crack of creaks sounded as the door pivoted on dusty hinges. When he stepped inside, the smell of burning herbs and flowers turned his stomach, and the smoke assaulted all of his senses. A tiny saucer held the burning pile of incense next to a bowl of water with rose petals and orange peels, and above that was a painted statue with exaggerated body parts and wild eyes. The mixture of the incense and the humidity-bludgeoned foundation was a lot to take in all at once.

It was a small shop. Jars of various herbs stood on shelves along with bowls of chicken feet, and skeleton keys and coffin nails filled some of the many display dishes on the tables. Leo ducked his head to miss the sea of handmade dolls constructed of burlap, cloth and Spanish moss. They were beautiful and unsettling all at the same time—the same way he felt about his powers. A large man, dressed in all white, looked up from behind the counter. There was a nod followed by a gracious smile. The shopkeeper returned his attention to piling roots, shells and powders onto a square of bright red fabric. Leo looked around the shop, trying to figure out what it was that he needed to see. *Well, I'm here...Now what? All of this looks ridiculous. Maybe* maji *isn't what the voice said.*

Then the shopkeeper spoke. "Is there something I can help you find?" he asked with an accent so resonant that it pained Leo's ears to listen. Whether it was Creole or Cajun, Leo couldn't decide. Even he wasn't really sure what the difference was.

"I don't know yet," Leo said candidly.

"What brings ya in here?" the man said as he dropped a small chunk of copal resin into the pile.

"Never been in here before. I'm new to this whole voodoo…hoodoo…stuff," Leo announced, his fingers exploring a string of alligator claws. "Someone told me I should check this place out."

"Let me know if ya have any questions," the man said, wiping a few lonely beads of sweat from his forehead.

"What's that?" Leo said, pointing to the items laid out in front of the shopkeeper.

"It's a gris-gris bag," the man answered before taking a drag off a hand-rolled cigarette and blowing a puff of smoke over the pile. With expert quickness, he pulled the corners of the fabric up around it and tied it shut with string and a short, whispered prayer.

"I've heard of that before. What's it for?"

"Anything. Everything. What's inside is different, depending on what you need. Customized for a specific purpose or for a specific person." The man opened a small bottle of amber-colored oil and drizzled a few drops over the bag.

"What does that do?"

"Anything alive has to be fed. These have as much life as they do power. Never open it once it's sealed. That would be—"

"Like gutting a live pig," Leo said frankly.

Just then, a woman emerged from behind the red velvet curtain on the other side of the counter. Leo's awareness was heightened at the very sight of her: a young woman with rabbit-brown skin, eyes as lustrous as tiger's eye and uneven dreadlocks with tips dipped in ruby red. A few strands danced alongside her smooth face as she retrieved a backpack from the floor. Leo compared her sweetness to that of a vine-ripened blackberry, one too high to reach but one he really wanted to taste. For a moment he thought he would say something stupid, but he was tongue-tied. His expression of shock didn't go unnoticed. The woman turned to look at him, smirked and then began to whisper to the shopkeeper.

Leo shuffled away from the counter and pretended to browse the handmade soaps. Then, without even trying, everything was amplified. He heard her whisper as if her voice were coming from a blaring speaker. The word *temazcal* rang out loud and clear. Then the gift dissolved. Leo found himself unable to move, uncertain what to think and do next. The woman continued the conversation at a delicate volume. There were smiles, giggles and an exchange of looks between her and the shopkeeper. A short minute later she made her way toward the door. As she stepped out of the shop, she turned to look at Leo. The suggestion of a smile was upon her face, as if she were only trying to be polite but also felt the urge to get a second glance. When she rounded the corner out of view, Leo turned back to the shopkeeper.

"What's a temazcal?" Leo asked. *Maybe that's why I was supposed to come here. Could be the girl. But probably not.*

"Where'd you hear about that?" the man asked, narrowing his eyes.

"It's a small shop. I didn't mean to eavesdrop or anything—like I was sayin', I'm still really new to all of this voodoo stuff. Just curious."

"It's not voodoo."

"Witchcraft or what?" Leo pushed.

"Aztec for 'house of heat.' It's a ceremony led by shamans."

"What kind of ceremony? Like a wedding or something?"

A darling laugh. "A cleansing ritual. For your spirit."

Leo's interest was piqued. "I'm down for something new. Where can I do it?"

Another chuckle. "Naw. I don't think you're ready for it."

"Is that what that girl who was just here is going to do? She looked a lot more delicate than I am!"

"At first glance, maybe. Besides, it's private, by invitation only."

"Well, can I get an invitation? I'm really interested in cleansing my spirit," Leo said unconvincingly.

"Try some Florida water—it's cheaper." The man picked a bottle off the shelf and set it in front of Leo.

"I'll give that a shot too, but how much is it? The ceremony." Leo pulled out a twenty-dollar bill to pay for the Florida water.

The man took the money, finished the transaction and handed Leo the change.

"I'm not the happiest person, you know," Leo said. "I think that's why I ended up in here in the first place. I feel like I've tried everything I can, but some things just can't be fixed, I guess." His voice was sullen.

There was truth to what Leo said, more than he actually intended to convey. What was meant to be just a desperate attempt to get his way was actually a glimpse into his true self, beyond the sarcasm and cynicism. A sharp stab of despair coursed through his body. Again, another reminder that he couldn't feel happiness. Even though he was all too familiar with it at this point in his life, it didn't make the reality of it any easier. He had only gotten more accustomed to it.

As Leo tucked the bottle of Florida water into his pocket, the man reached out to touch his shoulder.

"Here," the man said as he scribbled something on a scrap of paper. When he finished writing, he folded the paper twice, grabbed the gris-gris bag and handed both to Leo.

"What's this?" Leo said, both shocked and pleased with himself.

"A lagniappe for my first customer of the day."

Leo had no idea what a lagniappe was, but whatever it was, he was glad he had gotten it. He unfolded his fingers, and next to the gris-gris bag was the name, address and phone number of the shaman for the temazcal. He was breathless as excitement buzzed through his veins.

It was late afternoon when Leo returned to the house. A bee swooped in front of the door as he entered. *I guess Avery got her bees all set up.* A second bee flitted by and danced in circles before buzzing off into the distance. The rush of cool air was a welcome treat after the bike ride through the steamy streets. He wasn't going to call the number he'd been given. Instead, he planned to just go right over and show up at the address. It seemed more…Leo.

Over dinner, Nina told the coven that an old friend of hers, Merlot, would be joining them for dinner the next weekend, along with her coven. Merlot was an old acquaintance, one who had become Proctor of another coven in Houston. They had been introduced by the Advisory as support for each other while they learned about witchcraft. They hadn't spoken in many years because life had gotten in the way, but now that their lives were starting to take shape, Nina wanted to rekindle the friendship. What better way to do that than opening your home and sharing a meal?

By midweek, the coven had gotten into the habit of setting aside time to study powers and abilities that were shared between all witches. Even Leo, who had been taking less and less acid as the days went by, was on board. They practiced spellwork, and discussed potion making and the power of dedicated practice. Mitch and Leo continued their physical banter—a towel whip in the bathroom, a slap on the butt as they walked by each other. It was a friendship that neither of them had expected or truly understood, since they didn't have much in common. Over time, though, that's what they enjoyed about their dynamic. It was a balance of light and dark, and they existed somewhere in between.

When Mitch set aside his bizarre sexual attraction to Leo, a new world opened up before him. Leo took him camping, something Mitch had never done but had always wanted to do, and drove him to New Orleans East to see the drag races, something Mitch thought involved drag queens. He was slightly disappointed when he realized the races were beefed-up cars racing down a long stretch of road in the middle of nowhere. There were no drag queens, and without being presumptuous, he felt confident in saying he was the only gay person for miles.

Leo always had to take an activity and push it over the edge. Driving across the bridge to the drag races wasn't enough; he had to do it at 90 miles an hour. Going camping wasn't sufficient without tripping and venturing into the deep woods with only a flashlight and a machete. Everything needed to involve a significant amount of danger to be satisfying. Mitch put aside their differences and aimed to illuminate Leo's melancholia by being present. After finishing a bottle of Russell's Reserve bourbon one evening as the moon entered Pisces, Leo admitted to Mitch for the first time how much he appreciated his friendship. Later, Mitch didn't remember much about that evening, but he remembered Leo curled up on his bed, holding his hand and trying not to throw up. The liquor flushed all the emotions out of the depths of Leo's mind, and it all came rushing out in a hurricane-like flood.

"You're a good friend. You're a really good friend. I mean it. You're a G," Leo slurred as he tried to keep his focus. "I know you get sad sometimes. I feel that, and it makes me sad. I wanna be able to talk as friends, but you don't talk to me."

Mitch, who also had trouble seeing through the whiskey, cupped Leo's hand with his other hand. "I'm just…well, it's like…I don't know."

"And I know you want to fuck me. *I know* you wanna fuck me. I know we mess around a lot and it's all in good fun and whatever. I know you're always pushin' the boundaries, seein' how far it'll go. Slappin' my ass, lickin' my cheek. I see the way you look at me, I'm not stupid. I wish my ex-girlfriend had looked at me like that." Leo stared deep into Mitch's eyes. "But it's cool. You know? You're my homie. You're a G. If anyone ever tries to fuck with you, I got your back, you know? I mean that. If I ever get married, dawg…you'll be there."

Mitch didn't even know what a G was and had to Google it later, but he knew Leo cared about him. *I do care about you,* he thought, *and I really do want the best for you too. I don't think I've ever had a friend like you before. Not someone straight, but just, I guess, someone like* you. *But I mean, I still want to go down on you like a dam in Katrina. Get it? Because you're from New Orleans.* Mitch finally succumbed to his intoxication and passed out.

CHAPTER 20

Bowie and Buckshot surprised the Bonners early in the morning. Edie and Joshua had been wrapped in prayer when the door to the church opened. Edie recognized the familiar sound of jangling keys and presumed it to be Ben—or Buckshot, as he preferred to be called now. As the footsteps approached, Edie was rosy with anticipation. She heard the second-most-familiar sound that usually accompanied the jangling keys—that Oklahoma twang. Edie and Joshua rose from their knees and hurried toward the door to meet them in the hallway. Joshua swung open the door to see their team glowing with pride.

"We did it, y'all!" Buckshot squealed joyously.

Although the Bonners were excited to hear the news, the hallway wasn't the most ideal place to discuss how the events had unfolded. In a firm voice, Joshua asked them into the office. They weren't quite the same eager trainees who had left with the lunastaterum but were now accomplished soldiers. Even Bowie, who never cracked a smile, had an unusual cheeriness to his face. Once the office door was closed, Edie first collected the lunastaterum for inspection. They had returned it completely untarnished, and once she determined there was no need to panic, she politely asked them to sit. Buckshot removed his hat, ran his palms over his wispy, tousled hair and sat down to tell them every single detail.

"So, it's done?" Joshua asked, raising a single eyebrow.

"It's done," Bowie replied.

Buckshot let out a tart laugh. "It's well done, if you know what I'm sayin'! Here I thought I couldn't cook. Turns out I can burn more than my roux!" Another torrent of hissy laughter through his rotten teeth. "I could flambé a bananas Foster better than anyone at Brennan's now!"

"Easy. This isn't a joke, this is serious business. This isn't just another dead"—Edie lowered her voice to an off-the-record level—"nigger."

Buckshot paused for a moment, cleared his throat and then looked at Bowie, who had been staring right back at him in disapproval.

"You right. Sorry, ma'am!"

"Now…walk us through everything that y'all did. I really hope and pray to God that y'all were discreet about this."

Bowie leaned forward. "I made sure of it. It was very clean. When they find him, no one will ever know a thing."

"I don't know why, but I believe you when you say that. Call it my intuition. So, break it down for me. What all happened up there in Mobile?"

Bowie glanced over at Buckshot and then smiled at the Bonners. "We can show you. We filmed it."

There was complete silence in the room while Buckshot pulled out his phone and opened up the video file. He handed the phone over to Edie, his wiry arm stretched out over the desk like a line of fishing wire. Edie clicked Play, and the Bonners watched as Bowie and Buckshot listened. Joshua's expression instinctively cringed at the brutality, but he couldn't look away. Edie, however, wore a face that was passive—apathetic, even—and above all, hard to judge. The video ended with a still of Buckshot's face right before it was shut off. Without making eye contact, Edie returned the phone to Buckshot by sliding it across the desk. After an uncomfortable minute of silence, Edie looked over at her husband. A flash of horror struck her face, and tears started to pool under her eyes. She quickly dabbed the tears with the edge of her knuckle, sniffed back emotion and fixated her attention on Buckshot and Bowie. She looked stunned and moved with grief.

"I'm sorry," Edie said. "I don't know what to say. I am…in complete shock." She pulled back a final tear with a swipe of her hand, her eyes dry but weepy. "That was just the most beautiful thing. I can hardly stand it."

The uncertainty in the room vanished.

"It just proves that when you have faith in something, and truly believe and trust in God, he will deliver what is right," Edie said. "He will answer your prayers. When he brought y'all to me, he delivered a miracle. One that will change this world. I had my doubts, I admit—Lord, forgive me, but I had my doubts. But both of you came through for us. You came out victorious in the most glorious way. This is only the beginning. The book of Genesis says, 'Let us make humankind in our image' and that is exactly what we are going to do. And we will succeed. This is proof of that."

Each of Edie's doubts and hang-ups surrounding whether what she had set out to do was right were at that very instant cleared away. She knew her path as a wife, as a leader, as a messenger of God. She licked her lips with confidence as she ran through the endless possibilities to come.

"Can I just add that, from this point on, we need y'all to be a little cleaner about this," Joshua said. "I know the goal is to eradicate the devil and his partners on this earth, but torturing leaves room for error. We can't have that." He was on board with his wife, but he didn't believe it was necessary to be cruel just for the sake of being cruel. Something about the video had rubbed him the wrong way, something that proved to be unshakable.

Edie looked over at Joshua, partially disgusted by what he had said. "Honey! Have you been drinkin' or somethin'? Why would you say something like that?"

"I'm just saying that isn't it enough that we exterminate them?"

"No. Honey, no. They aren't fit to be on this earth among those who want to be in God's light. Every minute, every second they are here, we risk losing our pure children to their clutches. They deserve it. That boy, that…homosexual nigger witch…got exactly what he deserved. They're bugs. You should think of them as such. That's exactly how they start to sway people, with that kind of liberal, merciful thinking. We can't show any mercy. Losers and weaklings show mercy. We are not weak."

Edie turned to Buckshot and Bowie, her energy overwrought, her twinkling eyes demented and ferocious. "Y'all did the right thing. Remember this moment, and keep doing what you're doing. You two will single-handedly help deliver God's will and help change this community, this country, this world to what it was always intended to be…pure and free from sin. You are the messengers of God's whole truth, and you hold the power of his true light in your hearts. Praise his light and truth!"

Joshua leaned back in his chair and allowed Edie to take the reins. He turned toward something that might have been the feeling of guilt.

Edie clapped her hands, noticing that it was perhaps time to get her nails touched up. Now would be the time to do it. It was time to celebrate and treat herself. "From now on, I want you to give me a call with the details about what you're doing with the body before and after you do it. I need to be on top of all this for all our sakes. We can't have any of this coming back to us. Bowie…I'm trusting you with this."

"I can do this," Bowie reassured her.

"Good. Great! It's important because Joshua and I are fixin' to expand our reach and open up another, small campus for the Whole Truth and True Light. We're commencing a fund-raiser during this Sunday's service to help cover the costs. It's gonna be a small church, but big dreams come in small packages. If we are truly going to succeed, we're gonna need to continue to spread the word as far as we can, while remaining under the radar. The rest of the world won't understand what we're trying to do right away, so we need to keep that to ourselves for the time being. Well, now would be a good time for a bathroom break if y'all need to go. We're gonna move right on into your next task."

SMOKE

Ollie bit into an apple and positioned himself in the breakfast nook to bask in the light of the waxing moon. He arched his neck for a glimpse of the patio covered with his jungle of plants. It was unseasonably cool that evening, which made the air smell a little less wrathful. He usually didn't mind the heat. The hot air carried the fragrance of jasmine a little farther than cooler days. He scrolled through various apps on his phone, switching from one to the next, finding them all equally unsatisfying. With his head in his phone, he strolled through the house, passing other members of the coven along the way to the great room. Everyone was on their phone, all possessed and entranced by the glowing drug in their hands. None of them looked particularly happy or satisfied, and given the abilities they were developing, he thought at least one of them would be practicing.

"I'm bored," Ollie said after he tucked his phone into his pocket.

The coven looked up from their devices only to immediately drop their eyes back to their screens.

"What do you wanna do about it? Wanna go for a ride? Go play pool?" Leo suggested half-heartedly.

"Not really."

Nina stood up, locked her phone and headed toward her room. "I'm going to take a bath. There are a ton of books here. You guys are more than capable of exercising your abilities on your own. Self-teach something new." It seemed that everyone had the desire to learn new things but didn't actually want to have to do it. Not every single ability was as simple as snapping their fingers. They still needed to learn, they still needed to study. Things were always at their fingertips, quite literally, but when it came time to do something extra, even something exciting, it wasn't easy to motivate themselves.

Ollie sat on the couch and tried to cheerlead his way toward a group activity. They talked about Avery's grimoire, Mitch's inability to focus well, and Ollie's garden. They had all worked so hard on those single things that they didn't have much energy for anything else.

"Let's go get spirit animals," Leo suggested.

"It's not something you can just go out and buy," Bisa informed him.

"Well, no shit. Let's get up and do something. Put down our fuckin' phones, stop liking photos from people we haven't talked to in years, and actually do something. Now that he said it…yeah, I'm fuckin' bored too."

With a little more motivation and manipulation, Leo managed to persuade every single member of the coven to apply what they'd learned so far, together—in the woods. The weather was cool, the sky was clear, it was perfect. They piled into the car with Leo behind the wheel, much to Mitch's disapproval. He feared they might not make it to the woods if Leo was allowed to drive. Leo always seemed to get his way. It made sense for him to drive, though, because as the only local in the coven, he knew the perfect place to go where they wouldn't be disturbed. They brought everything with them: books for reference, flashlights, firewood, newspaper and bug spray. Even witches needed something industrial to keep the insects at bay in Louisiana.

Leo drove south to Luling and through the neighborhoods until he found a tiny unnamed road, a place where he had been before, back in his heavy druggie days. They parked the car on the side road and walked into a dark forest.

"Where are we, anyway?" Avery asked.

"The woods, stupid," Leo said with wide eyes.

Mitch looked at the location on his phone. "Somewhere near Garland Canal, I guess."

"Should just be right up there a bit, not far," Leo said. "Turn your flashlights on."

Within a few short minutes, the dense forest opened to a rectangular clearing, where a tall and lonesome oak tree stood near the middle.

"Right up there! See, buttercup? I told you I knew where I was going," Leo said sweetly to Avery.

Being an Eagle Scout had taught Leo a few things, but the two that remained clearest to this day were how to properly build a fire and that gays were bad. The latter was mostly because fellow scouts, while on retreats, would informally notify all members of the cabin that if anyone was gay, they wouldn't be allowed to shower and would get their ass beat. Leo never beat anyone's ass, nor did he really have an opinion about gays, but he sure knew how to finesse a fire. There was a certain amount of irony in the fact that he often referred to gays as flamers. Further, Mitch helped him build the bonfire near the oak tree. Leo, Mitch and Avery made a circle around the pile of wood and held hands. As soon as their intentions equalized with one another's, the bonfire flared to life.

"That shit never stops being cool as fuck," Leo said in amazement.

Avery was less concerned with the fire than with the vulnerability of being in the woods. "Is it safe to be out here? Isn't this like, the bayou, where alligators and snakes and stuff are?"

"I think we're okay," Ollie said softly.

"You don't know that! There are probably tons of snakes and wild animals out there staring at us!" Avery said as if she sensed something strange in the air.

"Well, probably. But you're a Primordial! Own it! We should be able to communicate with 'em! Just…tell them not to eat you. Besides, that's what we're here for, right? To try and get our own spirit animal!"

"Well, yes. I am willing to bet money that my spirit animal isn't an alligator," Avery said in a whisper, as if one would hear her.

They cleared some space, sat down on the rough ground and discussed the whole purpose of trying to secure a spirit animal in the first place. Avery consulted her book, and after realizing that they were in fact trying to identify a *totem* animal, they understood more clearly that they were hoping to gain a guide, a mentor, one that encouraged self-development. If the bond to their totem was strong, they might be able to transform themselves into their totem, but that was far more advanced than any of them were capable of—for now.

The sounds of the woods intensified as Mitch drew a circle with a stick. Each of them sat at points along the circumference and closed their eyes to sit in silent meditation. Their bodies warmed in part from the flickering fire but also from their heightened frequencies as they aligned themselves with the higher consciousness. The breeze stopped.

Leo grew impatient. "Does anyone…get anything?" he asked with one eye open.

"I think so?" Avery breathed.

Suddenly there was a sound from the forest, beyond the reach of the bouncing light from the fire.

"I think we're going about this wrong," Avery said.

Leo opened his eyes, looked at Avery, then at the black woods, then back to Avery. "I think maybe we just need to focus more," he countered. "Come on—head in the game." He snapped his fingers at her.

Bisa held out her hands like a referee. "Stop! Stop! Just…stop talking." Her eyes were still closed. "See…feel…listen. Remember what we just read in the book. We need to make a request. Everyone just repeat what I'm saying. 'In shadow and in light, I ask for us to unite. As one soul, one mind and one heart, in service together, never to be apart.'"

"There is no way you just came up with that," Mitch mumbled under his breath.

Leo laughed. "So you're Dr. Seuss now too?"

"Shh!" Bisa snapped. "Like you said, if we want to get better and be stronger witches, we have to…do the work."

Bisa began the chant and let the others trickle in organically until they were in perfect unison. Once it felt right—a feeling she couldn't explain, but understood—she slowly decreased the volume at which she chanted. Ever so slowly, her words became a whisper and then audible only in her mind. The others followed suit until they all sat in silence. There was a rustling in the near distance.

"I think…I think that worked," Avery said quietly. A smile grew on her face, and a sense of accomplishment washed over her.

They waited. Even Leo was a pillar of patience.

"Maybe it takes some time?" Ollie suggested.

Bisa shook her head. "Well, magic is immediate…but that doesn't mean they will just…show up."

Before there was a moment to react or even think, a wild boar cut through the clearing, ran past Avery and continued alongside the fire. Avery screamed in horror: what she had feared most was actually happening. Everyone jumped in terror. A choir of shrieks and screams echoed into the sky as they all tried to catch their breath. Like a colony of busy ants, everyone rose to their feet and scurried away from the boar, which was running toward the oak tree. Its size shocked everyone. It was less like a large pig and more like a small adult rhino. Despite knowing they were extinct, Avery was certain that it was a triceratops.

As the beast charged toward the tree, it lunged past Leo. He tripped over his feet and raised his hands for balance. The boar squealed while its feet scrambled inches above the ground, and then smashed into the tree with inexplicable momentum. The coven grouped together for safety and watched the animal leap back to its feet and dash off into the trees. It was gone. They stood, spooked and panting and very confused.

"I *told* you there were crazy wild animals out here! I knew it!" Avery shouted.

"Well, what the hell! Mitch is the one who is supposedly all gifted with animal mind reading or whatever!" Leo said.

"I don't know how to talk to a charging boar like that! I didn't even know it was there!" Mitch screamed back.

"Can we talk about what just happened?" Bisa suggested sternly.

"Why don't we talk about how this was Leo's idea in the first place," Mitch chided. "Out here, in the woods, with ravenous animals, probably rife with diseases, and one of them almost killed us!"

"Oh God! Oh God!" Leo said as he rolled his eyes. "So much drama."

"Well, do you know how to talk to animals? Do you make weird grunts and snorts and hope they understand? Or what?" Mitch questioned, furious.

Leo held one palm out toward Mitch and lifted the vape to his lips with the other. "I can't explain your alleged gift to you, dude."

"Can you explain how to get us back to the car then?" Mitch said, completely serious.

Bisa looked at everyone and leaned forward to gain the spotlight. "That boar just ran into the tree like something knocked it off course. Did anyone else see that? I'm not making this up. It literally just flew into the tree!"

"It jumped! It was hella spooked and it ran into the tree!" Leo snubbed.

"I know what I saw, and that boar didn't just run into the tree, *something* forced it," Bisa repeated.

Leo kicked out the fire and snuffed the rest with a swoosh of his hand. He started making his way back to the car in the dark and assumed everyone would follow. Everyone rushed to get their phones and turned on the flashlight so they could trail behind. Avery hobbled in fear at the tail end of the group.

"I'm not kidding," she said. "I hear hissing. I think I hear snakes. We have to hurry. Go, go!" She shoved Ollie farther ahead and quickened her step. "Ollie…I think they're following me. I still hear hissing. Ollie, what sounds do angry snakes make?"

CHAPTER 22

Mitch slept horribly but still woke up early, thinking he would be greeted by his spirit totem, or at least find out that someone had acquired one. Over a lazy breakfast and a couple of pots of coffee the general theme of the morning was one without totem animals. It was a small disappointment, one that made Mitch in particular feel like he was being denied something he deserved, as if the universe was simply withholding yet another gift, like that of divination. There was a lot of speculation over breakfast about what animal would be linked to whom and why, if the conjuring spell had worked at all. Oh, how he hoped it had. How could it not?

"I bet it's because you want it so bad—that's why one hasn't showed up for you yet," Leo suggested arrogantly.

There was a ring of truth to that statement. Mitch wanted lots of things. He wanted the gift of psychic sight that he obsessively tried to summon through tarot cards. He wanted Leo, even though he would never admit that out loud. What sort of gay would he be if he never got to seduce a straight guy, especially one who was absolutely positive he had no sexual feelings toward the same sex? He always wanted things he couldn't have, and not once did he ever question what drove the wanting. Some things he could explain, like Leo's pancakes, or red beans and rice, for that matter. He would have to, for the time being, accept the consolation prize of Leo cooking dinner.

Nina had taken a liking to rice-based dishes ever since she'd tasted Leo's red beans and rice, so when it came time to prepare dinner for her guests, she opted for another one-pot rice dish—jambalaya. She wanted it to be a group effort, like how families handle Thanksgiving prep over a few days. Nina couldn't tell if she wanted to give the impression that she had the coven under control and they were working together flawlessly, or if that was actually the case. After all, she was very new to being a Proctor. Nina and Leo tackled the Creole jambalaya* with andouille sausage and shrimp. Avery and Mitch worked on the cornbread*, salty and sweet. Bisa and Ollie paired up to make an okra salad*, setting some okra aside to add to a cleansing okra bath* Bisa wanted to take later on.

There were only so many hours in the day, and holding the morning meeting, prepping dinner and preparing the house for guests took away valuable time Nina could have used to rehearse how she was going to react to seeing Merlot for the first time in years. At one time, they had been very close—on the verge of being sisters, really—until the position for the Advisory opened up. It wasn't a secret: Merlot loved discovering she was a witch. The more she learned, the more it corrupted her very being. Her charms and spells no longer aimed for the good of all, but were used for personal gain in the most despicable ways. She wanted to achieve greatness at whatever cost. As Merlot began to dabble in the shadows more over time, her relationship with Nina suffered. Nina believed Merlot meant well, which was admirable. But at what cost? She and Merlot spent many evenings discussing how Merlot would change the way magic was used and regulated. Merlot believed magic was a gift, but one that came with rules, guidelines and laws that limited one's potential.

The stronger her powers became, the more she wanted to push their limits. Ambition and ingenuity grew along with her powers as she set her sights on taking down the Advisory by dismantling it from the inside out. The split between Nina and Merlot happened the morning the current members of the Advisory were scheduled to elect their fourth member. Merlot had done all the groundwork to ensure she would be selected. She exhibited extreme ambition and a love for witches, and already had a tremendous presence in the magic community. What the Advisory didn't see were her true colors, and they were as dark as the wine she was named after.

Later that afternoon, Nina requested an emergency meeting with the members of the Advisory. She shook their hands and thanked each of them individually. For a moment, Nina thought she was too late when the members said they had already made their decision and had informed Merlot the night before. Without hesitation, Nina divulged every single detail that Merlot had told her in confidence, all of which made no difference to the Advisory and was dismissed as pure hearsay. Without hard evidence, her accusations were nothing but rumors, although Nina knew they were true.

Nina dawdled for a brief moment and considered the repercussions of what she was about to do. She was haggard, with dark circles under her eyes, but not without reason. Her hands had been dipped in a potion that she had spent half the night preparing, one that needed to be continuously stirred over four hours. She applied it a few moments before she entered the room only as a last resort. The potion remained active for only five minutes, maybe six, but there was no way to be certain.

She looked at her watch. She was four minutes in. There she was, staring her final recourse straight in the face with a single word dripping from her tongue. There was no more time. She had to trust her instincts. Her lips parted, and she uttered,

"*Cupio.*" Nina's skin had a distressing tautness to it as she hung in suspense. The members of the Advisory reminded her one more time that their choice had been made. *Had the spell worked? Did they hear me say the word?* Nina eyes were spinning with abject horror as she waited for a reaction. There was only one final way to tell, and that was to ask them to appoint her in Merlot's place. They would either send her away or arrange for her to assume the position.

"I ask…I want…" Nina lifted her chin and spoke brightly. "Choose me as the fourth member of the Advisory."

The members of the Advisory all smiled gamely in unison as the watch on Nina's wrist struck the five-minute mark. The vote was unanimous. Nina had been selected as the member of the Advisory and stolen the position like a shrewd businesswoman. She never told Merlot the truth, but she didn't have to. Right after Nina met with the Advisory, they apologetically rescinded their offer to Merlot.

The two hadn't spoken for years. Nina always appreciated good manners, and it would be the height of adulthood if she were the first to try to mend their relationship. They were meant to be allies, not enemies cut from the same cloth.

The table's centerpiece was a bouquet of magnolia blossoms from the tree in the backyard. Magnolias, one of the oldest trees and traditionally symbolizing gentleness and nobility, were the perfect and most accessible option to encourage unity. If a tree could survive the test of time and produce such beauty, surely there was hope for Nina and Merlot.

Merlot pulled up to the house as the corn bread was being pulled out of the oven. When the doorbell rang, Nina felt a surge of guilt and uncertainty. She couldn't lose her cool now. Dinner was ready. She opened the door and held her breath. There she was, Merlot Cascadia, standing dignified and in control with a cryptic smile that suggested there was a story behind her eggplant-colored glasses. She had the very same face, Nina thought, one that was both enigmatic and erratic. A seductive exoticism to her clothing made her seem not at all suited to lead a coven of inexperienced witches. Perhaps that was Nina's old blueprint, one that she was projecting onto this person whom she used to know. Maybe Merlot wasn't who she used to be. Nina most certainly had grown since they had last spoken, so it would be foolish and arrogant to assume that Merlot hadn't.

"I thought Houston was hot," Merlot said in an accent Nina had nearly forgotten about, with piercing vowels and incorrectly emphasized syllables.

"I learned real quick that it's not the heat that gets you, it's the humidity!" Nina said, her mind a little more at ease. "Come in, please, come in!" Nina had been so preoccupied with meeting Merlot that she hadn't even noticed the two witches behind her. At Merlot's right shoulder was a man—stocky, clean-shaven and well dressed instead of dressed for the weather. On Merlot's left stood a woman younger than her eyes suggested, with a body shape that hinted at recent self-reinvention and an energy so vivid, it was as if she had consumed the sun. They both smelled like the forest floor in a rainstorm. "I'm so sorry—I'm Nina. Please come in!"

"I've never been to Louisiana, but I have to say, this house isn't exactly what I was expecting," Merlot declared.

"I didn't know what to expect myself," Nina replied.

"Nix always talked about this property, but he made it sound like a shack in the swamp."

Nina rolled her eyes. "He does have a rather informal way of describing property value even as Keeper of Books and Assets, huh?"

"Yeah, it's not quite as hillbilly as I thought," the woman to Merlot's left proclaimed tactlessly.

Merlot smiled. "This is Blake. She has no filter. I love that about her." She turned to her right. "And this is Andy. He only likes cheese pizza." She sniffed the air. "Is that corn bread I smell?" she said delicately.

"The very same recipe you and I made! Remember that potluck for the Advis—" Nina cut herself off in midsentence, fearing the Advisory would be a sore subject.

"I do remember," Merlot said as she nodded. "Dry! Crumbled like a sad sandcastle."

Nina arched her neck back at Merlot's bluntness. "Well, thankfully, Avery and Mitch made it!"

Nina brought the witches into the kitchen, where they met the rest of the coven. She introduced everyone by name and then said why she was proud of them. The dynamic between the two covens was more split than oil and vinegar. There was something off about the group from Houston, something that set Avery's skin on edge. Avery wasn't wary of strangers; in fact, she had always been quite the opposite. She took a whiff of each of the three as she walked by them and smelled things that she didn't expect: anger, pride and even some she couldn't articulate but that gave her goose bumps.

Avery clung to Ollie and spoke softly into his ear. "I don't think they like us."

"What makes you think that?" Ollie asked, his eyes fixed on the group of Houston witches.

"I can smell it. I know Leo thinks I make that up, but I don't. It's true. They don't like us, and I don't know why. Can't you smell that? I mean, I know you're different—a Transcendent and everything—but it's just so strong, I don't see how you couldn't smell it."

Ollie inhaled through his nose and exhaled through his mouth. "Yeah, I don't smell anything other than corn bread and sausage." What he didn't smell, he felt. If he'd been completely honest with Avery, he would've told her that he heard some kind of message from the divine telling him something was awry with that coven. Yet he said nothing. "But honestly, Avery, they don't live here. It doesn't matter that they're witches too. They're here for one night, and if they don't like me or my salad, I don't care." Nina's advice ran through his head on a loop: *trust your vibes, trust your vibes, trust your vibes.*

Dinner proved to be just the unsettling experience that Ollie felt and Avery smelled. Blake sat in the seat where Mitch had put his water glass to hold his place, and Andy took the tray of corn bread and failed to pass it along. They were rude, without manners, and their conversation was as dry as the corn bread. *What kind of life are they living over there if this is any testament to how that coven is run?* Nina wondered.

Bisa swallowed a gulp of water and cleared her throat. "So, Merlot, I can't place your accent. Where are you from?"

Merlot leaned back in her chair, crossed her legs and poked at the jambalaya with her fork as if trying to stab it to death instead of eat it. "I'm from everywhere. I've lived in New York and California and now Houston, but I was born in Almería,

Spain. The climate in Houston reminds me very much of home. Humid. I don't know if I'd like a dry climate."

Blake dropped her piece of corn bread onto her plate. "Dry like this corn bread," she said with a smile.

"Don't be rude," Merlot said as she picked a cigarette out of her pocket. "They put a lot of time and effort into this meal." Merlot made no effort to conceal her sarcasm. She put the cigarette to her lips, waved her hand over the tip and watched it catch fire.

Nina calmly placed her forkful of food down on her plate and held out her hand. "Oh, I'd really prefer it if you didn't smoke at the table—or inside, actually," she said, her patience beginning to wear thin.

Merlot took a long drag from the cigarette, blew the smoke into the center of the table, and, after letting it disperse throughout the room, put out her cigarette on the side of her plate.

Leo took a drag from his vape. "I like her."

"Have you ever been to Spain, Bisa?" Merlot asked.

"No, sadly, I haven't ever had the pleasure. I've heard the people are…very kind. I can't remember where I heard that. Maybe I'm wrong, I don't know." For a moment, the only sound was that of clinking silverware against porcelain. "Do you miss it?"

"A city is a city. Once you've been to enough of them, they all start to feel the same. I do miss the food though—nothing can compare. Especially the paella. My grandmother used to make the best seafood paella. It's what jambalaya wants to be." Merlot wet her lips. "I hate to say it," she said in Spanish, "but it's really just a bland, trashy substitute."

Nina constricted her eyes. "Can you not do that, please? You're the only one here who speaks Spanish."

"Sorry, sometimes it just slips out." Merlot held Nina's gaze, aware of how concerned Nina was with her behavior. "I'm not the only one. Andy here speaks Spanish, don't you?"

Andy nodded in agreement. "Sí."

Ollie cleared his throat. "I mean, I do too. I'm part Argentine."

Oops. I should have remembered that, Nina thought as her eyes slipped over to look at Ollie.

Merlot smiled, then unexpectedly set loose an excited gasp. "How's the Advisory? Is it everything you dreamed of?"

"It's been fine," Nina replied quickly.

"Have you told them about how you got the position?" Merlot inquired, her eyes so deep, they looked like they could drown someone.

"Yes. I was appointed by the Advisory. You know that."

Merlot ran her finger along the edge of her mouth, outlining her bottom lip. "Why?"

"I guess they felt I was the best for the job. Why don't you ask them?"

"Maybe they don't know why," Merlot suggested darkly.

"What does that mean?"

"You know what it means," Merlot said in Spanish.

Avery dashed into the conversation, completely unwelcomed. "So, what kinds of spells have you guys done? Nina said that you guys have been practicing longer than we have."

"Transmogrification," Blake announced freely.

"What's that?" Avery questioned.

"Changing shape, transforming things, kicked up a notch with some techniques used in things like bloodletting."

"You drain other people's blood?" Avery asked, horrified.

"Usually our own. But sometimes, yeah," Blake said, her voice full of shadows.

Bisa chimed in. "Sacrifice?"

"No—well, not yet," Blake said as she shrugged.

Merlot laughed hoarsely at the mild hysteria spreading in the room. "You really need to start teaching them that *they* are the ones in control, not everyone else."

"I'm setting them up to succeed, not self-destruct, Merlot," Nina said, her gaze fixed on Merlot's dicey eyes.

"I'm glad I never had the goal or the grades to make it into somewhere like Yale," Merlot said. "Even with your fancy education, you don't know anything. You've spent your entire life trying to create success. You've done a lot, except be successful. You're naïve, scared and as fragile as your belief that you're a good leader. You have nothing to teach. You may have a degree, but you have much more to learn. The universe will keep giving you lessons until you learn it, my dear." She stood from the table.

"My God, you're still the same energy," Nina bellowed gently. "Maybe you should go!" Then she added, "Why did you even come here?"

Merlot pressed her wine-red fingernails into the table as she leaned in toward Nina. "Why did you invite me?"

"A lot of time has gone by, things in the world are changing, and it's crucial, especially now, that we work together. I wanted to put everything behind us, be adults. I wanted to make fucking corn bread you'd like."

Merlot glared at Nina and her coven. The corners of her mouth lifted as she smiled ever so slightly. "Our goals have always been different. If you think we're going to wash away the past over a shitty meal, you're insane. But you're right, the world is changing. That's *exactly* why I came here. Fuck your corn bread." She waved toward Blake and Andy, calling them like dogs as she walked away from the table. Before she reached the doorway, she turned her head back toward the table. "The jambalaya was okay."

Leo filled his mouth with food. "You know what? I changed my mind. I don't like her flip attitude. She was rude as fuck. Just okay? Man, fuck her. My jambalaya was the shit."

Bisa turned toward Nina, concerned and bewildered. "What does she mean, *that's why I came here*?" Silence. A raw and deafening silence. The front door slammed shut. "Nina? What does that mean?"

Nina took a sip of wine and excused herself from the table without a word. She opened the patio door and stepped out into the darkness. Merlot's declaration of slights stung deep, because part of it was true. Was Nina a good leader? Or was she just pretending to be? The struggle to find value in her actions and character suddenly was crippling. Surely there were people better suited for the role she filled. What if by faking it she was doing more harm than good? Maybe there was someone who would not only be a better leader but would excel at it.

An unknown feeling washed over her. Her heart thumped forcefully, followed by a light pulsing in her head. Nina's hand bolted to her chest as she caught her breath. She was a Transcendent, a type of witch celebrated for their link to the divine ether, but never had she experienced a sensation like the one that had just passed. Magic was being performed nearby, but what kind and by whom, she did not know.

CHAPTER 23

At the mere mention of the swamp, it was all he could do to prevent his stomach from turning, a loathing so intense that it enraged him, not just how he could taste the bitterness upon his tongue when he spoke of it, but that he couldn't deny the magic of it. Behind the smells of mud and algae, thick as the bayou was vast, was a spell so heavy that only nature itself could have cast it. There was a heaviness to the air, packed with the sounds of buzzing insects, snapping twigs and gurgles of water. Its voice—a whisper, like the preternatural mutterings of a fiendish creature. The half-light of the moon was hidden under the canopy of leaves.

Nix exercised caution as he slowly stepped across the bayou floor. A Primordial witch with a flair for divination, Nix was not a tower of a man, but he was tall enough to have to duck under the low branches of the trees. Slender, with lips as thin as his frame, he had a cascade of dark hair that naturally looked professionally messy and eyes the color of acorns in the fall. The deep indentation lines that ran from his nose past the corners of his mouth hid behind a stubbly beard. He was embracing forty with elegance, like a sophisticated distressed leather jacket that wears handsomely over time. His eyes, so sharp they could cut a diamond, looked into the brush near the water's edge. Something was there. Staring back at him, a glowing rusty-orange eyeball. Finally, what he had been looking for.

He smiled. Under the darkness from the canopy of cypress leaves, he lifted his hand and drew his fingers into his palm in a slow and magnetic wave. The air between them seemed to move, like heat rising from the desert floor on the horizon. The gator shuffled among the mud and dead plants, stepping out from the water and onto the land. Nix called him once more with another generous curl of his fingers, a charm beyond communication and swollen with persuasion. He could hear the gator's heartbeat as if his own ear was upon the animal's flesh. When the gator reached his feet, he instructed it to roll onto its back with a swirling of his finger. The creature, once so predatory, had been reduced to an obedient dog performing tricks. Only there was no treat to reward it with; it was all a trick.

Nix unsheathed a twelve-inch dagger, a handle constructed of silver and bone with an ornament of Pluto's planetary symbol strutting out from the pommel. A skull engraved in black marked the blade just above the heel of the knife. Nix knelt down next to the body of the gator, still and silent. He was neither surgeon nor poacher, but he would have to hang and gut the creature all the same. There were many truths in blood-based divination. Visions were clearer, cleaner—but the deed was dark and stained. Whether used for good or evil, blood magic's curse is its price that gives the illusion that it hasn't one. Magic is infinite, and its capacity for time is beyond that of a lifespan. Its power lies in that—it can collect when it wants. The larger the creature, the clearer the message. He didn't specifically want an alligator, but like substituting shortening for butter, one works with what one has.

Nix collected a few shards of broken trees and placed them in a pile. He touched the base of the pile, and a stream of sparks raced along the bottom until the wood grew limbs of fire. Nix then pulled out a long rope coiled inside a bag, wrapped it around the gator just underneath the back legs, and spiraled it up the length of the tail. He attached the loose end of the rope to a long vine that dangled from a nearby tree and tied a solid knot with the two ends. A trail of sweat dropped down his forehead and sank into his eyebrow. It was time. Nix dropped to his knees, fit his elbows snugly against his side and turned his palms up toward the sky, his lips mouthing words for a few moments before he began to chant them aloud.

First in English. "A gift of blood for what's to come," Nix chanted with a pervasive yearning. Then, in Latin, "*Quid enim ad sanguinis donum.*" A cold smile appeared on his face as he continued to repeat the spell a total of three times to connect to the divine. He raised his arms slowly. The vine began to crack and rustle as it retracted toward the treetops. Bits of foliage and leaves fell like snow from the limbs as the vine coiled around branches, hoisting the gator into the air. Nix's face was swathed in firelight, a disturbing mural against the stunning blackness of the woods. He drew a series of lines and symbols upon the ground with a chalky white powder, rose to his feet and in one heavy-handed swing, sliced clear across the belly of the alligator. The entrails spilled out in a shower of blood. Nix probed the tip of the knife into the wound and examined the cavity, pulling away at the flesh to release the flow of fluids. As the spurting slowed to a trickle, Nix bent down and observed the patterns created upon the floor. A messy constellation of blood, powder and sand. His tight and irregular lips twisted with pleasure that was almost carnal, like the satisfied grin of a sex addict watching someone undress. It was all falling into place. What he had wanted and desired for so long was in the future.

Nix kept his eyes on the blood spatter for a moment, sensing that someone might be watching. But there was no one. He was alone. "There will be life…in death." Another creepy smile. What he suspected had been validated. His eyes darted over the mess as if reading a map. The knife was wiped clean with a black cloth before he stepped back a few paces, his eyes so concentrated, they were on the edge of catching fire. Then, all at once, the fire grew tall and the gator burst into flames. Rolling smoke filled the umbrella-like treetops as the fire grew white-hot like the death of a star before turning light blue. The fire burned and burned as Nix walked away. The gator fell to the ground as the vine snapped. In a roaring rush of blackness, the fire was extinguished, leaving nothing but ash.

CHAPTER 24

Mitch's intuitive block made a massive turn for the better the very next morning after their morning meeting and before a lunch of pretzel sticks. As he walked out of the dining room with the bag of pretzels in hand, he glanced through the half-open door to Nina's bedroom. She stood in the center of the room, placing large chunks of African amethyst around her in a circle. Before he could knock apprehensively on the open door, Nina spoke.

"You can come in—you're not disturbing anything," she said serenely.

"Sorry, I didn't mean to stalk," Mitch said as he entered.

Nina completed the circle and turned toward Mitch. "What's on your mind?"

Mitch shook his head as if he didn't have a question. Only he did. His eyes browsed the circle of crystals, then glanced at Nina, then went back to the crystals. "So, okay. I mean, I've always kind of used crystals for things. And everyone has always made fun of me for thinking that they hold mystic powers. Like, I'm delusional or something."

"You want to know if they actually do possess power," Nina asserted.

Mitch nodded. "Do they? I mean, obviously now things are a little different from how they were. I mean, I've seen things in just the past few days that should be impossible. But that doesn't, shouldn't, mean that everything I think in my mindskis is like, legit. Can you explain it?"

Nina's eyes were wide and earnest. "The act of ritual through intention is a mighty and potent force. When the gene we possess was activated, it created—well, amplified—our ability to manifest our intention through ritual. Crystals themselves are just rocks, just like we are just people, but we both have power, both have energetic vibrations. Why is one real and not the other? Think of marriage, for example. It's a ceremony, a ritual, but is it something tangible, outside of a marriage certificate? Its impalpable existence doesn't mean the marriage isn't real. It's real to the couple that's married. The power of crystals, whether science or *MythBusters* has proved it or not, is valid, mostly because of the belief in the power we have given them as a collective effort over time. It's like speaking a language. Once you learn that language, you're able to communicate in ways that you weren't able to before and maybe never even knew you could. Or doubted was possible." She trailed off about the types of crystals she had chosen for her circle and why she chose to wear a garnet necklace. "Tell me, how do you feel about your powers? Do you feel you're developing them? Getting stronger?"

Mitch considered the evolution of his life, from when he was powerless to when he possessed power. He dug back into his youth when he wasn't sure if being positive alone was enough to survive to adulthood. His parents were a mess of a couple in the end. His mother knew it, his father knew it and Mitch knew it better than both of them put together. He was the victim of it. There was a darkness in his family, and he always tried to find the light, hoping that light would be a way out. His mother hated that she had a gay son, his father was mostly emotionally unavailable, and he was surrounded by peers and a sibling who didn't understand him and in fact, constantly tormented him. Maybe that's why he could never be content and settle down in one spot: he was always looking for that feeling of home but could never seem to find it. Perhaps he was a lost wanderer, one who only wanted to believe he had a positive outlook but suffered from career underachievement, poor social skills and delusions. It made him wonder if he was bound to end up just as dysfunctional as the rest of his family. But there he was now, clearly gifted with divine power…Was that divine intervention? Was this the home and the family he had been searching for all his life? Maybe he was the only one holding himself back.

"I think so?" There it was, there was that doubt he was so familiar with.

Nina took a deep breath. "Mitch, you are one of the most positive people I've met. I know things haven't been easy for you—they aren't for anyone—and although I may not know the full span of the specifics, I know that amidst all that, you still have this optimism that's just…infectious. That's how you become a powerful manifestor. That's how you encourage your powers to bloom…You keep that optimism alive, at whatever cost. Don't worry about what others think, don't compare yourself to other people. That's a death trap." She grabbed his hands and pulled him into the circle. "A solid meditation practice will help open so many doors for you. And you being a Primordial, you have the gift of heightened senses, so let's start with that as our foundation."

"What about healing? Can I learn to do that?" Mitch questioned.

"Primoridals often can mend physical wounds, but how well they can heal depends on their skill level and the severity of the wound." Nina felt that Mitch had a different type of healing in mind. "But emotional wounds or breaking karmic cycles are typically conducted by Transcendent witches."

That was exactly what Mitch meant: the emotional wounds and karmic cycles that he and his family suffered from and were trapped—no, imprisoned—by.

Nina looked over the features of Mitch's face, but she didn't need a facial expression to read his feelings or thoughts. "Having said that, sometimes things are totally out of our control. Some things even magic can't truly fix. We can't be responsible for the entirety of our family. That's a really difficult and unrealistic burden to carry."

"But what about you? Aren't you as the Proctor kind of responsible for the entirety of this coven?" Mitch asked sharply, hoping he had found some kind of loophole in her logic.

"We can be influential as we invoke the energy of opportunity for change. We're all in control of how we handle movement, and every one of us has choices, including you. We can accept or reject those choices. I'm here to guide and help, but I can't make those choices for you. Change is hard. Even when it's simple, it's still really hard. Change doesn't always feel good. But that doesn't mean that it's not good. I know that you struggle with divination and you really want to connect with the tarot. And that'll come to you. It's a hard skill to learn. It's like painting. Anyone can pick up a brush and throw some paint on a canvas, but some people are just more naturally talented, whereas others need a little extra practice. Your senses and powers work the same. So, what I want us to do now is to work together on developing your senses."

Nina guided Mitch through a series of prompts to help awaken his body and stimulate his senses. With his eyes closed and his attention focused, he unlocked a higher sense of hearing. He described what he heard in the next room, the room beyond that, then outside the house. He transitioned on his own to his sense of smell. A few minutes passed. Mitch's sense of smell grew stronger. He could smell the sweet, chalky scent of Bisa's makeup and that it had suffered some heat damage. Leo's sweat was the next strongest scent, spicy like hot paprika.

"Now try the same thing with animals. Look for that," Nina suggested. As Mitch concentrated harder and deeper, his grip on her hand tightened. She had meditated countless times and usually experienced the same few sensations. This time was a little different. Her mind changed gears without her permission or expectation. *Probably because of the joined meditation*, she thought. Nina had been in group meditations many times, but she'd never experienced anything quite like the stirring sensation between her brows. She assumed it was only her third eye in overdrive, powering not only her own consciousness but Mitch's as well. The tingling swelled into a hazy blend of colors and patterns and then took shape in the form of Leo. There was no mistake: the vision was of Leo. She concentrated on Leo's body as it levitated into the air and then slowly melted into an electric vapor, filling the black space around him. The vision ended in a flash of white, not unlike the color of her knuckles. She opened her eyes to the sight of Mitch staring back at her.

"I couldn't feel anything. Maybe there aren't any animals nearby or something," he said, sounding disheartened.

Nina exhaled and released her hands from Mitch's grasp. For a moment, she considered that she had no business being a Proctor. How could she justify it when she couldn't explain what had just happened? In that flash of an instant, she was reminded just how rickety her grasp on the world of magic was.

"Don't stress about it. There are probably lots of reasons why you couldn't pick up anything. Not every gift is always available to every witch. You never know until you practice."

Nina congratulated Mitch on his efforts and quickly escorted him out of the room. When the door closed behind him, she began searching for the meaning of her vision. There were no immediate answers, only instinctual urges that involved some private study time. She cracked open a book from her bookshelf and started to skim the pages.

CHAPTER 25

A couple of rooms away, Leo was in the study, browsing the books on the shelves. There were more magical possibilities than there were books in the room. Leo didn't need a psychic vision to show him that he was unhappy and always had been. It was something he knew, something he felt, something he lived. There was darkness, and its reach was scary, but it didn't deter him from searching for a solution in the pages of the many books. He'd had no way of knowing as a child all those years ago that he would end up like this. Was he where he thought he would be? Absolutely not. He felt like a failure. How could he have known he would be so unhappy? How could he have known his daughter would die tragically? How was he to know that his entire life would be endless unhappiness?

He couldn't have known. Only now there seemed to be a way out. Maybe. If there was a way, it had to be in a book somewhere. His success as a witch had already given him more confidence than his entire life as a man. Perhaps he was the one witch, in the history of all witches, who would be able to do what was thought to be impossible. It was this drive that distracted him from his ceaseless vaping and steady acid drops, at least temporarily. Spells for his specific blood type, Ayurvedic ointments and crystal baths, he tried them all that afternoon. It was a day full of a combination of spells, procedures, potions and mantras all ending in the same failure. Although Leo felt satisfied with his ability to successfully perform spells and design potions, it didn't make him any happier. There was still an emptiness, a void that had only gotten wider with time and deeper with persistence. His efforts left the datura plants without their flowering trumpets, the bottle of geranium oil bone dry and his soul space unchanged.

After Leo had accepted the fact that he was unsuccessful, he started on his way back to his room to sulk in private. The door to Bisa's room was open, and he stopped to peer inside. Bisa was listening to music and painting. Without invitation, Leo entered her room with the boldness of a squirrel forcing itself into a bird's nest for eggs.

"What do you want?" Bisa asked briskly.

"What are you painting?"

"It's not really about what I'm painting but how I'm painting. I'm trying some new…techniques."

"I can't paint for shit," Leo said as he slipped his vape into his pocket. I remember my grandpa painting. I think it was my grandpa. He always painted these sad clown portraits."

"Was he mentally ill?" Bisa asked as she continued to paint.

"He was Catholic."

"Is there something you need, Leo?" Bisa glanced back at him over her shoulder.

"I was workin' on some *magic* earlier." He made quotation marks with his fingers when he said the word *magic*. "But no, I was just walkin' by, thought I'd say hi."

"You don't strike me as the type of person who just casually chats to people for the sake of conversation."

Leo sat down on her bed and rested his elbows on his knees. "What, I'm distracting you or something?"

"You were just walkin' by and thought you'd stop in to chat, huh? You made it a point to tell me you were practicing magic, so I'm assuming you either want an audience or advice. What were you working on?" Bisa looked over at Leo.

"Same as everybody else, just tryin' to be a better person, I guess. Tryin' to be happy."

She raised her eyebrows. "Your commitment to *fantasy* is inspiring," she said sarcastically.

"It has to be. It's all I have goin' for me right now." It was the most honest thing Bisa had heard out of Leo's mouth since she'd met him.

"Have you tried painting?" Bisa asked as she dipped her paintbrush into a well of crimson paint.

"For what?"

"For whatever it is that you've been working on all day." Bisa watched his expression as her hand moved down the canvas. "Painting can be spellwork too. Artists are magicians in a way."

"So you identify as both?" Leo asked.

"The line between them is a little fuzzy, if you ask me."

Leo stood up, walked over to Bisa and looked at the canvas. "I like it!"

"I did too, until a few minutes ago."

"What happened?"

"I got distracted," Bisa said tightly. She resisted the urge to recite a small charm that would send him out of the room, or humiliate him, and instead invited more conversation for reasons she couldn't explain.

Leo considered for a brief moment that he could try to utter a chant that would stop Bisa from being so guarded, yet he resisted. "I did just kinda barge in here like a wild boar. You right." He made his way toward the door.

"It's a portrait. A self-portrait. That's what I'm working on," Bisa said swiftly.

Leo swung around and walked back to the canvas. His eyes looked over the abstract painting and then into Bisa's eyes. For a moment they both felt the need to say something, but they hadn't the words to do it. The silence said more than any amount of words they could have said. It wasn't an immediate attraction, for Bisa was mostly repulsed by Leo; it was a recognition. It was an exchange, like the glance between two strangers on either side of the street who recognize each other's plight. A recognition that existed beyond explanation, like an inexplicably known secret. It was a connection of the cosmos behind their eyes.

"Have you ever tried painting?" Bisa asked.

Leo smiled, holding her gaze. "You asked me that already."

Bisa felt vulnerable for the first time since they'd met. "I did, didn't I. I blame the spirit of the brush and pen."

"Is that why you've been so nasty to me? Spirits?" Leo joked.

"I'm just like that with most people. Especially men. I don't trust people easily."

Leo was unaccountably fascinated by Bisa. "I guess I'm just a gambler."

"Danger addict," Bisa corrected.

"Living life is dangerous. People make it tolerable."

"Coming from the most intolerable person I've ever met," Bisa said as she took a step back and put her paintbrush into a jar.

"I guess it's a defensive thing. I've tolerated a lot of people and most of them have let me down, but none of them have been as interesting as you are."

Bisa smiled and crossed her arms over her chest. "Do you remember how much of an ass you were the first couple of days? Where is that guy?"

"Tied up and gagged in the back of my head," Leo said sweetly.

Their conversation—dynamic—previously so guarded, was now warmed by the energy of their banter-rich ebb and flow. They were more interesting to each other than they had been mere moments ago. As they continued to talk, they both realized they were able to detect and feel each other's weaknesses, and with that realization came a sense that through their relationship, whatever it became, the energies that prevented them from being their true selves would be washed away. The more they talked, the more they simultaneously enlightened and irritated each other. Their connection would always be surprising and intense, and it would never be easy. Bisa represented the light side of Leo and he embodied the dark side of her, a mystifying juxtaposition that neither of them could explain or articulate, although they still questioned it.

Bisa waved her finger back and forth between them. "What is this?"

"I don't know. I can't figure it out. I was hoping you'd tell me."

Bisa looked deep into Leo's eyes one more time before she shrugged the question away. "Well, I should really finish this up before it dries and I have to start all over."

Leo nodded, winked and left the room.

The clouds covered the moon just after midnight. A little after 2:00 a.m., Ollie woke up and kicked off the blanket. Even with the air-conditioning and the cover of night, it was hot. It wasn't often he got out of bed in the middle of the night for anything other than a quick pee or a glass of water. So when he awoke because of overheating and a sudden surge of hunger that ran through his belly, he knew it was something serious. He stumbled to the bathroom naked, assuming everyone was in bed. After a quick trip to the kitchen to snack on a peanut butter sandwich, he stood in front of the open fridge to further cool down.

With his hunger satiated and ready to get back to sleep, Ollie walked back to his room and covered half his body with the sheet. He could usually fall back to sleep, but not always; it was the one talent that Leo excelled at that Ollie truly envied. Sometimes he had to masturbate to get back to sleep. Other times sleeping in another room did the trick. Sometimes, despite his best efforts the only thing he could do was wait for his mind to tire on its own and endure the insomnia, often falling asleep only an hour or two before he woke for the day.

He fell out of consciousness just before three and woke back up a few minutes after. He raised his head from the pillow, a little groggy and with a light headache, the kind one gets from not enough sleep. Ollie rolled his eyes and looked around the full darkness of the room. For a moment, it looked as though someone was standing in front of the door. He knew he had closed the door, so it wasn't someone in the hallway. He rubbed his eyes as his sight adjusted to the dark. The door was closed, and there *was* something there: the outline of what looked to be a human figure. Ollie wasn't quick to panic, but he was as hot as a freshly fired pistol, and between the heat and the lack of sleep, the discomfort was enough to wrestle his composure away. He tried to focus, but the dark made it impossible. What he would have given to be a Primordial right then, to be able to throw a little flame here and there so he could put his mind at ease and get back to sleep.

Then the outline moved. Then there was the sound of a footstep. Ollie's nerves exploded in terror, as if he had stepped on a live electrical wire. He sat up in bed, hoping it was just his imagination caught somewhere between a dream and reality. Ollie held his breath as his pulse quickened. With a sweaty, shaking hand, he grabbed hold of his phone and switched on the flashlight. The beam shot out, pierced through the darkness of the room and landed on the back of his closed door. There was nothing there. Was he seeing things? He'd heard something. He'd *felt* something. He zigzagged the flashlight across the room, filling the corners with light. He was alone. When he felt his breath return to normal and felt the sweat on his body turn cold, he leaned back onto his bed and fell against the pillow.

"Boo!" a voice shouted into his ear.

Ollie screamed and jumped out of bed in a storm of tossed sheets and blankets. He screamed again, this time with the guttural panic of someone about to die. His feet shuffled across the floor as he grabbed the phone once more, this time to point at the bed. Nothing but a sweat-stained mess of sheets. There it was again, this time on the periphery of his vision. Something moving out of view. The more he turned to see what it was, the faster it moved away, sending him into a cyclone of terror. When he circled back to face the bed, he was met directly with a face distorted by the flashlight in his hands. The light shone toward the ceiling against the features of the man's face and through his hair, sending strange shadow puppets across the ceiling.

"Boo!" the man shouted as his head jolted toward Ollie.

Ollie jumped as he recognized the face beneath the warpings of the flashlight. It was Andy from the Houston coven. Ollie stumbled again, falling against a chair full of folded clothes.

Andy laughed fantastically. Suddenly, the door opened and the light flicked on. It was Leo.

"Dude, what the fuck!" Leo said with sleepy eyes. Then he saw it—he saw Andy too. Before he could even make sense of it, Andy vanished within the time it takes to blink an eye.

"Did you see that?" Ollie asked, shaken.

"Yeah, I fuckin' saw that! What's he doing in your room?" Leo shouted, and then looked down at Ollie's naked body. "Dude, put some fuckin' pants on."

Ollie slipped on some shorts as Mitch entered the room.

"My God, what's going on in here?"

"Ollie's in here jerkin' off with that guy Andy," Leo said cheekily.

Mitch rolled his eyes. "No, seriously. What's going on? Are you okay?" Mitch rushed over to Ollie to comfort him.

"The guy from dinner the other night. It was him. He was in my room," Ollie said as he wiped his forehead. "Go wake Nina."

CHAPTER 26

Despite the abnormal hour, it wasn't long before someone made a pot of coffee.

"I know everyone is all riled up about last night," Nina said as she cupped her third mug of coffee with her hands. As suspected, everyone was a little uneasy, and for good reason.

"How did he get in?" Avery asked with panicked eyes.

"Are we safe here?" Mitch asked next.

Nina lifted her hands to encourage everyone to calm down. "I know there are lots of questions, and you have the right to be concerned. Not everyone is going to be as understanding as we are. Witches are just like any other types of people. They may not like that we are the ones who have been prophesied to help usher balance into society."

"Why would they even care? That sounds like a stupid reason to harass people," Leo said as he slurped a mug of black coffee.

"Oh, it sounds stupid? People have done a lot worse for a lot less," Nina said. "It's no different from gangs and turf. Only in this case, it's covens and powers. Gang activity is senseless and futile, but that doesn't stop the behavior. And if witches are clustered in covens and mixed with a chaotic leader or Proctor, the same sort of hostile madness can happen."

"So what does he want?" Leo asked.

"I don't know yet. It might help us to ask what *they* want. I know you didn't sign up for this. I gave you a choice, to be here or to leave. To be here is to live with that danger. It comes with great reward, too, but it's not always going to be easy. Or safe."

Nina looked around the room and saw lots of jitters and restless bodies.

"How did he get into my room? And where did he go? What kind of spell is that?" Ollie asked.

"It's not a spell, it's astral projection—basically being out of your physical body," Nina said. "It's an advantage Transcendents have over Primordials. Bisa, Ollie and I are the only ones in this coven who naturally have that capability."

"What about us?" Avery asked.

"What do you have? Heightened senses. You can smell other witches. It's an auric smell. Auras can be detected by scent. The stronger the witch, the stronger the smell. Primordials tend to smell like the element they have the strongest connection to. Usually pine or moist earth, the ocean after a thunderstorm with the faintest hint of cucumber, the air in the dead of winter or smoke and sulfur."

"You should be a sommelier," Mitch said, half serious.

"What about Transcendents?" Ollie probed.

"We tend to smell like amber or rosemary. I don't know why, we just do."

It was precisely moments like this that were best for hands-on experimentation. Additionally, it would help encourage their success as witches and bond them as a coven. Nina instructed them to stand, and then ran Leo and Avery through an exercise to help strengthen their craft and channel their ability to smell auras. All Avery had to do was sniff and she was able to determine that Nina smelled like freshly rubbed rosemary needles, Mitch like amber, and Ollie like cucumber and rain. When Leo stepped up to try, he smelled rosemary on Bisa's skin, and Avery was rife with the stench of sulfur. He lifted his hands to his face and inhaled deeply through his nose.

He smelled different. "Yo, why can't I figure out what I smell like?" he asked after he'd pulled his shirt out from his chest and sniffed the fabric a few times.

"I can't figure him out either," Avery said with a puzzled look on her face. "It's like he doesn't have a smell. But…" she buried her nose in his chest and sniffed, "he does though. I just don't know what that is. What is it?" She turned to Nina for clarification.

Nina ran her nose along Leo's body, trying to pick up a scent like a dog would track the ground in the woods. Avery wasn't alone. She couldn't decipher what his smell was either.

Avery inhaled through her nose. "I mean, I smell it. It's like…I dunno, I want to say gold. But that doesn't make sense. It just smells, yeah, golden. I dunno, that's all I got."

"We'll work on that. Let's move on for now," Nina said as she went to the cabinet and took a brown glass bottle off the shelf. She unscrewed the top, placed her palm over the mouth of the bottle and tipped it over as if dabbing a cotton ball. She rubbed her hands together and wiped her palms over Ollie's and Bisa's foreheads.

"What's that?" Bisa asked.

"It's an elixir I made during the full moon. It'll help you connect with the astral plane."

Nina led the two through an exercise to activate their ability to astrally project. She brushed the crown of their heads rhythmically, remembering how Merlot had once done the same to her when they were first learning how to project. When she felt it was appropriate, Nina stepped back and allowed them to reposition themselves. Bisa stood, and Ollie lay down and spread out on the floor.

"Go beyond what you know, beyond where you go when you meditate. See the world around you through your eye inside," Nina instructed. "If you need to, repeat in your mind the word *proiectura*."

The radiance of Ollie's ambition suddenly fell dull. "I don't even know how to spell that, let alone pronounce it."

"Connect with it, speak it. It will fix itself as you concentrate," Nina said.

Bisa frowned. "I don't know what that means either."

Bisa's brow began to twist and quiver. Suddenly, a second version of Bisa entered the room, her face glistening with satisfaction. The moment everyone noticed her, the doppelgänger vanished in a whip crack of soft light. Bisa opened her eyes as her knees gave out beneath her. Nina rushed to her side to catch her before she fell to the floor.

Ollie clenched his eyelids tighter as if to seal them forever. "She did it, didn't she? Fuck."

There was a dampness to Bisa's skin that almost made her glisten in the light of the room. "It worked. Why am I wet?" she inquired strangely.

"It's astral fluid*, kind of a by-product of astral travel," Nina said. "Our power and our life force are embedded in it, and it tends to seep out onto our skin during projection."

Ollie sat up and opened his eyes. "I can't do it." He brushed off his hands. Instead of enjoying the success of Bisa's accomplishment, he was lost in a world of defeat.

Bisa had occupied the same physical plane through an alternate version of herself, her spiritual self. In doing so, her head buzzed, and for a few minutes afterward, everything seemed to have a halo as if bathed in direct sunlight. Her awakened state didn't go unnoticed and was celebrated by all, except Ollie.

"Rest a little. Here, sit down," Nina said, motioning toward the couch. She rubbed the side of Bisa's cheek and winked at her before she turned to Ollie. "It'll come."

Ollie ignored Nina's comment and looked straight at Bisa. "How'd you do it? How'd you get back?"

Bisa shook her head, still a little fuzzy. "I don't…know. I just did it. I didn't choose to come back, it just kind of happened. It was like when you suddenly trip over something."

"In the future, as you build that muscle, you'll be able to hold your grip on your astral body and return to your physical body by using your own will," Nina said. "It'll be as second nature as blinking after a while."

"Does it get easier?" Ollie asked.

"Well, yes and no," Nina said. "I still have a hard time doing it. The less you do it, the harder it becomes." As she spoke, she realized that she hadn't practiced it herself in a very long time. "It *can* help to be completely nude. Clothes can hinder astral travel. They interfere with the ether."

Ollie scoffed. "Okay, well, I'm not about to just strip down in front of everyone."

Leo laughed and started picking at his nonexistent fingernails. "Good."

"So, what are we going to do about Andy? Nothing?" Avery asked.

"I don't think we should react," Nina said. "He's teasing. You saw what they were like. We can set up some enchantments to prevent them from crossing into our space, but I think it's best to just ignore it for now. They're bullies. We have to pick our battles, and right now that isn't one we need to waste our energy on."

"What if he comes back?" Ollie asked.

Leo waggled his head in agreement. "Yeah, dude. Bullies just keep going and going until someone stops them. Trust me."

"Well, you'd know, wouldn't you?" Mitch jeered.

Bisa wasn't listening anymore. She was rolling in the splendor of her new view of the world. "I think I need to go lie down for a bit."

Nina nodded. "Of course. In fact, why don't we all just take a break for a bit. Maybe figure out what we are going to do for dinner." As Leo and Mitch started to walk away, Nina called out loudly, "Or maybe we can start cleaning up the mess everyone left in the kitchen. I'm not a maid!" *I told myself I wouldn't turn into their mom!*

A couple of hours later, the battle for bathroom time began. Bisa and Avery occupied the bathroom in the foyer and Nina's master bath while Leo was hogging the bathroom between his and Mitch's room. Leo was by no means a metrosexual. His showers were always quick, like it was a bad thing to be too clean or well groomed. All he needed was some shampoo and body wash and a good five minutes. Soft-boiled eggs took more time than he did. However, he had been in the bathroom for nearly twenty minutes, which was absolute madness in terms of Leo's bathing routine. Mitch occupied himself on his phone as he pounded on the bathroom door with his other hand.

"Leo, hurry up, I have to pee," Mitch said as he browsed Instagram.

No response.

Mitch pounded three more times. "I'm just gonna come in if you don't open the door." No response. "I don't care if you're naked or not. You might, but I won't. Obviously. And I *will* look." There was nothing but silence on the other side of the door. Mitch put his ear to the door and listened for something—anything: the sound of running water, the clinking of the toilet paper roll on the metal holder or even something a little more private. He twisted the door handle and cracked the door open, just enough to get a reaction if Leo was paying attention. When he didn't get the expected result, Mitch pushed the door wide open. It was empty. *Wait. I know I saw him go in here.* Mitch pulled back the shower curtain and looked behind the door. Leo was gone. Mitch left the bathroom and looked around the house, peeking into every room. He wasn't tripping—that was Leo's thing—but he knew for a fact he had seen Leo enter the bathroom.

It was only when Mitch returned to the great room and stopped to look outside that he found what he had been looking for. Underneath the magnolia tree in the backyard sat Leo, legs crossed. Mitch opened the door and walked out into the yard, indifferent to the fact that he wasn't wearing shoes or socks.

"Am I crazy or were you in the bathroom?" Mitch asked loudly. He wanted a solid answer, one that would prove he wasn't losing his mind.

"That was so awesome!" Leo sang.

"Taking a dump?"

"I was just sitting here, thinking about meditating, just *thinking* about it. And then I thought I should've gone to the bathroom. And then I just…got up and did it. But I did it while sitting here, dude! It was just like what Bisa did earlier!"

"Astral projection?" Mitch asked, slightly afraid of the answer.

"Hell yeah!"

Mitch watched Leo clap his hands to celebrate himself as a sense of anxiety rose up in his stomach. Instinctively he stepped back and raised his chin in confusion. *But he's a Primordial like me...*

Nina watched from the window at the breakfast nook. As she watched the interaction between Mitch and Leo, an eerie feeling wove itself into her mind and triggered the memory of her vision of Leo. She had to remind herself that people always ask for signs and then don't see them when they appear. Even she needed to run that by herself every now and then. Perhaps it was time to seek some outside counsel from the Advisory on the matter.

It had been a while since Nina had conducted a summoning spell to meet with the Advisory. It wasn't always necessary, but the spell was in place for situations like the one she found herself in. She hesitated, but only for a moment. The spell was cast with the lighting of a candle and a few chanted words. Once she was connected to the higher consciousness, she sent her request to meet, complete with suggested time and place. The sounds she heard were indeed voices, those of the other members in the Advisory. The spell acted as a sort of spiritual telephone. It was nine in the evening when Nina arranged to project herself into the meeting space. Surrounded by candles and bathed in moonlight, she closed her eyes and prepared to enter the space with a few deep breaths. The spell began with a visualization, one that connected her imagination to that of another plane.

She was tuned in to her consciousness now and found herself in the middle of an open field. A large oak tree not too far in the distance sang the tunes of leaves in the wind under the moonlight. As she walked toward the tree, the mesmerizing sounds of heavy wind chimes filled her ears as the wind began to blow. She organized the details of the story she was about to tell the Advisory while her hair told its own story in the unforgiving breeze. The clouds that patched the sky above were blushed with a deep amber color.

Halfway to the tree, the breeze stopped, and a single purple leaf flittered down in front of her face. She held out her hand to collect it, and as her fingers closed over the stem, the ground beneath her feet fell into the earth and created a short stairwell of grass and dirt. Tongues of ivy and star jasmine curled around the base of the stairs and bloomed with each step downward. A humble door of gray wood appeared at the bottom of the stairwell. Nina's vision began to flicker in and out like an old television struggling for a signal. It had been a long time since she had projected herself for this length of time, and she was rusty. She was behind in her psychic sit-ups, and it was high time she got back in shape. Teaching had caused her to neglect her own psychic self-care.

Nina reached the door and pushed it open. As she walked through the doorway and into blackness, the door swung off the frame and began to dissolve into silvery smoke that plumed out from where her hand made contact. The smoke intensified and soon she was engulfed by it. When it started to dissipate with the sound of hushed and whispering voices, she no longer saw the blackness or the grassy staircase, but instead the Symposium meeting room. It had been a very long time since she had stepped foot inside, and the room seemed to rise before her as if she were much shorter than she actually was. It was undeniably a wonder to behold. No matter how many times she visited the room, it always took her breath away upon entering.

Nina stepped onto the mosaic floor made of hardwood with stone inserts and gold gilding. It was more than a floor: it was high art, an elegant pattern of vines and leaves. The walls were solid concrete the color of Barcelona at dusk, and a strong fire burned brightly in fireplaces at both ends of the room. The only piece of furniture was a large fourteen-foot table, vine-like wooden legs under a thick, uneven boulder slab of polished stone with malachite, chrysocolla, azurite and swirls of native copper. It was Nina's favorite part. The rough, hewn edges were softened by the vibrant colors of blue, gold, green and toasty brown. Nina stepped closer to the table and pulled out a chair to sit. She felt a slight rumbling, and then in trickled the other members of the Advisory.

First to arrive was Rosemary Cherry, a Primordial witch from Northampton, England. The eldest of the group, yet the most stylized, she possessed an effortless beauty that made everyone assume she was years younger than she actually was. She was free from the falsities of makeup, apart from some black eyeliner. Her silky, straight white hair, flat-ironed into a museum-quality bob, made a stunning frame for her emerald eyes. Rosemary walked into the room with authority in a long floral skirt under a zipped-up lambskin jacket. She was every bit as fragrant as the herb she was named after but with none of its needles.

The second plume of smoke appeared, and Per Kaji emerged from the gray. His face was smooth, with a kingly nose and thick arched eyebrows. Half Japanese and half Swedish, he spoke only English. It was unimportant, as his preferred language was being of service. His earth-brown eyes looked over Nina and Rosemary as his delicate hands pulled out a chair for Rosemary. A gentleman of the highest regard, his manners were as transcendent as his powers.

Nina had hoped they could begin immediately, but they were still short a member. Nix was perpetually late, but he was also a very talented witch when it came to divination and spirit work. He was excellent, actually, which allowed everyone to tolerate his tardiness. Where was he when he was always late? Nina was always early, so she figured that the day would come when she would have to suggest that he speed things up or be late somewhere else.

"It has been a day, let me tell you," Rosemary said as she adjusted her chair. "I don't understand how I got stuck in New Mexico. It's always sunny. I don't know how I haven't burnt to a crisp. My poor aging skin can only take so much. It never rains there! How are you, dear?" she said to Nina. "It's been ages. Hobnob?" Rosemary pulled out a package of cookies—biscuits, rather—from her pocket and waved them in the air.

"No, thank you!" Nina replied, checking her watch.

"It's funny, Hobnobs. You know that word refers to mingling amongst friends. This is sort of a hobnob."

"It would be if we were all here," Per said. His voice was clean and crisp, void of any accent.

"Shall we start?" Rosemary questioned as she took a bite of her biscuit.

The voice that responded didn't belong to anyone at the table. It was Nix. "I hoped you'd wait for me," he said as he appeared at last from a puff of smoke.

"You have many talents, Nix," Rosemary said. "It's a shame that being late is by far your greatest talent. You must have even been *born* late. It's the only excuse."

"What can I say, I enjoy life. I have no intention of rushing through it," Nix said as he sat in the closest seat, his hands running down the length of his all-black outfit to smooth it out. "I would have to say that I believe my greatest talent is not being late, but keeping our finances in order better than the rest of you."

"I don't want to sound too wanky, but I held that position for years, far longer than any man *or* woman, and the position chose me, it wasn't given to me like some kind of sad consolation prize. If we rewarded intellect over charisma, the position would have gone to someone like Nina, who deserves it. The irony of that is that she didn't want it."

Nix sat with a smug grin on his face, completely unfazed by Rosemary's jab. In the flicker of the firelight, Rosemary looked almost demonic as she shot cross stares at him.

Rosemary turned her attention back to Nina. "So, Nina, tell me, why are we here?"

"As you all know, I'm Proctor to a coven in Louisiana. I'm still quite new, but I have some concerns about one of my witches. Normally, I wouldn't think twice about it, but there have been certain idiosyncrasies with his powers that I can't make sense of. As if that weren't enough, I've also had a vision that involved him. I normally don't have visions, and I certainly have never had one like this one before. I wanted to bring it before you to see if it's something I should worry about. Or maybe it's nothing. Maybe it's just that I don't have all the answers." Nina took a breath and thought that maybe she'd been a little long-winded about something that might very well be nothing at all.

"Right then," Rosemary said. "Out with it. What's been troubling you?"

"I've been going over and over it in my head. And I dare to say that when I think something, I feel it."

She had the room's attention, and they all listened attentively as Nina recounted the events that concerned her and finished with the recap of her vision. By the end of her story the Advisory had nothing but enigmatic expressions on their faces. Rosemary, who had her arms crossed on the table with a wild look in her eyes, wore a look of shock. In the realm of magic where many things were within the realm of possibility, Rosemary's expression was something disconcerting to experience.

"I have to say I don't feel anything out of the ordinary. I don't think every vision means something significant. I've had many visions, and I've interpreted loads of them wrong," Per said.

"You're wrong," Rosemary said sternly. There was a coldness in her voice, a tone that bordered on both fear and exhilaration.

"What do you mean?" Nina asked.

Rosemary held her gaze without so much as a blink. She slowly shook her head as if some unbelievable fact had come to light. "There's no denying the severity of your concern. You were right to come to us."

Nina shook her head and gave a nervous smile. "You almost look a little scared."

"Do you still get scared at your age?" Nix asked Rosemary facetiously. "Haven't you seen everything by now?"

"It never goes away. In fact, the things that are truly terrifying only become much worse."

Rosemary was a snacker, though you wouldn't know it from her slender frame. She had a hard time going a few hours without a snack, and if there were snacks at the ready, it was hard for her to go more than a few minutes without gobbling them up. Yet she had lost interest in the chocolate-covered cookies before her on the table. This situation was much more important. "Have you, any of you, ever heard of the Corporeals*?"

Nina shook her head and let the word sink into her thoughts. *Corporeal.* She had never heard the word before and hadn't come across it in all of her studies. She wondered if Merlot knew. They had been study buddies at one time. Surely Merlot would have shared something as significant as this with her.

"Is that some kind of cookie?" Nix said softly as he smiled.

"Don't be daft. This is serious," Rosemary said as she broke eye contact and looked toward the ceiling as if listening to some stream of mental dialogue unknown to anyone else. "My family has a history of witchcraft that goes back further than most people I know." Her eyes moved to the center of the table, as if seeing the distant past in the space in front of her.

"Well, that would be you. You're the oldest," Nix added.

"Before my ancestors moved to England, they lived near Salem. Right before the great witch hunt of 1692. They were witches, powerful ones. They kept a grimoire, passed it down through the generations. I grew up being read excerpts from it, like some kind of fairy tale. There were spells, recipes and all sorts of other things. But there were also stories. Journal entries. Documented results of spellwork. Some of it was dark; much of it was extraordinary. I got older, and I began to read through the book on my own. That's when I came across something I'd never heard before. Near the beginning of the book. Or somewhere in the middle. I can't remember. But it was the legend of the Corporeal. Well, it became a legend because it was deemed to be so. It was thought to be just ramblings of a witch who liked to experiment with talents far beyond what they were capable of. I asked my mother. That's what she told me. Just a legend. But it wasn't. It was a prophecy."

Per shrugged. "What was it?"

"It was about the third and final nature of witches. It was supposed to happen during the next shift. But it never did. So, it was dismissed. The shift after that…still nothing. Nothing and nothing and nothing. There was and always has been only the two kinds, Primordials…and Transcendents."

"Surely someone must have tried to connect with that energy, right? A skilled Transcendent?" Nix suggested.

"Oh, of course they did. All manner of witches of all levels of skill. Everyone received the same answer from the divine, which was no answer at all." Rosemary ran her finger down the slick edge of her bob.

Nina's heart began to race as Rosemary told her story. "What kind of powers were Corporeals said to have?"

"They were said to be the most powerful of all. Energy witches…alchemists. They could manipulate energy and affect matter. Extreme levels of telekinesis. A Corporeal could even obtain invisibility through aura manipulation."

Nina leaned in, her face fully illuminated by the roaring fire. "What else? What about shared powers? Could they successfully mimic the powers of, say, a Primordial? The elements?"

Rosemary stuttered, as though she were uncertain how to answer. "I'm not entirely sure. I remember something about— well, I believe they could control the elements but there was some kind of cap to it, like they couldn't create or summon them."

Nina raced through her memory and tried to piece together whether Leo had controlled or created the elements he experimented with. Had he created the fire in the candle or had a candle already lit? It had been raining when he'd made it stop. Did that mean he could be a Corporeal? She hadn't seen any other evidence of it. Just then she remembered seeing Mitch and Leo outside near the tree. Something was awry. What was it?

"So, they're dangerous?" Nix asked.

Rosemary dismissed it, but only enough to put everyone at ease. "What do you consider dangerous? Even the most responsible person in the world can misuse magic and have it be dangerous. Even those with the purest of intentions can change in an instant. Whether a Corporeal is a danger—to us or an ally—lies in the kind of person they are and how they use their power."

"Surely not every witch or Corporeal—if they actually exist—is going to be dangerous," Per said.

"They can move energy, and with that comes the ability to open and make portals as they see fit. Which may seem great if you find yourself in a jam in another dimension and you need a quick escape before your imminent death, but what about the other situations?" Rosemary sat up straight in her chair. "Before any of us get too far ahead of ourselves, Nina…you need to determine if this witch is in fact a Corporeal. Any way that you can. Now, unless anyone objects, I suggest we adjourn for now. I'm bloody starving."

CHAPTER 27

Edie was standing on the corner of the stage in her sleeveless dress, pink from top to bottom like a glass of pink lemonade, when Joshua began the service. Every seat was filled, and the air-conditioning was having trouble cooling the room. As at most services, the temperature would continue to rise until someone fainted from the heat instead of the Holy Ghost.

She looked at her watch. There were goals to meet, and Edie was bathed in ambition as much as she was Christianity, if not more. When the two mixed, she became a nearly unstoppable force against anyone or anything that challenged her. It was something she was proud of, and she used it to her advantage in every service she led and with every soul she brainwashed, all for the sanctity of her faith. Or perhaps it was privilege masquerading as ego and dressed up as faith. Behind her persuasive words was a woman of power, a force that was only encouraged by her followers, condoned by her husband, a woman whose complicit ideas were held up high and supported. It was that support that she and Joshua intended to discuss in their service.

Joshua removed the microphone from the stand at the pulpit so he could move about the stage with ease and keep the audience engaged. They weren't members of a church during their sermons, they were audience participants, contributors to a show a little less glamorous than one would see in Vegas but just as surreal and illusory.

Joshua scratched his sweating brow and looked out into the rapt audience. "Now. Today we're going to mix it up a little.

For all of you worried about the devastation that comes with changing things up, it's going to be a good thing, trust me. We want to talk about the strength of your faith. Now, last year, y'all helped us raise $248,678, and"—Joshua looked over to his wife—"how many cents was it?" He motioned to her with his free hand, his wedding ring glistening in the light like a holy relic.

Edie smiled as she walked toward the pulpit and retrieved a second microphone and switched it on. "Twelve cents." A blissful giggle followed.

Joshua repeated the total amount. "That's how much you gave to us during our last fund-raiser, funds that allowed us to expand our church." Clapping and cheers. "Funds that gave us the opportunity to create new programs such as our Small Group for Truth and Light that allows people to come together"—Joshua closed his hands together over the mike—"and explore their common interests and explore their faith *together*. A program that has only grown in size since its inception, grown to a size that even I thought wasn't possible, isn't that right, Edie?"

Edie nodded proudly. "It's true!" More loyal clapping and encouraging cheers.

Joshua pumped his fist into the air as he spoke. "It allowed us the funds to establish our own youth scouting organization, the Boy and Girl Trailblazers of America, a group that holds the true values of our country and our faith in the highest regard, a group designed to help guide our youth away from sin and instill in them the knowledge and life skills they need to survive in today's hurting world!" Another surge of lively applause. "We were able to meet with the president of the United States of America only a few weeks ago, and you know what he said?" An outburst of "What?" rang out from the audience. Joshua looked over at Edie.

"He said…keep on making America great," Edie said, closing her eyes as if moved by the sheer beauty of the compliment.

Joshua responded as quick as lightning and just as loudly, "Yes he did! *Yes he did!*"

"It's true, he did!" Edie confirmed.

"And that's what we're gonna do…*together.* Come on, put your hands together, just like in prayer." Joshua was feeling it now, the true power of religious celebrity. "We're gonna do it, whatever it takes. Say it. Say 'Whatever it takes.'" The audience recited the phrase like a choir of zombies. "I love it. I just love it. The combination of church and a vision coming together for a purpose. My wife has a phrase she likes to say, and I want her to share it with you now. Edie!"

Edie took a few steadying inhalations before she spoke. "I always say if you can do it all by yourself, then you aren't risking enough. And I really mean that. If you want more, you need to risk more. Is our faith worth that risk? Are our children worth that risk? Is all that we stand for worth that risk? We need to stretch as a church, with new ideas and programs that help save our country from those who aim to destroy our homes, our souls and our children. You are more than just members of this church. Y'all have gifts and talents that God wants us to help you identify and put to good use. Together we can raise the bar and step up to achieve that life that is out there waiting for you to live. There is a truth that needs to be spread across our nation and around the globe! Can I have a good amen?" An eerie harmonious "Amen" sang toward the stage.

"Thank you, Lord, thank you, God, thank you, Jesus…for giving us the opportunity to help lead these people toward the light." Edie found herself pacing back and forth across the stage as she took control over the sermon. Her body began to sweat from the strength of her conviction, and right then she noticed she was getting another headache. She seemed to be getting headaches more often lately no matter what she ate, how long she slept or how much water she drank. It was beginning to become a nuisance; it was something she couldn't control, and the thought of something she couldn't talk her way out of only made her headache worse. The least she could do was ignore it for the time being and hope to God that by the end of the sermon, when the room was cooler and everyone had left, she wouldn't need to bury her head under a cold rag and have a lunch of ibuprofen.

"I want to transition to the next part of our sermon today. Ushers, will you please come forward? Let's prepare for our offering. I also want to say that following this sermon is our yearly fund-raiser. The power of giving is what makes us free. If you believe in the power of your God, give what you can. I understand not all of us have the means to give much, but give what you can and you will be rewarded a hundredfold in heaven and during your time on this earth! Checks, money orders or good ol' cash will do just fine now. If you feel more comfortable, there is an offering box just outside in the hall where you can discreetly add whatever you like. There'll be lots of snacks and sweet tea, and I know how y'all look forward to Ms. Boudreaux's pecan pie*. I know I do. There'll be lots of that to go around too. Come on, everybody, let's do this together!" The offering plate was more of a bowl, really, deep and cavernous. When it reached the stage after making its rounds around the room, the Bonners nearly had tears in their eyes at sight of it. Their cup—no, their bowl—truly did runneth over.

"Praise his light!" Edie shouted. "God bless y'all! His presence is here in this church! Lift your hands, because he is here. Father, bathe us in your light! We thank you for the truth in our words today, we thank you for the love of everybody in this church, we receive it! We *receive* your love! Show us the love, show us the power of giving, show us, dear Lord." Edie's shouting made her head pound even harder. It was worth it, though. The gain was more than the pain. Beyond the headache were the words she wanted to say but carefully avoided: *show us the money.* "Touch somebody next to you and say to them, 'God bless you, give what you can!'" As if the overflowing amount of donations wasn't satisfying enough, the organ music swelled and Mrs. Harris fainted into the arms of her husband, overcome this time by the power of faith instead of the heat.

CHAPTER 28

The coven continued to practice magic over the next few weeks, both together and privately, but always progressing at their own pace. They were no longer just people with abilities; they now identified as witches and accepted the gifts they had been given, which grew stronger by the day. It wasn't just magic that had an effect on them, but each other. Bisa fed off Avery's carefree attitude, Mitch taught Leo how to take better care of his skin and the importance of face masks, and Oliver's influence filled each of their bedrooms with houseplants.

Avery was the most open-minded and impressionable of them all, with a learned ritual of a deep cleaning clay mask—infused with her own enchanted honey—every Thursday night. By Halloween, which she now preferred to call Samhain, she had as many braids in her hair as she did potted plants in her bedroom. In a sense, she was the next best version of herself, one she thought she would achieve by trusting her spirit. It always helped her, whether it reminded her to water her maidenhair fern or how to braid her hair like Bisa's.

They observed Samhain in the traditional sense, which for the coven meant by their own traditions. The members threw a party for themselves because they had a lot to celebrate. They decorated the great room with herbs and incense, and they ate honey cake and drank the moody cocktails Ollie crafted in the kitchen. Dancing was inevitable. Mitch knew how to throw a party, and given that Halloween was his favorite holiday as a child, he was going to make sure they had fun. He didn't order the fog machine and strobe lights for nothing. Ironically, the place looked like what a normal person would think a witch's house looked like, with its carefully designed fake spiderwebs, strange feather decorations and a lot of moss. In the glow of the candlelit room, one could hardly tell the difference between the fog and incense smoke. It was fabulous. It was the new pumpkin carving. There was so much dancing. And their hearts were open.

When the oppressive Louisiana heat fled for winter, Leo started to spend a little more time outdoors. More than usual. He had grown up in the South, but it didn't mean he preferred being hot or even liked it. Winter was his favorite season. It was the foggiest time of the year and seemed that much more magical because of it. Temperatures dropped low enough to wear a light jacket, and with Leo's new knowledge of skin care, he started using a heavier moisturizer. He had learned a lot over the past month. Yet nothing interested him more than the information he uncovered while researching the nigrum pullum, or black pullet. Nina had mentioned the ritual that invokes the nigrum pullum when he first arrived, she called it the Union of the Divine Dualities, but she hadn't fully explained it. Leo may have seemed dim-witted and forgetful, but when he wanted to remember something—he did. Nina unintentionally made it more interesting by refusing to discuss it, therefore making it seem more dangerous, and danger to him was like a warm bath on a cold night. He was a Primordial, perhaps one with exceptional gifts, and he was certain he could conduct some clever animal magic on his own, for his own selfish needs. He finally felt successful, and proud of himself. If he'd been his parent, he would have had one of those bumper stickers that proud parents slap on their rear bumper, the ones that read *My Child Is an Honor Student*, only his would read,

My Child Is a Gifted Witch or perhaps more appropriately, *My Son Is the Fucking Shit at Magic.*

Leo pulled a chair underneath his south-facing window and opened it halfway. The cool, dead scent of winter in the swamp flowed in. He had learned enough about the basics of moon phases, colors and candle magic to be pretty successful at creating spells of his own. Leo crafted a small nest made from an abalone shell, moss and twine. He felt around his dresser drawer until he grabbed hold of his tiny glass pipe. He hadn't smoked weed in a while, but that's not what it was for, not that night anyway. Into a tiny mortar and pestle he borrowed from the kitchen he dumped cilantro leaves, marjoram, dried fennel seed, peppermint and bay leaves. He became more confident of his skills the more he pounded the herbs into a chunky powder. It wasn't quite the same as the sticky weed he usually packed into the bowl of his pipe, and it required a new level of finesse to handle it.

There was a tiny corked bottle to his left. He pulled the cork out, and it popped like a new wine bottle. He brought the lip of the bottle to another, one that held a Full Moon Elixir and Essence of Solomon's Seal, both borrowed from Nina's potion cabinet. With utmost precision, he poured the mixture into the smaller bottle. He lit the pipe, inhaled just enough to fill his mouth with smoke and then blew it into the tiny jar and corked it. The smoke swirled like an apparition over the potion. With a few violent shakes, he blended the smoke with the liquid. He poured the liquid onto a small piece of paper and waited until it was fully dry before dropping it into the center of the makeshift nest and lighting it on fire. The flakes of ash swirled under the breeze from the window slightly before they escaped out into the world. If it worked like he thought it would, it wouldn't be long before he'd be visited by a magpie bearing gifts.

Leo wasn't the only one practicing magic that night. Mitch was alone in his room listening to old Grimes, working with the power of water. Much like their connection to animals, Primordials were also blessed with a strong connection to nature. He painstakingly concentrated on a glass of water until he connected with it in a way that allowed him to whisper to it and have it whisper back from the pitcher it came from. It was his third success of the evening, but the second one that went unacknowledged by the rest of the coven. The first magical triumph came around midday while taking a bath. Through happenstance, he learned that he could choose whether he wanted to stand on the surface of the water or sink below it. Of course he had to concentrate hard to make it last—or happen at all—but it was something to celebrate nevertheless. With a towel wrapped around his body he invited everyone to come witness his success, albeit short-lived, as he was able to remain on the water's surface only long enough for them to see before his feet sank.

It was during dinner that he carried out his second successful spell. He had spent a few days perfecting an enchantment over a bowl of water filled with rue and angelica root. Once he determined the water had reached its full potency under the moon, he spiked everyone's drink with a teaspoon of it during dinner. The remaining mother water he stored in a jar in his room. It was a water-based protection spell that came with a few bells and whistles, and was there if he ever needed it. He felt a surge of success, finally.

That success encouraged him to take his spellwork a step further. What good was magic if you couldn't have a little fun every now and then? He knew it might be unethical to craft a potion that would boost his power of influence, but how could a harmless gay boy with a big heart wreak that much havoc? He knew that Transcendents had the power of influence, but it didn't stop him from *attempting* to acquire that gift himself. It sounded useful. Especially as someone as eccentric as he was, someone who would be called a faggot from a speeding car on the regular if he walked down the street. Perhaps he could change that, discourage those with that kind of ignorance in their heart from acting, thinking like that.

The potion was white like milk and rich like wine. It was fruitier than expected and thicker than he would have liked, but if Mitch were to be honest, he'd admit that he'd willingly swallowed things far less appetizing and much thicker, so he drank it all. A smile emerged from his white-painted lips. As he licked them clean, he realized that he felt absolutely nothing, even though his mind repeatedly told him he felt something. For a moment, he saw himself back in the office of the therapist he'd seen during his early twenties, the one who told him that his headaches were probably psychosomatic and to try yoga. He decided to let that go as he remembered that another doctor had given him a diagnosis of migraines. However, those migraines had stopped around the time he became a little more magical. So maybe he did feel something and the potion did work. Only one way to be sure.

By the time of the winter solstice, the coven had finally decided whether they were going to celebrate pagan holidays. They were in Louisiana, a state that celebrated everything from catfish to Shakespeare, and that wasn't including the outrageous Carnival season that lasted weeks. It only made sense to celebrate as much as they could, but in ways that meant something to them. Granted, the pagan holidays didn't mean a lot, if anything, to any of them, but they opted for some good revelry. It was kind of like experiencing Mardi Gras for the first time: one tries to go to as many parades as possible before going to a select few if any in the years that follow.

Nina started the morning meeting with craft time instead of lecture time as she walked them through the creation of the Ab Initio Talisman*, a sort of magical inkblot created with elixir-infused ink. "A talisman provides power and energy. Its purpose is to attract a specific benefit to its owner. This one is one of my favorites," Nina said as she flipped through a stack of papers. She pulled out a large piece of paper stained with black ink. Its shape was completely abstract. "I made this years ago, under the light of the first new moon of the year. So there's a nice parallel there for us." She gazed over the unframed talisman with mature eyes and let her mind wander. "The purpose of this talisman is to shift the perspective of its owner, to see positive developments in one's life through the use of an inkblot."

"Like a Rorschach test?" Bisa asked.

"Same technique, different intention. It's supposed to be hung where you'll see it every day, so I kind of failed in that way, but you get the idea. The purpose is to look at it every day throughout the entire year—the rest of your life, really—and see what you see as time goes on. Here it's the allegoric intention we add to common objects like ink and paper. Our intention transforms it into something unique. The power of our intention is what gives it life."

"Making its worth…illimitable," Bisa added as she organized her items on the table.

Before Nina could praise her for her wise words, the doorbell rang. Nina had spoken to Rosemary earlier and knew the Advisory was planning a visit, but she hadn't expected them so early in the day. Part of her considered that their early arrival meant that they weren't bearing great news. As she turned the handle on the front door and opened it, the grandfather clock rang aloud: 11:15. She had forgotten that Avery had asked to reactivate the clock chimes before they sat down to meet moments ago. Before her stood the three other members of the Advisory in a solid frieze against the foggy gray of the looming afternoon.

"Good morning, Nina," Rosemary said with a nod.

"Good morning! I wasn't expecting to meet so early. We've only just started our daily meeting." Nina was a little on edge. She could feel something in the ether that was somewhere between ominous and dangerous. Rosemary sounded chipper, but her energy was serious, more solemn. Nina looked at Nix, dapper and glowing with an everything's-all-right-but-it-isn't face. She opened the door farther and invited everyone inside. A few moments later, the strange expression on Nix's face was completely gone and replaced with a more stoic one. There was a lot of energy among them. They were all skilled in some way, and with skill came higher vibrations. It was like having a lot of magnets in one spot. It was hard to tell what direction the pull was coming from.

"Is the entire coven here?" Per asked.

"Yes. I can have them stay in the dining room while we talk," Nina suggested.

"Oh, absolutely not. That's why we chose to meet here. This concerns you and your coven directly," Rosemary declared with an undertone of foreboding.

Nina paused for a moment. At last, she said, "Have a seat in the great room. I'll let them know."

The Advisory made their way to the great room with Rosemary leading the way. Nix, who was characteristically late, lagged behind, admiring the new furnishings, decorations and personality that Nina and her coven had brought to the once empty house. It had been under his ownership as Keeper of Books and Assets until it was awarded to Nina to lead the coven. He moved a few candlesticks, adjusted a few books and impolitely poked his head into places that guests typically stay clear of unless invited.

Nina collected the coven from the dining room where they were working independently on their talismans and brought them into the great room. Before she sat down, she looked around for Nix, who was missing. Always late. Always distracted. She wondered how it was possible to be late to something he was already on time for. Only he would be capable of that.

Rosemary cleared her throat and nestled her hands comfortably across her knee. "My name is Rosemary Cherry. I am part of the Advisory. Your proctor, Nina, is a member as well. I would—"

Nina interrupted, "Where's Nix?"

The entire room swung their heads with their eyes peeled.

"Like the lice shampoo?" Leo asked, half serious. It was the only Nix he knew.

"Nix De La Fuente. He's another member of the Advisory," Nina said softly as she continued looking for him.

"Bloody hell," Rosemary said. "Every single time. It's always the same thing. Always late. Always *distracted*. Nix! Nix! Where the hell are you?"

Nix rounded the corner and entered the great room.

"We're starting in here. Is there something you need?" Nina asked politely, but with authority.

"Sorry—just taking a look at what you've done with the house," Nix said. "It really does have a personality now. It tells a story like a beautifully written song."

"Have you been drinking?" Per asked. "The last time I heard you say that was at my Beltane party."

"That was different," Nix replied as he sat down on the couch.

"Yeah, you were drunk. All night you stumbled around like Bradley Cooper in that movie with Lady Gaga."

"Enough already!" Rosemary screeched. "Sit down and shut up." She made introductions around the room. "I'm Rosemary Cherry. This is Nix De La Fuente, the Keeper of Books and Assets. And Per Kaji. Together with Nina, we make up the Advisory. I know this is the first time any of you have seen us, but we aren't a group that is ordinarily seen." There was a long pause. At last, she began to tell them why the Advisory was meeting at their house. "There are witches coming into their own all over the world. Not hordes of them, but enough. Every day there's potential for another witch to *be born*, now that the gene is active from the shift in energy. We came here today to discuss some very alarming news with you. We try, as a whole, to keep an eye on the magic community. It's no easy task, and you'd be grateful never to have to be in our position. It has come to our attention that a witch—a budding witch, completely unaware of his own power—has been killed. Murdered. For the very fact that he was a witch."

The room fell silent. Even the air outside seemed void of all noise and wildlife.

"We don't know who exactly is behind it," Rosemary said. "But we do know that it isn't entirely safe. For any of us."

"We don't mean to scare you. That's certainly not why we're here," Nix said reassuringly.

"In fact, it's quite the opposite," Rosemary added.

"We came, as a group, as the Advisory, to let you know you have allies and support," Per said before he took a moment to meditate on the severity of the issue. "Sadly, this is common during a shift."

"What do you mean we're not safe?" Avery asked, her white face now almost ghostly.

"It could be any manner of person, or being," Per said.

"Could it be other witches?" Bisa asked.

"I wouldn't like to say yes, but if I'm to be fully honest, I would have to say that it's entirely possible. There are other witches out there, and around the world for that matter, who don't always agree with the common principles that are of the majority. In fact, in my experience, some actually despise those principles," Rosemary said.

Leo took a hit from his vape. "Y'all don't think you're just overreacting a little? I mean, do we know for sure this is like, a hate crime against witches or whatever?"

"Yes," Rosemary said absolutely.

"How?"

"You'll just have to believe us when we say that we know it is. Have you not seen enough that allows you to have faith in that?" Rosemary added.

"I don't know. I still think this one incident isn't really, like, something to start boarding our windows up over or anything," Leo said casually.

Avery rolled her eyes before she used them to stare at Leo. "Are you seriously that apathetic about this? Someone's dead. Another *witch* is dead. You're a witch. Don't you feel anything? Ever?"

Leo blew some smoke into the middle of the room. He leaned back in his chair, ripe with indifference. "I'm just not that deep."

"I don't care what I'm able to do, I don't want to be killed over it. It's not like I signed up for this and agreed to have a bull's-eye on my back!" Avery squinted as she ran through the different possibilities of death in her head, hoping that none of them would come for her. "I don't mean to sound…however it is that I sound right now…but I think we all need to be on the same page with this. I mean, we should work *together*. As much as you drive me insane, Leo, I don't want you dead. I don't want to be dead either!"

Mitch sat forward in his seat and timidly scratched his head. "I don't want anyone to die either, but Leo might be right. We could just be jumping, like, the gun, a little bit. Maybe?"

Avery's mouth dropped in horror.

Bisa's head flip-flopped back and forth, as if deciding between viewpoints. "Maybe we should just really figure out what we know first before we make any huge decisions."

Avery's head, which was overcrowded with emotion and thought, was allowing anything and everything to spill out. She spun around, rotisserie-style, and then took a deep breath in through her nose. "You know, I can smell your attraction to him." Avery indicated Bisa and Mitch with her finger. "And it's frustrating because it's clouding your judgment about him being so careless. That's a dangerous way to think with what we were just told. You both have a blind spot, and blind spots come with denial. People who are in denial make bad choices. We need to maybe prepare ourselves for this and be a little more cautious until we figure out who the fuck is out there *hunting witches*! We might be next, and with that attitude, we will make easy targets. Life is way too short and I care way too much about living it to be picked off and murdered because no one takes this seriously."

Nina stood up and walked over toward Avery to soothe her. "Avery, we're going to figure this out before it would ever come to that."

Avery turned her head with tornado-like speed and caught Nina off guard. She hadn't seen Avery this riled up before. "Nina, all due respect and everything, but one of my biggest pet peeves is not being taken seriously. One of my biggest loves is life and being able to experience as much of it as I can."

Rosemary stood up from her seat. "Avery, dear, I assure you, Nina and the Advisory are taking this seriously."

"No one ever said we'd be in danger!" Avery spat.

"What do you think life is?" Leo said. "I don't know where you grew up, but in the real world where everyone else lives, things are dangerous and shitty and people die and you can't save anyone or protect anyone from anything."

"That's exactly the type of attitude that probably got your daughter killed," Avery said.

Leo stood up and threw his vape into a vase with earth-shattering force. "You need to shut the fuck up about things you know nothing about! Who the fuck do you think you are?"

"I'm not your ex-girlfriend. I'm not going to let you take me down with you!"

Nina stepped into the swirling tension between Avery and Leo and shouted, "Stop!"

"Man, you're lucky Nina is fuckin' here right now or I'd fuck you up like the little cunt that you're being!" Leo shouted, his words as cold and toxic as the memories Avery had unearthed at the mention of his ex-girlfriend. The endless, rage-fueled, inarticulate arguments with a vocabulary that consisted mostly of *fuck*, *fucking* and *fuck you*. That same anger filled him up and spattered out in all directions like an oil spill in a nature reserve. Avery's words stung because part of it was true and he knew it. But he would never admit it. Not yet. He couldn't. He wasn't ready, he wasn't able.

"Oh, go drop some acid and escape again," Avery uttered.

Rosemary clapped her hands together and the room was filled with an ear-splitting crack of thunder. A quick strobe of esoteric light flashed before everyone's eyes with the blinding power of the sun upon waking—the kind of light that could disinfect things if they were exposed to it for too long. Everyone, including the other members of the Advisory, struggled to regain composure as Rosemary approached the dispute. She had always been affable, and people usually felt at ease in her presence. Even people who didn't like her forward personality still enjoyed being in her company. Only now she unveiled a different side of herself, one that saw the nastiness in the world and responded to it with intensity.

"This stops *now*!" Rosemary said bluntly. "We will never survive with this kind of behavior, and if this coven is so hell-bent on being at each other's throats, we might as well do whoever is after our heads a favor and rip ourselves to pieces before they have a chance. Because if this is how we react to a different perspective, well, frankly, I don't believe that's even something worth fighting for. So before either of you, *any of you*, speak another word, I want you to think long and hard about what you say. This world is fueled by examples, and people repeat the patterns they learn by example, unless we break that wheel and create change. That is what our powers are for, and if we can't agree on that, then no one here deserves the gifts they have. What kind of world do you want to live in? Is this how you want to continue? Is that how you prefer people to act? If so, then everything you've learned and done is a waste of time."

Thirty minutes later, the members of the Advisory had said all they needed to say and left. Nina's stomach struggled to settle down as she ran over the argument between Leo and Avery in her head. She retreated to her room and ran herself a bath. Her energy had been sapped during the discussion along with her confidence to competently lead the coven. It was an idea that polluted her mind every now and then and one that proved to be difficult to quell.

Most of the coven found that they needed some time to themselves to let Rosemary's words sink in deep. Ollie watered his plants and spent some time in deep meditation in his room. Bisa mixed a few special elixirs and potions into her paint and continued working on her painting. Mitch was about to consult the tarot in his room when he suddenly felt a surge race through his body. He stopped in his tracks. He felt warm like when he took a shot of whiskey, only the warmth was everywhere. He ran his hands over his body, feeling for temperature changes, but his skin felt completely normal.

Mitch took a breath and walked to the bathroom mirror to check for anything physically out of the ordinary. Nothing new. Same old Mitch. Then all of a sudden, he had a rush of thoughts, followed by a feeling of confidence. It transitioned into what felt like a dream that had been draped over the waking world. For a moment he thought perhaps he was the victim of some kind of dark magic and was going to be the next witch to turn up dead before he even knew what was coming. He looked deep into the eyes staring back at him in the mirror. It suddenly all made sense. The world around him hadn't changed, but he felt—knew—that he had some sort of sway over it. Everything around him looked slightly more interesting than it had before. It sounded like something Leo would say, something an acid lover would say when trying to describe what the world looks like while on drugs. But he wasn't on drugs. Unless you counted a potion being a kind of drug.

In that instant, he remembered the potion he had drunk and everything fell into place. It had worked. Or at least he was finally starting to feel the effects of it. Whether it was serving its purpose was up for debate. Suddenly Mitch darted out of the bathroom and into Leo's room with a new kind of coolness. Of course, he was unwelcome, and Leo desired nothing more than to be left alone, listening to "Effervescent" by All Them Witches on repeat. Neither of those things mattered. Mitch began a conversation, delicately at first, as Leo would have expected, but slowly pushed the boundaries of Leo's free will as he looked into his eyes, over his lips and down the length of his legs. It was difficult for Mitch to be around Leo at times, especially when he wore sleeveless shirts or gym shorts. That was not the case this time. Mitch was in control and abnormally unflappable. It was how he dreamed he could be around Leo, only this wasn't a dream; it was real. If anything, it felt more like a lucid dream, one where he called the shots and always got his way.

Mitch continued to control the flow of conversation and directed it from the frustrated energy that arose out in the great room to a more romantic one. He shut the door and sat down on the bed next to Leo. He felt like Leo was giving him a sort of permission. It was undeniable, although he couldn't be certain whether it was truly consent or only what he wanted from Leo. Mitch could smell Leo, and quite strongly, more than he'd ever been able to before. *Did that potion boost my senses too?* he wondered. As Leo continued to talk as if reciting a monologue, Mitch continued to scoot closer.

Leo reached into his pants and scratched his balls, indifferent to Mitch's presence. "Let me smell your fingers," Mitch demanded with a seductive undertone, his eyes bright and unashamed.

Leo looked back at Mitch with a puzzled and amused expression. "No," he answered, laughing.

Mitch was going to get what he wanted. He knew it like he knew the potion had worked. "Let me smell your fingers!" he said again, this time with a crippling sense of command. But in a nice way.

Leo reached up and slapped Mitch's face, but slowly, so his fingertips brushed teasingly under his nose. From the corner of his eye, Mitch noticed something move inside Leo's shorts. Something that could only be one thing. The smell in the air was sweet and spicy, the smell of heterosexual experimentation, sloppy kisses and naked skin. It smelled like what Mitch dreamed of during his moments of lust when he stared at Leo just a little too long. It was better than anything he had imagined this moment would smell like. Leo rose from the bed just enough to slide up next to Mitch. Their thighs touched, their faces only inches apart.

Mitch eyed the features of Leo's face as if looking for hidden treasure he was desperate to find. He hadn't ever dreamed of finding treasure, but he had dreamed of moments like this. The power of influence coursed through his entire body and pumped through his heart, which beat with the entrancing rhythm of a drum circle in Congo Square. His breath was disrupted by the overwhelming percussion from inside his chest. His lips parted expectantly. Finally, in a soft, hot gush of air, from the very crux of his desire came a tender request.

"Can I kiss you?" Leo asked.

Mitch said nothing. He was utterly speechless. His eyelids flickered as he struggled to come up with a response. Mitch reached up and stroked the length of Leo's dainty ear, from the top down to the lobeless bottom. When his fingers reached Leo's face, his hand pushed around to the back of his head and he locked Leo's cinnamon hair between his fingers. Mitch braced himself for what was about to happen, what he had only dreamed of happening. He looked into Leo's amber-green eyes as Leo leaned in toward his lips. Mitch's lips touched the side of Leo's face, and with a trembling lip, he approached Leo's mouth. He had kissed many people in his life, some of them women, but none of them compared to this encounter. Not by a long shot.

The kiss, gentle at first, transitioned into longer and more passionate kisses. For the first time in what seemed like ages, Mitch felt successful at something. He'd achieved something. This kiss wasn't just another item on his list of failures or under-achievements. Minutes became hours in the fantasy-turned-reality that was Leo's kiss. Mitch explored Leo's body with his hands, feeling the erection that throbbed in his gym shorts, now a little wet. Had Leo always been this open-minded or was this just the power of influence? While Mitch removed Leo's shirt and trailed his mouth from the neck to his nipple with a series of kisses, he had but one thought: *magic is fucking awesome.*

By the time they were both in their underwear, Leo had started to take control, as if he finally had found the food he had been starving for his entire life. It was extraordinary. They tumbled together onto the floor, naked. Mitch, no longer holding back apprehensively, looked down and stared at Leo's dick. It was harder than he had ever expected a straight man's to be, and curved just enough to not be straight. Mitch laughed as he considered the irony of that. Over the next thirty minutes, their faces were wrapped in pleasure, amazement and otherworldly ecstasy. There were no words, only slow and heavy breaths, nothing like the gay porn that polluted the internet and spoiled his expectations. It was exactly everything he wanted. It was oral exploration beyond casual connection, and spiritual in form. Graceful kisses and soothing tongue strokes that left him wet in places even the humidity couldn't reach.

Mitch was edging toward climax when Leo finished all over Mitch's chest in an unexpected yet explosive ending. A few minutes later, they rested on the floor together, limbs curled around and tangled with one another. Mitch caught his breath as he watched the blades of the ceiling fan spin. Leo was unfazed by the intimacy and showed no signs of being uncomfortable. A dubious expression fell across Mitch's face as he wondered how long this would last. Fearful of the result of his actions, he gathered up his clothes, wiped himself clean with his socks and got dressed. *Did I just trick him into having sex with me?* Mitch asked himself as he avoided making eye contact with Leo. *How long is this potion good for?*

While Mitch was deciding whether he should stay and explain or just pretend it hadn't happened, the effects of his influence wore off.

"Dude, what the *fuck*?" Leo shook his head and held his hands out as if trying to stop a moving train.

"What?" Mitch asked. But he didn't have to ask. He already knew. He knew full well what had happened.

"I think you need to leave. Just get out."

Mitch's shoulders tightened up as he struggled to find what to say. "Do you hate me now?"

"I don't know how you did it, or why you did it, but I know for damn sure that I wasn't in complete control. I'm not stupid. I'm not gay, dude!"

"I know you're not gay!"

Leo peered sternly from the middle of the room, where he picked up his clothes and slipped them back on. "Then why'd that happen? I don't even wanna know how you made that happen. That creeps me out even more. I've never had a friendship like this, you know that!"

"You don't have to remind me," Mitch said. "I already feel bad." That was partially true. He was conflicted over how guilty he actually felt. He would have been lying to himself if he'd said he believed Leo was completely straight. Leo was too comfortable with his sexuality.

"I never in a million years thought you'd do something like that. I mean, at least if you were drunk or fucked up, I could pass it off as that. But you're clearly super sober! And I mean,

I feel like I've been pretty cool about all of this. I'm not a very tolerant person when it comes to most things, but I've been pretty tolerant and accepting of all this gay energy you keep throwing at me. But it was always like, in good fun, and I *knew* there was a line, even if it was a little fuzzy. I never thought you'd cross it, or cross it like *this*! That's how I know you did it! Because I know I wouldn't have done that."

Although he identified as—knew he was—straight, Leo had found the kissing, oral and touching more satisfying with Mitch than with any woman he had ever been with. He would never admit that, but he was into it. So much in fact, that it wasn't Mitch's potion that held influence over Leo, it was Leo who held influence over Mitch. The potion could have worked, but Mitch wasn't quite skilled enough to mix and activate it. "Dude, I love you, you're my friend, and I've never had a friendship like this before with anyone. You've been a really pivotal person in my life. All the stupid crap aside, you've been there for me and you've tried to help me see the positive in my hellhole of a life. You really showed me what it means to be a *friend*. That's why it's so fucked up, dude!" His eyes lowered to the ground as he suddenly thought about all the times he had manipulated women into sex, women who probably would have given him a speech very similar to the one he was giving now if any of them were to have said something. For a moment, Leo felt like a hypocrite and thought he should stop judging Mitch for doing what he had done out of love, or whatever he thought it was. But what could he actually say? *I know how you feel. I've wanted someone so bad that I just…had them. But what you did was different.* That wouldn't exactly make a whole lot of sense. So he kept his mouth shut.

Mitch agreed that his actions were appalling and that their friendship was special, but couldn't bring himself to say anything in return. Leo stared at him with the intensity of the connection they had shared only moments earlier. He wasn't angry, but he wasn't exactly at ease either. It was like being under a ceiling fan in a sweltering room. There was a long bout of silence as Mitch stood by the door and Leo by his bed, finally in underwear.

"Look, dude," Leo said. "I don't hate you. But I also don't really wanna see you right now. Can you just get out? Please."

Mitch—who had had the luxury of getting exactly what he wanted—turned toward the door with a spin in which shame and satisfaction were felt equally. He left the room and closed the door behind him. His shirt was crumpled, and he stuck his soiled socks into the pockets of his pants to wash later. He reached the door to the bathroom but stopped in the doorway. Avery was inside applying lotion to her hands. There was utter silence as they looked at each other in the mirror. Avery turned to face him. She could smell what had happened, the emotions, the radiance of pleasure, the anguish of being attracted to someone who would not and could not return the attraction. It emanated from Mitch like the smell of burnt toast in a kitchen.

Avery let out a sigh. "You know, you can't save him. Not even by forcing him to fall for you," she said without reproach. Avery placed an emboldened and understanding hand on Mitch's shoulder as she passed through the doorway and left the bathroom. The empathic exchange was over, and Mitch was alone. He entered the bathroom, shut the door and sat in silence on the toilet. In the middle of shifting thoughts, he heard a sound. He took a moment to determine whether he had really heard something. Silence. A minute later, the sound returned.

There was no mistaking it. He knew what it was, but it made absolutely no sense to be hearing it, not in the bathroom. He stood up and walked to the sink. It actually was there. If not by chance, then by magic.

Ribbit! Ribbit! The frog croaked as it jumped to the counter.

There was so much inside Mitch's head that he found it increasingly difficult to make sense of what the frog was doing there. He couldn't even speak. He just stared at the bulbous eyes of the slick, green frog.

Ribbit! Ribbit…Ribbit!

He concentrated on the frog's movement and shook off his sense of drama. Then the frog made another noise—not the familiar and repetitive *ribbit* he'd been hearing, but a voice. The frog had said something, but its mouth hadn't moved. It was a voice like honey, much different from how he expected a frog to sound.

"I am here to help you. I am here to teach you…" the frog said.

"Teach me what?" Mitch asked, feeling half crazy.

Ribbit!

"Oh, come on!"

Mitch reached down to collect the frog, but as his finger made contact with the smooth, slick skin, the frog disappeared. *Was that my totem animal?* Mitch thought. *Oh my God. All that crazy shit in the woods really did work!*

CHAPTER 29

T he next morning, Avery made banana pancakes and bacon for everyone. Ollie, Nina and Bisa were chatting while Avery listened closely. None of them actually realized that Leo and Mitch hadn't said much of anything to anyone.

"I'd like for us to do a peace and protection ritual tonight," Nina said as she cut into a fluffy pancake.

Everyone remained quiet. Leo rolled his eyes a little, assuming that the ritual was to help put everyone's mind at ease about the murdered witch. Nina repeated herself to make sure she had everyone's attention.

"I'm going to take a spell I already know and personalize it by having all of you contribute. Avery, I'd like you to make a gem elixir—infuse it with your honey. Ollie, make up some kind of anointing oil, anything you'd like. Bisa, please prepare a ritual salt and bottle it. Mitch, I want you to do some water spells, make something that can amplify our power. And Leo, I need you to make a sachet of some herbs. Make sure you pick the ones that are best for protection. If you don't know which ones, I'm sure Ollie can help you with it. It's not enough to just know something. We have to actually *do* something to get better at it."

Leo finished his pancakes and stood up from the table. He grabbed a single apple from the center of the table and placed his dishes in the sink.

"Leo, are you listening?" Nina asked.

He hated it when someone asked if he was listening. "Yes! I heard you!"

Later, when the evening sky had turned black, they conducted the ritual in the great room. It was cool and moist, the backyard covered in a post-rain fog. Everyone had done their homework, and as they carried out the ritual, the wind outside picked up and started to rattle the windows. It sounded like pebbles against a wooden fence. The coven had found their rhythm with rituals, seeming more cohesive than like a circle of people with nervous smiles that said I-have-no-idea-what-I'm-doing. Their organized fashion led them to finish seamlessly and faster than expected. Leo always left the circle earlier than anyone else, passing time by not helping with the post-ritual cleanup, and eating snacks, although it wasn't unusual to see him playing with ritual items while everyone else was gathering them up to put them away—with a half-empty box of cereal in one hand—like a junior high boy. After a while, everyone stopped trying to force him to help and just acknowledged his presence with a shake of the head, roll of the eyes or muttering under their breath. Leo never seemed to mind.

However, his demeanor was a little different this time. He participated in the ritual without any smug comments, and he cleaned up the ritual space without anyone having to ask him to help. It was as if he had become someone else entirely, someone with manners. Clearly, something was wrong—something was on his mind. Nina was the first to reach out to him.

"Leo. Everything all right? What's the matter?"

Leo looked up at Nina, surprised that someone could tell something was wrong. "Nothing."

Nina tilted her head. She didn't need Avery's ability to sniff out a lie. "Now, I know that's not true. You've been acting strange all day. What's going on?"

"I've just been thinking a lot about stuff."

"Like what?" Nina asked in a low voice.

"Lots of things. I'm just tired of being unhappy. You know? I feel like I've been like this all my life, no matter what I've done. I just can't fix it. I can't change it. I feel like a fuckin' loser."

"Where is this coming from?" Nina asked, astonished.

"The world! Everyone in it! My past!"

"Do you know how much you've accomplished just by being here? Think about what you've done. You have wonderful gifts. Sure, maybe you could work on smoothing out some of your rough edges a little more, but that doesn't mean you're a failure."

"I've been thinking about my daughter and my ex a lot. Even that…even then…I don't think I was really, like, happy. So what good is all of this magic if it only makes me successful at magic but doesn't change how I feel? And I'm so tired of the way everyone looks at me—not just everyone here in the house, but everyone who has ever known me. The older I get, the more I feel it. This look like, *That guy is a lost cause. He's never going to achieve anything.*"

"It's not going to help if you keep it all in. We can work on this together. Now, I don't have all the answers, but I sure as hell can help you try to find some. If you want. If you need help…ask for it. You know that." Nina looked down to see an apple sticking halfway out of his pocket. "Why do you have an apple in your pocket?"

Leo shrugged and winked. "Not enough room for another banana." He smiled and left to go for a ride on his bike.

CHAPTER 30

The swamp was empty, just as Leo had hoped it would be. He biked to a secluded area and followed a tiny path through the grass, carrying a flashlight and a burlap sack, the sounds of the woodlands buzzing all around him. He looked around at the encasing forest, so alive it seemed to be looking back at him. It wouldn't have surprised him if the forest had spoken.

The farther he walked, the deeper he went into his own memories. He saw himself at seventeen, dropping acid and getting a blow job from that trashy girl from Alabama. Memories of himself at twenty-three, candy-flipping and watching old Adult Swim videos on YouTube with people whose names he couldn't remember now. Then the memory of himself only a few years earlier, holding his daughter only thirty minutes after shooting up with his now ex-girlfriend, Tonya. At times like this, he often regretted all of it but was content with it all the same. There was a strange sort of comfort in being uncomfortable. It was the norm. It hadn't ever been anything different. Who was he to try to change nature? How many people could say they'd lived a life like he had and come out alive? If he had changed anything about it, would he have gotten as much pleasure out of life? He wasn't sure how to answer any of his own questions.

Leo's feet snapped a few branches that fell across the path as he proceeded to a small clearing. The night sky was fixed with a few stagnant clouds, reflecting the urban light from the nearby cities in colors of rust and mauve, and tinges of gray. From his pocket, he pulled out the apple and split it nearly in half with a knife. From his other pocket, he removed a piece of paper with illegible words that bled from having been doused in an elixir he had made earlier. He folded the tiny scrap of paper and slipped it deep into the crevice of the apple.

There was another ripple of memories steeped in emotions he wasn't prepared for. He remembered his daughter. Her smiles, the way she had preferred rattles over stuffed toys, the sound of his knees hitting the pavement when he learned she was dead. He recalled a street of red, stained with blood and bathed in police lights. Leo had told Tonya to pick up more booze and take Krystal with her. She was already drunk. And high. By the time she collided with the tree, she had already passed out.

Leo's eyes were bloodshot as he tried to choke back his emotions. He placed the apple inside the burlap sack and looked around for the best place to bury it and cast the spell. It was a small patch of soft ground, cold and wet from the winter rain. Leo closed his eyes and saw the image of his daughter. He commonly referred to her as his *daughter* instead of as Krystal because her name was too difficult for him to say out loud. He dropped to his knees in the same fashion as he had years ago at the crash site. He twisted the burlap tight and began to dig with his bare hands. Leo lifted one fistful of dirt out of the earth after the other. His hands hooked like lobster claws.

Deeper. Deeper.

It didn't matter how high he had been the night of the crash: the sight of Krystal on the road, surrounded by shattered glass, plunged him into a sobering misery.

Deeper. Deeper.

His hands were black from the mud. So much hadn't changed since that night, he realized. Leo was stuck in unending grief. Continually covering up reality was the only way he could deal, all while hoping that his reality was passing itself off as a lifelike and convincing nightmare. There was a sudden uptick in the wind.

Deeper.

Tears welled up in his red eyes. It was an event so rare, like seeing a comet, that he knew he would have little control over it once the floodgates opened.

Deeper.

And then a rock. A sizable gray stone was embedded in the earth. As tears began to roll down his cheeks, Leo tried to dig it out with his hands. He was eight inches deep and couldn't go any farther. In a fit of frustration, he pounded the rock with his muddy fist. A few more tears seeped out and fell into the hole. Leo fingered the sides of the rock a second time, hoping for the best, but he had gone as far as he could go. There were feelings he wished would go away, feelings that all the drugs in the world couldn't wipe clean. The only hope he had left was that the pain would just go away, just this once. He broke down in sobs, drool oozing out of his mouth and hanging from his bottom lip like a spider's first web strand. When his dirty hands had given the sack a final twist, he slammed the apple against the rock, and rivers of wetness erupted from his eyes.

Smack!

He curled over the hole the way a caterpillar curls when someone disturbs it. Then, he suddenly whipped back and slammed the bag into the rock—violently—like a man who had run out of options and lost all chances for happiness.

Smack!

Again. And again. He hit the rock over and over, as he would hit a pipe or shoot up, again and again. The dirt that was snugly fastened to the rock began to sputter like the surface of boiling water. He dropped the bag and began using his hands instead. His fists collided with the rock, and the dirt erupted, sending sprays into the air and leaving a zigzag crack down the center. Leo drilled his fist into the rock once again, this time jeopardizing his eyesight as fragments splintered off and shot into the air. Every emotion he was capable of suffering, even some that he hadn't discovered yet, awakened—all at once. They were the kind of feelings that only intensified over time and fed on repression.

The energy behind Leo's unearthed depression put new strains on his composure, his mask of apathy that was stretched too thin and crafted from a lie. He tossed the chunks of rock aside and added the bag with the apple to the hole. Leo had cried maybe fewer than five times in his life and had always felt relieved afterward. Not this time. He could feel his pulse in his eyes as his hands shook with rage, sadness and regret. Maybe the emotions were so strong because he was sober for the first time in a long time. Magic had become the perfect substitute. There was a drawback to it: it didn't numb him. It was a distraction, but a sober one, and with sobriety came the harrowing truth of his reality. His daughter was dead, and there was nothing he could do about it. He had failed her just as his parents had failed him in ways he had vowed never to repeat.

Leo's face leaked and drooled uncontrollably as he buried the bag and filled in the hole with dirt. The seed had been planted, the spell had been cast. When there was no more dirt and he knelt before solid ground, he pounded his fists against the newly turned earth, packing it solid. It was as if he were burying his daughter all over again, his hands soiled from dirt he had thrown onto the coffin, only this time that coffin was a burlap sack that he hoped to bury forever along with his guilt. The truth was he didn't even fully know what he wanted from the spell or what he expected to achieve; he just wanted things to be different.

Leo struggled with the word *father* and what it really meant. In his mind, a father was someone who had no life of his own because he had given it up to care for and nurture his child. He didn't remember truly doing either of those things. The only true thing he could remember in solid detail was the number of times he had had the chance to be a father and hadn't been. That was easier to remember because there had been so many chances.

Leo looked up into the weeds ahead of him and saw a single cattail swaying in the breeze. It was like some kind of sick joke that it was there staring back at him: his daughter's favorite thing to play with in the marshes. Why could he remember that above all else? It only made the pain worse. With the flood of tears came all the memories of things he had considered trivial, like debris carried by rushing water during a hurricane. Without something to stop the current, the debris would be too weighty to bear. It wasn't the debris that saddened him most, it was who it belonged to, a figure in his life he had neglected out of selfishness and could never make amends to, no matter how many tears he cried.

After Leo had been a professional line cook, he had been a masonry worker, not a construction laborer who did all the digging. He dug and filled that hole in the ground regardless. There was a large chunk of rock now by his side. Without thinking twice about it, he scooped the rock up with his hands and began to pound it into the dirt, packing the soil tight. He no longer worked in construction, but the insane-with-grief Leo, years after the drugged-zombie, horrible-father Leo, years before the new Leo of whom he was not yet aware, was determined to use the small list of skills he had picked up in construction to make sure the ground was flat. The sweat on his body froze his skin in the night air.

With one final thump, Leo slammed the rock into the ground, and in what sounded like a reheated meal cooked for too long in a microwave, the rock popped, sizzled and began to melt. Streams of a mercury-like substance poured over the sides of his hands and erupted from the ground all around him. He stopped crying, got out of his head and looked around. Steaming rivers of shiny fluid made it seem like he was in the middle of a geyser that had just risen to the surface and was ready to blow. *What's happening? What did I do?*

It was mercury. He couldn't smile, he couldn't cry, he couldn't react until he caught his breath. Leo forgot about the spell. His eyes were bursting with amazement, not because of what happened, or how, but because of what was unearthed by the fissures in the ground. Perhaps there was light at the end of a very long and dark tunnel. Maybe there was some hope for him left. Maybe he had just turned over a new leaf when he released all that grief and pain, and was being rewarded for doing so. He didn't care. If anyone had known what had just happened, they might've been shocked or a little jealous, but he was sure as hell they wouldn't have realized why he was so thrilled about it. He needed it. It looked like mercury, just like the mercury in the old thermostat on the wall at the house where he grew up. It would make for the first addition to his list of metals to obtain.

Leo wiped his hands on his pants, dug into his pocket and pulled out a tiny vial. It was the remainder of the elixir he had used to consecrate the paper that was inside the apple. He dumped it out feverishly and began to scoop the molten metal into the vial with a dead leaf. His breath was heavy as he collected the mercury like a squirrel after nuts. He grinned, the corners of his mouth wet from tears. One metal down, six to go.

CHAPTER 31

The Bonners had received more money than anticipated from their fund-raiser. Edie counted it three times just to make sure her numbers were correct. The math was as right as her members were loyal.

"Joshua, dear, I know that you have some plans for the Baton Rouge campus and all, but I want to talk to you about some plans I have of my own!" Edie said.

"What more could you want?" Joshua said as he shook his head at his wife's insatiable appetite. It extended beyond pie and into the beyond.

Edie explained her plans for the new campus and added in renovations to their current church, which included a new "office." All through their relationship, Josh had known that Edie was a go-getter with ambitions as high as the temperature in August, but at times it was truly exhausting. He was content, and even slightly overwhelmed as their operations within the church continued to grow. It was hard work being in control of so many lives while still trying to control your own. There was a certain kind of coloring that Edie's skin took on when she was excited about something, a rosiness that he often saw, especially when she wore that one pink suit that looked like raspberry frosting. She was just so darling, how could he ever tell her no?

She ran through her plans for the new campus and even showed him pictures of listings online that she thought would be excellent places to invest in—not just for financial reasons but based on demographics. The longer she talked, the more he was convinced. It may have been out of sheer fatigue from having to listen to her energized and motivated pitch, but mostly it was that he wanted her to be happy. She had flaws, but he still wanted the best for her, for them, and at his age and at the height of his career, he was content with letting that be the way it was.

"I've already talked to the architect…"

"Who? Charles?" Josh asked.

"Oh Lord, not him. That man is all hat and no cattle. Don't you remember the mess we found ourselves in when he tried to renovate the youth wing? I was certain that roof was going to cave right in on all those kids! Remember? That's when I found Mr. Roland, the architect who did that snowball shop over in Denham Springs—remember the one we used to stop at on the way to the other campus? He looked at it and found all sorts of issues, and that's when I went back to Charles madder than a wet hen and called him out for it."

"Ah yes, I remember." Josh nodded, but he was only half listening.

"That's why the roof had to be done twice. Anyway, so I called him, and he's agreed to do some work for us to add on a new…office."

Joshua looked up from the papers on his desk, brow wrinkled. "A new office? What's wrong with this one all of a sudden? We just got new carpet in here and everything!"

Edie stuck the tip of her tongue out and pressed it to her upper lip. "Honey, it's not that kind of office. It'll be for our *other*…office work."

Oh Lord, that woman is going to outlive us all with ambitions like that.

Edie winked. "Excuse me, I need to go find some ibuprofen. I've got another nasty headache. I don't know what's going on. The barometric pressure or whatever, stress or, I don't know what. We'll talk after I hear from Mr. Roland." Grinning, she left the room.

CHAPTER 32

Bisa had scaled back from taking two showers a day to one now that the weather had cooled off a bit. It was bittersweet, because it was her time to relax as much as it was to bathe. She was one of those people who took forty-minute showers but spent thirty of those minutes simply standing under the running water. She had been thinking a lot about how she had ended up in Louisiana, the job she left behind and whether she was actually still employed. She hadn't been able to figure that one out yet, no matter how many times she brought it up to Nina. Every so often she would think about her native Nigeria and how wild her journey had been from then to the present. She was somewhere doing things she had never, ever expected or even deemed possible. Nigeria was a thought that came and went faster than the weather in New Orleans. It wasn't exactly the prettiest bit of nostalgia to mull over. That was usually when she turned off the water and slipped out of the shower, which was exactly the case tonight.

She stood in front of the fogged mirror, wrapped in a large towel. She removed her shower cap and began to blot her skin dry with another free towel. Bisa reached forward and wiped her hand across the mirror like a car's wiper blade until she could find her reflection. Something caught her eye in the mirror image of herself. There was a strange aubergine-colored section on her left shoulder—a ring, no larger than a silver dollar. Bisa had gotten used to seeing strange things and having bizarre dreams, but she was awake. After it didn't go away within a few blinks of her eyes, she looked down at her shoulder. It wasn't a hallucination, it was real. It hadn't been there in the shower, but there it was now, a bulging loop under her bruised skin.

Bisa breathed out a panicked gasp and reached up with her right hand to touch it. Her fingers pulled back as if electrocuted. Then she noticed the tail. The ring wasn't a complete ring at all. It would've been had there not been a strange spongy tail the color of rotted pumpkin spiking out from her skin. First, Bisa tried to pluck it out with her fingers, only to find that the segment broke off under the pressure of her fingernails and the body slithered farther inside. She could feel the movement under her skin like a piece of glass being flossed through a wound. Then, she attempted to remove it with a pair of tweezers. She should have known it wasn't going to work. For years, people had been telling her that her tweezers sucked. They were cheaply made ones from the drugstore, without a brand name, nothing like the high-quality stainless steel tweezers by Anastasia Beverly Hills that she used to sell to customers at Warpaint. She would say they worked flawlessly no matter how small or fine the hair was and plucked and shaped brows so well that you couldn't even feel it.

Bisa stuck the tweezers into the small flesh wound on her shoulder and tried to catch the remainder of the worm. As she suspected, another segment broke off under the dull, flat tips of the tweezers. The worm repositioned and slithered in a little farther. Clusters of rings started to sprout like branches from a tree. It burned, and no amount of digging could remove whatever was under her skin. Not even the most expensive beauty equipment at Warpaint could have done the trick. Terror coursed through her veins as the burning sensation began to expand down her chest and out to her arms. Before she could think of what to do next, her equilibrium was thrown off and she started to topple under the strength of her dizziness. Her stomach turned in agony, and her heart began to change its rhythm. *Am I dying?* she thought in the moments before she called out for help.

"Avery!" she yelled. Then a few coughs shot out from her throat. "Nina!" Bisa screamed with all the energy she had, the kind of scream that expanded the rib cage and required honey to heal the throat. It was beastly and rippled with fear. She had screamed like that only one other time in her life, and it was a scream she never wanted to scream again. As her knees finally gave out, the door opened and she collapsed into Avery's arms. Avery fought to keep Bisa on her feet as she asked what was wrong, but it wasn't long before Bisa had taken Avery down to the floor with her.

Then Avery saw it—although what, she couldn't say. Bisa's shoulder looked bruised and alive as the worms continued to slide under her flesh. Bisa scratched and clawed at her shoulder, and then at her clavicle as the worms started to spread toward her throat. A horrible, clotted sound gushed from Bisa's throat, similar to that of water trying to squeeze through a congested drain. Her eyes were everywhere, looking for help, white and protruding.

"Nina! Help! Hurry!" Avery shouted in desperation. She had no idea what was wrong or what to do. "You're going to be okay," she said to Bisa, stroking her forehead. "Everything's okay."

Bisa's rich color began to drain from her face. Avery held a shaking hand over the affected area. Primordials were supposed to be physical healers. She hadn't been trained, but if there was ever a time to try, it was now. Avery was concentrating as best she could under pressure when suddenly she saw her hand surrounded with a hazy, almost illusory energy. The energy flowed from her hands and fell onto Bisa's body like the softest of snow. Avery waved her hand over Bisa's body and slowed the infection, whatever it was. But it wasn't enough. The cluster of worms continued to spread, as if their slower pace were only teasing Avery. Suddenly, Avery felt a sharp sting in her palm. She had been accidentally stung by her bees before and had grown used to it. But this sting was worse, as if the entire colony had stung her palm all at once, all in the same spot. Avery turned her hand over and saw the exact same patterns embedded deep within her skin, a tail sticking out and waving from the center of her palm.

She screamed and immediately attempted to pluck out one of the worms, but with no more success than Bisa had had. The ring started to spread, but faster than it had for Bisa. Avery convulsed and fell to the floor, her throat clicking and her tongue tossing in circles as she tried to scream. Bisa let out a syrupy cough and struggled to catch her breath. Avery was shaking, and Bisa was choking and turning purple.

Hustling footsteps were heard approaching from around the corner. A stream of blood began to run from Bisa's nose as she faded from consciousness. Leo, Mitch and Nina entered the bathroom to find Bisa motionless and tangled in Avery's jerking limbs. Leo knelt down, quick to try to help.

"Don't! Don't touch them! Get back!" Nina shouted.

Mitch and Leo wailed suggestions at each other as Nina tried to collect her thoughts. *What do I do?*

Avery's eyes met Nina's as if begging her to save her. Leo was shoving Mitch and shaking Nina, telling them to get someone to help. Then, Nina's pupils dilated as she stretched the limits of her power of influence to possess both Leo and Mitch. Suddenly, both of them were calm as Nina forcefully suspended their movement. Nina's irises became fluid-like and swirled in circles of purple. She stood over the two women and held her hands out over them. A quiet chant left her lips as she brushed her hands through the air from head to toe over their bodies. The swirls of worms began to shrink, leaving only dark purple bruises on their skin.

She turned to Mitch, who was still under her influence. "Go find Ollie, and make a salve of coconut oil, tea tree, turmeric, goldenseal and eucalyptus. Add Avery's honey to it." She took a deep breath. "Now!" Next, she grabbed Leo's shoulders and looked into his eyes with the utmost seriousness. "Bring me a glass of water and my tree-of-life essence from the cupboard."

Leo shrugged out of Nina's grasp and ran to grab the supplies. The two women were alive, but only barely. They were breathing but unconscious. Nina straightened both of their bodies on the floor and applied the salve to their skin. When they opened their eyes, Nina forced them to drink from the glass of water. She didn't need a spell to help them fall back to sleep. She and Leo carried them to their beds. Nina called Mitch and Leo out into the great room to give them some answers.

"What happened to them? Are they gonna be okay?" Leo asked with frightened eyes.

"They're going to be fine. They were cursed. With what's called an Exhauriat worm."

"What the hell is that?" Leo asked.

"Are we gonna get it?" Mitch pressed.

"You won't now. It is contagious. I think that's how Avery got it, from touching Bisa. It spreads really easily through physical contact."

Leo looked at Nina, perplexed. "Well, where did Bisa get it?"

"That's what I'm going to find out. It's a nasty spell. Simple. Deadly. But not a lot of people are…witchy…enough to cast it. It takes a toll on the person casting it, so a lot of witches would never attempt to do such a thing."

Leo scoffed. "Please. Murder takes a toll on your psyche, too, but people run around doing that shit all the time. More than half the population of New Orleans are murderers, for fuck's sake!"

"What does it do?" Ollie asked.

"It's a worm that multiplies under your skin. Its skin is toxic. Just touching it with your bare hands can kill you in a matter of a few minutes if you're not careful. So, Bisa and Avery were very lucky." She knew that if the infection had spread—enough to cover their entire torso, in a solid, bruised mass—they surely would have died. A smaller infection like the one that ran down Bisa's neck and along Avery's arms meant there was a good chance they could survive. Nina trailed off into an explanation of the healing process that would follow. She had never seen the curse before, but she had known about it. If she hadn't connected to the higher consciousness for advice from the divine, her coven might have suffered the deaths of two very gifted witches. Who would have cast such a curse was something she wanted to know. It had to have been a skilled witch, one who knew what they were doing and how to do it. It wasn't the careless bumbling of a beginner. This was personal and had been done with purpose. Whether the intention was to kill or only wound someone, it was repulsive all the same.

Merlot had to be behind it. There was only one way to be sure…Nina had to look her in the eyes to see for herself.

CHAPTER 33

Edie and Joshua were used to picketing. For a church with commercials that ran at least twice a day and more than one campus, they sure were cheap as shit when it came to the quality of picket signs. Edie had a thing for neon poster board and chose to use only pink, blue or solid white, depending on what they were picketing. If it was a lesbian, they used pink, if it was a gay man, she preferred blue, and anything else fell under the safety of white. Their signs were always handwritten with a thick, black permanent marker. It was Edie's second favorite black object, the first was her pulpit microphone.

Picketing was more than just standing in the sun and shouting nonsense until there wasn't anyone left to read the picket signs—much more than that. It was an activity that Edie and Joshua both enjoyed and that seemed necessary to look predictable and consistent with their actions. If everyone underestimated them and thought they were just predictable yet amazing Americans, no one would ever suspect them of anything. Edie always told Joshua, "We need to keep our enemies either confused or disinterested enough to have no idea what we're gonna do next."

The witch they had murdered in Mobile was actually a New Orleans native, so when they learned the funeral was going to be held only a few miles away, it took Edie only twenty minutes to prepare enough picket signs for six people, since she was able to reuse a few from the last protest. With her pretty blue picket signs—plus two white ones that read *Mystic Perverts* from when they had protested outside a Catholic church, which didn't make a whole lot of sense, but in the end she considered gays perverts, too, so it was a small, insignificant detail—she was ready to go stir up some controversy.

Nina was driving back from the grocery store in the city. She had given up going to Rapp and Boudreaux Food Market. It smelled, and their produce just wasn't as good as the produce at Whole Foods. It was this change of location that placed her in the position of driving a little farther on the 10. Had she gone to Rapp and Boudreaux, she would've been stuck with some sad and spotty bell peppers and wouldn't have seen the Bonners picketing from the traffic-laden highway. She had a lot on her mind lately: the well-being of her coven, how much longer the refrigerated items could last in the back seat before they started to warm up, and now whether she was going to stop an injustice that was out of her way and perhaps not her fight to fight.

That's when it hit her: it *was* her fight. The whole purpose of the coven's mission was to promote balance, but that didn't mean it always had to be achieved through magical means. She put on her blinker and took the next exit so she could make a quick pit stop at the funeral. Nina hadn't the slightest idea what she was going to do or if it would make any difference, but she had to do it, and hope the strawberry rocky road ice cream didn't melt. Even if it did, a pint of melted ice cream would be worth it if she could make a difference or, better yet—change someone's perspective. This was the Whole Truth and True Light Church, though…Their name was spread across the side of their picketing van in gold…Perhaps she would *need* to use magic. They were pretty much beyond rescue.

Go 2 Hell!

All fags deserve to die! Sinners, SHAME, Boo!

WE'RE GLAD YOU'RE DEAD!!!

GAY = RAPIST

Those were the key phrases that Edie had come up with in the craft room of the church, minus the two about mystic perverts, which, of course, still applied in her mind. What Edie chose to leave out was the fact that the deceased was a witch. She could have written that on a protest sign and people probably wouldn't have thought much of it. A witch in the literal sense isn't something that people often take seriously. But she left it out, just to be safe.

Nina parked her car and walked across the cemetery toward Edie and the protesters. Edie could've branded that and advertised in the church community—Edie and the Protesters—like Prince and the Revolution or Bill Haley and the Comets, with hate speech for lyrics and groupies in place of backup dancers, ones that all showed up to foxtrot to an insufferable rhythm. A good protest truly was music to her ears. She had the fame, the followers and the message, and people loved her for it. People also hated her for it, but God's destruction would come for those who opposed her soon enough, and she would be there to hold the hands of those whose faith was true and whose hearts were righteous.

The protest was in full swing by the time Nina arrived at the site. They didn't want her there either—she was black—but they weren't going to say that out loud. Their racism was more of a private affliction, at least until it didn't have to be top secret. There weren't many people at the funeral, and from what Nina could determine from a few concentrated dips into the higher consciousness, even the parents weren't there. They had dismissed their son, but paid for the funeral. To them, that *was* love. Nina wasn't planning to use any magic or power of influence, but the hate was so strong, so thick, so ingrained in their brains that for a moment she thought there wouldn't be any other way to stop the concert. A man, rednecked both from the sun and from birth, raised his sign as high as he could. His eyes were hidden by the large sunglasses that slid on his chapped and sweaty nose. Those eyes were probably as red as the Confederate flag print on his shirt, she guessed.

Nina always had the best of intentions when it came to battling injustice—and when it came to protests, for that matter, for which she had been on the other side of that sign herself. Sometimes, though, it didn't always go as planned, like the time she was arrested for criminal trespassing and taking part in a riot in North Dakota in 2016 against the Dakota Access Pipeline. It was a very cold day and she was battling, peacefully, for the truth. Here she was doing the same, but whether it was going to be peaceful had yet to be determined.

Nina targeted the redneck man in sunglasses, a man twice her size in height and weight, and marched toward him. Right as she figured out what she was going to say, another woman beat her to it. A woman with a short natural Afro with a hard part on the left. *A college student*, Nina guessed. Words were exchanged between the two, words that quickly twisted into an argument as they naturally only could. Nina walked faster. The argument switched from verbal to physical as the plucky young woman grabbed the picket sign from the man's hand and smacked the side of his arm with it. Again. But harder this time. Again—but faster.

Nina pulled the woman away from the group of tall white men, all of whom had left their pointy hats at home. The woman wasn't just anyone, and she wasn't there by chance: she was there to mourn the senseless death of her brother. Nina just *knew* it. As much as she knew she adored fresh pasta.

Nina turned back to Edie and the protesters. "You all have no right to be here."

The redneck opened his chapped lips and let out a gutsy sigh. "We have every right to be here. Just as much as y'all! Louisiana law says we can protest all we want, long as we don't disrupt the service."

Edie appeared from between the men like a snake in tall grass, her sign bending against their elbows. "You're right," she said to Nina. "There is a funeral going on, and none of us want to break the law, now, do we?"

"We follow God's law, Pastor Edie!" the redneck said.

"Yes, we do. And he would want us to hold true to our cause and not get arrested. So let's step back a bit. Let the…*many*…in attendance for this funeral carry out the rest of the service." She motioned to everyone to scoot back a considerable distance to abide by the law. "We'll be over here, nondisruptive, in plain sight. A reminder that God is watching."

If the victim's sister had been carrying lighter fluid and a pack of matches, there would have been a barbecue. She had no tears. Her sadness had been replaced with confusion and rage. Nina managed to calm the woman down, first with her sharp vernacular and then with a little help from magic. When Nina caressed the woman's shoulder, she suddenly understood why she had been drawn to the funeral. It wasn't strictly in the name of injustice, but because the deceased was a witch. It was the very witch that the Advisory had come to tell them about. It was all too close. Too real. This time the cause she was fighting for might end not in her getting arrested, but possibly in getting killed.

Nina kept the conversation short. Sometimes she would assert her power of influence and press for some information.

If her brother was a witch, this woman might very well be one too. She couldn't detect anything, or smell the witch on her. Yet it didn't discount the chance that it hadn't blossomed yet. A few minutes later, Nina declared herself a "grief counselor" and offered her ear in case the woman ever needed to talk. Right before she left the woman, she smelled something. It was fleeting, strange and indiscernible, like the smell of a stranger's house when entering it for the first time.

Nina caught a glimpse of something out of the corner of her eye. It was so camouflaged that she thought her eyes were playing tricks on her. She looked across the burial plot and saw a young man, vibrant, healthy, but completely stoic. Only he wasn't really there. Nina stared at the man, who was just as fixed on her. A shiver ran through her body as she realized that he wasn't a man at all, but a ghost, a spirit. Then the man— ghost, spirit—smiled lightly. It was his funeral. The woman was his sister. Nina looked back at the woman, then back across the plot, but the spirit was gone. Nina hadn't had many visions. In fact she wondered if she'd ever had any like the one she had just experienced. They had been, for the most part, in her head. It was as if her psychic muscle had been working out and she hadn't noticed because she was with it every day. But there was no doubting it: something was stronger. Only she had a hard time believing that was the case. *My powers have peaked...haven't they?* Obviously, she was mistaken. For that spirit was as real as her criminal record.

CHAPTER 34

*K*nock! *Knock! Knock!*

Bisa turned her head toward the door to see Avery hovering in the doorway.

"Can I come in?"

"Of course! You're supposed to be resting."

"I can handle only so much sitting still. Besides, I wanted to come check how you're doing." Avery hobbled into the bedroom and found a spot near Bisa on the bed.

"It hurts to move my arm a little, but I'll be okay." Bisa placed a hand over Avery's on the bed. "Thank you for…trying to help me."

Avery surprised herself by giggling. "Don't be silly. Anyone here would have done that."

"I don't think that's entirely true."

Avery looked over Bisa's bruised skin, where patches of purple were finally starting to fade. "I wish I could've done more. This is still new to me and I have a lot to learn."

"Stop. I know." Bisa sat with her thoughts for a moment to consider just where she was and how she had gotten there. "It's wild, isn't it? How much we don't know yet, how much more there is to learn, *still*!"

Avery's eyes lit up as she smiled. "I know! It's overwhelming sometimes, just how much."

Bisa nodded. "I do love learning though." Her eyes wandered into the past.

"Were you one of those kids who just loved school?"

Bisa grinned. "I was. My dad was an artist and my mom valued education a lot, I think because she didn't have many options growing up. They didn't always agree, but they tried to be good parents."

"Are they still together?" Avery asked.

Bisa adjusted herself on the bed and sat up. It was the most open she had been in a long time. But she felt safe with Avery. "No. I think when they first met, they were really young. I don't know how old, but young enough to think everything is a good idea. My dad was gay, actually. He was discreet about it, but people knew. My mom knew. I knew. Other people did too. It's not something that's accepted in Nigeria. My mom wasn't a hateful person, and they didn't raise me to be one either. It was a part of who he was, you know? It was in his DNA, and he wasn't able to live out his life as himself. He was himself, but not completely. Coming here to the United States and feeling so much…hatred, just for being black, something I have no control over, really made me understand that you can't change who someone is, and you can't beat it out of them. They are going to be what they are regardless. But they both loved me very much. My dad taught me a lot about art.

"I think about them sometimes. Like what they would say if they knew me now, and who I've become. I'll never have another mother or father, and the chance for them to see me succeed in a world where they couldn't is gone." Bisa was a little misty eyed.

"I know I'm not your mother or your father, and I know that I come from a completely different place and am completely ignorant about much of the world you come from, but"—Avery used both hands to hold Bisa's—"as your friend, as your sister witch, and even as a stranger who barely knows the whole truth of who you are or the struggles you've had to go through…I'm happy to have met you, and I admire you. I do! I may not be as intuitive as you, but I know you have a soul that's good, and it makes me happy to know someone like that. Because you love to learn, and that makes you the perfect teacher for a world like this, with people like Leo."

They both laughed.

"My God, Leo," Bisa said, rolling her eyes. "I don't even know where to start with that one."

"I'm sorry about what I said before. In the great room, about you and Mitch being attracted to him."

"Don't be. I'm glad you said it. Sometimes people need to hear the truth."

"I didn't need to say it *like that*."

"Okay, that's true," Bisa said, laughing.

"It's true, though, isn't it?"

"I think so. I don't know what it is, really. He gets on my nerves so much and sometimes I even think I hate him, but I care about him, probably more than he even cares about or likes himself. Or maybe I just feel sorry for him? I don't know. He's not really the type of guy I would *ever* be interested in. We have nothing in common, and we're just—very different."

Avery looked over Bisa's face as she thought about Leo. The only thing Leo liked more than danger was Bisa—at least that was Avery's impression when she sniffed him out.

"He reminds me of someone," Bisa said. "I feel like I've met him before. Maybe in another life or something, as they say. It's funny: my mom told me that's how she felt when she first met my dad." Maybe that was why she was so unnerved by Leo. She associated that feeling, regardless of whom it was attached to, with suffering and misfortune.

"Do you ever talk to them anymore?"

That was it. That was the question that tipped the conversation. It was like when you're on the verge of crying and someone notices and asks, *Are you okay?* which causes you to burst into tears. But she wasn't going to cry. She didn't have any left.

"I wish I could. They lost nearly everything in the Nigerian Civil War. After that I somehow managed to finish one year at the university, studying fine and applied arts. It was a way to make both my parents proud. I was getting an education and I was learning about art. I had dreams of coming here to America to study. There were so many programs, so many opportunities, so many people who felt as strongly about art as I did. I thought, anyway. I remember I had just gotten the results of my exams and was going to have dinner at home with my parents to share how excited I was. My father was caught kissing another man by some people in town. He would have been sentenced to death once it got out."

"*To death*?" Avery shrieked in horror.

"But that never happened. The townspeople got to him first. People I knew. People I saw every week. They attacked us. At home. They broke through the door, grabbed my father and beat him and beat him and beat him. I couldn't even see his eyes, they beat him so hard. All while the others cheered and held us down to watch. Then they pinned my mother down to the floor and kicked her over and over." A tiny bit of vomit inched up and burned Bisa's throat before settling back down to her stomach. It had been one of three times she'd even tried to recount this story. The first time, she had left out most of the details. The second time, she had been about to tell it exactly as it happened, but right as she'd started, she'd changed her mind and kept quiet. She was ready now. "They killed them both and made me watch. And then they held me down and raped me. One of the men said it was to make sure I turned out right. I can't even describe how that felt. Looking back it feels like I just went numb."

Avery wiped at the bottom curve of her eyes. "My God, Bisa."

Bisa shook her head at the memory of it all. "Anyway, I managed to get out of there and transfer to Chicago, where I continued to study art and design at Columbia College Chicago. I got a job as a makeup artist, took out as many loans and grants as I could and put myself through school."

Avery's face was a flurry of awakening. "I can't even begin to imagine what that was like. I would never want to try, either. I'm sure that isn't even the half of it. And I'm so, so angry and disgusted that happened to you and your family. I admire you. You're a stronger woman than I will ever be. You're so brave."

"I don't feel like I am."

"You're doing what most people who haven't gone through half the things you have only dream of doing."

"What?"

"You're living your life. You're not living in the past, you're strong, you're a survivor. Hearing what you just said and seeing who you are now…it gives me hope. You're completely authentic and it's beautiful, and I can smell that it was not an easy journey for you. You deserve to be happy. And I want you to know that you can talk to me about anything. And I'll tell you anything about me! No secrets. Just good friends. I want to be able to see the world from as many perspectives as I can, so I can be half as amazing as you, so I want us to be friends."

"All right…witch," Bisa said, laughing.

A half hour later, Leo walked past the door to Bisa's room on the way to the front door. He hovered in the doorway just long enough to check how the two were doing and to say he was going to go for a ride and would be back later. He hopped on his bike and rode off.

Nina closed her bedroom door, cleansed her space with palo santo, then sat down and prepared herself for astral projection. But there was one task she had to complete first. She wanted to confront Merlot and her coven, to send a word of warning, but she had to be prepared. Words could only go so far, and if Merlot was wrapped in a nasty hive filled with wild and unstable witches, she might need a little extra protection. As a Proctor, Nina didn't hold a lot back from her coven. She wanted them to grow and surpass her expectations and their own if possible, so keeping things secret didn't seem constructive, unless of course it was to protect them. Because she wanted to protect them from handling magic they weren't capable of handling yet, she had never told them that powers coupled to a type of witch could be shared—no, borrowed—by another kind. It was also in her best interest to carry out a spell that would do such a thing if she was going to confront the other coven. She had no idea how they would react or what they were going to do. Nina was smart, not reckless.

She lit a red candle and stared into the flame. It was in the calm, wispy flame that she gained the courage to harness power that she had never experienced, to experiment with spells that were only theoretical. Naturally, there were a lot of uncertainties with conducting this type of magic. She had a hunch about how long the spell would last and what its limitations were, but no actual idea how solid those hunches were. Again, everything was theoretical. She found that theory was pointless without application and experimentation. The coven was in danger, possibly quite serious danger, and this wasn't the time to debate about risk.

Nina brought a small cauldron to the floor. Into it she dumped a chili pepper, a shot of rum and a handful of crushed twigs that had been soaked in rum and cinnamon and then bathed in sunlight until dry. Nina drew a sigil on the floor with the ashes of burnt paper and leaves. Magic was messy sometimes. Nina sat in front of the cauldron with the red candle in her right hand and her left palm facing the ceiling. After a moment of silent meditation, she dipped her finger into a bowl of crushed herbs and freshly grated ginger root and scooped up the pulp. In a single stroke between her eyebrows, she wiped the liquid over her forehead. Nina closed her eyes and began the incantation.

"Invoco te, Tatewari," she said aloud. Twice more in her head. *Invoco te, Tatewari...Invoco te, Tatewari.*

The room fell silent until all she heard was the first sound her soul ever remembered, the sound of a heartbeat. Only it wasn't her own, just as it wasn't hers before she was born. It was the heartbeat of another. Nina felt a sudden blast of heat against her skin and saw a flash of light beneath her eyelids. In a poof, the cauldron's contents burst into flames. When Nina opened her eyes, the flame was gone. *Was it ever there?* she wondered. But of course it was. Smoke was rising from the pot. She extended her hand toward the rising smoke. When the smoke pooled around her palm, a flame zipped up the cord of smoke to her hand, which burst into flame as well. It didn't hurt, but it did surprise her enough to make her gasp aloud. She watched in amazement as her burning hand absorbed the flames like spilled water into a dry sponge. It was complete. She had the power of Tatewari. But would she need it? She hoped it wouldn't be necessary, but unlike car or health insurance, this kind of insurance wasn't a total rip-off. She actually needed it, and the price was small. Unless she were to abuse it. Then her premiums would go up.

A few minutes later, Nina was astrally projecting herself onto the front lawn of the coven's house in Houston: a new build, remarkably centrally located, with a few large trees that shielded it from the neighboring houses. It was the type of house that was so stylishly lit that you could never tell if someone was actually home. That probably came in handy, because the house was beautiful and there would be a lot of peeping eyes nearby, especially because it was down the street from a grocery store, a juice bar and a performing arts theater.

The sun had set, and the scent of dusk was in the air along with the heavy scent of witch. Nina wasn't exactly ready for conflict, but she wasn't about to turn back now. With a confident stride, she swaggered up to the front door and rang the bell. The door was opened by a woman Nina assumed was another member of the coven, but one she hadn't met or known of. Her name was Maisie, but she never told Nina that. Nina just knew. Nina stared at her with devious curiosity, trying to determine what kind of witch she was. Peanut-colored skin, congenitally sweet, with a face and spirit of the only person on the entire planet who should ever be allowed to answer a door. Politeness was ingrained in her like racism in the South. It caught Nina off guard. She didn't seem at all the type of person who would be involved with Merlot's coven, if she was. Maisie nodded and stepped aside, but said nothing. It almost felt like she was apologizing for answering the door. Nina had the sense that Maisie knew why she was there too. It was when Nina got that hunch that she entered, uninvited.

She made her way farther into the house, past the bizarre knickknacks and exotic sculptures. It was the kind of house that suggested you might have a hard time getting out alive. Nina passed Andy in the dining room as she made her way to the kitchen. But it was at the end of the hallway, where the living room connected to the screened-in patio on the back, where Nina stopped. Outside, in an assemblage of poofy pillows, surrounded by a dozen large lanterns illuminated with candles, sat Merlot and Blake. Nina could smell the incense burning out on the porch. As she approached, Merlot stopped midsentence and looked at her. It would have been predictable if she had smiled, but instead she breathed a cutting greeting into her mysterious eyes. Nina opened the door and stepped out onto the porch. Two black stone bowls of incense burned and smoked behind her on either side of the door.

"Uh, what are you doing here?" Blake said roguishly.

"I came to talk to you and Merlot about your futile bullying," Nina snapped back.

"Bullying? I don't know what you're talking about," Blake pretended badly, deliberately.

Merlot cocked her head back and watched.

"You could have killed her," Nina said. "And Avery! Who almost died trying to help. That's two people you put in danger, and that kind of behavior is unacceptable. You should be ashamed of yourself, Merlot."

"Of what should I be ashamed?"

"Enough of your bullshit! I can smell it. I don't need any kind of magic for that. We both know that Blake attacked my house."

"Attacked!" Blake laughed.

"Keep it up! You think I don't know you? I know you. I've known lots of girls like you." Nina suddenly heard and saw all of Blake's psyche as if it were on a live transmission into her brain and behind her eyes. "Now that you know you're a witch and have found someone like Merlot here to spoil you, you don't have to go back to sliding up and down poles in that hellhole where the only place you thought you would get to go in life was into the private room with the highest-paying customer. Only you did it out of pleasure, not necessity. You did it because that's where you learned you had power. The more sex you had, the more your power grew. The stronger your arousal, the stronger your power. All someone had to do was dream a little dream about you, and you grew stronger. Which only led these people to you, wanting more, paying more, needing the real thing because the dreams weren't enough.

"You drew people in, used them, manipulated them into giving you anything you wanted, leaving people within an inch of their sanity. And you knew your magic was eating their mind…but you didn't care. Why would you? For the first time in a long time, you were on top of the world and could ask for and receive anything you ever wanted. Then you met Merlot, and what a pair you two make."

Blake stood up, smiling, ready to taunt Nina with more of her bullshit. "You don't know the half of it. You think you're all wise, and good, and noble, but you're just like everyone else. You're just like us, you're just like me. That's what I hear…"

"Sit down," Nina said sternly.

"Yeah, I know all about you…snake…Should we talk about how you became part of the Advisory?"

"I said, sit back down."

Merlot watched with boiling excitement, feeding off the tension as Blake drew closer to Nina.

"What are you gonna do? Teach me how to sit down, shut up and take shit from other people?"

"Is this what you're teaching them about magic, Merlot? How to push buttons?" Nina asked as she stared at Blake.

Merlot didn't answer. She only watched more intensely.

"You gonna punish me? Teach me how to play dirty like you did with Merlot? Come on...play dirty. I know you can." Blake's voice dropped to a raspy whisper. "Like I said, you're no different. You're just weaker."

Nina felt something in the air between her and Blake. A force. The words spewing out of Blake's mouth weren't just words. They were laced with persuasion, sexualized, spiked with manipulative command. As soon as she realized what was happening, Nina raised her hand into the space between them and opened her fist.

"Don't!" she said, but what she really meant was *bitch, please.*

The candles flared out all at once, and the sheer fabric of Blake's caftan billowed as a small puff of fluid-like fire appeared from Nina's hand and went into the air. Inexplicably, there was no combustion. It was as if the flames just materialized. It was a type of controlled fire in the shape of a sphere that one normally never sees. There were no flickers. It was just a slow-burning fire, yellowish white, feeding on the fuel of its genesis point as the fluid fire burned around it on its perimeter, like fire in space. Nina's invocation spell had functioned as she anticipated, and her aura was blessed with the power of Tatewari, the god of fire in Huichol folklore. The power was borrowed, not given, and allowed to be handled aurically with the spirit occupying her outer aura and connected to her psychically, reacting instantaneously according to Nina's intentions.

Blake stepped back in surprise. Even Merlot was stupefied. Neither of them had anticipated or detected the magic that Nina possessed.

"What is this? You're a Transcendent. You borrowed this power. Forgive me, I'm impressed," Merlot said with arrogance.

With the surge of spirit running through Nina's aura, she unleashed a threat upon them that attracted the other coven members to the porch to see what all the fuss was about.

"You've always teetered between insanity and reality, and look at you now, surrounded with clones of yourself," Nina spat.

"Is my perspective really all that insane?" Merlot asked. "Is it so wrong to want people with the means to actually shape the world and help others like them, instead of protecting people who kill each other, rape and destroy the world they live in? Humans aren't witches. They aren't divine. We need more witches. Everyone else is disgusting. Blind. Ruled by fear. Your methods are no different." Merlot stood up to face Nina, her hair falling off her shoulders. "Why is your method acceptable and mine is not? Who is to say whose method is valid and whose is wrong?"

"I can only imagine what chaos you would have created had you been in the Advisory. You would have gotten everyone killed," Nina said.

"You really think people aren't doing that already? Why do you think the world is so out of balance? Why do you think we have these powers to begin with? You've seen just as much as I have. You really think humankind is going to save this world? They don't care about the world, they care about themselves. And having *more*. Taking. Stealing. Lying. At least I do it openly and not for myself. I wanted to kill you when I found out the position had been given to you. I was going to turn all that shit around. I don't need the Advisory to help me now."

"Stay away from us," Nina said. "Stay away from my coven. This is the only time I'm going to say it." She stood in the darkness of the patio with only the burning flame in her hand to illuminate the conflict between them. Her eyes dropped down to Blake's bare arm, where something alarming and unusual caught her eye. On the upper end of her smooth forearm was a cluster of three hive-like lesions, red and swollen. They could have been bug bites, but it wasn't the first time she had seen them. She had seen the same trio of pus-filled legions on Andy's arm during dinner. It was more than just coincidence. It had to be. It had to mean *something*. Nina blinked, and in that split second saw all that could and probably would happen. A gift from the divine, a vision. One to be worried about, and prepared for. Nina didn't speak Spanish, but Tatewari did, and as the spirit coursed through Nina's aura, their skills were one. *"No necesito leer tu mente para saber qué va a pasar,"* Nina said fluently as if she had spoken in her native English. I don't need to read your mind to know what will happen.

Blake exchanged a look with Merlot before she turned back to Nina. After a moment of silence, Nina could feel the spell beginning to weaken and fade. It would be best if she returned to her body. Nina took one last look into the darkness of Merlot's eyes and showed herself out of the house. Past the coven, through the hallway and out the front door. As the door swung shut behind her, Nina dematerialized instantly and returned to her body, damp and gasping for air.

"I thought she didn't speak Spanish. What did she say?" Blake asked Merlot.

"She doesn't need to read my mind to know what's going to happen," Merlot translated.

Nina caught her breath and processed everything that had just happened. She was back in her bedroom, safe and surrounded by positive vibes. She could instantly tell the difference between the vibrations at Merlot's house and her own. Although positive energies overpowered negative ones, they were also created, and the beauty of creation takes time, whereas the force of negativity is instant and catastrophic. It gave negativity an advantage. It was easier to annihilate those who challenged you than it was to create change within them.

Was everyone safe? Nina wondered. She checked up on Bisa, Avery, Ollie and Mitch but couldn't find Leo anywhere. She asked around and discovered that he had left on his bike, saying he would be back later. Only, he hadn't returned and no one knew exactly where he had gone.

CHAPTER 35

Leo had traveled across a lot of Louisiana but had never spent much time in any of it. Now he drove his motorcycle through New Orleans, zipping through rush hour traffic, leaving only the scent of burnt rubber behind as he peeled between the lanes onward. He passed by Bayou Sauvage, where he used to go with a couple of joints packed in his pocket and explore through the tall grass. He had once found a rusty old 1972 Chevy Nova with two windows busted out and bald tires. They were the kind of tires he was familiar with, ones that had been rubbed smooth by excess speed and careless driving. He revved his engine and increased his speed from sixty-five miles per hour to eighty-one. Next was Slidell, a city he raced straight through because it reminded him of when he worked at a restaurant there. One where the dishwasher made more than he did. That's where he had met Tonya. Nothing but bad memories there.

From Slidell he continued on 59 North straight to the outskirts of Pearl River. He passed two churches and a dingy tavern and turned onto Sugarmill Road. The town disappeared behind him as he continued to bike down the vacant road. It wasn't entirely empty—there were a few small homes spaced out every couple of minutes, but they weren't close enough to borrow an egg if you needed it. He made it to 5691 Sugarmill Road, the address he'd been given by the shop owner at Maji. There was less than a quarter tank of gas in his bike, but he had passed a gas station at the corner of Sugarmill Road and Beech Avenue, so he wasn't worried. When he hopped off his bike, he thought, *This better not be a waste of my time or my gas.*

Leo walked down the gravel driveway toward the poorly painted white house, his motorcycle rattling behind him as the engine cooled. The lawn was mostly dead and covered in leaves. *What am I even going to say to these people when they open the door? Hi! I'm a total stranger, and I want you to invite me inside and give me a temazcal ceremony even though I have no idea what one is or what it does. By the way, your lawn's dead.* Although it didn't seem like he was going to start off on the right foot, it was pretty much exactly what he planned to say.

When Leo reached the door, he searched for a doorbell. It had been painted over with the same kind of laziness a maintenance man of an apartment complex would paint over hinges and light fixtures whenever the apartment turned over. Leo had had all sorts of construction jobs, even ones that included painting. He recognized a half-ass, I-don't-give-a-shit-about-this-job job when he saw one. Leo could see that kind of work a mile away. What he couldn't see was the doorbell. In that moment he realized how laziness affected other people, such as himself when he was looking for a doorbell at a strange house.

The door opened, and a man half his size with nutty-brown skin stood before him. The man's bushy eyebrows drew together as he stared at Leo, but he didn't speak.

"Hi, I was given this address by a guy at Maji, in New Orleans. He said that you, or someone here, did a…temazcal ceremony. Or whatever. Am I in the right spot?"

Silence. The man didn't even blink.

"Right. This address here." Leo indicated the scrap of paper with the man's address in his hand. "The store…Maji? The guy told me to come here and talk to…you? To arrange it for me?"

Leo wasn't sure if he was asking questions or making statements.

The man looked at the piece of paper and then back into Leo's eyes.

Maybe this guy doesn't speak English. Fuck. He looks Mexican. "Do you speak English?" Leo's excitement was fading quickly. "Spanish? English?"

No response. Finally, a blink.

"Never mind. Sorry," Leo said as he tucked the paper into his pocket and turned to walk away.

"You're in the right spot. I was just playing around," the man said, and Leo could hear the grin in his voice. "They called me and told me they referred someone. Surprised you showed up."

Leo turned back around and rolled his eyes. He had basically said everything he thought he was going to say except one thing. "You need to do something about your lawn. It's dead."

The man brought him around to the side of the house and opened the garage. He pulled out two green folding chairs, the kind people watch fireworks from on the Fourth of July, and set them on the concrete.

"Sit. Let me tell you about the temazcal. It's been a long time since I've had a random person come all the way up here and not know a thing about it." The chair made a farting noise as the man settled into the seat. "It's also two fifty."

Leo opened his mouth to respond, but his bulging eyes said more than any words he could have said.

"Dollars," the man said. "Two hundred and fifty dollars. For the service."

"How long is it?" Leo asked, wondering how much the man would make per hour.

"About an hour. Maybe a little over. Depends."

So, this guy makes two hundred and fifty dollars for an hour of work? I mean, I knew I was getting screwed when the alcoholic dishwasher was making sixteen while I made twelve, but shit, I should've gotten into this witchy shit a hell of a lot earlier if that's what this guy makes. "Fuck. I don't have that kind of money on me." He was disappointed. He hadn't thought that far ahead. He hated to admit it, but he'd assumed it was the type of thing that would be free. He had no idea why he'd thought that and felt stupid for assuming.

"I take Venmo. Or PayPal. Whatever is easiest. Or even Zelle. I know lots of people have that service now too."

"You take Venmo?" Leo asked, shocked.

"Yup!"

"And you're a shaman?"

"Twenty-two years. My wife—twenty-four."

A shaman who accepts Venmo and PayPal. Didn't expect that.

"I might have to come back," Leo said. He knew he had the money, but he had the money for other things, not necessarily for spiritual growth. For an instant, he thought maybe it was time to change that.

"It's up to you. Decide if it's worth it to you," the man said as he waved to his wife, who had been watching from the window.

"Is what worth it?" Leo truly didn't know what he had meant.

"Your spiritual health. Your soul."

That was all the man needed to say. It was as if he had read Leo's thoughts. It seemed like divine intervention, like it was supposed to happen, like things were going to change for the better for once instead of for the worse. He had already come so far and learned so much, and although he was still pretty good at this whole witch thing, he knew deep down inside that he had some flaws—serious ones—flaws that went beyond the laziness of painting over hinges and light fixtures. The kinds of flaws that shaped your future, that prevented you from being your best self, toxic, self-sabotaging flaws.

"Gimme your Venmo," Leo said as he took out his phone.

Meanwhile, Nina had been worrying about Leo's disappearance. She wasn't satisfied with the answers the rest of the coven gave her and just had to know where he was. She could feel something changing, but it wasn't clear whether it was good or bad.

There was a labradorite pendulum on her dresser. Nina retrieved it, unfolded a map of the state onto her bed and pulled back the pendulum with her thumb and index finger. She had never tried this method of scrying before; she was used to black surfaces, or shiny ones like water or a crystal ball. But those were for something more obscure. She needed—wanted—to know where Leo was and why. The pendulum swung in circles, small at first, then in large rounds, ones that drew the chain nearly parallel to the map. Then, the pendulum shot like a bullet out of Nina's hand and landed on top of Pearl River on the map. *Why would he be up there?* she wondered.

Nina extended her hand over the now immobile pendulum and closed her eyes. It was a full moon, the best time for psychic activity. Perhaps it would amplify her strengths enough to see where he was, maybe even why. There was a series of images and fades to black, as though she were watching a montage in a film, but none of it made any sense. The pictures in her head were fish-eyed, like a convex mirror. He was in no danger, but she didn't recognize anything or anyone around him. Then the image faded to black indefinitely. She could get only so far. It was as if a barrier deliberately limited her from seeing exactly what was going on, but let her see just enough to let her know where he was and that he was fine.

Judging from their short stature, Balam and Itzel, the husband-and-wife shaman team, appeared to be of Mayan heritage, which Balam confirmed while giving Leo a little history on the temazcal and where it had come from. It had been passed down through his family and become an annual ritual that he and Itzel did together on the first full moon of the new year. Although it wasn't the first moon of the year, it was a good night for Leo: he had arrived on a full moon and the sky was astoundingly clear. It wasn't the same moon he would have seen from the house—surely not from New Orleans, where the neon signs and streetlights polluted the sky. It was a bright, cosmic moon rising into Gemini, Leo's zodiac sign.

Leo expected Balam and Itzel to ask a lot of questions about him and his history or belief system, but refreshingly, they hadn't asked any. The shaman and his sweet-natured wife instead asked him to wait patiently while they prepared for the ceremony. Balam shuffled some rocks around in a burning crucible while Itzel laid out a bed of palm leaves and atop that, a circular purple cloth on which she placed several ritual items and instruments. Leo sat in the folding chair near the garage and watched them prepare in the backyard as the moon rose higher into the sky. He could barely make out the sweat lodge in the dim light of the crucible fire. It was a round hut with a chimney and a wooden door, and looked like the surface of the moon. Balam had built it by hand himself. The craftsmanship of the hut boasted a pastoral stylishness and put Leo's construction skills to shame. When Leo tried to do rustic, it just looked sloppy.

The shamans looked like different people as they rustled around in traditional garb—well, traditional to them. They were modern, but still true to their roots. Balam was dressed all in white, with a beaded brown belt around his belly and a red sash tied around his head. Itzel, a little more accessorized, with flowing garments of white, pink and blue. Shells and feathers hung from her necklace. A vibrant crimson patterned scarf hid her hair from her face. At first, Leo wanted to laugh. *What kind of bullshit is this?* But the thought faded, and he immediately felt bad for even thinking it. It was getting a little cold, something he loved about winter in Louisiana. He had stripped down to his underwear and huddled up in the chair, keeping himself warm while they prepared. Then, it was time.

It began with the blowing of a conch that trumpeted out into the cool evening air. The sound knew no bounds and seemed to trail off into space. Itzel lit a chalice of copal resin and held it in her right hand like a torch, guiding Leo toward the hut. Again, the honking sound of the conch, louder still. For a man no taller than five foot five and somewhere near sixty years old, Balam had one powerful set of lungs. The conch sounded out louder and louder with each call to the spirits as they walked through the thick copal-scented smoke into the yard. Leo looked around. They were all alone. But they weren't. He could feel something—someone perhaps—in the air. His heart began to flutter in ways that even driving ninety miles an hour over a bridge couldn't bring about. *What am I so nervous about?*

Before he could make sense of his anxiety, they had reached the blanket of palm leaves on the ground. The shamans stepped ever so delicately around the circumference of the blanket to the other side. Leo could feel the heat from the crucible, where an enormous amount of volcanic rocks were being heated. He looked toward the hut. The door was open. The space inside was the blackest black he had ever seen. Cavernous. Womb-like.

"Now, pick up an instrument," Balam instructed Leo. Leo was so overwhelmed with the experience that hadn't even fully begun yet that he heard *Pick up something.*

Leo looked over the items laid out across the blanket: jars, maracas, handmade pouches and instruments he had no idea how to use. He lifted the sides of his underwear and stepped forward to the edge of the blanket. His knees cracked as he bent down to select something…anything. Allowing instinct rather than his intellect to take over, he picked a beige-colored bag tied with a bright purple string. It looked like the kind of bag people would use to carry gold during the Renaissance, or at least that's what he assumed from his one and only trip to a Renaissance festival ten years earlier.

The shamans exchanged a look, one that spoke without words.

"What?" Leo asked. He tried to hide his anxiety and uncertainty, the vulnerability, but it shone as brightly as the moon above his head.

"An *instrument,*" Itzel repeated. "Something to play." She smiled with the sweetness of honey. "You can carry that with you too. That just means…" She struggled with finding the words in English. "You need a big hug." She pointed to the string around the top of the bag. "Purple. That means…transformation." Her English was actually very good. She certainly spoke more eloquently than he did.

"Oh!" Leo said, a bit embarrassed. He knelt down a second time and chose a wooden maraca fashioned in the shape of a pear, adorned with Mayan symbols and decorated with strings and feathers that tickled his rough hands as he picked it up.

"Now we will invoke the cardinal points," Balam said quickly before beginning to pound on a relic of a drum. The rhythm frightened Leo, not because it was eerie, but because it was real. It was something primal, a repetitive beat that pounded through all his walls and into the very thing that made him who he was. Balam and Itzel raised their hands, and Leo followed their example. Balam drummed, Itzel chanted and Leo stood with his arms in the air, holding a tiny pouch and a silent maraca. Then he began to shake it. Timidly at first, politely, even, as if a baby were sleeping nearby. The drumming intensified, and Itzel's piercing yelps and howls were strong and unsettling. It was a powerful force that surged through Leo and encouraged him to make music with the instrument in his hand, to shake it more rapidly and with confidence—unapologetic. The stronger he shook the maraca, the more unraveled he became, the more his walls began to crumble *(I am so uncomfortable right now)* and topple back and forth. That was no easy task; those walls *(I feel things; I just want to be in the dark hut already)* were high, thick and reinforced, but they were about to come crashing down, and he realized he wasn't as prepared for that as he thought he was. *(Maybe that guy at the shop was right. I wasn't ready for this.)*

The drumming stopped. The chanting ceased. The copal burned. Leo's anxiety spiked high.

"We are now ready to enter. Inside," Itzel said delicately.

She guided Leo to the door, which was only a little higher than his knees. Inside was nothing but approaching blackness, and with it was all his fear, his anxieties, his pain. There was a small exhalation of air as Leo dipped down through the door and into the hut. He was surprised by how much he could actually see at first, while the door was open. It was as round as it looked from the outside, and the brick walls were black. He couldn't decipher if they had been painted black or they were black from soot and smoke. Itzel encouraged him to walk to the left and around the room because *that's the direction energy flows.* In the center of the hut was a deep pit that sank into the earth. He sat opposite the door and the world outside looked wide and safe, even under the cover of night. A wave of panic like an electric current ripped through his body.

"Can I sit by the door?" Leo asked.

The shamans stopped in their tracks and spoke to each other in Mayan.

"Do you feel…fear?" Itzel asked.

"Yeah. I don't know why, though."

"The temazcal represents the womb of Mother Earth, and we enter to be reborn," Itzel said. "You need to ask why you feel scared of that. Come sit by the door." She motioned for him to continue around the room to the other side.

With the first part of the ceremony finished, Leo took a few deep breaths to calm himself. But no amount of breathing could have eased him into what he was about to experience. His hands were fists, hammers that rested upon his knees as he sat cross-legged on the floor. He heard the digging of a shovel outside.

Then the fresh air that seeped in from the open door changed temperature. A shovelful of volcanic rocks, glowing orange, entered the room like a prince being carried by servants. Balam dropped the stones into the pit in the center of the room as another ripple of emotions shot up Leo's spine. A few moments later, another sizzling pile of glowing rocks entered and topped the previous pile. The temperature rose. Hotter than any August in Louisiana under the direct sun at noon with no sunblock.

(*Oh my God. This is so hot. I don't know if I can do this.*) Itzel opened a bottle and poured a liquid over the rocks (*Holy shit...I can't breathe. This room feels like an oven*), and steam balled up out of the pit like a ghost rising from a tomb (*What if I don't get out of here? No one knows I'm here. What if I die?*) and cascaded down the walls from the ceiling.

Leo's pulse was fast. *How long is this going to be? How hot is this going to get?*

Balam entered the hut a final time, only now holding the chalice of burning copal and a wooden bucket filled with a tea made from Mayan herbs. The incense smoke intensified under the dome and thickened the air. Itzel leaned in and wrote with what looked like chalk, or wood, or perhaps more copal resin— he couldn't tell—on the rocks. Sweat poured out of Leo's body as though every gland in his body was working on overdrive. It was hot, so hot, and the heat was terrifying. Leo's gut wrenched as if trying to expel emotions that he swallowed and swallowed so many times, it was making him sick to his stomach. His body shook. His knuckles were white, but he couldn't see them. He needed *something*, but he didn't know what.

(*I'm so scared...*)

Then Balam closed the door. A blanket that was strategically hung above the door fell and draped over the entrance. The light from the cracks in the door was gone. It was black as pitch. It wasn't exactly what Leo had expected, and he felt childish and arrogant for envisioning a different experience.

"Let everything come out. If you need to scream, then scream…If you need to cry, then cry," Itzel said.

If Leo had had the chance to gather his thoughts, he might have been able to avoid *feeling*, but that wasn't possible. It felt like he was holding the hand of someone who had only a few breaths left, like he was seeing his own death right before his eyes. Then, at that moment, he unleashed a stream of tears, and those tears were legion. *I don't cry*, Leo thought. But the tears expelled themselves from his eyes in the heavy blackness as if he had no choice, like vomit after a night of drinking. Sick and weak—but better out than in. Leo looked around the inside of the hut. It all looked the same: black upon black with a lungful of pungent steam. Drumming. Chanting. Glorious and frightening all at the same time.

Itzel stopped chanting and remained quiet while the drums continued to beat to an expelling rhythm. "Your daughter…she's not alive?"

"No," Leo said through a wave of tears that covered his lips.

"What do you want to say to her? She can hear you," Itzel said.

Drumming. Drumming. Drumming.

"I miss you. I love you," Leo said, choking on his own words, his chest heaving up and down under the pressure of his emotions rising to the surface. "I'm so…so sorry. And I know that's not enough. I lost my baby girl. It's all my fault and I'm sorry." He repeated *I'm sorry* until his words were unintelligible.

"What do you want to let go of?" Itzel asked.

Leo lifted his hands to his face and wiped his eyes. *What* do *I want to let go of?* He remembered the death of his daughter, he thought of his sarcasm and his closed-off heart, he pondered how he craved connection but pushed it away when it presented itself in someone. *I'm so fucked up.* Leo ran over the memories of putting aside time with his daughter to sit around and get high with people he had no connection with. There were many things he wanted to let go of, parts of his personality that he felt were ingrained in his very makeup. Guilt. Shame. Addiction. But he uttered, in a sad falsetto, "Fear."

Itzel splashed a ladleful of tea onto the rocks. They hissed like a pit of angry snakes as they yielded another asphyxiating amount of steam. Another hissing noise sounded as more tea was tossed into the pit. Sweat and tears became the same thing on Leo's face. What a sight he would have seen if he had been able to see his reflection. He couldn't remember ever seeing himself cry. He had been so sad for so long that tears would have seemed wasteful. Tears were for grieving things that would eventually get better, but he remained unchangeable, stuck in a deep well of hopelessness and unhappiness.

The drumming stopped, and there was a shuffling noise. The door opened, and Balam slipped through the blanket covering the opening. A gush of cool air spilled inside and refreshingly chilled Leo's wet skin.

(Thank fucking God it's over.)

Leo plummeted forward over his crossed legs and placed his forehead *(Get me outta here)* on the floor where the air was a little cooler. He waited for someone to say something, to give him permission or an invitation to get up and leave. Itzel walked over toward Leo and handed him a bowl of honey and coffee grounds to rub over his body and exfoliate his former self.

(This isn't over.)

Balam returned with another teeming, steaming pile of rocks and dumped them into the pit. Higher and higher the temperature rose. Just when Leo thought it couldn't get any hotter, the temperature soared beyond anything he could have imagined. For a moment, he wondered if he was even safe inside the hut, or if his body could handle the extraordinary, sterilizing volcanic heat. *How the hell are they not even sweating?* He was drenched as if he had recently surfaced from a pool of water.

His cynicism slipped back in for a moment with the opening of the door. He had sweated his ass all over Louisiana, inside numerous restaurant kitchens, outside in the sun at many construction sites, under the stars on drugged-out acid trips, absolutely obsessed with the idea that one day things would naturally fall into place for him because…they had to. He had suffered through the death of his daughter and drug busts, all with the hope that one day he would get his shit together and figure out what to do with his damn life. *Where did going through all of that get me?* Apparently, back to sweating his ass off in Louisiana with no idea what the hell he was doing with his life. But that was just the cynicism talking. It was a hard villain to defeat. Nevertheless, Leo rubbed the honey mixture across his face, chest, arms and legs. He even dabbed some between his toes.

Balam closed the door again, and the drumming resumed.

"This is the scariest part for most people," Itzel said. "This is when you confront your fears."

Leo uncrossed his legs and lay flat on the floor, his eyes staring into the blackness of the unseen ceiling. When the door closed again and he heard Itzel speak, his cynicism disappeared. He had to go through this. At this point, there was no turning back. He had to commit—even though it was so hot, he thought he might die. Then, he considered that he might, and that it might be better for everyone if he did.

"You have to die…to be reborn," Itzel said.

It was as if she knew exactly what frightened him. Leo liked danger, but this was the closest he had ever been to the feeling of death, although he was also completely alive for the first time. The drumming picked up, and Itzel sang and yelped shrilling falsettos into the air and struck an instrument made of chimes. Leo began to calm down, giving in to the experience. He relaxed and melted into the floor. Balam handed the drum to Itzel, and now it was her turn to play. Leo didn't understand how either of them could see. Perhaps shamans had their own set of powers that he didn't know about. Balam arrived at Leo's side and poured fresh water over his forehead. It trickled through his hair and under his head, settling among the palm leaves that covered the floor. He lost control of his body and urinated on himself as he released and relaxed. Despite all the drugs Leo had taken and the number of altered states he'd been in, nothing had ever triggered such a reaction. Yet it seemed natural—necessary, even.

Plants, possibly herbs, maybe even flowers, were set upon his chest and stomach. Leo remained completely still, like someone under anesthesia. He stared into the darkness as Balam lightly slapped a bundle of herbs across various parts of his body, almost like performing an exorcism.

"At the count of three, scream. Scream as loud as you can and let go of everything you don't need to carry anymore," Balam instructed as he backed away, leaving the piles of vegetation on Leo's chest.

Leo prepared to scream. He inhaled, and in that moment, he couldn't tell if his heart had stopped or he had just been desensitized to it. But he was still alive.

"One…" Balam said.

Another deep breath in.

"Two…"

(I want it out. All of it. I want things to change. Let me be strong. Help me be better.)

"Three!"

Leo opened his mouth wide and screamed a burning, heartbreaking scream. It was as loud as the hut was hot. His exhausted breath trembled in the aftermath. A few strained moans seeped out as he began to discover a whole new set of sensations. Then he began to see something other than the pitch black that surrounded him. As he stared upward, his eyes caught the sight of tiny purple dots floating through the air. They were hazy, like the floaters that pass over the surface of your eye, the ones your brain has grown accustomed to and learned to ignore. More dots appeared, giving the stretch of black the appearance of being studded with violet stars.

He closed his eyes and saw a purple aurora on the inside of his eyelids. His eyes darted back and forth as he soaked in the imagery. Then came the warmth. He could feel it in his eyes. As the shifting waves of violet curtains evolved into a mysterious shape, Leo breathed in deeply. The shimmering, diffused light formed into what looked like a lion—no, a wolf. The longer he stared at it, the clearer it became. Even when he repositioned his gaze, he was forced to look at the afterimage, like when staring too long at a single spot. Without warning, the image formed into what looked to be a human eye.

The door opened. Leo opened his eyes, and the colors, the wolf, the eye—were gone. Balam encouraged him to exit. Leo sat up and crawled out of the hut. A little dizzy, a little lightheaded. Itzel lifted his arms out from his body as Balam poured a bowl of chilled water over his head. Leo closed his eyes and listened to the sounds of water dripping to the ground. He didn't want to open his eyes. Not yet.

"Come back…come back…" Itzel said lightly.

Another deep breath, and Leo opened his eyes as Itzel ran her hands down both of his arms. He looked into Itzel's smiling eyes, then up at the large moon in a star-sprinkled sky, then back into her eyes.

Balam wrapped a clean towel around Leo's shoulders.

Itzel smiled. "Welcome…to your new life."

When Leo regained his composure a few minutes later, Itzel offered him a plate of fresh pineapple and papaya. They watched him eat as they spoke in Mayan to each other. After Leo had eaten half the fruit, Balam spoke.

"My wife and I could feel your energy during the ceremony…like a wolf."

Leo's heart began to race.

"Thank you for allowing us to…share…this with you," Itzel said.

They let Leo dry off and get dressed, although for some reason his clothes no longer felt like his. By the time he was fully dressed and back in his own shoes, Balam and Itzel were already back inside. It was quiet, the fire was only a pile of coals, and a green floodlight shone over the lawn. He walked across the lawn back toward his bike, lost in thought.

A rustling caught his attention, and when he looked up, a wolf was standing in his path. It wasn't a dog or a pet of any kind. It was a wild wolf, one with no collar and a razor-sharp stare. Leo became still as a statue and returned the stare.

What is it gonna do? What is a wolf even doing out here? I can't believe it's just staring right—

Then as quickly as the wolf appeared and with even more surprise—Leo gasped—a thought rose up from nowhere. It came first as a feeling, then a thought, and then he saw it like he had seen the purple dots on the cusp of reality. The vision became a voice, and that voice spoke words that instantly made sense. It said, *Your soul is incomplete. You cannot feel...cannot experience happiness...because part of your soul...is absent...is missing.* The voice, reminiscent of a whisper, stopped. There was a stretched-out silence, as if he was waiting for more. Leo met eyes with the wolf once more *(wait...)*, and as he did, the wolf shot into the darkness and out of sight. Leo's eyes whizzed back and forth across the night as he tried to see where it had gone and what it was doing. But it was gone.

Leo wiped the trickle of water dripping from his hair and continued back toward his bike. *My totem?* Leo began to consider all sorts of things as he tried to justify the appearance of the wolf so mysteriously soon after he had had a vision of one. Of course, it was only the beginning of a stream of consciousness, one loaded with the unusual insights and realizations that come as a gift from having an open mind. He remembered reading that as you became more psychic and your third eye cracked open, it was common to see waves of color, specifically purple dots, and orbs...and to see a human eye.

Was he becoming psychic? He made no immediate assumptions about any of his thoughts except for the bit about his soul. *How could that be possible? Nina told me I couldn't feel happiness because I was born in an area that prevented that from happening. Something to do with the sea level, or something like that. What if that wasn't true?* As soon as he reached his bike, he began to consider what and how part of his soul could be missing.

CHAPTER 36

Nina confronted Leo as soon as he walked through the door. His first instinct was to lie and Nina detected it, as Leo had suspected she would. She had a talent on par with Avery for sniffing one out. Leo told her about the shaman and the temazcal, and reminded her once again about the absence of happiness in his life.

"Don't I deserve the chance to try to find that?" Leo asked.

Nina nodded. "As much as anyone else, if not more, considering your…magical handicap, being born below sea level."

She politely asked him to let her know when he was going to leave in the future. It was the all-too-familiar, please-tell-me-where-you're-going speech that went absolutely nowhere. Leo had turned to head toward his room when he mistook a sense of knowing for being dehydrated. He had sweat a lot during the ceremony and hadn't had any water to replenish what he'd lost. But it wasn't that. He realized it wasn't dehydration or lightheadedness, but instead the feeling of a powerful energy boomeranging toward him. He rushed to his room and opened the window.

Leo waited by the window with his makeshift nest before him. A few moments passed, and then a magpie fluttered to a stop on the windowsill. *Another animal? Is this my totem?* But that didn't feel right, mostly because the bird held an old but shiny, silver bullion coin in its black beak. The markings on the coin were ones Leo had never seen before and couldn't decipher. The bold bird hopped twice toward the nest, dropped the coin inside and looked at Leo. Neither of them moved. Then the magpie cocked its head, and Leo could have sworn it winked at him before it flew off into the night, much in the same fashion as the wolf earlier. It wasn't his totem animal; the wolf was. His spell had made the magpie his servant, a collector. Leo reached into the nest and retrieved the silver coin. He now had two of the seven sacred metals that he desired.

The scent of rosemary wafted into the room. Leo turned around and wasn't at all surprised to see Bisa standing there. He was getting the hang of this whole witch thing.

"What's that?" Bisa asked as she pointed to the coin.

"Just something I found." Leo shrugged. "What's up? How you feelin'?"

"Better…" Bisa said. Her forehead wrinkled as she processed the idea that Leo actually thought to ask how she was doing after the attack—and cared enough to do so. "Nina said I should be back to normal by the morning." There was a pause. "Where did you run off to earlier today? You were gone a while."

"I met with a shaman. Tried to figure out how I can…fix what's wrong with me."

"Because you can't feel happiness?"

Leo considered that Nina might have told her, but more than likely, she just knew. "Yeah."

"Sorry, I didn't know if that was private or not. I just felt it."

"It's all good."

Bisa invited herself into his room and sat on the chair closest to the door. "What did the shaman say? Was he able to help you?"

"There were two of them, actually. Husband and wife. So short! I think they helped. I finally found my totem animal."

"So that spell *did* work!"

"I'm not just a pretty face, it turns out," Leo said as he rolled his eyes, making light of his own joke.

"What was it like?"

Leo had been trying to make sense of it himself. "The ceremony? I don't think I have anything I could compare it to. I've never experienced anything like it before. Those people who are in some fatal accident but somehow don't die, and they talk about a near-death experience…It was kinda like that."

"Sounds dangerous."

"So, of course I had to do it, right?" Leo said, grinning.

Bisa felt something under his masked words. "Something has changed. I'm getting a new kind of vibe from you. It's not happiness, though. What did the wolf tell you?"

"I never said anything about a wolf," Leo said, shocked.

"You didn't have to." Bisa looked deep into Leo's eyes and saw something she hadn't seen before, something she recognized but didn't fully understand. Whether it was to be feared or valued, she didn't know yet.

"What are you thinking about?" Leo asked as he noticed the pensive glaze that covered her eyes.

"Maybe we aren't all that different. Perhaps from different worlds, maybe."

Leo chose his words carefully as he pondered what she actually meant. A full minute passed before he spoke again. "I heard something. After I left the ceremony. I've talked to Nina about this before, and it made sense at the time. But I don't think it's legit. Not like I think Nina is lying or anything, I think she just doesn't know. I mean, I think her explanation is wrong.

Not that what she's saying isn't legit, but it's not when it comes to me."

"About your handicap?"

Leo nodded. "I'm not a religious person. I'd probably burst into flames if I entered a church, and I don't know much about souls, either, but I think part of mine is missing."

"Your totem gave you this. The wolf."

"It doesn't make any sense to me."

"Is there anything you've seen since you've gotten here that makes sense? What in either of our lives has ever made sense?" Bisa said with a hard sense of truth.

Leo vented every thought and concern he had kept quiet about his entire life. Each sentence was more heartbreaking than the one before it. His eyes were lined with tears like a mug of tea that had been filled just beyond its limits. "Even if part of my soul is missing, I don't know how I would go about trying to get it back. If I can even get it back. What if I can't? Shouldn't everyone be able to be happy about something? To feel that? I've made some dumb-ass decisions in my life, but I can't even enjoy a beer and a grilled cheese after a shitty day and feel good about it. I watch all these movies where people are deliriously happy about things—small things, big things, everyday things—and I just don't have that. And those are bad examples, I know, but it's the same shit I see every day in real life. I can see what people feel when they're happy; it shows on their faces. And now…well, now I really *understand* what I don't have. And I know I'm not just making it up. What kind of a life is that?" Leo's voice trembled.

He looked deep into Bisa's eyes, and for the first time, Bisa was able to see past the only version of Leo she had ever known—perhaps the only version he himself had ever known.

"When I first saw you, I thought, *What the hell is that guy doing here?* But then I got to know you, and I thought, *I really don't want to know this person.* And it just got worse the more time I had to spend around you. It was like you were the epitome of every single repulsive trait I had ever encountered."

Leo's eyes shrank. "Is this supposed to be making me feel better?"

"The more I tried not to judge you, the harder you made it. But I don't know you, and you don't know me. I understand you more than I thought I ever could. I empathize with you in ways I thought I couldn't. And that itself doesn't make any sense. That alone goes against any sort of logic that I know of. After hearing what you just said, and knowing all of that, and feeling all that I feel from you now, I would say with one hundred percent certainty that if you were only the version I saw when I first met you…you wouldn't have said even half of what you just told me. You would be a lost cause. Everyone's made stupid decisions. No one is immune to that. There isn't a person on this planet who could say otherwise, and if they did, they'd be lying. I don't think you're a lost cause. If I don't think that, I don't know how you could."

"Someone who gets high while their daughter's dying on the side of the street doesn't sound like someone with a hopeful future."

Bisa could feel the pain. It was the kind of pain that she had felt herself. Pain was only a form of energy, an emotion; the origin of it was circumstantial. There was an unusual luminosity to Leo's pain, one that allowed her to see and feel all the colors and facets of its complexity like a sunbeam hitting the inside of a geode. Bisa walked over toward Leo, touched his chin with her thumb and forefinger and lifted his head. She placed a kiss upon his lips and then rested her forehead against his. It was the type of kiss that was shared by neither lover nor friend—but between starseeds*, souls that have origins in the stars and are all cosmically linked to one another. Leo's body relaxed for a moment, like a balloon that had finally lost all its air. They doted on each other for a moment, one without question or the need for explanation.

It was a short-lived break from Leo's self-loathing. Bisa slowly embraced him, her arms wrapping around his neck with the genuine empathy of someone who understood him, if only for a moment. It was in that brief moment that Leo realized that everything Bisa had said and done should have induced happiness, yet he still couldn't feel it. Her words, kiss and embrace inspired neither happiness nor hope—only a dark wave of wretched misery. It served as a reminder that he was broken, that something *was* missing. He felt the physical sensation of her lips against his and yet an absence of emotion, something he knew he should have but didn't. *This is something to be happy about. Anyone else would be happy about this. I hate myself for being like this.*

Leo released himself from Bisa's arms. "If I had had my head on straight and had met you years and years ago…I think I would've had a very different life. If I'd fallen for someone like you." Leo left the room as he wiped the evidence of a cry from his eyes. He raced out of Bisa's arms, away from the bedroom and into where he felt the safest and most comfortable: the enveloping arms of risk and danger. It was the closest substitute for what he thought he *should* have felt when Bisa kissed him. Leo hopped onto his bike and drove off into the night.

The moon was high when Leo parked his bike on the side of the road. He had no reason to stop other than the intuitive draw he felt that he couldn't explain. His eyes were dry and he could see clearly. There was a hiking trail ahead of him, or at least that's what it looked like. A makeshift one, the type of trail made by youngsters who sneak out after curfew to drink with their friends in the woods. It was winter, and spring's hatching snakes weren't upon him yet, making it seem a little less dangerous, a little less interesting. He entered the woods regardless.

On a sunny afternoon, the forest ambience was nearly perfect: the tall trees, the angled slope of the ground and the rustling of the wind through the branches. Under cover of night, it was eerie and ominous. It fit in faultlessly with Leo's state of mind. He wasn't looking for anything specific, but it was in that aimless stroll that he found something. He heard a sound as spooky as the forest. He stopped and listened. Voices. Not chatter, but chanting, singing and yelping. Leo had always struggled with verisimilitude, but the likelihood that there were people gathered in the middle of a forest late at night seemed slim. On the other hand, he remembered that he had brought the coven into a dark forest to chant by a fire, so perhaps he was being a little too dismissive.

He'd already walked for what felt like an eternity, and he had no idea how far into the forest he was. It only made sense to check out who or what was having a party. Maybe it was a bunch of drunk teenagers and a twenty-four-pack of cheap beer. Maybe they'd offer him one. It could be a bunch of destitute squatters who chose to live in the woods rather than in the tent city under the Ponchartrain Expressway. He might actually know some of those people. He also might get stabbed to death, but it was a risk he was willing to take.

The chanting synced with the drumming, and he could smell campfire smoke now. He was a few feet from the wall of branches and leaves that blocked the fire. When he was close enough to see through the netting of tangled branches, he stopped to stare in secret like a stealthy Peeping Tom. A good twenty feet away was a group of six people. It appeared to be a voodoo ceremony. Leo had seen enough films to know when there was some voodoo going on. It helped that he had taken a brief look through the Voodoo Museum on Dumaine Street too.

A large man dressed in white greeted a large wooden drum with symbols painted in blue on the side like it was an esteemed king. He dropped to his knees and kissed the ground before he retrieved it with his hands and signaled to a woman behind him. She was dressed in shades of blue and white. Barefoot, she walked toward the drum with a shiny sequined bottle in her grasp. She poured what Leo assumed was a mess of wine in front of the drum as the rhythm changed. A man drew closer to the fire with a black goat strung over his back, its front legs hanging over his left shoulder and the back legs over his right, like a tender embrace from a lover.

Everyone was dancing. But it wasn't a type of dancing that Leo had seen before. It wasn't the sloppy, alcohol-induced sluttery where people shoved their asses into someone's crotch, or the style of sandwich that involved two guys and a girl with a GHB cocktail. Leo had seen all of that before, and this was nothing like that. It was a frenzied, wild type of movement that caused one woman to fall to the ground in convulsive spasms. The dancers appeared to be completely entranced, possessed.

The woman's feet left a circle in the dirt as she spun and popped up off the ground like a pebble during an earthquake.

They danced, all except one: she who held a red clay jar on the edge of the group. She had the same coloring and shape as someone he'd seen recently. The woman turned around as if she had heard Leo's thoughts. Her hair, red-tipped dreads that hung in a sort of messy perfection. He *had* seen her before. She was the woman who had smiled at him at the voodoo shop. This time she wasn't wearing any makeup. Not that she needed any to begin with. The fire only seemed to bring out the gold in her eyes. *Shit. She just saw me.* Leo was so distracted by her that he hadn't even processed that she was aware of his presence at what looked to be an intimate and private gathering to which he most certainly was not invited and would never have been invited, and where he might suffer the same fate as the goat if he made his presence known. *Shit.* He had let himself be seen. The woman turned back to the ritual fire, waited for a moment, then turned back toward Leo and stared. It felt like hours. When the decade was over, she began to walk toward Leo, the red clay jar in her hands.

"What are you doing here?" she asked, sounding both alarmed and intrigued.

"I'm sorry, I'm not spying or nothing, I was just walkin' in the woods. I didn't mean to interrupt or anything."

"I've seen you."

"No."

"Yeah. At Maji. You walked in. I was leaving. Right?" She insisted on an answer.

"You smiled at me."

She was quiet for a moment, and when she determined that he wasn't dangerous and had actually stumbled onto them completely by accident, she smiled.

"Just like that," he added.

If it hadn't been so dark, Leo could have seen her blushing a bit.

"Okay, well, you can't be here," she said as she looked back toward the group by the fire. They were too possessed to notice her absence. She turned back to Leo and flashed him a cautioning stare. "Please, just go. This is *really* private, and you have no reason to be here. So you need to go."

Back at the hysterical dance circle, a woman poured out a powder into a symbol. She stood before a table covered with dripping candles, bells and bones.

"Why? What's going on? Is this voodoo?" Leo couldn't help but be fascinated. It was beyond his sense of danger. He felt a spiritual pull—one he didn't think he would have felt before the temazcal.

"We're paying back some spirits. We have to." She wasn't quite sure why she had told Leo that.

"Why is that woman on the ground?" Leo was even more insistent about getting an answer than she had been that he leave.

"Spirits can't eat, drink, fuck or dance…They want to, but they can't. But we can. It's how we communicate. Spirits aren't on the same plane as we are. They're everywhere, all at once. They aren't restricted to a place or time like we are. This is how we connect and communicate with them, because we can't communicate with words. The language is rhythm…music. Time is a concept that humans use, not spirits. It's not the same for them. So we set aside a time and a place and a method to call them. They do a lot for us, and we give a lot back for what they do for us." It flowed from her lips like she had been talking in her sleep. Slightly aware, but unaware.

Leo looked down at her hand. "What's in the jar?"

"It's a govi jar. Spirit jar. When you die…your little angel or little spirit stays in your body for three days. A lot can happen in three days. Sometimes we collect that spirit, to protect it from others."

"What would they do with it?"

"If someone has that, has your spirit, they can resurrect your body and make you a slave. You're a zombie like that, and you do whatever that person wants you to do. You're stuck until they set you free. If they don't, you'll never get to the otherworld, and you'll be a slave for eternity." She blinked as if a veil had been lifted from her face and brushed her eyelashes.

"How do you do it?" Leo asked as he reached out to touch the symbol etched into the side of the jar. His finger came in contact with the red clay and he saw its contents across his eyes. It was as if a movie projector had suddenly turned on and beamed onto the inside of his eyes. Graveyard dirt, twigs from twelve different trees and fragments of bone.

"Do what?" A newfound sense of urgency and awareness surged through her. "Look, you have to go. Now. Get out of here. Go!" Her voice trailed off into a whisper as she shoved him back into the trees.

Leo stepped back up to the web of branches. "Wait! What's your name?"

"Tambala," she said as she broke away from his clutches, unaware of the information that she had divulged, and slipped back into the ritual.

CHAPTER 37

Mercury retrograde was in effect and Avery felt anger and hate, but it wasn't hers. It didn't belong to anyone in the coven either. It belonged to someone, no, *someones*. It was dark, destructive hate and it felt like sharp needles. The conclusion that those emotions belonged to someone else was rooted in instinct. Avery looked at the clock. It was late. Then, the emotions turned into scents. She could smell the hate and anger, and it was getting stronger, coming closer. Avery ran through some possibilities in her mind for a few seconds, and then, as if pushed by some unseen force, leapt from her bed with urgency and ran into the great room. Ollie, Bisa and Mitch were watching television. They turned around to see Avery, struck with some kind of unknown fear.

"What's wrong?" Ollie asked. He didn't need to know specifics; he felt it too. But he felt something new, something different. The smell of a wet forest floor filled his nose. He had smelled that before.

"Quiet," Avery said quickly. She held her hands out, begging them to stay motionless. "Someone's here."

Right then, the door to the back patio opened. The door swung sluggishly to reveal nothing and no one. Mitch switched off the television and stood up. The house was silent. Too quiet. Avery lifted her hands and lit all the candles in the room. She uttered something she recalled from the book on her nightstand, and as her words filled the room, the mystery of who had opened the door was unveiled. Maisie, Blake and Andy stood next to the door, stylized for battle, or execution.

"Nina!" Avery shouted.

Blake lifted her hand as if she were about to swat a fly, and Avery rose from the floor, sailed through the air and smacked into the wall of the study. Her body stuck to the wall like a fly in a hanging flytrap.

Andy's hands filled with flames as though his palms were a pack of matches that had been struck all at once. He reeled his hand back and took aim at Mitch, but before he could deliver his blow, the sound of a blast sprang from the front door, and wood and metal exploded across the floor. Before the debris even had time to settle, the door was kicked open and Bowie and Buckshot entered the house. A smoking shotgun was rattling wildly in Buckshot's hands, and Bowie unsheathed his knife.

The gunshot distracted Blake's concentration, and Avery fell to the floor like a marionette whose strings had suddenly been cut. The witches of both covens broke off and took cover behind furniture.

"Come on out, you fuckin' witches!" Buckshot screamed. He raised the shotgun, steadied his aim into the candlelit room and cocked the gun to shoot once more.

Bowie took a few steps into the house and into the hallway, where he saw Avery slowly recovering from having the wind knocked straight out of her lungs. She raised her head, but before she could even form a solid thought, Bowie reached down, grabbed her by the neck and lifted her off the floor. Her feet dangled as they tried to find footing, her toes grazing the hardwood as though doing some twisted kind of ballet. Avery saw a glimmer run down the edge of the knife in the candlelight. Bowie grinned, nearing the moment of satisfaction, but as his arm plunged forward to stab, Nina dashed from the dark hallway and landed a blow to his arm with a large brass candlestick. It hardly stunned him, but it was enough for him to drop Avery. Bowie kicked like a wild horse and nailed Nina in the stomach, sending her doubled over and grunting back into the hallway.

Buckshot's gaze swayed across the room. He turned toward Bowie and saw Avery on her knees at Bowie's feet, gasping for air. Avery reacted faster than Buckshot could squeeze the trigger, and a purple flare of pint-sized lightning, or perhaps fire, shot out from her hand and struck Buckshot's hands. He released one hand from the gun and waved it in the air to soothe the burn.

Andy appeared to materialize out of thin air, quickly swung his hands, and sent Bowie and Buckshot down the hall like a couple of bowling balls bouncing in and out of lanes.

"Who the fuck are these assholes?" Andy said as he started to charge his hands back up with fire. They were the assholes who were out to hunt and destroy all witches, including them, if they could. They had unintentionally lucked out and stumbled onto a jackpot of witches to kill. All they had to do was actually do it. The witches had a lot of power between them, so Buckshot and Bowie would have to outsmart them if they were going to be successful. They had one hell of a task at hand and an even more hellish disadvantage.

Blake clapped her hands, and the furniture rose from the floor. Mitch, Bisa and Ollie scattered to their feet and tried to find cover in the house. Mitch and Bisa ran into Ollie's room, and Blake narrowed her eyes and sent a chair and some firewood after them, which exploded against the door as they slammed it shut. Ollie found himself at the potion cabinet and chose a bottle at random to use as a weapon. If there was something inside it that would function as a weapon—great! If not, he could always aim the bottle at their face and knock them out. He uncorked the bottle, and the smell of the liquid was stronger than his sense of fear. He trusted that it was something useful. With one quick and fortunate throw, he pitched the bottle at Blake and it knocked her in the head, fell to the floor and shattered. The liquid spilled out around her feet.

Buckshot raised his gun once more and tried to take aim, but the gun was too hot. Instead, he turned the gun around to wield the butt of it as a bludgeon. He ran down the hall, screaming, holding the gun back and ready to hit a home run, until Andy waved his hand once more and flung him straight into a pillar in the great room, knocking out what few front teeth he had left.

Bowie bounced to his feet and tossed his knife through the air. Like a pinwheel in a windstorm, it sailed down the hallway and struck Andy in the arm. Andy stumbled back a bit and screamed out in pain.

Maisie stood by the door and watched. She slipped back into a dark corner and hid.

Avery ran to the puddle of potion and stuck her hands in it. The potion clung to her palms as she rose to her feet, and she released it with a pendulum-like swing of her arms. The potion slipped from her hands and formed a seal over Blake's face, like the bulbous formation of water a split second before someone breaks its tension from underneath. Blake tumbled back and scratched at her face, leaving little wakes in the water after every pass. Avery reached back into the spilled potion and spread her fingers, and crystalline patterns began to form. A hazy gust of expelled air rose from her hands as the water cracked and crunched and solidified into a frozen pond of ice on the floor. The ice spread toward Blake's feet, and when it hit the bottom of her boots, icicle vines shot up around her leg like tent stakes and locked her in place. The icy vines grew and spread across Blake's body like a storm cell over a patch of land. If she didn't drown from the water covering her face, she would surely freeze to death.

Buckshot, bloody and fuming, picked up his gun and brought it down on Avery's back with the force of a single gunshot. Her back cracked as she fell toward the floor in agony, wriggling like a worm left out in the sun. Her hands went to her back as tears trickled out of her eyes.

Nina sprang back from the darkness and grabbed hold of Buckshot's gun. The struggle didn't last long, because Blake cast her hands toward them both. In a single blast she propelled them across the great room and into the corner nearest Ollie's room, where Mitch was hiding. Avery distanced herself from the pain as best she could, and concentrated on the sounds outside. She heard the bees, and she closed her eyes and called to them in her mind until her thoughts became words. From the marriage of her bedside book of magic and her intention, she created a summoning spell. Then it happened: a buzzing drove of angry bees rushed in through the patio door. She was one with them. Like an army of loyal soldiers, the bees swirled into a cyclone and dashed toward Bowie. Avery just wanted the pain to stop, the attack to stop.

Bowie looked up at the swirling tornado of bees, illuminated by the candlelight. He ran toward Andy, and with an adrenaline-fired leap, crashed into him and wrapped his hand around his knife. The bees drew closer and began to wrap around both of them.

Bisa was on her knees in Ollie's room with her eyes closed, chanting a mantra over and over, trying to gain control over the minds of their attackers. She tried as hard as she could but she just couldn't concentrate enough to take hold. Ollie's door opened, and the piles of wood and broken chair pieces tumbled inside. Buckshot wiped his eyes and saw Mitch. He reached for his gun, cocked it back and fired. Mitch would have been hit had the gun not been slapped to the side by an unseen force. It was Maisie. She had saved him. The gun's barrel was crushed under her will as she brought her fingers into a tight fist and stepped out of the shadows and into the light.

A bee stung Bowie, and two pierced Andy with their barbs. Another few bees trailed out of the cyclone and stung Blake, who had nearly passed out from holding her breath underwater. It was clear that this was not a battle Bowie was going to win, not like this. He grabbed hold of Andy, using him as a shield, and broke through the swarm of bees. As he breached the wall of bees and broke into the clear, he elbowed Andy, sending him back into the bees screaming in terror. Bowie didn't look back and didn't wait for Buckshot. He didn't have to. Buckshot had had enough. His favorite gun was broken, and he couldn't seem to land a single blow if his life depended on it—and clearly…it did. He shuffled around on the floor and rolled away from the witches. Buckshot raced out the door at a speed that would have been admired by gold-medal-winning Olympic athletes. The truck was already pulling away when Buckshot hopped in the back and grabbed hold of the sides to stabilize himself.

Maisie helped Mitch and Nina up from the floor. Blake looked around the room in horror, realizing she'd been moments away from drowning. Andy rose from a small pool of blood on the floor, his right hand clutching the stab wound. The bees had dispersed and he was free. Blood gushed through his fingers and soaked his clothes. No amount of pressure would be able to stop the flow of blood. He needed help, he needed magic—Blake's magic. She was the strongest, and she would surely know what to do. After all, this had been her idea. He stumbled to his feet like a deer that had just been hit by a car and survived. He arrived at Blake's side, and after a few moments of panic and lightheadedness, he placed his hands on the sides of the water bubble covering her mouth and tried to break through it.

Avery released her power over the bees and sprinted forward a few steps. She threw her arms up, and the room was immediately filled with a warm, blowing wind. It was the kind of wind that one would experience if a typhoon ever met a volcanic eruption. Debris rose from the floor as the wind grew stronger. Above Avery's body was a small flowing mass of blackness. That's all anyone could see, because the wind had blown out all the candles. There was a bright flash of light above her, then another, like lightning from the center of a dense storm cloud. Avery's hair lashed out like tiny whips. The air in the room grew balmy, like right before a storm hits. Then, a sharp, thin vein of lightning jutted out from the black cloud and illuminated the room. The wind howled and whistled.

Blake scratched at the impenetrable water covering her face while Andy desperately tried to save her. Another few threads of razor-thin lightning bolts spat out into the air. A few more shot out in random directions with tiny branches of their own electric stingers. The room illuminated with each mystifying spark. The lightning didn't crack and thunder, but sparked in micro-booms like untapped forces of nature that had just awakened from slumber. The electric shocks continued to stab out into the room with the unpredictability of a live wire chock-full of high currents. The sparks buzzed and popped reminiscent of a blown circuit breaker until one sliced through the edge of the water covering Blake's face, popping the bubble. Blake gasped for air. Another bolt quaked through the air and jolted the ice that had formed at her feet.

"Maisie! Go! Now!" Andy called out over the howling wind and sputtering electricity. He bowed his head toward Blake and muttered something under his breath, and moments later he and Blake were gone.

Bisa stepped forward and held her hands out towards Avery. She spread her fingers and with a gentle nudge of influence, she disrupted Avery's spell long enough her to sink to her knees. Nina rushed toward Avery and grabbed hold of her arms. In a matter of seconds, Nina's influence dissolved Avery's output of energy. Mitch flipped on some lights and looked around at the mess.

"Is anyone hurt?" Nina asked. "Avery? You okay?"

"My back. It really hurts."

Nina spun around toward Mitch. "Mitch! Come here and try to heal her."

Mitch emerged from the corner. "I don't know how to do that. I don't even know if I can."

"Try. Please?" Nina asked. She pointed to Maisie. "You!" She tore across the floor toward Maisie like a rattlesnake. "You better have a damn good reason why you're still here!"

"I do." Maisie backed away from Nina like a scared child.

"I knew your coven was dangerous."

"That's why I'm here. To help."

"You're a little late for that. Someone could have died. A lot of help you were. What do you even mean? Help with what?"

"I wasn't sure what they were going to do," Maisie said. "I didn't think they were going to actually go through with anything. But I came along in case they did."

Mitch was still holding his chest and feeling the beating of his heart. "She saved my life. She stopped that hillbilly from like, shooting me in the face."

There was a pause. "I'm listening," Nina said calmly.

"Merlot recruited me into the coven early on," Maisie said. "It didn't feel right, but I had nowhere to go. She was the only one who knew what I was going through. But I never felt comfortable with them."

"She's telling the truth," Avery said. "I smell oak—"

Nina cut her off. "Yeah, oakmoss, I know. So then why go along with it? What was their plan?"

"They don't see the point in your plans. They think your trying to achieve balance is stupid. They think they should be encouraging witches to use their powers to get what they need to survive, not helping a thankless world. Those are their words, not mine."

"Their powers," Ollie said. "What kind of witches are they? I didn't even know we could do things like that."

"Normally, we can't. But they're all amped up on drugs," Maisie said.

Leo entered through what was left of the front door. "What the fuck happened here?"

"We all almost died!" Mitch shouted. "Where were you?"

Nina kept her attention on Maisie. "Drugs? Like what? Drugs don't...amplify our powers."

"I'm not talking about coke and heroin. I mean magical drugs."

Naturally, given his past—Leo began to feel a familiar sense of curiosity. After the temazcal, he had stopped dropping acid and taking all other drugs. But when he heard the term *magical drugs*, it not only intrigued him, but left him wondering what he could achieve under the influence of magical drugs. Old-school drugs like weed and heroin were a thing of the past, his former self, but now there was something completely new to explore, and possibly for good reason.

"Merlot dosed us with it during our initiation to the coven. I don't know how you were initiated into this coven, but Merlot used ants. She fed the ants the drug and then used ant bites to initiate us, which gave us our first…*hit*. The bites take a really long time to heal and I never liked how it made me feel; it didn't vibe with me. Everyone else loved it. It made them feel—alive. Happy and powerful. Whatever she gave us enhanced our powers, gave us abilities we normally wouldn't have. Blake and Andy kept using the ants to keep their power. So they were all amped up, acting on irrational impulses. I don't even think Merlot used it herself. She just used it on us."

"Where did they get it?" Leo asked.

Nina looked back at Leo, trying to gauge where his curiosity was coming from.

"A guy named Evan. He's some kind of dealer."

Before Maisie could finish telling them about the drug dealer, Leo was asking more and more questions until he arrived at the answer to his question: "How can I find him?"

"It's hard to explain," Maisie said. "It's not like you can just go visit this guy. I mean, you can, but he's not local. He wasn't in Texas either. He can give people access to his place, but he can't leave. It's a strange kind of magic. Even humans go to him for drugs. All kinds, not just magical."

"But how would they know where to even find him if it's like…accessed only through magic?" Leo asked.

"He hands out business cards."

"Seriously?"

"Yeah. People can get freebies with every referral. For humans, it's different. They don't even know that he's magically restricted. Once they touch the card, the address on the card changes according to whatever is convenient and discreet for the customer. If there's an abandoned house somewhere, the card will show that address. They show up, knock, and the door opens to his house. I'm not really sure where he is. But that's all I know about how it works. Merlot has known him for years."

Leo grabbed her arm to inspect Maisie's ant bites. Those sores looked oh so familiar. But that wasn't what he was interested in. He was interested in the imagery he received from Maisie's mind when he touched her. Like a psychic download, he knew how to contact Evan. Not for a delivery, but for a social call, where he lived.

"I don't want you going back," Nina said to Maisie.

"I can't."

"Stay here with us until we figure something out. We can set you up in the study for now after we clean up some of this mess." Nina knew they were in very real danger, and she had to figure out a way to protect the coven. *Why didn't our protection spell work?* It had been carried out perfectly, but it was ineffective. She walked around the house with a cauldron of burning incense and cast a few more protection charms, hoping it would be enough to protect them from another attack.

The next morning, Ollie and Nina collaborated on the patio to create a sort of antidote to the drug that Maisie was given: a powdery mixture of cornstarch, sweetgrass, black henbane, wormwood and hibiscus. A concoction that could potentially be fatal if mishandled, but restorative if executed correctly. The powder was administered over Maisie and left to marinate for ten minutes to draw out the drug. Fifteen minutes later, she felt like herself again. All she needed now was a good shower and some fresh clothes.

"So, what do we do now?" Maisie asked.

"I think it's time for another chat with Merlot," Nina said.

"They'll kill you the moment they see your face."

"Then I better wear a mask."

Nina touched the gate to Merlot's home and instantly felt something was awry. *Did they know I was coming? They couldn't have.* Nina fingered the bag of powdered antidote in her pocket. The spell would be a little weaker than if she had gone in person. But Houston was too far to drive, and projecting was the only "flight" she could get on such short notice. Nina passed through the gate and saw the door to the house was open. Something seemed wrong. She pushed open the door, letting it hit the wall. Nina entered and listened physically and energetically. It was unexpectedly quiet, with no sign of a threat. She proceeded inside slowly and carefully, keeping her hands on the antidote in her pocket for easy access. Then, she smelled something foul—the scent of death.

Nina raced to the room by the patio. The hairs on the back of her neck spiked as she saw the bodies of Blake and Andy on the floor. Andy was slouched up against the wall with gauze draped over his stab wound and spilling onto the floor into a pile of coagulated blood. Blake was a few feet away, supine, dead from an unknown cause. Nina hadn't seen a dead body in a very long time, and upon seeing the pale witches, she flashed back to the first lifeless body she had ever seen. Her grandmother had died peacefully in her sleep, and Nina remembered her face, which looked like she was resting or dreaming.

This was different. Andy's eyes were wide open, and Blake's were bulging out of their sockets. Nina walked over to Blake and knelt down beside her. With two fingers, she tried to pull the cold eyelids down, only to find that they immediately lifted back up like cheap roller blinds, just like the kind in the nursing home where her grandmother had passed. *So that doesn't actually work like it does in the movies,* she thought. Nina had no reason to believe it was death by magical means. Only…it had to be. *Right?*

She had no sooner registered the fact that Blake and Andy were dead than she realized Merlot was gone, but…*was she dead?* Nina searched the rest of the house. It then occurred to her that maybe this was the work of those who had attacked her own coven at the Barrow House. Maybe they were responsible for the death of the witch in Mobile too. She immediately began to miss New York, a place she had lived long enough to call home. There was so much death in the South…so much hate. She thought she'd never feel at home in a place like this.

Moments before she returned to her body, she caught another scent, that of wet rock, like the walls of a moist wine cellar. *That's a Primordial smell.* But witches retained their smell only when they were alive. It dissipated almost instantly when the lights went out. It belonged to someone outside the coven. Not human, no—a witch.

When Nina returned to her body, she considered this was all more than she could handle and she was, as they say, in over her head. She would have to meet with the Advisory immediately, and she didn't feel prepared for that either. They had asked her to determine if Leo was a Corporeal and she wasn't even able to do that. Nina walked out into the great room to meet with everyone.

"This sucks!" Mitch said as he tossed his deck of tarot cards on the ground. "Why does Avery have such good luck with divination? Like, *I'm* the one with the tarot cards! I'm the one who's dedicated and committed to learning them!"

"I'm not trying to outdo you, Mitch! It's just intuition!" Avery said with a grin.

Mitch looked up at Nina. "You're back? What happened?"

"They're dead."

"You killed them?" Avery asked in horror.

Nina shook her head. "No. Not me. They were already dead when I got there. Except for Merlot. I don't know if she's dead or alive…She wasn't there. But…I smelled a witch. A witch killed them. So now, I think we should think about how we are going to protect ourselves. I've requested a meeting with the Advisory, and we're going to figure this out. There's no need to panic right away."

"Mmm-hmm…" Mitch said as he collected the tarot cards, shuffled them hurriedly and selected a single card at random. The Tower.

"Someone should be out today to fix the front door and the bedroom door. Thank you for cleaning up what you can. Let's, for now, try to just get back into our routine and be mindful about our environment and those in it. It's Imbolg, not that anyone actually cares…It's Carnival season. Go see a parade, have some fun. You guys deserve that after all this."

Avery rubbed her hands together to channel her excitement. "Yes! I *love* that idea. Chewbacchus is tonight. Let's go!"

Mitch rolled his eyes. "I hate parades."

"What? No one hates parades. Do you not like fun?"

"That's not my kind of fun! It's way too crowded and everyone's drunk. How is that fun? Parades are just a bunch of people throwing trash into crowds of people who like to catch trash. And they have like forty of them, right? Like, why do they have to have that many parades? Isn't one, or like, maybe even two, good enough?"

Avery scoffed and shook her head. "Don't be such a curmudgeon. We're going. All of us. I'm telling everyone that's what we're doing. We're going to do something fun as a group for once!" Avery picked up the tarot deck, spread the cards out in front of her and picked one. She smiled before she flipped it around to show them. "See! Four of Wands! It's time to celebrate and have some fun."

"I'm not convinced," Mitch said reproachfully.

Avery was determined to get her way. She locked eyes with Mitch, reached into the pile and pulled out another card. "Mmm-hmm," she said, bursting with satisfaction. "Why does no one listen to me when I say something? Look, see! Three of Cups! Fun, friendship, be nourished by those who back you up. You don't *have* to sit home alone and mope unless you absolutely *want* to. And I'm telling you right now, you don't want to. We're going."

Ollie entered the room with a half-eaten apple in his hand. "I'm with Avery."

"Good! Two down, two to go," Avery said.

It didn't take much effort for Avery to convince Leo. If there was anything he didn't like, it was sitting still doing nothing. Even though he'd spent much of his life in Louisiana, he'd never truly tired of Carnival season. Chewbacchus was for weirdos, and he was a weirdo. Bisa felt it was the best thing for the group. She wasn't crazy about parades either. They seemed like a bunch of white people on pedestals choosing who got a prize. Other parades like Muses and Zulu had a different energy, but that wasn't the point. She was also not going to go unprepared into a public place knowing that they could potentially be walking targets. Bisa prepared a little defensive potion and secured it in her pocket, a sort of pepper spray for witches. If they were to be attacked, she would be able to defend herself, after a fashion.

Chewbacchus started at seven, so they planned to be there by five to accommodate for parking and time for a to-go drink from one of the bars near the parade route. Leo dragged them to Lafitte's for a purple drink, and they walked from there. Mitch turned out to be mostly correct—the streets were filled with crowds of drunk people—but he had neglected to predict that there were a lot of people in costume for no apparent reason other than to be at a parade.

"What am I drinking?" Mitch asked, his face puckering after the first sip of the alcoholic slushie.

"I told you, a purple drink!" Leo shouted.

"Yeah, but like, what even is that?"

"Man, can't you just enjoy it?" Leo said.

"Can I *not* like something?"

Avery swallowed a big gulp of her purple drink and wiped her lips. "Yeah, but you tend to not like something just because everyone else likes it."

Mitch scoffed, thinking that she had no place to call him out because it was mostly true. "That's not true!"

Ollie took a sip of the drink, pondered the flavor and texture for a moment, nodded and then took another sip. He looked up toward the street, his eyes open and bright. "Let's go wait for the parade over there!" He pointed to a spot near the corner where there were just enough people for Mitch to be comfortable.

The other members of the Advisory arrived just after seven thirty. A detailed rehash of events followed soon afterward. They had no answers, only a lot of speculation.

"If a witch really is behind this, I have no idea how we are going to figure out who it is," Nina said. "It could be anyone!"

"What about the Corporeal issue? Have you found anything that would lead you to believe he is one?" Rosemary asked.

"Nothing new since we last discussed it. After the attack, I became a little preoccupied with that."

Per looked around the house and noticed it was empty. "Where is everyone? Are they here? I'd like to meet with Leo."

"Yes! I'd like to speak with him. Perhaps we as a collective can determine this," Rosemary added.

"How would we even do that?" Nina asked. "Do you know something I don't?"

"Are they here?" Rosemary questioned.

"No, everyone went to see the parade."

Nix looked uneasy, or perhaps piqued, but said nothing.

"Is it Carnival season already? I've always wanted to experience Mardi Gras. It seems so wildly unnecessary and wasteful!" Per said.

"I feel the same way about Nix, but we still celebrate his birthday every year, now, don't we?" Rosemary jibed.

"How do they even have parade floats with all the potholes here?" Per asked.

"It's why they have the parades, dear—so they can fill them up with beads," Rosemary said.

The parade wasn't a seamless succession of impressive floats. It was more a float-wait, wait some more, float-wait-wait longer-float type of event. It was the delay between floats that tested Leo's patience. The excitement of the anticipation wore off very quickly as the pace seemed to slow down after each float passed. But he had faith in his home state and was irrationally proud of it.

Bisa and Mitch left the parade and walked back to get another purple drink. Mitch liked the taste now. They took a shortcut to avoid the large crowds that plagued the streets. Halfway down the block, Bisa felt a message coming through the divine. When her vision was clear, she looked up to see two men—boys, really, bored little boys with nothing to do except entertain themselves at the expense of others. It was why they had busted the windshield of a car on Toledano Street the previous night, and the window of a small yellow house on Chestnut Street the night before that. Boredom and ignorance were the biggest influence on their idle hands. As Bisa and Mitch walked closer to the two boys on the sidewalk, their laughter turned to chatter and then became whispers.

"Show us to his room, please," Rosemary asked.

As Nina led the group down the hall toward Leo's room, she said, "I don't know what you're hoping to find. I don't see how anything of his would help us decide whether he's a Corporeal. I also don't think it's right to be snooping through his things without permission."

Rosemary lifted a finger in the air like a beacon of reasoning. "It's not quite as scandalous as that, Nina. We're simply taking a cursory glance to see if there are any warning signs."

"Rosemary, with all due respect, it seems like you think I've missed something or I'm not able to detect something really obvious."

"Don't be absurd, Nina! Being a Proctor is much like being a parent, and sometimes parents want to believe the best of their children, leaving them blind to the fact that they're actually nasty little twats behind their back. When all witches, even those outside your own coven, are in danger, we can't be too careful."

Nina opened the door to Leo's room and stepped inside. Per, Nix and Rosemary followed close behind. Rosemary took a look around the room and clasped her hands together.

"What exactly are you looking for?" Nina asked.

"I'm not entirely sure. Ask me again when I find it," Rosemary said.

"*If*…you find something," Nina added.

"Correct! Again, just a precaution."

"I'm sorry, I wish I could be of more help," Nina said.

"You can get me a sample of whatever it is you're using on your skin. Your face is positively radiant."

"Faggot!" one of the thugs shouted in a loud, clear megaphone-like voice from the other side of the parked car that separated them.

Mitch, who had never been one for conflict in the past, normally would have kept walking and decided it wasn't worth his time. But those days were over. He was a witch now. With that came confidence, a sense of self-worth and a strength he'd always had but never bothered to exercise. He always tried to see the beauty in things, as long as it wasn't a parade or ignorant people. Being called a derogatory term was by no means something new, but it had been a long time since it had happened. Maybe it was because he always surrounded himself with more open-minded people, or because he was now in the

South, where progress was so slow, it practically moved backward.

"Faggot-ass bitch!" the other hooligan said, and then snickered at himself.

Mitch didn't know if it was the sense of empowerment that made him react, or the memories of his God-loving family and asshole brother who called him a faggot, or the purple drink, but it took less than a second for his heart to skip a beat and his pulse to accelerate. He saw himself in one second as a doormat, and in the next, as the shoe for once.

Mitch stopped in his tracks. "Excuse me?" he called back as he turned to face the two boys on the sidewalk.

"You heard me, fuckin' shitty booty bitch!"

"Who's the bitch? Why don't you come here and say it to my face instead of hiding behind some parked cars?"

Bisa grabbed Mitch's hand and started to pull. "Come on, ignore them."

"No. I've been ignoring assholes like this all my life, trying to be the better person, but you know what? Sometimes assholes just need to be shown that they're assholes. I'm not a fucking doormat."

The two boys pulled their pants from their lower thighs to their upper thighs and let them hang loosely around the bottom of their butt cheeks.

"All right then, come on, faggot," the boy with the red underwear said as he waddled through the space between the parked cars and into the street. He pumped his fist into the palm of his other hand as he clicked his tongue.

"Let's go," Bisa said as she continued to pull Mitch away from the budding fight.

Per rustled through a few drawers while Nix checked the closet. Rosemary investigated the small nest on the windowsill for a moment and then moved on. She ran her hand along the unmade bed, scanning for something—anything—but found nothing unusual. Despite all her knowledge of the legend of the Corporeals, she couldn't find one determining factor that led her to believe that they were anything more than legend. Her black boot wedged itself into a pile of dirty clothes on the floor. "Messy boy, this one," she said.

"Leo is one of the most talented witches in the coven," Nina said. "He's a little rough around the edges. Gifted people are often the most eccentric. Beethoven famously hated being clean. People had to sneak his clothes away just to wash them. Picasso! He fired a pistol filled with blanks at philistines or at people who tried to interpret his art with endless questions."

"Steve Jobs ate only carrots for weeks!" Per added from inside the bottom dresser drawer.

Rosemary reached down to retrieve a dirty T-shirt and held it in the air like a dead ferret. "Yes, and Freud was a cokehead."

Mitch pulled his arm from Bisa's grasp and shouted at the boy, "Come on, smart-ass!"

The red-underwear thug smacked his fist into his palm two more times and dashed forward to land a punch. Mitch lifted his chin and blew a gust of air from between his lips. The force of the blow was so strong that it sent the boy onto the ground, leaving him sprawled out like a starfish.

The other boy, who wore gray underwear, rushed over to defend his pal, but Bisa was already a step ahead of both of them. She pulled the potion out of her pocket and chucked it at the ground between them. The bottle shattered at the gray-underwear boy's feet, stopping him in his tracks.

He laughed. "You missed, you dumb bitch!"

Bisa entered a meditative state and uttered, "Butio." The potion exploded with the force of a small homemade bomb. Debris and pavement flew into the air and busted a window out of a parked car. The two boys tumbled back like weeds under the force of the explosion. She'd made another pothole people would have to avoid in the future.

Leo felt his mind slip into an alternate space of awareness. He concentrated as best he could among the bead-crazed parade patrons and the disco-charged parade float. Every day there seemed to be a new advancement in his powers, and he could add this to the list. He felt a rush of fear and exhilaration all at once, a sort of fight-or-flight response. He blinked and saw the source of the feelings. He saw Bisa, Mitch and the two boys with pants falling down to their knees. Leo blinked again and the double vision was gone. He would now have to react on instinct and impulse...and be guided by intuition. He had never been that great at acting intuitively, but it felt like everything was beginning to change, especially since the temazcal ceremony.

Rosemary brought Leo's favorite T-shirt—the extra-large, psychedelic, tie-dyed shirt with a large skull on the front—to her nose. She inhaled the musky aroma. Aside from his natural human scent, she couldn't detect an odor that distinguished the type of witch he was. She sniffed again, like a police dog being given a scent to track. If she hadn't chosen the path of the witch, she most certainly would have become a police officer. She loved a good investigation. The sniffing was as close to that career as she would ever get. The scent was special, one beyond the common odors of a witch.

"What is it?" Nina asked.

"The smell. There's something odd."

Rosemary pulled the T-shirt away from her face and tumbled it around between her hands, searching for the next best spot to sniff. She peeled back the folds of the cloth to reveal a clear shot right to one of the armpits. Rosemary closed her eyes, brought the T-shirt to her nose once more and sniffed. Her brow furrowed, and she opened her eyes. The words escaped her for a moment, like someone trying to describe what a near-death experience felt like, or the beauty of Snowdonia, in Wales, where she would go on holiday as a child. Rosemary pulled the shirt away from her face, her thin lips parted. There was only one way to describe what she smelled, and it didn't make sense, but she had found what she was looking for.

Leo zipped away from the parade and left Ollie and Avery on their own.

"Where are you going?" Ollie shouted as he watched Leo push his way through the crowd and into the street.

Leo continued to run toward an unknown destination. He turned right and swung into a smelly side street, where he caught his breath for a moment between two overflowing garbage cans. It was almost as if he was being controlled by another force, like his decisions were not his own. But he had only grown more confident in what he could accomplish and why, like some sort of primal instinct as natural as how to breathe. With his awareness kicked up a notch, he felt exactly where Bisa was. He closed his eyes and leaned back like he was participating in a trust fall with the wall. Leo knew he had complete confidence in what he was about to attempt. It was perhaps unlikely, but he knew it wasn't impossible. A breeze picked up as he focused on Bisa's emotions, and he fell back toward the wall and sank into it as though it were made of water.

"What do you smell?" Per asked. Everyone waited.

At last, Rosemary looked up and said, "Gold."

Leo opened his eyes and found himself falling onto the pavement. Only he wasn't in the alley anymore; he was on the street, falling onto the hard pavement behind Mitch and Bisa. When he landed on the ground, his eyelids fluttered until his vision was clear.

Mitch turned around to see Leo on the ground. "Where did you come from? What are you doing on the ground?"

Leo sprang up. "Bisa, move!" His voice was hot and ready.

"She's got it!" Mitch said as he held Leo back.

Bisa stood with her back toward Leo. "I don't need saving," she said with her eyes fixed on the two boys.

"How did you know something was up?" Mitch asked.

"I don't know, I just knew." He walked toward Bisa. "What did you do?"

"I sort of…reset their intentions. While I have them under my influence, I'm poking around to see if I can help heal some past wounds."

Mitch gasped. "Oh my God, Leo! You're bleeding!"

"What? Where?" Leo reached up to his nose and felt nothing.

"No, here, on your ear."

Leo brought his fingers to his tiny earlobes and felt the slick stream of blood oozing out of his left ear canal.

"What's that from?" Mitch asked.

"I…don't know. I feel fine though."

"Well, that's not something that people normally like, have happen. So I think we should get you checked out. Maybe let me try to heal you or figure out what is wrong."

Leo swatted Mitch's hand away from his ear. "Later." He turned back toward Bisa. "Everything okay?"

Bisa turned around, in complete control of the two boys. "It is now. They won't remember anything about this, and they'll probably throw themselves into traffic before they ever insult someone again. Trust me."

There was no way to know for sure what exactly Bisa had done to change their mind-set, but there was also no reason not to believe her.

"Can we go do something else?" Mitch said. "I'm so over this parade thing. It's just not for me."

"I'm with you on that. But what about this guy's car window?" Bisa asked.

"Bisa, I don't feel great about it either, but it's probably only going to cause a lot more trouble for us if we try to fix it. We can't be responsible for like, the entire world. Let's go."

Leo instructed Bisa and Mitch to go back to the car while he went to find Ollie and Avery at the parade. When they were out of view, Leo turned his attention to the two boys, who were slowly recovering. They were opening to a new way of thinking, as if a drain had suddenly unclogged itself and fresh water was being allowed to flow through. Leo rubbed his fingers together and stared at the boy with red underwear. As he circled around his thumb a second time, he heard a cracking sound as the boy's skull imploded and caved in on itself. He switched his focus to the other boy, and with a mere rage-fueled glance the boy caught fire. Leo didn't act out of cruelty…It was out of anger, like a wrathful lioness defending her cubs. He turned to run as fast as he could to go collect Ollie and Avery.

The members of the Advisory didn't make any quick judgments. Rosemary wanted to check as many sources as she could before she dared say another word. Ten minutes after the Advisory members left, the coven returned home. Leo cleaned the blood from his ears, and with no source of a wound he assumed he had gone a little too hard too fast. His magic was lit, turned up, and he needed to relax a bit until his body acclimated to his new strengths. Patience had never been one of Leo's strong suits.

CHAPTER 39

Instead of making dinner, Nina ordered a pizza and kept the evening meeting short. There were a lot of thoughts and concerns within the coven, and she wanted to give them time to discuss the topics that fell outside the loosely organized syllabus she was working through. Naturally, the subject of death was a hot topic. If they had been playing a game of *Family Feud*, the survey would have said that death was the most popular answer on the board. They agreed that death was inevitable for everyone, and resurrection was simply impossible under all circumstances. However, Nina said, that shouldn't suggest that communication with other spirits was impossible. It was quite possible through mediumship, invocation or the cleverness of a very skilled witch.

Ollie suddenly felt Bisa's emotions shift. A wave of sadness covered her. Leo, on the other hand, saw it as colors. Bisa was thinking of her parents. That in itself wasn't odd; she had been thinking about her parents a great deal ever since she'd told Avery about her past. She had gotten used to the idea that they were gone, and she had lived so much of her life without them that she had nearly forgotten what they were like. When she'd pricked the bag of memories, it had popped, and every memory of them she'd ever had had spilled everywhere. She wasn't sad about the fact that she couldn't resurrect her parents. If anything, she was excited about the fact that she now had the means to try to communicate with them. But it wouldn't be the same. It would be some kind of sad, muted version of reality, and that just wasn't good enough. If anything, it would make her feel more alone, more isolated, more parentless.

Bisa excused herself from the meeting without any explanation and retreated to her room for the evening. Not to cry, but to make her very first attempt to communicate with her parents. Sure, she would stumble through it and possibly make a mistake, but eventually, she would figure it out. How dangerous could it really be? Nina had said nothing about the dangers of spirit contact, and although Bisa subconsciously knew there were dangers involved, as there are with most magical processes, she intentionally overlooked them.

As Bisa prepared, rashly, to begin her descent into the spirit realm instead of connecting to the spirit of her parents, Avery had plans of her own for the evening. If death was the most popular answer on the survey, then strength was the second-most popular. Avery ran her fingers through her hair and looked at the tarot cards on the table in the great room. She didn't want to sit in a circle and talk about strength as a theory; she wanted to be able to push the boundaries of how strong she was and prove that she was getting powerful. She shuffled the deck a few times, cut it twice and then shuffled once more. She flipped the top card over to see the eighth card of the Major Arcana staring right back at her—Strength. It was a beautiful card, one that she rarely ever saw in a spread, much like Death. The deck depicted a woman, who looked stunningly similar to herself, holding a lion's mouth open and inserting one hand between its powerful jaws. The woman on the card, delicate and compassionate, hadn't conquered the lion, but instead acted from a place of restraint, grace and cooperation that allowed her to develop a sense of well-earned trust. That was it: that was exactly what she needed to do as a Primordial witch, as a woman, as herself.

Avery grabbed her phone and Googled Audubon Zoo in New Orleans. She summoned a Lyft, and while her ride was on the way, Avery considered the dilemmas of the real world. Just because the coven worked with magic didn't mean there weren't security cameras or guards patrolling the zoo. She was ambitious and spiritually guided, not dumb. She dug through her closet and found something that only made her look and feel more like a witch. She ripped the hooded cloak off the hanger and held it out in front of her. She hadn't a single reason to carry this with her when she traveled, but she always did. Nor could she get rid of it. It had originally been priced at three hundred dollars, but she'd bought it with her employee discount for twenty. *My God, retail markups are so criminal.*

It wasn't the cheapest ride, but forty minutes later Avery arrived at the zoo, now well outside their visiting hours. She walked along the side that faced the park and followed the chain-link fencing until there was a clear spot into the zoo. There was only starlight, and it illuminated the frosty layer of winter mist that churned across the field behind her. Avery unsheathed her hands from the cloak and held her palms out toward the fence. The milky fog around her hand became translucent as a spherical band of air began to pulse inside her hands. As the wind whipped faster, like tiny windmills out of control, a ring of fire, like a circular sparkler, shot threads of light into the air. Faster and faster they spun as the chain-link fence began to burn and melt away against the pressure of her magic. When she closed her fists, the circular chunk of fence met the ground, leaving a doorway into the zoo that was edged with smoldering-red fencing.

Bisa wiped her eyes and repeated a chant she had made up only moments earlier. *If Leo can do that sort of thing, then surely I can as well.* The room was dark apart from the rising moon that poured in through the window and fell across her chest. After seconds that felt like minutes had passed, Bisa opened her eyes. She was no longer in her room, but instead somewhere entirely new. Or was it? There was an uncomfortable familiarity to the world around her. She had intended to thrust herself into the spirit realm and be reunited with her parents (assuming that's how it was done or at least how she could make it happen), but she knew she was somewhere else. The sky was black and filled with millions upon millions of tiny stars like a sea of glittering diamonds. Beside her was a forest of birch trees. *I've been here before.* Behind her was nothing but an open field, and against all better judgment, she entered the forest and darkness returned.

It wasn't like the dark forests you see in films that are ridiculously lit for the cameras; it was hard to see. She lifted her hand in front of her face and could barely make out the outline of her fingers wiggling back and forth. Still, she proceeded, holding her hands out in front of her to avoid stumbling and falling. Then, as if a light had been switched on, her vision adjusted, and within the blink of her eye, the blackness was brightened just enough for her to see where she was going. It was a ghostly shade of dark blue, as though early morning snow had been captured on Instagram and had the brightening and warming Nashville filter applied to it. It was quiet except for the sound of the sighing leaves and her footsteps shuffling over the forest floor.

Soon, she caught sight of something ahead: a clearing in the forest. Bisa quickly walked straight toward the opening, and when she ducked under a few branches, she found herself at the edge of an enormous meadow of tall grass. It was what she expected somewhere like Montana to look like. The grass bent against the breeze like gentle waves over an ocean. It went on for what looked to be miles. In the far distance, the air began to clear. Her vision sharpened further and allowed her to see a mountain in great detail…and the figure dressed all in black that stood upon the summit. As a Transcendent witch, Bisa took sight more seriously, the mundane observations of the real world, the suggestive highlights in the Somnium plane—the dream realm, glimpses of the beyond from that space between sleep and awake. It all made her more aware and sometimes a little more frightened of something that was indeed—frightening. It was precisely why the dark figure on the mountain, which would have roiled the bravest stomach, felt so ominous. She saw a cloak rippling like black flames in the breeze. A cold chill ran down the length of her body, and in that moment, the figure descended as though it were a cascading body of water flowing down from the mountaintop. From there, it moved into the edge of the forest, out of sight.

Avery toured the paths of the zoo, walking past the sea lions, the cages of spider monkeys and the gorilla enclosure.

"Hello, everyone!" she announced to the animals, as though she were a guest they'd been expecting.

Squack! Hummf…Hummf…Roo-roo…Rrrack! The animals called back to her, swinging along vines and hopping along their landscapes, releasing cheerful grunts. They were conversational, friendly and curious about her presence in the park. She had such charisma and they were eager for someone who spoke their language.

Avery followed the path until she arrived at the lion habitat. She needed to be calm and show restraint…That was the message she needed to express with her energy, or this whole situation could go very, *very* wrong. She approached the lions' paddock and stopped to observe the landscape, her vision as honed as that of the creatures in the nocturnal habitat. She took a few deep breaths and asked for protection from her guides, her angels and whoever else was watching out for her. She was confident, but not that confident. Her eyes breezed over the den and she spotted a lion—no, four lions, one male and three female. She had never been superbly athletic, but she did manage to scale the fence, climb onto a thick tree branch and drop herself into the den. Already she was doing things she hadn't thought she'd be able to do. If only her high school gym teacher could see her now. The grass was mown and the ground was flat. In the center of the den was a large dead tree that looked as if it had been treated for preservation, like the tiny pieces of aquarium décor one would find at Petco. Beside that was a large rock with two smooth mounds. Surrounded by fencing, a moat or high, man-made cliffs, Avery realized that she was in the lions' house now.

The lions looked up at her. The females were huddled together near the wall, and the only male was alone on the grass near the smooth rock. Avery began to breathe faster. There was a level of wonder that you felt only from behind the fence at a safe distance. Once inside the fence, that sense of wonder became all emotions all at once. The lion, with its tousled mane and enormous face, turned its head to look Avery straight in the eye. He had been sleeping before she arrived—typical—but now he was wide awake, strong and stoic. Her proximity to him in particular inspired a sort of magnetism in her that was unparalleled.

There was a brisk swoosh as the zoo became void of all noises, calls, squawks and grunts. After a few minutes of being absolutely mesmerized, Avery took her first step toward the lion. Her shoes crunched over the stiff, cold grass. She could feel them, all the lions. She felt the lions' thoughts swirling around in her mind as if they were her own. She couldn't decipher what they meant, but she could feel them. As she drew closer to the lion, she expressed an energy of pure divine love. She took another step forward. One lioness fell back asleep. Another step. The second fainted back to sleep. A few more paces. The last lioness, totally disinterested in Avery's unexplained presence in her home, battled insomnia and instead pretended to sleep.

Avery drew closer to the male lion fearlessly. The breeze blew lightly. She was close enough to smell the unusual musky scent of the giant cat. A rich and distinct scent, intoxicatingly regal, with notes of honey, popcorn and chicken soup. The smell was hypnotic. It had been a long time since Avery had been to the zoo, any zoo—they made her sad—but she couldn't remember and hadn't anticipated a scent so complex and mystifying. The perks of being a Primordial witch, no doubt. She was only a few feet away when she removed her hands from underneath her cloak.

Bisa looked up into the starry sky and then back at the world around her. There was no sign of her parents, or any other spirits, apart from the mysterious figure that had hidden itself among the birch trees. She circled in place as she tried to connect to a spirit energy of any kind, but there was nothing. The breeze stopped blowing and Bisa turned back to the forest. The cloaked figure was now at eye level, standing still at the edge of the woods. The flames that were its robes billowed slowly as if underwater, even though there was no breeze. Bisa blinked, and suddenly the figure was gone. She squinted, but there was only a clear path into the forest. Was it the ghost of one of her parents? Maybe even another spirit she had known over the course of her life? Or was it something different altogether?

Suddenly, the starlight began to fade. Bisa looked up into the sky to see a cloak of the truest black eat its way across the sky. The cloak spilled with the chilling rumbling of an approaching storm. There was an eerie undertone to it, like guitar strings being teased with a knife's jagged edge instead of a pick. In a matter of seconds it was too dark to see.

Avery reached out toward the lion. Her hand did not tremble, and she felt no anxiety in her approach. The tips of her fingers tickled the wiry fur of the lion's mane. She took a step closer. Intention was everything at this point. There was a sort of camaraderie, an understanding that existed only between them. A trust. She moved her hand closer, up through the jungle of mane and around the lion's soft ears. Avery smiled. The lion's sadness, boredom, frustration and depression all came rushing in, and Avery instantly felt imprisoned. If there was anything she could do, it was express compassion. She expelled tiny breaths from her mouth, ones filled with exhilaration. She ran her other hand along the lion's back, through the coarse hair that reminded her of the family dog with its rough, thick coat. She didn't care where she was, how she had gotten there or what existential problems the world was in: in that moment, Avery cherished only the bond she had created with the lion.

The lion huffed and grunted with contentment as Avery ran her hands around his head. She stroked the lion's face around the eyes and down to his mouth, and placed a hand on both the lower and upper jaw.

Bisa looked frantically around the blackness. There was no sign of a way out or a way through. Her feet stumbled over each other as she tried to find her way back toward the forest. She spun around again, hoping against hope for a light. Then, she found one. She found two, actually. A few inches from her face stood the black figure, black as death, with two glowing black orbs for eyes. It seemed impossible for black to glow when there was no light for it to reflect, but in this realm…it did. There was no time to scream. Nowhere to run. She felt the coldness of the figure upon her skin like air from a freezer door left wide open. Bisa's voice quivered as she stumbled back. The flowing hood fell from around the eyes, and the figure's face was transformed from a shadowy clump of flowing fabric into a gray face with no features other than a mouth with wet, glistening lips. The wrinkles on the face grew wider under the glowing eyes, as though someone were holding a flashlight underneath their chin in a dark room.

The figure lifted an arm and leaned toward Bisa.

Avery could smell the lion's oddly sweet breath as she opened his jaws. *I'm not going to hurt you,* she thought—communicated. Avery was not controlling the lion but working with it. She had persuaded him to cooperate with her command and had earned his trust. His jaws were strong, like the metal traps she'd often seen out in the woods in rural Wisconsin. But these jaws weren't a trap. They wouldn't snap shut and tear away her flesh. Avery looked into his eyes and opened her fist inside his mouth, extending her fingers over the tongue as she stroked the top of the lion's head. Her heart beat inside her chest, fierce and uninhibited.

The cloaked figure revealed a single finger of solid bone, tapered at the tip and sharpened to a needle-tip point. Bisa's eyes opened wide as the finger stretched out to touch her.

Then, quick as a cat, the fingernail scratched Bisa's arm. She tipped her head back and into the sky that now blended in with everything else. She couldn't see the mark the scratch made, but it felt cold and hot all at the same time, a dual-sided pain compacted into one sensation.

Avery's fingers touched the rough, wet tongue of the lion. Suddenly, another lion appeared from behind the rock and stood above her. It made no noise. It didn't have to. She had found—earned—her totem animal.

CHAPTER 40

Bisa sat up from the floor of her room in a cold sweat and with a stinging wound no thicker than a paper cut on her arm. Much to her surprise, the person she immediately sought out was Leo.

"Who do you think it was?" Leo asked after Bisa recounted the tale of her trip to another realm.

"I think I should be asking *what* it was. It wasn't human."

After a long debate full of controversy and even some name calling, the two reconvened in the study. Forty minutes later, Bisa found her answer in a book on the shelf. She had heard Nina talk about bibliomancy, the act of performing divination through the random choosing of a book, but she had never witnessed it. Her hands were browsing the shelves in the study when, as if pulled by string, her hand linked to the binding of a book on the middle shelf. She stuck her finger into the pages at random and opened the book directly to page 123. The descriptions of the Land of Perpetual Midnight* were identical to what she had experienced. It was uncanny.

"Well, how did you get *there*?" Leo asked.

Bisa continued to flip through the pages and by chance ended up reading aloud a passage that answered his question. "Listen to this: 'Astral planes can be accessed through more means than one. Common techniques are intense meditation, ritualistic use of substances in various forms, chanting or repeating words believed to contain strong esoteric power and even sex-induced trance.'" Then it all made sense, like a puzzle piece fitting into the last open space. *Sexual trance*. The realm felt familiar because it was. She *had* been there before. The night at the hotel, that strange flash that made her question her reality for a split second, had been real. She had accessed that plane accidentally through a deeply sexual experience. "It doesn't say anything about the figure I saw. The one that scratched me."

"Maybe could've been something that followed you in," Leo suggested. He was clear-headed for the first time in a long while. Even his nails were starting to grow back.

Bisa shared a little bit about her past with Leo, mostly about her parents. She wanted him to know why she was so determined to connect with them in the first place. It was this topic that planted the seed in his mind about his own parents. Suddenly, something felt suspicious. Everything that he had experienced recently only seemed to be adding up to the discovery of something major. Only he didn't know what it could be.

The next morning, Leo filled up his gas tank and made a surprise trip down the bayou. Not for pleasure or a moody and pensive bike ride, but to pay a visit to his parents. He was starting to get the hang of trusting his vibes. Here all this time he'd thought Nina was just being dramatic.

When Leo was finally "home," he looked over the sad lawn that looked like so many of the rotting cemeteries across the state. He had forgotten how unglamorous his parents' house was. It was dull, a kind of ugly that couldn't even mimic happiness under the shining sun. He knocked. They didn't have the kind of relationship where he was welcome to come in as he pleased without their permission.

His mother answered the door. She was plain, but not in a vanilla type of way, and looked nothing like Leo. Her strawberry-blond hair had a certain mommy-ness to it—short and a little dry from a scorching flat iron or repetitive dye jobs. Short and slender with a set of rosy pink cheeks like two flowers. She had more wrinkles around her eyes than he remembered. *Has it really been that long since I've been down here?*

"Leo! My God. What are you doing here?" she said.

"I was just out for a drive, thought I'd stop—"

A husky voice from the other room. "Who is it?"

"It's Leo," his mother said, sounding neither excited nor unhappy.

There were a few heavy footsteps, and then the door opened farther.

"Well, hey," his father said. His face empty, his eyebrows raised.

"I was just tellin' Mom that—"

"What do you want?" his father said, his manners having vanished immediately.

"What do you mean?" Leo wasn't exactly sure what his father meant. But when he really thought about it, he realized his father had good reason to ask that. He did contact them only when he needed something. This wasn't any different. He needed something, he just didn't know what.

"We haven't heard from you in, what, months now? I gave you five hundred bucks to help you out with whatever it was you said you needed—that time—and then we never heard from you. And we called!" His father slipped up next to the screen door between them.

Leo could see through the screen that his father had gained about twenty pounds and had been spending a lot of time outside. There were more sunspots on his shoulders and hands, and he had clearly given up on wearing socks. If his dad had been more handsome, more well groomed, perhaps Leo would've ignored the fact that he was standoffish, but he had a reason to act that way. For the time being, Leo decided, he was going to accept it. He probably deserved it. After all, he had taken the money and not called in months. In his defense, it would've been difficult. His phone had been shut off temporarily right after that. The five hundred had been just enough to bring his balance out of the negative. Things were starting to look up for him. He wanted his parents to at least get wind of that.

"I know. You're right," Leo said, surprising even himself.

His mother sighed the way a mother does when she has no choice but to love her son. "Are you doing okay? You look different."

"I am. I'm doing really well. I think. I'm living with some new roommates in a really nice place. Learning a lot."

"Like in school? What are you doing for work?" his mother said.

"Sort of. It's like a work-study thing. Like a trade school."

"Well, maybe you can start paying us back one of these days," his father said. After a disheartened sigh, he changed his tune and opened the screen door. "Come on, come on inside."

The place hadn't changed much, but his mom was wearing nail polish again, and his father's toenails were perilously long. Despite a few aesthetic disturbances, they were actually a pretty cute couple. His father had once been a redhead, back when he had hair. Another quirky gene that had managed to miss Leo. They sat down at the kitchen table, and his mother offered him a can of Coke. He preferred Pepsi, but he wasn't going to complain.

"I know you like Pepsi, but it's all we've got," his mother said.

Leo smiled, pleased that she remembered such a trivial detail.

"Sorry to hear about Tonya," his father said.

"What do you mean?" Leo asked. "I haven't talked to her in a long time. What happened?"

His parents glanced ruefully at each other, uncertain what to say next.

"Leo, she died," his mother said gently. "Not too long ago. I thought maybe that's why you were here. We tried to call, but your number was disconnected, and when we finally got through, someone else answered, so we realized you had gotten a new phone number."

"Wait…what?" Leo said quietly.

"Some police officers came by to talk to you," his father said. "I guess you were listed as her emergency contact at this address or whatever. Couldn't help them, though—had no idea where you were." He scratched his rust-colored stubble as he spoke.

Leo didn't need to ask why or how: he knew. His apple spell. She had died the night he'd buried the apple in the earth. Suddenly he went numb. Conflicting emotions rolled around inside him. He hadn't seen her or talked to her in perhaps a year, and he hadn't ever actually loved her. But he was looking at the situation with a new set of eyes and an even newer awareness. He hadn't intended for her to die, but he hadn't exactly thought she was the best person on the planet either. Neither was he. But he wasn't the same person he had been then. He was special now. There was a long, uncomfortable silence.

His parents were starstruck by the seemingly adult version of Leo who sat in the chair in front of them. They had never seen him so calm and collected. It was like he was finally an adult, someone they could talk to, reason with and perhaps come to respect or even be proud of. Leo's father reached up to scratch his beard once again, and a small cut on the edge of his hand caught Leo's attention.

"I haven't talked to her in a…very long time. What happened to your hand?" He was genuinely concerned about his dad for the first time in…maybe forever.

"Oh. I was trying my hand at some things in the kitchen."

Leo laughed. "What? Since when do you cook?"

"Since about Friday. I've got a little more time now, and I thought I would try out some new hobbies. I had no idea that a knife as dull as ours could cut so deep."

His mother shook her head. "I told him! Don't try to cook unless it's absolutely necessary! It looked like he murdered an onion in cold blood."

"She's right. I went back to crocheting," his father said.

"No shit. One of my roommates crochets." Leo reached out to grab his father's hand. "You've gotta get some better knives, ma—" He stopped. He had an elucidating feeling that he got when he had a hunch about something. It was the kind of feeling that Transcendents usually talked about, one he had always wished he could experience—except he had experienced it twice now. Leo ran his thumb gently over his father's cut, and everything suddenly became clear. As if the fog had finally lifted and the sun had beat down every shadow. "You're not my real parents."

For a brief moment, his parents thought it was a joke. Only, of course, it wasn't. They soon realized that Leo knew the truth. How he knew was the mystery.

"Tell me the truth. Tell me everything. Don't lie," Leo said with a dark effervescence.

Richard and Linda Sullivan had been his parents as far back as he could remember, but over the next hour they told him every detail about where he had come from—well, as much as they knew, anyway. His biological parents had given him up for adoption and died from an overdose shortly afterward. That was back in Massachusetts. A few years later, when Richard's mother fell ill in Louisiana, the Sullivans had moved so he could take care of her. Leo had been too young to remember and they had opted to tell him when the time was right, but it never felt right. They answered every question Leo had truthfully, civilly, but also regretfully, because they feared it would further alienate him. They wanted only the best for him, and they had become so comfortable with the lies they'd told that it was going to take a lot of effort to reverse all of them.

Leo handled the information stunningly well. He didn't lash out, or make a scene, or even cry. Linda half expected him to shed a few tears, at least, if only out of anger. But there were none. There was only a sense of intrigue. *I knew it. I knew what Nina said couldn't be true...about my magical handicap. I knew there had to be another reason why I'm just not happy. Maybe you're just fucking depressed, Leo...Ever think of that?* Cynicism and realism crept in, but only for a moment. *No, there's more to this. I need to know more.* Leo folded his arms, attempting to hide his nervous energy.

"What are their names?"

"Leo, do you really wa—" his mother began.

Leo accosted her in midsentence. "Tell me their names…please."

"Jim and Tina Perkins. They lived in a garden apartment over in Whipple Pines, about twenty or thirty minutes from where we lived in Boston."

Seriously? My dad was named Jim, like the bourbon Jim Beam, and my mom had the same nickname as crystal meth. That explains a lot.

When his mother said the words *Whipple Pines*, Leo could see the apartment in his mind. He wasn't sure if he was imagining it or it was a real memory. Sometimes it was hard to tell. It was a dingy basement apartment, labeled a garden apartment to attract—no, mask the fact that it was a shitty place. Low ceilings, the scent of mildew and small rectangular windows near the top of the wall just below the ceiling. The actual building itself wasn't half bad…from the outside. It rested right on a tree-lined corner that faced south. It would have gotten a lot of light during the early parts of the day, if the sunlight had been able to find the windows. The front door wasn't even at the front of the building. It was down the alley, halfway to the back of the building, like something reserved for the help or people who didn't deserve or couldn't afford a real apartment.

Leo stood up from the table. "Take care of that hand."

CHAPTER 41

Ever since Avery's night at the zoo, she had wanted to further explore her powers. She had also started taking more naps during the day. It seemed she shared more in common with lions than she'd initially thought. It was during an afternoon nap that she woke up suddenly, gasping for air. She was hot. Not the kind of sticky heat she had grown accustomed to from living in the South, but the searing kind of hotness from a burn. She checked her body: no burns, but it felt real. She had been dreaming of the Barrow House. In the dream, she walked down the driveway to the house and saw a truck parked beside it. Inexplicably panicked, she rushed toward the house, only to see it burst into flames. Naturally, being so gifted with fire, her first instinct was to try to control it. But it raged beyond her control and consumed her instead.

Later, over some iced tea, Avery told Nina about her dream in graphic detail. Nina had talked about the Somnium plane before, but it was one of those subjects that everyone seemed to think was useless, kind of like chemistry, advanced trigonometry or even history, for that matter. It wasn't like they actually taught *real* history in classes anyway. Everyone always knew about Thomas Edison, but no one knew about Lewis Latimer, whose innovation led to the creation of carbon filaments that extended the life of the short-lived light bulb. After the burning sensation finally started to subside, Avery found more credence in the study of the Somnium plane, where the results of common magic are often unpredictable and hard to control.

Avery wasn't the only one learning a few new things. Whereas her education was more lecture-based that day, Bisa's was more experimental and artistic. She had just finished putting the final touches on the self-portrait she had started several weeks earlier. A gold background and her skin as red as the blood in her cut. The painting's mystery was something she hoped no one would ever need to solve. However, just in case they did, the painting's *instructions* were written on a folded piece of parchment and slipped into the far back pages of Avery's grimoire where she would eventually find it one day. Bisa trusted Avery. It took more time for her to get in and out of the grimoire than for Leo to book a plane ticket to Massachusetts, another adventure on which he would embark completely alone, for his own purposes.

CHAPTER 42

When Edie was angry, people knew it. When she was disappointed, people noticed. When she was angry and disappointed, people ran. But Buckshot and Bowie had nowhere to run. They couldn't have run even if they'd wanted to, not with both of them being under Edie's influence. She would've hated to admit it, but she was thankful for that little bit of potion, even if it was bending the rules. Bowie and Buckshot entered the church office disappointed in themselves and left with cheeks imprinted with the shape of a crimson Bible. Whoever said the Word of God didn't hurt anyone hadn't ever met Edie when she was angry and disappointed. She always got her way, and if she didn't, someone paid for it. They would have to try again and again until they succeeded. There was no alternative.

Joshua was leading the service at their Houma campus while Edie stayed at their flagship and prepared for the ribbon cutting of the new room. It was Louisiana, after all, and they celebrated everything, no matter how big or small. But the real celebration came later after the service was over and the church had emptied out. Edie led her cronies down some new concrete stairs to a door with a keypad. Neither Buckshot nor Bowie could figure out what was behind the door. Edie clearly had her secrets. She loved her secrets as much as she loved her ambitions and her Bible verses. This is why, when she lifted her manicured finger to the shiny new keypad, she punched in 0 – 1 – 1 – 6 and recited a verse: "'They claim to know God, but by their actions they deny him. They are detestable, disobedient and unfit for doing anything good.'"

The door beeped three times and hissed like a dying snake as it unlocked. Edie turned her big head toward the two men.

"Titus 1:16. My favorite verse." The adjective *favorite* was a somewhat dishonest or inaccurate descriptor in addition to being absolutely true. Edie had many favorites, as if her taste was made up of all her favorites and nothing else. She knew she'd had many conversations with them in the past in which she'd quoted verses, and those, too, were her favorite. Perhaps it wasn't a lie but more like a statement that people learned to take with a grain of salt.

Edie flicked a switch on the wall, and the monochromatic room was illuminated by four mounted and backlit six-foot-tall, white onyx crosses. It was bright enough to reveal every imperfection on Edie's face, like those well-lit mirrors at Sephora that force you to look at every blemish.

"Behold the room of our future!" Edie said as she entered the room with the effervescence of a *Price Is Right* model about to showcase fabulous new prizes. She stretched her arms out in operatic pride as her stilettos click-clacked on the cold concrete floor. "Welcome to what I like to call God's Workshop. I have plans for this place. For you, for us, for this church! We're gonna collect those sinners, and we're gonna expose them to God's holy light. Now, these walls are two layers of concrete with one layer of heavy steel between them. I reckon this is the quietest, most secret room in all of Louisiana and maybe in this entire country, possibly even in this whole world!" *Let's find the next sinful contestant and bring them on down to God's Workshop! With your hostess, Edie Bonner!*

Buckshot pulled off his hat and scratched his sweaty scalp. "What are you gonna do in here?"

"Whatever is necessary." Her eyes went cold for a moment. Then a smile jumped back on her face. "I know it just seems like a tiny, cold little room. But it's just the starting point. It's a diving board into the pool of our dreams."

"No shit! You're gonna put a pool in here?" Buckshot said as he reviewed the room to gauge what size of pool would fit. "Like a wading pool or whatnot? My dad—"

Edie clapped her hands. "Buckshot! Dear! No! It's a figure of speech, darling. This country, this *world*, is spiraling straight to hell. Homosexuals are having parades in the street, people are making up new genders…confusing our children. There are witches out there right now, organizing, and plotting, ready to destroy all of us and what we stand for. So you know what? I decided we need to do the same. With the help of God, I am going to reverse the sin that is a plague among us." Edie tossed back a piece of hair from her face that had fallen out of place during her passionate monologue. *Next, we have a fascinating example of a radical Bible banger with a melting sense of reality.* "Now, do you know what I did just the other night? I was on my knees, wrapped up in evening prayer as I often am, sometimes for hours on end—that's how much I care about our salvation. Then it came to me. I heard the word of God."

"What did he say?" Buckshot asked.

"He said to me, 'Reveal your sins.' And in that moment I laid all my sins bare. I stripped before God and offered up every single sin I had ever done, and I gave myself to God and he rewarded me with enlightenment! All the answers we have ever needed are in this mighty book!" Edie picked up a copy of the Bible from the center of the floor. "All the instructions I needed to bring God to the world are in here. But I still needed more, I needed some clarification. So I asked—I prayed—on what I need to do next. And he told me. The answer was so simple, I was almost embarrassed.

"In this room, I'll conduct a ritual on a dark soul, in God's name, and I will be given the greatest gift of all…God's holy light. I don't mean this in the metaphorical sense, I mean actually. I will be blessed with his holy light and I will be able to disperse it as I see fit, to cleanse this world, send their awful souls to hell and bring myself that much closer to God until I finally reach him in heaven when it is my time. I will fight fire with fire, and y'all are gonna help me do it. It will be revolutionary. Trump would be so proud!"

And finally, you'll tour the church where the best lock-ins in all of Louisiana are held! The Whole Truth and True Light Assembly of God Church! You and a fellow sinner will be abducted to God's Workshop, where you'll enjoy a one-night stay with no food or water! This horrific chamber is the perfect place to experience radical religious rituals! Plus, enjoy being strapped to a cross made of solid pine, where your heart will be cut out with a large bowie knife and dropped into a flaming pot of fire at your feet, while the cavity in your chest is filled with…a live dove! So, it's a grand tour of the church belonging to the largest religious wackos in the South…a once-in-a-lifetime ritual killing…and, of course, a trip to hell! This package truly has the fingerprint of a sadistic psychopath!

Edie, overcome with emotion as the images of the ritual ran through her mind, dropped to her knees. "It will be so beautiful." She looked at the large pine cross in the center of the room. Her voice was a stream of trembling whispers. "If we walk in the light as he himself is in the light, we have fellowship with one another, and the blood of Jesus his son cleanses us from all sin. Yet even if I do judge, my judgment is true, for it is not I alone who judge, but I and the Father who sent me. He who sins is of the devil. I, Edie, of the **Whole Truth and True Light Assembly of God Church**, God's messenger of true light and warrior against all sin, purge this world of your sin, in the name of the Father, the Son and the Holy Spirit." Suddenly, Edie's headaches were gone. "I can feel it. I can feel his power inside me. It's time."

FIRE

Leo went from having drugged-out red eyes to taking a red-eye flight. It was the cheapest he could find on short notice. When he arrived in Boston, it had just struck eight in the morning. He had to make this a quick and efficient trip. With the last known address for Jim and Tina Perkins, Leo hailed a Lyft and made his way out of the Boston airport and to the town of Whipple Pines. He didn't need any coffee to keep him awake. Between the chatty driver and the anticipation of what he would find, it was the equivalent of sucking down a red-eye from the airport Starbucks. The farther into Whipple Pines he got, the more depressing the sights became. In fact, to him, it looked a lot like most of Louisiana. There was a soothing sense of symmetry between where he was actually from and where he had grown up. Almost like he was destined to live a certain type of way—although perhaps for not much longer.

Thirty-five minutes later, the car pulled up to the building Leo had seen in his head. It was almost exactly the same. He was starting to really enjoy the new powers he was discovering. It made life way more entertaining. When he stepped foot onto the sidewalk, Leo told the driver to wait; ideally he wouldn't be too long. Chances were slim that someone living in the building now had lived there at the same time as his parents, but Leo had a feeling there was someone. The driver agreed to wait. After all, he didn't want to get stuck in the crime-ridden town of Whipple Pines looking for his next fare. There had been several cases of drivers robbing or raping customers, but if anything, it would be the other way around if he picked up a fare in Whipple Pines, a city that generated more violence than a farm full of pit bulls bred solely for illegal dog fights. That weekend had seen the highest number of homicides of the year so far, including the eleven-year-old who had shot his own mother, the three people who had died in a shooting in the Family Dollar parking lot, the eighteen-year-old fatally shot at the intersection of Seventeenth and Garfield and the two men who robbed a couple at gunpoint at a downtown ATM only to shoot them in the head before they fled the scene. Needless to say, it was safer to wait in a locked car with the windows rolled up until Leo returned.

The building's landlady, a suspiciously chipper older woman with thinning hair and poor eyesight, answered most of Leo's questions about a couple who had lived there many years ago, to the best of her knowledge, anyway. Boy, did she like to chat. It was the kind of chatter that almost seemed like she was talking to herself. Perhaps it was out of habit. Leo couldn't imagine that she had many visitors. She did have a cat, though. He didn't see it, but he could smell the overflowing litter box.

After the landlady searched through her tired old brain, she remembered the couple in question. "Jim and Tina. They were always late on the rent. One day they were just gone. They weren't very friendly, not to me. I sometimes forgot who they were because I didn't see them enough. They weren't like Troy. He always talked to me."

"Who?"

"Troy Brown. He should have just moved into their extra bedroom and saved himself the rent on his apartment, he was over there so much."

Leo's expression changed. He no longer tried to avoid conversation and instead tried to get her to talk even more, with a little direction. He didn't have to try too hard…It happened…effortlessly.

"Troy Brown. He lived in the apartment above them. But he moved out a while ago. He works at the mill over off West Tracy Highway. He works for my husband there. Well, ex-husband."

Five minutes later, Leo was back in the Lyft and heading toward the mill on the outskirts of Whipple Pines. It was closer than he thought, a straight shot down the road, no more than ten minutes tops. Leo had gotten used to the expedited way of life he was living lately. Things happened more easily and quickly than they ever had in the past. If he'd cared about money at that point, he might have just walked into a bank and robbed them of every last dollar. That would have occurred to the old Leo, perhaps, but now he thought about and wanted different things.

When Leo arrived at the mill, the driver waited again, now almost enjoying the tour of the slums. He felt like those people who liked to drive through the bad parts of town like it was a trip to the zoo to see the animals, but all from the safety of being behind the glass.

Leo's powers were growing stronger each and every minute of every day, but he also seemed to be gifted with a bit of luck. He stuck his hands in his pockets and walked toward a man standing outside the mill having a cigarette. A real cigarette, like the ones Leo used to smoke before he switched to vaping and then quit smoking altogether. *Wow, that really fuckin' smells. Did I use to smell like that?* As Leo approached, he had a feeling he was in the right spot.

The man nodded. There was a quick moment where Leo judged the poor guy. The energy he felt reminded him a lot of his own, but in the past. He knew better than to judge someone who was so similar to how he used to be, but he just couldn't help it. It made Leo like the man a little less because he was such a striking image of who Leo had been only a few years earlier. Staring him right in the face was the personification of everything Leo would have been if he hadn't been a witch and made different choices. *You really lucked out, Leo. You really did.*

"What's up?" the man said as he raised a set of stained fingers with a half-smoked cigarette between them to his lips. His voice had a certain nicotine-soaked rasp to it, one that Leo now realized afflicted every single person who had run in his old social circles.

"I'm looking for a guy named Troy Brown. I was told he works here."

"What for?" The man stiffened up. The cigarette hung from his lip as he crossed his arms over his chest, and smoke billowed up over his face like a kind of camouflage.

"I was told that he knew my parents, Jim and Tina Perkins," Leo said, thinking it was best just to be honest and see how far that got him. He assumed that the man might have some sort of record or perhaps even a warrant out on him. That would explain his stiffness and apprehension. *That's how I would've reacted.*

The man's face lightened up a bit. He took a drag from the cigarette and removed it from his lips. "I'm Troy." His eyes searched Leo like he was looking for something, anything, that made him look suspicious. When he couldn't find anything, he looked back into Leo's eyes. "You're their son, huh? Well, fuck. I remember you. You probably don't remember a whole lot, huh?"

"What can you tell me about them?"

"I don't know, man. It's been a long time. I don't think I'm the right person you should be talking to."

"I was told you were at their place all the time. You're the best source I have." It was already taking too long, and Leo was getting impatient again. As he looked over Troy's face, covered with oil smudges from his soiled hands, he felt a rushing feeling, one that gave him bloodless cheeks and jitters like that airport red-eye would have. Suddenly, he had control over Troy's intentions. "What do I need to know?" Leo asked.

A softness fell over Troy's face as though he were about to sing a lullaby to a sleepy infant. "We were really close. We got high together, a lot. Jim tried to stop cold turkey. He kind of did, I guess. He was in recovery for a few years. But his addiction was too strong. He went back to using. I stopped. He didn't."

Leo was getting closer to the jackpot as he let instinct ask questions instead of his mind. "What kind of drugs did they use?"

"Everything. The guy had everything."

"What guy? My dad? Jim?"

"No. His dealer."

Leo chortled a curious little giggle as he felt another rush of whatever it was that was coursing through his veins. Power, perhaps.

"Who was that? Do you still see him?"

"That was ages ago, man. I only went with him to pick up just the one time. I don't remember where the guy lived. He was some kind of fancy dealer, like a professional one or something."

"What makes you say that? What do you mean…professional?"

"He had a business card. Jim showed it to me one time. But Jim liked to share, so I never had to buy anything of my own. I always thought it was kinda weird. What kind of dealer advertises where they live and what they do? I never understood that. But the guy had some good shit."

Hope and excitement fluttered across Leo's face. "What was his name?"

"Started with an *E*…Eddie…Ed…naw…"

Troy's memory was a little foggy. Fortunately, Leo knew just how to lift that fog. He snapped his fingers, and a ripple of unseen energy whooshed across Troy's face. "Evan—his name was Evan!" Troy said in an unexpectedly excited tone. It didn't even sound like him.

It had to be the very same Evan that Maisie had mentioned back at the house. The rushing sensation that had been streaming throughout his body slowly began to fade, and Leo's heart began to return to its normal rhythm. He now had answers, but he also had a splitting headache, a bloody ear and a wobbly sense of equilibrium. *I'll acclimate to this sooner or later*, he told himself.

Leo dug into his pocket and pulled out a pack of gum where his vape used to be. Regular peppermint gum, not the nicotine kind that smokers transition to when they're trying to quit. He poked the hard rectangle of chewing gum through the foil of the blister pack and popped one into his mouth. He did the same with a second piece, but offered it to Troy as he thanked him. It was the only compensation Leo could offer. He had no cash on him, and Troy's breath smelled. So it really was the best option, considering.

When Leo returned to the car, he was utterly euphoric. Yet he wished he had astrally projected himself to Massachusetts instead of actually flying by plane. He could've been back home already. He could already be trying to connect with Evan. He never considered whether it was dangerous to astrally project for long periods, or even at extreme distances, but Leo's own safety was never his highest priority.

It was, however, becoming more of a priority for Bisa, who had spent most of the morning convincing the coven that he hadn't simply abandoned them. She used every explanation, including the possibility that Leo might have left without telling anyone yet again. Bisa had become a voice of reason over the past few months, so when she gave her list of reasons why Leo wouldn't have just left them high and dry, everyone trusted her.

The major difference between Bisa and the rest of the coven was that she actually knew something was happening. It was as real as any event unfolding right in front of her. She could feel Leo's mind working as if it were her own. It only made her more curious, and with that curiosity came the invasion of privacy. Bisa wasn't a nosy person or someone who didn't respect boundaries. In fact, she was very much the opposite. With Leo, the rules were a little different. She related to him strangely, in a way that made absolutely no sense. If she'd had to simplify it, she would have said that opposites attract, but even that oversimplification wouldn't honestly explain anything. It didn't take a professional to see that they had nothing in common apart from feeling drawn to each other and having some darkness in their past. So when Bisa felt a sense of warning, she decided to ignore the boundaries, just for now, and search Leo's room. She felt like a concerned mother riffling through her wild son's things, hoping not to find something incriminating, but also expecting to.

Bisa had no experience with drugs, but when she opened the top drawer of Leo's dresser and found a stash of coke and a baggie full of dry, crumbly weed, she knew what it was. Disappointed, she looked at the stash tucked behind a pile of mismatched socks. Bisa didn't know what she had expected, or even hoped for, but it was a little bit of a turnoff nevertheless. *It's none of my business*, said her heart. *This guy is a mess and he's sleeping under the same roof*, said her brain. The only compromise she could come to was to confront him about it. Yes. She would have to say something. It was her duty as…whatever she was to him.

CHAPTER 44

Ollie hadn't played the piano since he was fifteen. Now, thirteen years later, he found himself sitting on a piano bench in the great room, wondering why he had quit playing. Only, he hadn't so much as quit as lost interest. He had a gift for playing the piano, there was no question about that, but Ollie had always known he wasn't passionate about it, even when his parents made him play for their friends and applauded when he finished as though he were some kind of musical prodigy. Other people always wondered why he hadn't chosen the path of music and become a concert pianist, but Ollie knew in his heart that it wasn't what he truly *wanted* to do. It wasn't fulfilling. The older he got, the more he was starting to feel like there wasn't a thing on earth that he would find satisfying enough to fulfill him completely. It was a given that whenever he played, he would attract people who marveled at his talent and watch in awe as his fingers danced along the keys. Sometimes, when he was at a mall or somewhere with a piano, he would spontaneously sit down to play. And always, people would flock to him like tourists to Bourbon Street.

The sound of Ollie's playing was irresistible, even for people who didn't appreciate the piano. Instead of attracting tourists, he attracted his Proctor, Nina, who had been secretly standing in the doorway watching him play. It was a sweet tune, both compelling and enchanting, but altogether unfamiliar. When Ollie finished the piece, he lifted his hands from the keys and rested them in his lap while he stared into space.

"I didn't know you could play," Nina said.

Ollie jumped at the sound of her voice and his hand shot to cover his heart as he let out a startled breath. "I don't really. Not anymore."

"That's not what it sounds like. That was beautiful." Nina stood next to him at the piano bench.

Ollie shrugged. "It's just something I came up with."

"You just made that up?"

"Yeah."

"Just now? You sat down and just…started playing something." Nina was almost starstruck.

"Yeah. It wasn't really anything. I'm a little rusty. It's been a long time."

Nina shook her head. "Wasn't anything?" she repeated. "Oliver, that was amazing!"

Another shrug. "Well, there are more important things right now than how well I pick up an old hobby."

Nina nudged him to make room for her to sit next to him on the bench. "What's on your mind? Talk to me. You know you can always talk to me."

"Things are just so different. My life is completely different from what it was a year ago. Even a few months ago. So much has happened, and everyone still kind of feels like…a stranger."

"You mean everyone in this house?" Nina said as she straightened her posture. She had never taken to seats without backs.

"Yeah. This…coven. Or whatever. I know it's supposed to be like a family, but it's never felt like that for me. It's a very lonely place."

Nina sat very still and thought long and hard about what to say.

Ollie spoke first. "What's going on with this plant, by the way?" He looked up from the piano and pointed to a pot of leggy English ivy on a stand to his left.

"What do you mean?"

"I don't think you have a green thumb. Look at it. Look how weird and leggy it is. It looks like a hairstyle from *Stranger Things*."

Nina's cheeks lifted and her lips curled as she let out a snorty laugh. "I know. It's very sad. But that's what I have you for, to help me with that. Look at that back patio. It's a jungle back there! Even in winter!" He was right: her plants were sad and his were spectacular, almost as breathtaking as his piano playing.

It was exactly more of what Ollie didn't want to hear. "What good are all these things I can do if they all just feel like…something I can do?"

"I'm a lot older than you, so trust me when I tell you that in all my years, I've had hundreds of interests. I'm like you in that way. Interested in so much. However, I'm not nearly as gifted as you, not at even half of my interests. Sure, I have some hobbies that I like, that pass the time and are good, well, hobbies—I guess. But after a while, I finally figured out what was best for me, what truly felt…satisfying."

"What was it?" Ollie asked with eyes so wide, they were about to water.

"What I found to be most satisfying didn't really have much to do with me at all. I was most fulfilled by helping others become the best version of themselves," Nina said. She had always prided herself on that above all else—helping others. Suddenly, she felt reinvigorated and confident about being a Proctor again. She quickly acknowledged the feeling and set it aside. She was here for Ollie, and he looked almost dementedly dispirited.

"What if I never find that?" he said sadly. "What if I just go through my whole life, however long that is, and I never find that? Or what if I do, but I don't recognize it?"

"This may not mean a whole lot to you now…in fact, I can almost guarantee it won't mean shit, and that's okay, because one day, it will. But I am telling you, I feel it. I *know* it. You will one day." Nina tilted her chin and looked away. She had the sense that something significant would happen for Ollie in the coming autumn. "Only it won't be anything like you expect, at all. As far as what it will be or how you'll recognize it, well…remember to ask yourself this each time you are considering a path…Do you *have* to do it? And if you don't *have* to do it, then don't. There's something more suited for you. But *always*…try something first, before you decide. Whatever it is."

They shared a moment of silence.

"Do you ever wonder what your life would be like if you hadn't realized that?" Ollie asked. "Or if you hadn't been our Proctor, where you're sort of forced to help us better ourselves?"

"Of course I do. Everyone does. Not so much these days. But sometimes. I don't get too wound up about it, though. It's not what happened, and not much good can come from being stuck in the past. The past is the past…It's over. This is where I am now. Life's short enough—too short to be worrying about what could have been."

Ollie continued to press for more details, more clarity. "Did you know that you were good at it right away? Or was it something you kind of figured out over time?"

Nina smiled and waggled her head back and forth. "Not really. Not right away. But I pursued it until…I felt I could really help people. I didn't really know I could until I started applying myself in ways that allowed me to practice it. Does that make sense?" Nina wasn't even sure what she meant and hoped her confusing response would be enough to satisfy Ollie.

Ollie placed the fingers of his right hand on the piano keys but didn't play them. "I feel like I've wasted so much of my life trying to figure out what I should be doing. You know? Something that…has meaning for me. Something that makes me feel like being on this planet is important. Or useful." His free hand jumped up to middle C, and he played something quick and dazzling. "I know I'm good at things…" And before he could finish: "It just feels like I've just wasted all this time when I should have buckled down and tried to work out what I was meant to do. I feel like everyone else does that. Or maybe people just settle. Or maybe I just overthink everything."

A faint memory crossed Nina's mind. She let it linger for a moment before she spoke. "I feel most at peace when I know that I've helped someone find clarity or peace or purpose. If I can help someone discover their own self-worth, that gives me purpose."

"Is that why you're so concerned about Leo?"

"We're not talking about him right now," Nina redirected. "But…there will never be another chance to do that for someone I really wish I could have…my mother. I'll never have another mother to help guide *me*. I wish I could've returned the favor. I wish I could have had the chance to influence her as much as she influenced me. She was strong. And being strong is hard. I know that is kind of a cliché these days: the strong black woman. But that's not at all what I mean."

Nina's eyes began to glaze over, and tears were close. "But that's the past, and this is where I am now. I just hope I can do that for all of you. I know we're not blood, but we're still a family. To me."

Ollie lifted his hand from his lap and gently rubbed Nina's back. "Nina…you have made more of a difference in all of our lives in the short time we've been here than I think anyone ever has for any of us. I can see it. I can even see it in Leo. And that's saying something."

Nina believed Ollie, or at least she pretended to believe him as she wiped the bottom of her eyes.

"Hey…" Ollie said as he lifted her chin. "I'm telling you the truth."

"I know you are. I just want to be better. I feel like I'm failing all of you. I know you just told me that I'm not, but it doesn't always *feel* like I'm helping. I don't have all the answers, and I can't protect you or even teach you the things you should know as fast as I should be able to. After the attack, the first thing I thought was that I had no business being a Proctor…Maybe I'm just pretending to be something I'm not."

"Well, that's fear talking. It sounds like you need to follow your own advice, huh? Your intentions…your soul…is nothing but careful and good. Everyone sees that. I see that. Lots of people see that. Why can't you?"

Nina had held in her emotions for as long as she could. A few tears oozed their way out of her eyes. "At this point, I just keep wondering, how can I inspire you *now*, when I have so much doubt?"

The piano bench squeaked as Ollie repositioned himself to sit a little closer to Nina. His hand moved to the other side of her shoulder as he wrapped his arm around her back. "I think you should be asking yourself why you deny all the progress we *have* made. Why are you making that harder for yourself? We all want the world to be better than it is, and together, we can make a difference. If we want to shift our reality and create that change, we have to focus on our gratitude." Ollie hardly skipped a beat to take a breath. "Slow down and focus on the abundance of your being, who you are and what you have created within all of us here. Awareness of being causes a ripple, and you deserve to be happy, and to realize the positive effect of your being on us, on the world—even here in Louisiana…where I hope we don't stay forever."

They both smiled and laughed.

"Don't look back to what you wish you could have done, or what you wish you could have been," Ollie said. "You're waiting on *you*. That spirit of your mother, that's part of you, but she can't take all the credit. You've taken that seed of what she gave you and nourished it and helped it grow. Growth is change, and sometimes change is hard and sometimes it sucks, and most of the time it feels shitty in the moment. This is something everyone struggles with, right? If there is anything that I've learned, that *you've* taught me, it's that being a witch doesn't magically wipe out all your insecurities. It doesn't allow you to bypass the lessons that you need to learn. I feel like, in my own experience, it does the opposite, and it highlights them with a big-ass spotlight and a neon marker. Like oysters. A little sand gets trapped inside an oyster and what does it do? It turns it into a pearl. Or Beyoncé. She took lemons and made *Lemonade*."

Nina had stopped crying. She was absolutely dumbfounded by Ollie's sudden burst of wisdom. She was convinced, now more than ever, that she actually was having a positive influence on their lives—Ollie's in particular. "You know, you have many gifts, Ollie, but this is by far your biggest talent."

"What?" Ollie asked.

"Your light." She stared straight into his eyes to make sure he was paying her full attention. "You're a healer."

CHAPTER 45

Edie had brushed her teeth, slipped into pajamas and fluffed her pillow before she and her husband knelt beside the bed for a quick evening prayer. Upon finishing, they both pulled back the sheets like they had thousands of times before, only this time, Joshua wasn't planning to go straight to sleep. After a few minutes of tossing and turning and before Edie slipped away into dreamland, Joshua pushed off the covers and sat up.

"I'm just not tired yet."

Edie would never stop him. She was a starfish sleeper, even though she would never admit it. She liked to spread out in all directions in the king-size bed. Most of the time she did, but now she had even more reason to do it without having to compromise.

Joshua wriggled out of bed and headed downstairs, where, he said, he would try to read or perhaps watch some appropriate late-night television. Actually, he didn't plan to do either of those things. Instead, he was eager to browse through his financial statements. He cared about a lot of things more than Edie did. Well—different things. The environment was one, which is why he had switched to paperless statements a couple of years earlier. Saving the rain forest wasn't his sole motivation for going paperless, though. He also wanted to keep a few financial secrets.

Edie liked to spend and to know there was money to spend. She couldn't be bothered with the actual numbers or, God forbid, any type of math. That was what Joshua was good for. He liked numbers. Except the ones he saw when he checked the balance of their checking and savings accounts...Those numbers were bleak. Their nest egg had been nearly sucked dry. The new campus had taken up the majority of their fundraiser money, especially since the contractors had had to scrap the first foundation and start again because of an architectural oversight. The fact that they had money to burn was a bigger illusion than the idea that they were the true messengers of God. Money was tight. It had been tight for a while. Joshua hadn't come up with any new solutions to build up their savings, but he had gotten better at hiding the truth, which was an unbelievable feat in and of itself.

Sure, Edie spent money like it was a job from God, but even she had trouble spending all their money. But now, their money was being swallowed up like a family trying to support children, only they didn't have any children. *They* didn't— Joshua did. That was the secret he was best at hiding. If that ever got out, it would destroy everything he had built. It was never his intention to struggle financially. It had just kind of happened. Over the past few years, he had been wiring money to a daughter he had from another woman. His daughter, an environmental studies major with a minor in religious studies, had just turned twenty and was about to finish school at Tulane, setting them back a good two hundred thousand dollars. As busted as New Orleans was, things were sure ridiculously expensive.

Her name was Angela, and their father-daughter relationship was kept top secret. It had to be. Whereas Josh had Scottish and Welsh roots, his ex-girlfriend Nicole had a father who was whiter than Joshua on a sunny day, but a mother with suspiciously honey-colored skin, a woman who looked like she tanned regularly and never missed a day. Perhaps it was

Joshua's ignorance that had allowed him to be blinded, or maybe it was how well Nicole had hidden it from him because of his upbringing, but her black ancestry was always there, like a stain that was set for life. At the time all he saw (wanted to see) was how beautiful she was. And she was. Physically, mentally and spiritually. That was the only thing he could see. She was different.

Back then, Joshua had been a little angsty. He had had a lot of questions, many of which were about God and his faith, which led him to become estranged from his parents and abandon the values they had drilled into him since his youth. The sanctity of monogamy seemed like everything he didn't want at the time. Then he had met Nicole, and all he wanted was monogamy. When she had become pregnant with their child, he was excited and scared about being a father. But it wasn't until he laid eyes on a baby girl with a complexion far darker than naturally possible if both parents were white that he also felt angry.

At first, he believed Nicole had cheated on him, and he did his best to hide the terror in his face and the angry screams held hostage in his lungs. He tried to make up scenarios in his head in a desperate attempt to make sense of the situation in a room full of doctors and obstetric nurses—scenarios even he didn't believe, thoughts he had never thought before that moment. But the only information she had ever withheld from him was that she was of mixed ethnicities.

Joshua met Nicole's parents that day, one black and one white, both good people. Yet he couldn't help but feel like he had been shortchanged, like everything had been a lie and he had been tricked into being with someone his family would never, ever approve of. While he was there in the hospital, he received a phone call that his parents, with whom he had not spoken in more than a year, had died. Quite ironically as well. They'd died in a fire started by a spilled incense burner full of frankincense, one of the gifts to the Christ child. The frankincense brought fire, which brought the death of extremely overbearing parents and an inheritance of three hundred thousand dollars. Joshua couldn't help but feel a little bit like Jesus with all those gifts. He chose to accept the new life at his fingertips.

Nine weeks later, Nicole's parents suggested Joshua and Nicole leave Angela with them and take a day trip up to Mississippi to help them find some peace of mind after the chaos of adjusting to a new baby and the death of Joshua's parents. It was more of a selfish act for Grandma. She missed raising a child about as much as Nicole loved having some time away from one.

They were a little over an hour into their trip, somewhere between Baton Rouge and St. Francisville, when Nicole wanted to take a slight detour and check out a secret lake she had heard about. She liked to swim, and didn't like sitting still in a car. It was also hot, so a dip in a secret lake sounded romantic. Joshua loved Nicole, but he didn't love good ol' Louisiana water. All of it, even Lake Ponchartrain, looked like a cesspool. He had taken a few trips to Florida, where the water was clear and blue. Why they hadn't gone there instead was something he would never understand.

The lake turned out to be pretty secret indeed. Nicole had suggested a route that seemed like way more work than it could ever be worth. They parked alongside the road, hopped over some Jersey walls, carved out a path through a patch of dense woods and finally arrived at the lake ten minutes later. There were more pebbles than actual sand, and a rotting fish had washed up on shore. There was also a mediocre view of a large lake surrounded by trees and marshlands. The only romantic thing about it was the tire swing near the water's edge. Josh was happy to see Nicole so excited, and was satisfied watching her enjoy the water all on her own. He wasn't going to go into that murky water, even if someone paid him to do it. Although the undisclosed location of the beach was indeed a secret, the bigger secret was that Nicole tragically contracted amoebic meningitis after swimming in the lake and died a few hours later. He had known it was a bad idea to swim in a Louisiana lake. He wished he had spoken up about it.

Nicole's parents took custody of the baby girl, per Joshua's request. There was minimal visitation for a while. Then none after he met Edie. She suffered from endometriosis and would never be able to have children of her own, no matter how hard she prayed. It would kill her to know that Josh already had one in the family, especially one of color. Joshua would pepper the baby conversation every now and then with comments about how he felt it was selfish to have a child when the world was so out of balance. That it was unnecessary and irrational and merely an illogical obsession because she felt she just had to have a child, for no apparent reason, as though it were a doll from the toy store.

After he had reviewed a few bank statements, Edie came plunking down the stairs in her floppy slippers.

"What are you still doin' up down here?" Edie asked. She was loving having the bed all to herself, but it didn't feel right without him in it.

"Just going over some bills for the new build. It wasn't cheap." He locked his phone, clasped his hands together and stretched his arms over his head.

"Well, we can figure that out tomorrow. Come on back to bed," Edie said as she held his eyes.

Josh turned off the lights and rubbed his wife's back as he walked up the stairs. Edie smiled and then looked back into the darkness with a puzzled look on her face.

CHAPTER 46

When Leo returned to the house, he explained his absence with total honesty. No one else in the house was adopted or had ever been through the life he had, so they accepted it and let him slip away to his room. A few minutes later, Bisa arrived at his bedroom door. He hid the spell he was about to prepare and answered her knock. She was going to offer to draw him a bath or get him something to eat. He looked exhausted, but it was the kind of exhaustion where one doesn't actually know they're exhausted. After she guessed he was preparing a spell, she decided against offering him anything until he 'fessed up to a few things that had been festering in her mind.

They bickered back and forth. Bisa insisted they talk about the drugs in his dresser drawer, and Leo defended his right to privacy and the idea that things are just a little better when one is under the influence of something. Life can be really dull otherwise. Having said that, he assured her that he wasn't using drugs anymore. Before he could explain further, Bisa launched into another anti-drug campaign and protested that drugs only took him further out of the present. She agreed with the idea that they could be used for personal and spiritual growth, but not when they were abused, and Leo had always been a habitual abuser.

Before the conversation turned into a heated debate over the use of illegal drugs, Bisa changed the subject. "So what spell are you doing in here in secret?" she asked, hoping she'd intuitively guessed correctly.

Leo rolled his eyes and then realized that he wasn't as discreet as he thought he was. "I know what you're gonna say, but it's not like what you think."

"Okay, see, that right there makes me think you're setting me up for a lie."

Leo rolled his eyes again and pulled out the bowl of salt and the oil-anointed candle from underneath the bed.

"I'm going to see Evan."

Bisa sighed. "The drug dealer?" she asked in a strained tone that suggested she was trying really hard not to be angry.

Leo explained Evan's role and that he was going there strictly to get some information. She believed him, but she also didn't fully trust him. She saw a darkness in Leo, one that he didn't.

When Leo finished telling Bisa the whole story, she said, "Well, I'm coming with you."

"No, you're not," Leo replied coldly with a babysitter-like authority.

"Yes, I am. Or I'll just have to go tell the rest of the coven that you're going to meet with the very same dealer who supplied witches with drugs that led them to try to kill us and feel good about it."

"They won't believe you. It's your word against mine!" Leo nipped back.

"Come on. Are they going to believe me…or an alleged *former* drug addict with a drawer full of cocaine?" Bisa knew she had won the argument.

"Yeah. You right."

Bisa shut the door and helped Leo prepare the ritual. Leo poured the salt into a pile. He hadn't used this much salt since the day he quit his job at the restaurant. The chef had come in and traded being hungover at home for a paycheck while she took a nap on the sacks of flour. That's when he'd opened a fresh box of kosher salt and poured it over all the prepped ingredients for lunch service, all the way from the oven station to sauté. He'd dropped the box of salt as a theatrical exclamation point like one does a microphone after a speech so exceptional, there's no way to ever follow it up. The salt in a pile before him now was not some kind of definitive act or gesture, but rather a conduit for spellwork. It was magnificent how much his life had changed…so much that even something like salt had a new purpose.

They held hands as Leo lit the candle. He said "Evan" and then dipped his finger into the flame. It happened so fast that Bisa didn't even remember what had happened when Leo touched the fire. They were now sitting on the wooden porch of a small house. A red door was before them. Leo whipped his head around to try to make out where they were, but it could have been anywhere. There were no immediate tells.

Leo stood and considered knocking, his balled fist slowly unraveling a few inches from the door. He reached down to the handle, twisted it and entered the house. Evan's house was surprisingly full for its size. Shuttered windows, stacks of papers and books, a jungle of wires running along the floor, the faint scent of nostalgia. Leo had lived in places that looked like this.

Before them, in a velvety-red armchair, Evan sat quietly. As Leo slammed the door behind them, Evan looked up, almost as if he had been expecting company an hour ago and they had only just now showed up. His eyes were barren and dark, but seemed to glisten like mint jelly under the light of the standing lamp.

"Who the fuck are you?" Evan asked in an uncouth but hypnotic tone, like the stinging voice of an ex-lover too chaotic to date but too delicious to turn away.

"Are you Evan?" Leo asked.

"Don't make me ask you again," Evan said.

"I'm Leo."

"Then yeah, I'm Evan. How'd you find me?"

Leo took a few steps forward, kicking a path out between the messes on the floor.

"A friend recommended you to me."

Evan laughed as he ran his hands through his hair, which was clay-like probably from a lack of proper washing, even though it looked clean—styled, even. His skin had very few lines. He wasn't the wiry specimen Leo had expected him to be. There was a spryness to his spirit that showed in his quick mannerisms, his cuddlesome voice and his taut face. "That doesn't sound like the truth. But I take it you know what I do or you wouldn't have been able to find me. So, what exactly do you want?"

Evan looked at Bisa, who was still standing by the door, observing.

"I'm not interested in whatever's on your menu," Leo said. "I came here because I think you might be able to tell me a little about my parents. Jim and Tina Perkins. Remember them?"

There were beats of silence as Evan looked back into Leo's eyes.

"I know it's been a while, but I know you used to deal to them," Leo said. "I wanna know what you were selling them."

"Jim liked everything."

"So you sold him what?"

"I said he liked everything, not that I sold him everything."

"So, what then? Heroin? Acid? What?" Leo started running through the list of his own vices.

"At first. But mostly they came to me for AFD."

Leo shook his head and frowned. "AFD?" He looked slightly disappointed, almost like he was upset that there was something he hadn't tried. The moment passed quickly. "What's AFD? I've never heard of that."

"I'd be surprised if you had. It's not something typically carried by any dealer I've ever known, other than myself." Evan turned his attention back to Bisa, who was still hovering by the doorway. "AFD. Astral fluid."

"And what's astral fluid?" Bisa asked as she took a few steps closer and sat on the armrest of Leo's chair. She already knew. Nina had mentioned it once.

"It's not synthetic; it's an organic substance. Everyone has it. You two have it. But it can be extracted and used."

"Like a life force? An aura?" Bisa asked.

Evan raised his eyebrows in surprise. "You brought a brain with you. Not just a pretty face."

Leo tightened his eyes at the phrase he had used once himself. He didn't appreciate the parallels.

"Thank you," Bisa said freely. "How long ago was this? Wasn't this twenty-some years ago? You don't look a day older than twenty-five yourself. I'm all for diet and exercise, but people still age. How does someone manage something like that?" And before Evan could respond: "Astral fluid?"

Evan shook his head. "Never get high on your own supply."

"What then? It's someone else's...stash? Someone else's...magic...someone else's spell?"

"Astral fluid doesn't keep you young. It gives you other things besides youth. Characteristics, emotions—powers. All of whomever the fluid is drained from." Evan looked at Bisa, then at Leo, then back to Bisa. "Are you his girlfriend?"

Bisa winced at the thought. "No," she responded. There was a slight hint of disgust in the one-word answer.

"So, you brought a friend along, for what? A quality check?"

"I told you, I'm not here for that. I just want to find out what you know. I just want to ask some questions," Leo said, becoming more frustrated with each passing moment.

"You already have. What else do you want?" Evan said, his voice like a slap in the face.

"The secret to your youthful glow," Bisa said. "If it's not astral fluid."

Evan shook his head. "Can't you smell it? I've smelled it for years. Maybe I'm just used to it by now."

"Smell what?" Leo asked.

"The magic." Evan pointed at Bisa. "Like how you…smell like summer-kissed rosemary." Evan swayed his finger over to Leo. "And how you…smell like…well, I don't know…What is that? It's a smell I haven't smelled in a very, very, very long time."

Bisa nodded. She *knew* he was older than twenty-five. She was content with keeping her satisfaction to herself. "I can't 'smell the magic,' as you say, but I can smell you. You're like me…a Transcendent."

"You got it," Evan said. "Boy. Leo must really be desperate for some answers if he's recruiting reinforcements to squeeze some information out of me like some kind of dry lemon."

"I'm not desperate," Leo said with a hot and heavy breath.

"Desperate to find out exactly who your parents were and what they were up to, as most adopted kids tend to do when they get older and find out the truth." Evan smiled as he swiveled his cozy chair back and forth.

Leo's head dropped back in surprise. "How'd you know I was adopted?"

Evan looked over Leo's body as if he had reconnected with an old nephew for the first time in years. "Look at you…you little bumpkin. All grown up now."

Bisa turned to Leo. "Do you *know* this guy?"

"Fuck no! This is the first time I've ever seen him in my life!"

Bisa wanted answers, and she wanted them fast. Every passing minute made her feel more vulnerable. If Leo was going to get anywhere with Evan, she would have to help him get there. "You said you sell astral fluid. Where does it come from? How do you get it?"

Evan ignored Bisa completely and focused his attention on Leo. His pupils widened. He was a gifted witch with more than just a talent for small-time drug trades. He had seen things, enough things to know power and presence when he felt it. "What do you want to know about your parents and where you come from?" Evan dropped his hands to his lap and held his fingers together loosely as if he were holding a thick rope.

"I don't know much. I'm from Massachusetts."

There was a rising shrill in the background, like the silent shrill of a dog whistle, too subtle to detect.

"You always thought you grew up in Louisiana, didn't you?" Evan asked, his eyes now polished and glistening like a wet street under the moonlight. "You thought because of where you were born that you'd never be happy. Someone explained it to you. And it made sense: being born in that area makes one prone to magical retardation. A handicap."

"But I'm not actually from there." As the silent shrill became higher in pitch, Leo and Bisa felt a sudden wave of fatigue. Leo ignored it and continued to push on, unwavering in his search for answers.

"Tell us how you get the astral fluid!" Bisa demanded as she suddenly felt herself melting into her perch on the armchair.

Leo nudged her to stop talking. She had to be quiet. He was getting closer to the answers he needed. His heart began to pound. "But I wasn't born there, so what caused it? Why can't I feel happiness? What is it? You know, don't you?"

A mocking laugh escaped from Evan's lips. "You're close. You're so, so close to figuring it all out. So close to finding what you've been looking for all this time, finding what you didn't even know you were looking for. And even with two brains, you don't know why you're so close."

Leo wanted to rise from his seat, grab Evan by the throat and punch him until his face slipped right off his skull. But he couldn't. It wasn't just that he wouldn't get any answers that way. Something was preventing him from doing it. It was almost a voice that told him to sit down and stay still. "Why? What the fuck does that even mean?"

Evan leaned forward gracefully, ever so slightly. The irises of his eyes were almost spinning. There was something strange about them, something that looked perverted and wrong, like the sickening twinkle in the eyes of a psychopath as he watches his prey struggle helplessly before him. "You weren't born with a magical handicap; you were given one. Your ability to feel happiness was stolen from you…and the memory of it was erased, or rather…replaced so that you wouldn't know any different, you would just continue to grow less happy as you went through life, always looking for a way out, trying everything you could, every drug you could, every woman you could, every job you could, hoping it would pull you out of it and make you feel whole again. But it never worked, did it?"

Evan held Leo's gaze as if he were reading all his private thoughts and uncovering every skeleton in his closet. Leo couldn't have turned away from him if he'd tried. It was too personal, too real.

Evan carried on: "You just continued to exist in constant agony rather than accepting it and trying to move on, because life was meant to be lived and that meant you needed more. You never felt the way you thought you *should* feel, filled with moments of joy. Everyone around you seem to be wrapped up in moments of happiness on levels you never felt you would achieve, could achieve. Danger is your greatest substitute. You were made to be this way, but the means by which you were made to be this way were even more tragic."

Bisa had the upper hand, but only if she chose to act. She searched the higher consciousness in a split second and returned to the present with a sense of awareness. She could hear the high-pitched shrill now. It was almost deafening. The heaviness in her core was still there. Bisa looked over at Leo and could tell he was under Evan's influence. She slowly turned her attention to Evan. He was nodding as if listening to a fascinating story.

That's when something below caught her attention. Evan's hands were open, palms forward. At the center of each hand was a small flickering ball of spinning white light. *Our souls*, Bisa thought. If she acted, Evan would surely react, and there was no telling what he was capable of. Bisa slipped her hand down and clutched the side of Leo's arm. *It's him*, Bisa said nonverbally to Leo.

Evan's eyes lifted to Bisa. He knew. There was a moment shared between them, but it was ever so fleeting. Evan stretched his fingers open wide, and the balls of light grew to the size of his hand. He would sap every last drop of their power if only given a few more seconds. It was like a full-on electric shock so painful that it almost made Bisa throw up.

Then Leo stood up without warning, free from Evan's influence. A shockwave shot out toward Evan, and the lights in his palms dissolved. His body went stiff and rigid like a corpse.

"Who buys the astral fluid? The souls?" Leo asked.

Evan struggled to speak, as if something was clutching his throat. "Many people. But there's one who always returns. He collects them. He told me he'd reverse the immortality spell on me if he eventually collected enough souls for his collection to be complete."

Bisa was now free to move as she wished, without Evan's influence. She took a few steps closer to Evan, against Leo's wishes. She knelt down beside him as his body trembled under Leo's mysterious control. She placed her hand on Evan's neck, and on contact, a vision seared itself into her mind. "Whoever he's talking about, he's the one who did it. He has part of your soul."

"Who is he? How can I find it?" Leo asked.

A muffled spittle of laughter spilled from Evan's mouth. "I'm not telling you that."

Leo tipped his head forward and tightened the pressure over Evan's neck, and then began to work on his rib cage. There was a shameful realization in Leo's eyes as he heard the crunching of bones and groans of suffering under his spell. He hadn't meant to crush Evan's chest, only to encourage him to reveal information. Leo released his grip on Evan and let out a sigh of disappointment. He couldn't speak. He had gotten in his own way. His rage had gotten in his way—again. The room was quiet. There were no more grunts of pain, and the shrilling noise had vanished.

Bisa stood up and looked at Leo, stunned that he had just killed a man. But it wasn't the murderous act that alarmed her as much as the blood rushing from his nose and ears. Leo fell back into the chair. His body temperature dropped as though he had plummeted into an ice bath. Then everything else followed: his blood pressure, his respiratory rate. He coiled up and opened his mouth to cough up a stream of dark, clotted blood.

"Leo! What is this? What's happening?" Bisa asked as she ran to his side. She had never seen something happen so suddenly. She immediately assumed the worst: *he's dying!*

Only Leo knew exactly what was happening. He had been a drug abuser for most of his life. He knew signs of use and abuse whether they were magical or not.

"I don't know what to do! What do I do?" Bisa screamed.

Leo closed his eyes and reached up to grab hold of her hand. When he opened his eyes again, they were back in his bedroom.

CHAPTER 47

Leo recovered quickly. Physically, anyway. Mentally he was still a little upset over how everything had ended. It all felt like a nasty kind of tease—one that left him no closer to where he wanted to be. After a tall glass of ice water and the bath Bisa had suggested earlier, Leo figured out what he needed to do. *Three days. A soul lives in the body for three days. That's what she told me.* He remembered the conversation he had had with Tambala, the woman who'd been doing a voodoo ritual in the woods when he interrupted her. The govi jars…That had to be the answer. It would allow him to retrieve Evan's soul, tap deep into his memories and figure out everything he needed to know. There was of course the benefit of being able to use Evan as a zombie, too, as Tambala explained. But that wasn't his priority. He'd remember it, though.

In the span of a few minutes, Leo was already on his way to Maji with hopes that Tambala was there. If she was, he would try to—no, he *would* have her tell him just how to extract a person's soul into a govi jar—whether she liked it or not. He had (perhaps unintentionally) gotten information from her before in the same way, and he would do it again.

Avery looked up from her beehive as she listened to the zipping of Leo's bike as he rode away. She had been at her tiny apiary for a while now, trying to perfect a new divination technique. Her relationship with the bees wasn't really all that different from her relationship with the lion in the zoo. She understood her connection to the animal kingdom and the divine, but she had no understanding of their relationship to the divine. Who was to say that animals and insects didn't have power of their own? Definitely not Avery. Especially bees, with their wings bringing them a little closer to the ether. Perhaps witches were only one part of the mysterious cosmos that had some kind of incredible power. She was an exceptionally talented witch when it came to her gifts, and she was sure this experiment, too, would yield wondrous results.

With the tip of her finger, she etched a symbol into the ground before her, and then placed a chunk each of kyanite, amethyst, fluorite and celestite around it. She dipped her finger in some of the bees' honey, dabbed a little on her third eye and then sucked the remaining coating off. Avery closed her eyes and listened to the sounds of the beehive. A few minutes later, she asked of the bees, "What do I need to know about our coven?" She had learned from practicing the tarot that it was always better to ask an open-ended question than to ask something that could be answered with a yes or no. Why, what or how were the best ways to formulate a powerful question that could be interpreted with greater accuracy. She observed the bees, taking note of their flight patterns and buzzing volumes. She detected a sort of energetic richness, but nothing deemed particularly noteworthy. Avery found the idea to be intriguing but unsuccessful, and she couldn't discern any sort of message that would allow her to interpret whether a message boded well. Then the bees swirled around the hive in a helix formation.

The buzzing intensified, and then a single bee droned away from the group and stung her arm. Avery's eyes opened wide, and she gasped. The stinger didn't bring pain, but a vision: the image of Leo's lifeless body upon the ground, followed by the feeling of death. Her psychic sight disappeared, and she found herself staring back at the beehive. The bees returned to their normal behaviors. Avery lifted herself up from the ground and ran inside to find Nina. She left the patio door open as she entered the house.

"Nina!" Avery called out. "Nina, where are you?"

A few seconds later, Nina entered the room, a bag of raw almonds in her hand.

"I think something's gonna happen to Leo!" Avery said.

"Slow down, slow down. What's gonna happen to Leo?" Nina popped another almond into her mouth and started to chew as she talked. "Did you…see something?" She waved her fingers back and forth over her forehead in an unofficial sign language signal for having a psychic vision.

Avery explained what she had seen and how she had seen it. She even included the feelings she felt during the episode and concluded with the method of divination she had used.

"Divination can be fickle. It's also not always literal when it comes to the idea of actual physical death. Do you think that's what it means?"

"Yes!" Avery said with an urgency that surprised even her, considering who the vision was about. She didn't *love* Leo, but she cared enough about him that she didn't want him to *die*. He was a member of their coven, and whether anyone liked it or not, coven now meant family.

Nina reached out and stroked Avery's shoulder as if she were trying to settle an anxious dog. "Sometimes our interpretation is off. Mine has been off a hundred or more times. I'm not discounting what you saw, not at all, and I'll look into it. I'm just saying that although the messages are always accurate, our interpretation of them can be off. It's like anything else: we get better with practice, with time."

It was then that Maisie entered the room. "Is everything okay?" she asked.

Nina smiled, nodded and popped another couple of almonds into her mouth. "Yes. Everything's good. I was just talking to Avery a little about divination and how interpreting is an art form. What about you? How are you feeling? Have you given any thought to what you think you might want to do? I don't know how you feel about wanting to join *our* coven, and we would all need to sit down and have a talk about it, but I'm sure we could work something out. No pressure or anything one way or the other. If you feel you need some time to yourself or need something else, that's okay too."

Maisie looked over at Avery and then around the room, as if the answer were written somewhere on the walls. There were a few shrugs and a couple of throaty moans, but nothing that was an actual answer.

Nina considered that Maisie might feel put on the spot, especially in front of Avery. She raised her hands and waved them in the air. "You don't need to answer now! You've been through…a lot. We all have!" She looked to Avery and then back to Maisie. "I want you to make the decision that's best for you, and I want you to feel comfortable making it, not rushed or pressured one way or the other. So *please*…take your time. It's really no trouble having you here, and whenever you want to talk about it, just let me know. Or about anything! Doesn't have to be about that at all. I'm always open to talk. That's my job—that's why I'm here."

"I don't mean you guys any harm or anything. I'm not like…the rest of them."

"We know that," Avery said.

"*I* wouldn't be crazy about having some random person stay in *my* house, and I don't want to get in y'all's way."

"You're not in anybody's way. Don't you worry about that one bit. So like I said, make yourself at home." Nina wrapped up the bag of almonds and started to walk away. "I'm making lentil and sweet potato stew tonight!"

Ollie had a thing for lentils and an even bigger thing for sweet potatoes. He certainly wouldn't miss it, regardless of what he was doing.

Ollie had taken his conversation with Nina to heart, and that meant he needed to test himself to see if he was any good. Transcendents were always more gifted when it came to spiritual work, and working with spirits was...well, spiritual. If he was indeed a healer, as Nina suggested he was, then what better way to test that theory than to visit a cemetery. He borrowed the car and, with the help of Google Maps, found a few cemeteries nearby that he wanted to check out. The first one was small, no larger than a tennis court, with gravestones that would surely sink into the ground during the next big storm. He paused for a moment at the entrance but decided he didn't feel a certain draw that he was looking for.

The second cemetery was a little farther out of the way, with wonky, lopsided tombstones like one would often see in a state that was slowly sinking at a Big Easy kind of pace. Only he didn't pick up on anything there either. *Am I being stupid? Is this even something I can do?*

The third cemetery was down an unnamed gravel road off Old River Road, which was off the 3213 Highway just outside Vacherie. Its location alone seemed to hold more secrets than any of those who had been buried there. The cemetery was nestled among a few low hills and a patch of trees. There wasn't even a Raising Cane's Chicken or 7-Eleven for another three miles. Louisiana was rather flat, and there weren't hills in the sense that people from other states think of hills. They were more like mounds, caused by the constant moving, sinking and flooding of the land. In spite of the mostly sunny day, there was a decent amount of low-hanging fog in the cemetery, the kind that one sees in a cemetery scene of a horror movie. But this fog held a sort of delightful essence. It made the unexpected huddle of cars parked alongside the entrance look all the more mysterious.

Ollie clearly was not alone at this cemetery. He walked through the entrance and along the path, listening for spirits. If there ever were a chance of it happening, it surely would be here, he thought. The farther he walked, the more his new interest in his abilities overwhelmed any doubt. He enjoyed helping and connecting with Nina. It felt natural, and he also felt fulfilled by it. As he passed by the first patch of large, aboveground tombs, he heard music. *Is that a second line?* The sounds of brass bands weren't his favorite, but he respected them. He respected all musicians. They were artists, and he loved art. Ollie believed that the world had certain ideologies built into its existence and art was the best way to decode and express those ideologies that people had been doing since art was even a thing. His gift also felt like art, and being so balanced between the classifications of masculinity and femininity, he seemed like the best person to embody such a gift.

Ollie slowly followed the somber sounds of "A Closer Walk with Thee" as if he were joining a second line himself. When he passed the last large tombstone, he could see the funeral. It was larger than he'd expected, but small enough not to supply any chairs. He stopped and stood behind the tomb, hiding from the crowd. In the far back, a woman was sobbing into a black handkerchief. Ollie could feel the emotion vibrating off of the woman like heat from a loaf of freshly baked bread that had just been pulled from the oven. He resisted his instinctual urge to try to soothe her grief. The music stopped, and the ceremony commenced. Ollie looked down to the ground and disconnected from the energy of the funeral. Over the next minute, the world around him went extraordinarily quiet. The funeral, the birds singing from the trees and even the sound of his own breathing dissolved. A feeling of nausea slipped over him.

Ollie stepped back from the corner of the tomb and rested his back against the cold stone. He could feel the rough engravings of the stone carving into his back as he allowed his body to melt. He closed his eyes and drifted away. Some undetermined amount of time went by, and then he opened his eyes again, slowly, as if for the first time. Without reason or logic, Ollie explored the sights that were before him. His head turned slightly to the right, and he could see the funeral in his peripheral vision. But that wasn't all he saw. On the outskirts of the cemetery, not too far from where the funeral was taking place, he saw someone else. He turned his neck and saw—with crystalline clarity—the spirit of the deceased. The man—or spirit, rather—was watching his own funeral. Ollie had always known there was some kind of afterlife, the existence of which was so controversial that it might as well have been labeled *actuality unknown*. However, he was always of the opinion that the amount we know about the universe is very small, and moments like this validated just how little he knew, not to mention how thin the veil was between the real world and the spirit world.

Ollie's mouth dropped open, and he blinked a few times just to make sure he wasn't imagining things. He wasn't. The spirit, a beast of a man with a large belly and a scraggly beard, was not dressed for the occasion: he wore orange shorts, a tank top that barely covered his bulbous belly and a fedora. There was nothing ghostly about him. He looked like, well—a man, alive and well. Perhaps a little overweight, but not like someone on their deathbed. There was a newness to the man. The spirit watched the funeral for a few minutes, as if it were a familiar television show in a different language with no subtitles. Then he turned his head and looked at Ollie with an expression of puzzlement, and began to walk toward him. His plump legs and bare feet tore right through the fog but left it completely undisturbed. Ollie held the spirit's gaze right up until the moment he stopped a couple of feet away from him. The spirit looked him up and down, sizing him up.

"Can you see me?" the spirit asked.

Ollie's eyes quivered a little as he thought of what to say. "Yeah…" he said hesitantly.

"Well, I'll be. Ain't that somethin'?"

A little grin formed on Ollie's lips but then slowly faded away. "Do you…wanna talk about anything?"

The spirit raised his eyebrows, looked around his feet as if he had lost some change, and then sluggishly took a seat on the ground with a raspy, exhausted sigh. Ollie sat beside him. The spirit smelled strange but familiar. Ollie tried to discreetly take a whiff of the spirit and deduced that he smelled like the crunchy, dry marshmallows in a box of Lucky Charms.

"So, I'm dead," the spirit said.

"Yeah, you are."

"Sixty-one years old. Never left Louisiana. Married only once. Never did a damn thing I wanted to, except raise my daughter."

Ollie looked out toward the funeral. "What else did you want to do?"

"Well…that doesn't matter now because I can't do it anymore."

"What is it…that you wanted to do?"

The spirit looked at Ollie for a moment, cleared his throat and then soaked in the funeral.

"I wanted to be on *Project Runway*. I got a thing about dresses. Not that I like wearing them, but I would look at the dresses that my wife tried on and think, *Damn…That is one sad excuse for a dress*. Too many ruffles, bad stitching, no silhouette. 'Course I never told her that. I only told her how beautiful she looked. And she is. Look." He pointed her out in the crowd: a woman half his size in a remarkably plain funeral dress. "She could make a pearl necklace look ugly and she's a good woman. I loved her. I know she was in love with me, but she loved me more than I was able to love her. I was in love with my dream of being a dress maker. How 'bout that?"

"Why didn't you do it?"

There was a moment of silence.

"I think I was afraid. It feels like that now. I don't even know if I would have known that…when I was alive. I knew that I wanted to leave, live somewhere else. Even for a little while. I thought it would give me the strength to make those changes that I knew I needed to make but never did."

"Why did you stay?" Ollie picked up a tiny weed from the ground and twirled it around his fingers.

A smile grew on the spirit's face. "My daughter. She's right there. See her? In the hat." He pointed her out. "I loved her. Gave her everything. Tonya, that's my wife, she always said I spoiled her to all hell." The spirit laughed as he remembered the exact moment his wife had said those words to him. "I stayed for her. I gave up everything, and I mean *everything* I ever dreamed of for myself, so that I could make sure she got what she deserved. I told myself if I ever had a child, I would raise them right. I wasn't gonna beat them or disown them, I wouldn't care if they was gay or anything, I just wanted them to be a good person. So the world would look at her and say, 'Damn, you're a good person…I want to be like you' and then they could live life in better ways because of her. But now it's too late. And I can't help no more."

"You're not gone. I know you're not, because I'm sitting here in this cemetery and I'm talking to you."

"You know what I mean. I failed."

"Your body died, sure, but you haven't failed. So much of this life…is about timing and what we do with our time. I certainly don't know why things work out the way they work out, or why people die when they do or why horrible things happen to good people, but you haven't failed. You made *her* life—better. Be grateful for that. I can tell she is. It's why she's crying. That I know."

The spirit blew a long-winded sigh out of his mouth and wiped the corners of his eyes. "Well, what can I do now?"

"You gave her a life with virtues. That will go further than any protection you'd physically be able to give. You did your best. Your daughter came first…even before yourself. No one's perfect. But you did the best you could with what you had."

The spirit rolled over all the memories and thoughts that were too painful to bring up in conversation. Every single thing he wished he had done differently or hadn't ever gotten a chance to do boiled to the surface and took shape in the form of a stream of tears. *Ghosts can cry...Ain't that somethin'*, the spirit thought.

Ollie reached over and touched the man's knee for some tactile comfort. Only it was more than that, grander. He took a deep breath in and felt a rush of hot energy fill his head. On the exhale, the heat drained through his body and into the man. Transcendents truly were gifted empaths, and emotional healing came as naturally to Ollie as breathing.

"That's not enough," the spirit said as he broke down in tears. His chin quivered, and tears dropped down onto his belly.

"Maybe...let it be enough," Ollie said.

Over the next few minutes, Ollie sat with the spirit, who never told him his name, and discussed a few more details of the man's life, ranging from trauma to death. With directed conversation, active listening and his unique healing abilities, Ollie acted as a sort of "witch doctor," healing emotional and spiritual wounds through a sort of empathic, psychic, energetic and auric form of talk therapy. Suddenly the energy in the air changed, and the spirit shimmered with a palette of colors that no longer included the troublesome hues of regret or worry. It was bizarre how easily Ollie knew what to say and when to say it. It even surprised *him*.

Just when Ollie realized that he couldn't think of anything else he could possibly say, the spirit stood up. Actually, it was more of a discombobulated wobble. The man had released much of the baggage he had carried over from his physical life.

Then, in the fierceness of a lightning strike, the man crumbled like dead leaves that had caught fire, and spilled into the sky.

CHAPTER 48

When Leo returned to the house with the information he had sapped from Tambala, he raced to his bedroom, shut the door and projected himself back to Evan's place. He entered and closed the door, but immediately reopened it when the foul stench of Evan's dead body overwhelmed him. With his shirt lifted over his nose, Leo begrudgingly walked over to the corpse. He pulled out a tiny jar from his pocket and set it on the side of the couch. He arrogantly disregarded all ritualistic preparations and went straight in for psychic surgery. There was no graveyard dirt in the bottom of the jar, nor were there any offerings or attractants. It was just an empty bottle…thirsty for a soul.

Leo placed Evan's finger in the top of the jar and began to speak the words that Tambala had told him in confidence. He placed his free hand over the crown of Evan's head. A few crackling noises could be heard from Evan's forehead. What was happening?…He hadn't even started. Leo pressed against Evan's head and moved along his body as if squeezing water from a sponge. He went down Evan's whiskery face, along his shoulder and down the length of his limp, cold arm.

Leo smiled as his hand approached the tip of Evan's finger that had been jammed into the jar. He thought again of how close he was to finally getting an answer to what he had been curious about for so long. His hand closed in on the finger as he wrung the soul out of Evan's body with the ease of a snake shedding its skin. Then, he could see it. Dangling from the tip of the man's finger was a pearlescent substance, neither liquid or solid but outrageously luminous.

"I take you, Evan. You are mine," Leo whispered aloud.

The substance spilled into the bottle and became transparent immediately. *Did I just fuck this up?* Leo removed the finger from the top of the jar and put the opening to his ear. He could hear Evan's voice. There were no distinct words, but it was his voice without a doubt. Leo capped the bottle with a cork, snatched the closest candle he could see—a black one—set it aflame and sealed the jar with the drippings of the hot, black wax. He'd done it. He had Evan's soul in a govi jar. Perhaps it was disrespectful to call it a govi jar, but he didn't care much. Leo looked back at Evan's lifeless body, now totally drained of any soul. Then, Leo was gone.

When he returned, he couldn't act fast enough. He needed the information faster than as soon as possible. It was eating him up. Leo tried several techniques to try to extract the information he needed from the jar, without success. He was able to do many things easily, but this was where his talent seemed to plateau.

Bisa entered the room, uninvited, right at the tail end of his last failure. "Two things: dinner is almost ready, and what are you trying to do that you can't?"

Once Leo explained why he had Evan's soul in the first place, Bisa was a little less acrimonious about the whole thing. She decided she would help him with his journey because she believed him and wanted the best for him. If anything, this could be the missing link, the tool to finally smooth those rough edges.

"Your technique isn't the problem, Leo."

"What, you think I'm not strong enough, maybe?" he asked, slightly disappointed.

"You're strong enough. I think you're bulldozing through this. Do you think doctors just rush into heart surgery without preparation?"

"Doctors in Louisiana might."

"You're missing the point." Bisa rolled her eyes. She had made somewhat of a habit out of doing that when Leo said asinine things.

"Okay, well, then, what is it?"

"This is a soul. It used to be in a warm body, and now it's in a cold jar. Change its environment. Then you might be able to coax it out. I think you underestimate the power of a soul. It's not a can of beans."

Leo looked up at Bisa for the first time with vulnerable eyes instead of guarded ones. "Will you help me?"

There was a slight pause. Then Bisa walked over toward Leo, knelt down beside him and stroked the hair just above his tiny ears. Her voice was calm and smooth. "Yes."

"Thank you," Leo said, genuinely grateful. "You're a really good person."

Bisa didn't know how to take the compliment, nor did she know whether she believed it. She snorted a little. "Thank you." She wanted to believe him, and to a point, she did. But the trauma of her past always got in the way. It didn't matter how many courses she took or what exercise routines she took on; she always felt haunted by her past, as though it were a burn scar that she saw every time she took a shower.

Leo reached up and touched her shoulder. "I mean that. You are."

Bisa smiled back. "Let's begin with setting the space," she said as she rubbed his knee. "Smudge out this area. Get some palo santo, start there."

Leo smudged the room, and they surrounded themselves with vibrational crystals and lit a candle. He held the jar above it. The flame licked the bottom of the jar, and the scent of Lucky Charms filled the air.

"I think it's working," Leo said. "Set it down here, on this plate."

Bisa moved her tongs over the metal dish and delicately placed the jar in the center. Leo closed his eyes and sat on his knees. There was silence. A moment later, Leo started to sway like a tall tree in a breeze, then began to rock in circles as he muttered words under his breath. His lips poofed out as his breathing intensified. A fit of convulsions overcame him, as if he were being electrified, but only for a moment. A deep, fluttering snarl escaped from his mouth, then a breath. Then came a lighter, abrupt growl that ended in a long-winded doleful yowling like that of a wolf at the moon. Bisa wanted to laugh at first; she thought Leo was joking. But he wasn't. His spirit was empowered with the energy of his totem animal, making him stronger, if only for a short time. Leo began to sweat and pant. His hair stuck to the side of his face. Then, his eyes snapped open. He leaned over and cupped the jar, close enough to feel the heat radiating off of it. Then a faint noise.

Crack...

A single hairline fracture slipped up the side of the jar as Leo tapped into the soul's memory.

Bisa realized that Leo's approach toward a goal was similar to how she made art: instinctual, impulsive and mostly uncompromising. It made her feel closer to him than she ever had before.

"Leo?" Bisa asked gently.

Suddenly, Leo straightened his spine and gasped as if he had been holding his breath underwater. He stumbled back and fell onto his hands.

"Are you okay?"

"I know who he is. I know his name."

CHAPTER 49

By breakfast the next morning, Maisie was gone. Her pillows and blankets had been nicely folded and left in the study. One of the first things Nina usually did once she'd had some coffee was make sure that everyone was still alive. Maisie had left sometime in the middle of the night and had probably taken an Uber or Lyft; Nina could never really figure out which one people used these days.

Nina patrolled the rest of the house with her coffee cup. She had to be certain Maisie was actually gone. She ended her expedition in the hallway just off the great room, where she stood staring into space. Everything was as it should be: the tall vase, the salt lamp, the decorative wooden box from the French Market, the sad little satin pothos that she couldn't seem to keep alive. *You should really just give up this fantasy of having a green thumb already. It makes Ollie look bad.*

She considered moving the pothos to a different location. A move did everyone good every now and then. *Right?* That's when she noticed another object on the table, one that didn't belong. Nina pulled the box forward to reveal a small cloth pouch tied with what looked to be thin wire, or possibly even hair. It was early and she hadn't finished her cup of coffee, so her mind was a little fuzzy. But for the life of her, she couldn't figure out what the bag was doing there. It looked like a gris-gris bag, what the local voodoo practitioners would call an amulet for a specific purpose. It wasn't something unusual, but the crafting and placement of it seemed irregular, suspicious— disturbing, even. She looked around her. No one was awake yet. She was alone. Nina held her hand over it and checked its vibrations. Icy cold, like frozen darts. She picked it up to inspect it. Normally, she would discourage her coven from ever touching a mysterious and potentially dangerous item. But—it was early, and that coffee cup was still half full.

The wire that tied the pouch shut wasn't wire at all, but black hair. *From what or whom?* she wondered. There was an unsettling aura about it. Usually these bags attracted good fortune, luck, prosperity and love. This little bag was full of death. As she held it, she felt unsafe. The vibrations felt like shockwaves that would topple any barrier like a Category 5 hurricane at the base of an ill-equipped levee system. *Is this why our protection spells didn't work?* Nina had never been through a hurricane of any kind and wasn't planning to be through one anytime soon. She wouldn't even tolerate a tropical depression…Having to live in Louisiana temporarily— now, *that* was what she considered a tropical depression. Regardless, a hurricane had made landfall right inside her own house and was now in the palm of her hand.

She tore open the hair-bound bag and inspected the contents. Using her prodigious intuition and exceptional knowledge of her craft, she identified every item. A dead and desiccated lizard, the eye of an alligator, the heart of a cat with a coffin nail pierced through it (surely one of the many stray felines that plagued the state), dirt from the ground where a fistfight had taken place, a quartz crystal (programmed for evil intentions) and dried gripeweed. The cloth was not just any small square of fabric picked up at the closest Hobby Lobby; it had a purpose, much like the contents it secured. *The pocket of a murderer? The T-shirt of a freshly killed child, maybe? It has to be something dark. Something truly evil. The handkerchief of Donald Trump. Okay…you're being ridiculous. Who put this here and why?*

Nina placed a small spell on the bag before she woke everyone up and called them into the great room. More importantly, no one seemed to know where the charm came from. Leo wanted to inspect it in case she had missed something, and Ollie wanted to try to collect some sort of psychic information from it.

"No!" Nina shouted. "This needs to be destroyed. Immediately. Then we should do another protection enchantment on the house, just to be careful. It's times when you feel you have nothing to worry about because it's nothing but sunny skies all day when a hurricane hits and you don't have any food or water and the floodwater washes your house away. No, I'm taking care of this right now. I'm taking this out back and burning it." She picked up the bag and its contents and did just that. Nina doused the bag with Florida water and salt and spit a mouthful of honey-laced vodka on it, and Avery set it on fire. Nina was going to protect them at all costs, and that included vanquishing the hurricane with intentions and vibrations stronger than any the gris-gris bag had ever had.

CHAPTER 50

Edie received a call from Bowie and Buckshot twenty minutes after she finished grooming her chamber for the ritual. They'd obtained a sinner. Edie didn't care about the specifics: a sinner was a sinner. It turned out to be a young man not even old enough to rent a car. He was a screamer, and even with the sound-swallowing walls, it was something Edie didn't want to risk—or listen to, for that matter.

"Bowie...shut him up!" Edie ordered as she primed herself to carry out the ritual.

As any well-trained crony would do, he did as she asked. He ripped a section of Buckshot's T-shirt straight off his back and stuffed it into the kid's mouth. It didn't matter how muffled his screams were, the blistering fear in his eyes was louder than any scream he was capable of. His arms were pinned to the pine cross, his hands nailed to the wood with Buckshot's nail gun. The kid's ankles, purple and bruised, were taped together at the base of the cross. Bowie was unflappable and hardly even blinked. Buckshot watched with the mania of a Saints fan watching them win the Super Bowl in 2010.

Edie took a few steps forward and began her speech. When she finished, she suddenly had a feeling of doubt. *What if this doesn't work? Are you one hundred percent sure, Edie? It can't be like that one time where you thought the Dalai Lama was an actual llama. You have to be sure.* Edie had to bundle the idea up and sell it to herself like some kind of twisted cult salesman. But she wasn't a cult leader, she was the messenger of God. *Yes. I am the messenger of God, and I am chosen to receive his holy light, and I will single-handedly turn this country—this world—right around and make America great again. I will heal the world of sin and deliver those evil souls who refuse the righteous one. Yes, God. I am ready.* Just like that, her nervous throat clearing and fidgeting went away as if by the grace of God.

Bowie pulled out a set of bolt cutters and his trusty knife and held them at the ready.

Edie's eyes looked at the kid flailing for mercy, and then she closed them. "Bowie…remove his heart."

She could have kept her eyes closed and waited for it to be over. But she couldn't. She needed to see it. It would have been disrespectful for her not to witness the ritual that allowed her to obtain God's gift. So she opened them, and her heart beat faster. The knife sank into the kid's chest and Bowie dragged it down through his flesh as though he were trying to pull a lever that had been jammed. Once he peeled the flesh back with the knife and exposed the ribs, Bowie pinched them with the bolt cutters and cracked the rib cage open. Fifteen minutes and a lot of blood later, the heart was removed and replaced with a live dove. Bowie dumped the warm heart into a bucket, and Edie set it on fire. It was the most otherworldly thing she had ever seen in her life, more trippy than any hallucinogenic drug trip she had endured all those years ago. This was pure magic.

"Yes. This is it. I can feel it!" Edie dropped to her knees, almost in tears. "Oh God! Bless me with your holy light! I am at your holy service!" There was a sudden flash of heat across her entire body. Her head whipped back, and she smiled a freakish grin that would have chilled the bones of any serial killer. Edie raised her hands as high as they would go and begged for more. Then a searing pain sliced through her head and sent her crashing to the floor. By the time she had regained her composure a few seconds later, the pain was gone, replaced with a sense of wakefulness, one she had never experienced before.

"Holy shit! Ma'am, you all right?" Buckshot said as he rushed to her side to help her up from the floor.

Edie smiled and rose to her feet with the stability of someone coming out of anesthesia. "I am more than all right. I am blessed. The renaissance is upon us."

"How do you know it worked?" Bowie asked as he wiped thick coats of red from his hands.

"I don't know…I just *know*."

"Now, my daddy, he always said women got this intuition thing," Buckshot said. "And it's mostly right. Spooky right sometimes."

Edie ignored him. She straightened her clothes and ran her fingers through her hair. A thought occurred to her. More of a craving. "Y'all clean this up. Be careful about it. And make sure to give our other guest something to eat. We need that one." She turned around cheerfully and headed to the door.

"We'll clean up!" Buckshot shouted.

"Where you going?" Bowie asked.

"I need a drink."

Truth be told (after all, she was one of the leaders of the Whole Truth and True Light…so if she wasn't truthful, then what good was she?) she didn't drink. Or at least she didn't until that moment. It was time to celebrate, and although the sting of some harsh alcohol would be painful, it wouldn't be nearly as painful as the moment her card was declined. Suddenly, the drink seemed less important. The bartender reran her card only to tell her again that it was declined. Embarrassed yet still polite, she left the bar and checked her balance, something she hadn't done in so long that she nearly forgot her account password. Checking your account balance was something poor people did, and Edie wasn't poor. *How the fuck am I in the negative?* She was not just poor—she was broke. If she was going to be completely truthful, she and her husband…were broke.

Edie had the accounting skills of a remedial math student with dyscalculia. Plainly, she didn't have any at all. As long as there was money in the bank, the numbers didn't mean anything. Now they did. Edie did know how to use her phone, though. She was a wizard with an iPhone and all the apps. She browsed through their account history until she found what she was looking for. Transfers—a lot of them. Not only that but a long series of checks made out to a woman whose name she didn't recognize but who had their surname—*Angela Bonner.*

When Edie returned home in a high-powered hissy fit, she said nothing about the woman but talked only about the being-broke thing.

"You tell me…you tell me right now…how are we broke?" Edie shouted as she prepared herself to crush the answers out of Josh.

"I haven't been fully honest," he said with a rueful sigh.

"Oh, I'm aware of that! How can we be broke? After all the donations we received at church! We just built a new campus! Can we not afford it? You better start explaining fast, and you better be fixing to set this right even faster!"

"We've been scraping by for a while now. It may seem like we're rolling in money, but we're really not."

"Savings?"

"We don't have any."

"The new campus?"

"All the donations we've received have gone into building it. I was hoping we could start and get some funding from new folks at the new campus, but bills just got to be too high."

He's not gonna tell me about this Angela Bonner woman. He's going to keep it a secret.

"I admit, I miscalculated some of our…schemes. So money is a little tight. We should be getting a check to cover us and bring us out of the negative. But that check won't get cut probably until next week. I'm so sorry, honey, I really am. I was trying to find a way out of it before you ever found out. I know how spending makes you happy, and I just want you to be happy."

"You mean you didn't want me to find out!"

The argument lasted eighteen minutes, longer than it took Edie to walk to the bedroom and lock herself in it. She paced back and forth and slipped into a chillingly soft silk nightgown that made her feel a little thinner and a little wealthier. After nearly cutting a path in the carpet from her pacing, she opened up her computer and did something she hated doing—research.

The beauty of the internet was that the entire world was available to anyone at any time. The drawback was that not everyone wanted to be available to everyone at any given moment. She logged on to a people-finding website, paid the fee for a report using her personal credit card and retrieved all the information she needed about Angela Bonner. There it was, plain as day: Joshua Bonner listed as the parent. The whole event took even more of a turn when she did a little Facebook stalking and found the very same Angela Bonner…and she was black. Well, not black, but not fully white, which to Edie meant that she was black enough. She was a firm supporter of the one-drop rule. Angela could be brown, mocha, mixed-race or any of the other terms people would call her, but Edie couldn't be fooled…Angela was a Negro and Negros were as black as coffee no matter how much cream you added.

CHAPTER 51

Now that Edie had the power of the holy light, she needed to test it. Who knows what she would be able to do! Maybe it would come with all sorts of added benefits. What if in addition to cleansing the world from sin she could also eat as many of Ms. Boudreaux's pies as she wanted and never gain any extra weight? If she could stay a size fourteen *and* eat as much pie as she could fit into her stomach, now, that truly would be a gift from God.

When she had Bowie and Buckshot retrieve and restrain not only her husband, but his daughter, Angela, she also had them swing by Ms. Boudreaux's house and pick up a couple of pecan pies. It wouldn't hurt to test that theory too. It didn't hurt that the pie was there to sweeten the situation. Torture and death were pretty sour acts. And when it was done in the name of the Lord, well, the pie tasted much sweeter.

She had finished a quarter of it as she sat in the corner of the chamber, dressed all in white. Bowie, Buckshot, Joshua and Angela were dressed from head to toe in white, too, per her orders. The room was white. Edie had even requested that the handle of Bowie's knife be covered in white tape. The only thing of color, besides Angela, was the pecan pie. Edie stood in the back corner and watched Bowie torture the young girl in front of Joshua. Slow torture, the kind that would make Joshua see the error of his ways, with a series of slow and meticulous cuts from her feet to her chest. When Bowie reached the chest, Edie ordered him to end it, which resulted in his knife finding Angela's heart.

Edie wasn't much for blood, but for some reason she couldn't explain, it didn't bother her all that much anymore. It was as if her brain had been rewired not to respond emotionally to the sight of it. Angela, who had planned to be part of the "green revolution," had just entered a promising internship program at Flora Teq, where she would analyze and interpret soil data. The minor in religious studies never could've prepared her for the wrath of the Whole Truth and True Light Assembly of God Church. She had graduated with a 4.0 and managed to hold down a full-time job working as assistant manager of the only organic food co-op in town. The blood that dripped from her body couldn't even reach the soil that she so desperately wanted to improve for future generations.

For a moment, Edie thought she wouldn't be able to finish half of the pie, but she did. That's when Joshua ran out of tears and Edie put down her fork.

"I have never been so betrayed in my entire life," Edie said as she walked toward her husband—or soon-to-be ex-husband. "You think you're clever? Keeping all these secrets from me? From our Lord! Well, you can't keep secrets from either of us. Not anymore. He's chosen me to lead."

Joshua stopped struggling to break free, and he stopped crying. He looked up into his wife's eyes and didn't recognize her. Or maybe he did and he only wished he couldn't see her for what she truly was. "What have you done, Edie? You murdered my daughter!"

"I'll tell you what I've done. I've liberated her from the filth she was created from. I'm lucky as all hell that I was never able to bear your children. You make me sick. Sicker than I've ever been in my entire life. I reckon you probably just want to die. I could just have Bowie do it right here in front of me while I watch the fear boil up!" Edie put her hand on Joshua's chest. "My Lord, your heart is beating so, so fast. But don't worry. Bowie isn't going to kill you. I'm going to save you. I'm going to purify you with the gift I received from God."

Bowie and Buckshot exchanged a look and then refocused their attention on Edie. They were partially in doubt that she had whatever she claimed she did. It just seemed a little too good to be true. God was good, but never in either of their lives had they seen the true power of God, and Buckshot's daddy didn't have a story about it, either. So they had their doubts.

"Edie…" Joshua said quietly.

"Shh!" Edie interrupted. "Quiet. Please." She ran her hands over his muscled body and then down his smooth, moisturized cheeks. She would have to throw out that Tata Harper moisturizer Joshua used. It would always remind her of him. That's what she told herself, but really it was out of jealousy. It always made her break out. "There will be things that I will miss. Your gray temples. The way you laugh. But every single time I think of it now"—Edie's smile dropped into a twisted mess—"all I think about are the lies." She started to cry. "So many lies. So many unforgivable betrayals." She wiped her face clean and knelt before him. "Oh Lord. I hereby cleanse this man with your holy light." Edie held out her hands as Joshua lifted his head to witness her speech. It was almost as if they were back on stage giving a sermon, only with more tears and a smaller audience.

Edie began to tremble, as if she were standing on a crumbling bridge. She closed her eyes, and the chamber began to fill with a strange smoke—wispy, like clouds in the evening sky. Joshua screamed as a slow-approaching fire festered at his feet and then slowly worked its way up his body. Edie giggled and cried at the same time, like a woman who had just cheated on her husband but enjoyed it. Joshua screamed harder than he ever had in his entire life. Then it stopped. Edie had manifested what she religiously believed to be God's holy light, and had burned Joshua's body from the inside out. What she didn't know…was that it was something else entirely.

CHAPTER 52

Edie pulled out her best Sunday-best and steamed it just as the sun was rising that Sunday morning. She changed the part in her hair from right to left and used Joshua's facial cream even though it made her break out (which usually didn't happen until the next morning) because it also made her skin glow like the lava lamps of her youth.

Edie opened her service with a speech about how her beloved husband was on a special—private—very long-term mission trip and would be taking a step down from his role as head pastor for the time being. The story was that he was a fiercely passionate Christian and had ideas and goals that stretched far beyond the limits of the Whole Truth and True Light. She spent the next ten minutes talking about how he would be concentrating 100 percent on his work. That meant no outside distractions, no communication and, more importantly, no questions for Edie to answer, at least for a while.

Somewhere between the long-winded lecture about Joshua's organized effort to spread their faith and her exaggerated examples of his humanitarianism involving the construction of orphanages, she almost had herself convinced it was actually happening. Edie truly was a master manipulator and brainwasher, so much so that she would have to exercise caution around herself.

The inspiring story only gave her audience more reason to stand behind them—or her. So when she flawlessly segued into the second part of her sermon, designed to persuade and rally support from her faithful followers, she hardly needed to try.

"I want y'all to listen carefully, because this next part is very important. But before we get to that, let me begin with a little prayer. Father. Lord. I pray that you watch over us. Give us strength to do what needs to be done. Your supreme majesty is humbling, and we ask that you give us your glory. We have challenges ahead of us, and I pray that you surround us with your holy light. Lord, show us that we are strong. Help us abandon fear so that we may do what's right in your name. Help us rise up! Yes, Lord. Help me find those souls right here in this room who are true and worthy of helping me carry your gospel, your light, your truth. Help me defend us all, and let us make this country great—again. In Jesus's name, amen!"

The room was flooded with an outpouring of *amens*, which transitioned into applause.

Edie smiled and paced back and forth across the stage. "I know it's a heavy burden to carry, I know it's a difficult road and not everyone is prepared to do it, and I'm here to say that's okay! I'm not here to shame you. Your support is what gives those who *can* help the strength to soldier on. So those of you here today—and I know there are many, I can see it in your eyes, I can feel it in the air—I ask you, rise *up!*" She held her breath for a moment. "I'm going to close with a prayer. But first I want to say that those of you who responded to what I just said…those of you who truly feel in your hearts that you have what it takes to do something good for our Lord, for our country, for our children, those of you who are devoted to making a *real* change…I ask that you please remain here after the service. I ask that you stay, because I have organized small groups that I would like y'all to participate in. Groups that will function as specialized divisions…each with a unique framework, objective and purpose. I will lead each of these groups, but each group will have a leader, so be thinking about if you are truly leader material." There was another booming pause as she soaked in the response from her thirsty audience. "Let us pray…"

It took Edie twenty minutes to shape the mass of curious people who stayed to hear what she had to say. She took a brief moment to head to the office and retrieve the potion she had used to recruit Bowie and Buckshot. Edie grabbed the small plastic shot glasses that they used for fruit-juice Communion that they offered sporadically. Although no one had intended to save some for later, there was just enough for one more use. Edie mixed the potion, along with her spit, into a pitcher of grape-flavored drink that contained less than 1 percent fruit juice. It was locally made, and Edie was proud of where she was from. She invited everyone to drink from the cup of God's holy light—insisted on it, actually—and administered the spiked drink to everyone present. Within a few minutes, the room was ready for her command and sworn to secrecy.

Edie enlightened them to the presence of witches and outlined what she had in mind regarding their capture, execution…annihilation. She gave the three task forces objectives and then waited for a moment with her arms crossed in front of her chest like a paradigm of dictatorship and tyranny. "Together we will banish these witches from the face of the earth, reclaim it from the grip of Satan and do it in the name of our holy Lord!"

Another flood of fanatical cheers rose as her supporters watched her with wild fascination.

"Come on. I want some suggestions. Any leader knows that any job can't be done alone, so tell me…what ideas do you have? I have given you the knowledge and provided you with the tools. Now y'all advise *me* on how we can do this…inconspicuously." Edie opened her eyes wide and waved tauntingly at her audience. "Come on, now!"

Buckshot stepped forward and opened his mouth to speak, revealing a few cavity-tortured teeth underneath his lip. "Say, uh…I have a suggestion," he said eagerly.

Oh dear, what has he cooked up now, Edie thought, seeing that Buckshot was so excited he could hardly stand still.

"The table is open, Buckshot! What's on your mind? There aren't any bad ideas, just ones that won't work and ones I don't like."

Buckshot placed his hands on his hips. "Well, I was thinkin' that since we already know where a bunch of them witches live and whatnot, instead of attacking them at home and hopin' for the best, why don't we try and lure them out into a place where they're more vulnerable. Like with that gator around my daddy's pond. Instead of just goin' in and looking for him in the weeds, he lured him out with some marshmallows. Dropped three jet-puffed marshmallows in and that little sucker came swimmin' out of his little hiding spot. That's when my daddy shot 'im! We called him King. We lived off King Road then. A-a-anyway! We had him for dinner later on, Gator à la King. Had some of my mamma's calf fries too…It was real good. A-a-anyway, I'm sayin' we lure 'em out like we did tasty ol' King!"

"Like I said, there are no bad ideas, just ones that won't work and ones I don't like. Buckshot, that sounds crazy…just crazy! The part about the marshmallows. But I like what you're thinking. I reckon we have a solid chance if we follow that plan, and in turn you can redeem yourself a little bit after y'all failed the first time!"

Buckshot pulled on the brim of his ratty hat so that she saw *Oklahoma!* Instead of his eyes.

"What would you propose we do, Buckshot?" Edie asked.

Buckshot lifted his head, looked around to make sure he was the only Buckshot in the room, then looked back at her. "Well, I think we wait for the right moment and get one of them to use as bait. I know all about bait, and I can guarantee that's just the type of bait that they'd flock to, one of their own." Buckshot placed his hands back on his hips as he regained some confidence.

"Then?"

"Then we lure them to a spot where they're at a disadvantage, get them out in the open, away from the comfort and shelter and safety of their house! Get those gators outta them weeds, you know what I mean? Then we, we, we strike! Take 'em down! Ambush-style!"

"I admire your ingenuity! I have to say, I actually believe we might be able to pull this off."

"Might?" Buckshot questioned.

"I say might because, well, even though it sounds easy peasy, I don't know where we would lure them to that wouldn't attract attention. I'd say here, but that could bring a lot of attention on us, and that's just a little too risky. So, unless you know of somewhere accessible and ready for Armageddon, then I say it rests on the line of being a good idea only in theory."

"I know just the place," Buckshot said as he winked.

Edie cocked her head to the side, heavy with intrigue. "Tell me more."

"Well, you know City Park, in NOLA? That place is thirteen hundred acres, ginormous, and I swear more than half of it isn't even used. Now, when Katrina came in and flooded it all to high heaven, it did over forty million dollars in damage. Katrina was a real bitch. That park has been slowly recovering and there've been some new attractions and whatnot, but there's still a lot of underdeveloped space or space that's just unoccupied for the most part. That includes Popp Fountain. Which I think is the perfect place for us to carry out our plan."

Edie was dumbstruck. She had never seen so many facts and informative tidbits fly out of his mouth. "Buck…how do you know all this?"

"I used to work there. I did some grounds maintenance for a while. I was the one who held the gate key for the fountain."

A jelly doughnut of a woman raised her hand in the air to interrupt him, her bright red nail polish flailing back and forth like a racing flag declaring an immediate stop to the race. "I've been to that fountain. It's open to the public now," she said matter-of-factly.

"Yes, ma'am, you're right," Buck said. "Partially right. It's only open on Sundays from ten to five. After that, the gates close and the fountain is off limits again until the following Sunday." He turned back to Edie. "I still have a copy of that key. I'm tellin' you, the grounds are perfect. All sorts of trees and cover. No one patrols over there."

"And what if they do?" Edie asked.

"Then I guess Bowie knows how to handle a situation like that, am I right, Bow-Bow?"

"Don't call me that," Bowie said, his eyes scary.

"Well, everyone, I think we have ourselves a plan," Edie said. "Buckshot, leave the lunastaterum on my desk in the office for now."

Edie ripped open a good smile and called the group over to the stage, where she spread out a large sheet of poster board. She had moved beyond protest signs and on to greater things, like attack teams, supplies and timetables. She could have been a party planner to the stars, everything was so organized. The two head honchos under her command were still Buckshot and Bowie, and she had to hand it to herself on her selection: they had turned out to be pretty amazing. The most important part of the operation was the stakeout on the house, which was why she elected her two prize disciples for the job. Buckshot would have the energy and eye for opportunity, and Bowie would bring stealth and patience. With them at the helm, they would strike when the time was right.

Right after they adjourned for the evening, Edie went into her office for some sweet tea. She picked up the lunastaterum, expecting to see the witches they had just talked about. The tool did fill with a milky white liquid, but she didn't like what she saw.

"What's the matter, Edie?" a voice said from the doorway.

Edie spun so fast, she nearly dropped the lunastaterum. *Nix. What the hell is he doing here?* "Nix! That kind of sneaking up on people can get you killed around here. What are you doing here?"

Nix entered the room a little frightened and even more disturbed. "I came here to meet with you and Joshua about your progress and to offer my services...but..." Nix rubbed his finger around his temple, as if to kick-start his psychic abilities. "I sense something has changed." He looked into Edie's eyes.

She smiled back at him. Her lip-gloss-covered mouth glistened under the bright office lights. "Where is he?"

"Joshua? That traitor? Don't worry about him. He's gone. He wasn't in line with our goals here…as it turns out. It's all irrelevant and trivial. I alone have been chosen. God has blessed me with his holy light."

Nix could see it in her eyes, feel it in the air and smell it on her skin…She wasn't blessed with God's holy light…No, she was something else. *Is she…a witch?*

"Thank you for your contributions to my cause, but your services are no longer required," Edie said as she narrowed her eyes. "I see right through you now. You're not sent by God. You're not one of his holy messengers…No, you're sent from hell…You're a witch!"

Nix shook his head and began to mumble a summoning spell under his breath. She was a storm about to hit.

"God has given me the gift of sight, and I see you for what you are," Edie said.

Edie lifted her hands to unleash her holy light, and looked upon his face. She had seen that look before: the look that gave her chills, the look of someone who knows they are about to feel the wrath of God. Edie opened her fist just as Nix threw a bottle of potion into his face. The clear liquid splashed across his face and dissolved his presence almost instantly, dripping over his body and transporting him away to safety, and leaving an awful stench of rotten milk and mushrooms behind.

CHAPTER 53

The Pickled Beet Co-Op was in a building that had formerly housed a CVS drugstore. It gave some hope to the city of Destrehan for people like Nina, people who liked food that wasn't fried in animal fat or scooped out of the mud. She arrived at ten, a mere hour after they opened, and brought Avery and Bisa along for a girls' morning out. Much to Nina's surprise, there actually was a health-conscious community in the area, and many local producers stocked the shelves with everything from bread to handmade soap. If she closed her eyes, it almost smelled like a Whole Foods, or one of those fancy vegan cafés in places like Portland, Oregon, where everything is artisan or craft, even granola. It was a place to stock up on some serious brain food and also a place to accidentally spend an hour browsing only the body and essential oils section.

While Nina was checking out the different kinds of sprouted breads, back at the house, there was a knock at the door. Ollie was taking a shower and Mitch was still in bed, so Leo answered it.

"Hi! I don't really know what to say…" the young woman said.

Leo smiled. She was *hot*. "You can start by telling me who you are and what you're here for," he suggested sweetly.

"Right. Sorry. I actually can't believe I'm doing something like this. For real, I can't. I'm always criticizing people on TV when they show up at someone's house unexpectedly and ring their doorbell to tell them something that people only call about. Or text about, now." There was nothing but silence and connected gazes for longer than the woman was comfortable with. Quickly, she revved up the conversation again. "I'm Sarah—with an *H*. Does Nina live here?"

"Nina?" Leo asked in a way that almost suggested he had never heard of her.

"I think that was her name. Maybe I'm wrong. Or maybe I have the wrong address. She said she was a grievance counselor and told me to stop by anytime, but now that I'm actually here…stopping by at random…uncertain about her name or address…I feel a little stupid."

Leo smiled again. "You're not stupid." The corners of his mouth seemed permanently hung on his cheeks. "You're in the right spot. You've got the right name too. She's just not here."

Sarah felt both confused and awkward, which made her immediate attraction to Leo both surprising and uncomfortable. "Okay. Are you her…boyfriend?"

Leo laughed and opened the door a little farther. "No way! We're family. Sort of."

Sarah nodded. "She was at my brother's funeral, and…I…Can you just tell her I stopped by? This is crazy."

"It is kinda weird, huh?"

"What?"

"People always show up places without warning in movies and stuff. No one really does that. Except you!"

"Except me!" she agreed as she nervously adjusted her hands in her pockets.

"You can come inside and wait if you want."

The invitation was both innocent and devious. Leo wasn't even certain if Sarah agreed to come in because she felt comfortable enough to wait or because he made her do it. He brought her into the study, where a pillow and blanket had conveniently been left on the floor. Leo was vaguely aware of her attraction to him for the first few minutes, but most of the time he was trying to control his own urges. He was a gentleman for a good amount of time, as much of a gentleman as he could be, but there was an undeniable chemistry. That's when Leo felt it, the tap, tap, tap on the shoulder from his old friend danger. This kind of thing happened all the time to people he knew, but never to him. He had heard stories of his friend inviting a Lyft driver in for a blow job after she noticed him giving her eyes in the back seat. Or his homie Danny, who had fucked that girl in the bathroom of Shamrock's during his birthday party while his girlfriend was playing pool. That's what made it so crazy—the risk that was involved. It made it more exciting, sexier. It didn't matter if it was crazy or raunchy or unfaithful if it was hot.

He was already kissing her when he realized he hadn't even thought about what he was doing. But again, that's what made it worth doing: they were strangers, someone could walk in at any minute and he had no idea if she was on the pill, so he would have to pull out…and that was hard enough for him to do in the moment. They didn't even bother getting naked…It was all about getting down to business.

What Leo didn't know was that by the time they ended up on the floor, Mitch had woken up and was on his way to the kitchen for a late breakfast. He stopped just short of the door to the study when he heard the panting and sticky slapping noises. He crept carefully across the floor in his bare feet, skipping the floorboards he knew for certain would creak, and peeked through the door.

Oh my fucking God.

Mitch stood there for a moment and watched, dipping into a reasonable amount of risky behavior himself. He couldn't decide if he was outrageously disgusted or ridiculously turned on. It was safe to assume he felt a little bit of both, and that middle ground led him to sneak back to his room and wait it out.

The moment they finished, Leo felt guilty and Sarah was appalled by her behavior. She was a Scorpio, so her passion and emotion were pretty fierce, but this was a little too much. They weren't even able to say a proper goodbye because Sarah picked up and left so fast. Leo tried to show her to the door, but stopped when he saw Mitch down the hall. He knew Mitch had seen the girl—he could see it in his face. What he couldn't make out was whether Mitch was supportive, revolted or hurt.

A few minutes later Nina, Avery and Bisa came into the house with a few bags of groceries.

"Was someone here?" Nina asked. "Who was that I saw driving away as we pulled in?"

"Some girl named Sarah. She was looking for you. She said she met you at a funeral," Leo said.

Nina sighed. *I knew I shouldn't have wasted so much time trying to decide which bread to buy!*

The crinkle of grocery bags brought Mitch back into the foyer. A trip to the grocery store meant a treasure hunt for snacks. It was one of the only things that would settle his stomach after what he had just witnessed.

"Mitch, there are a couple more bags of groceries in the car," Nina said. "Can you grab them, please?"

Mitch nodded, slipped on some shoes and left to retrieve the remaining groceries. Bisa stopped in the hallway for a moment: she felt something unexpected in the air, something uneasy.

"Everything okay?" Bisa asked Leo.

"Yeah! It's all good." Leo looked inside the grocery bag. "Did you get me any snacks?"

"Get out of there! Come help put stuff away."

By the time Nina had gotten to putting away the sprouted bread that had caused her to miss Sarah by only a few minutes, she realized Mitch hadn't brought in the last couple of bags. She was looking forward to one of them the most. It had a kombucha drink and a pint of mint chip ice cream that she had sneaked in for herself.

"Did Mitch bring in the rest of the bags?" Nina asked.

"No, not yet," Avery said as she began to open a bag of dill pickle chips.

Nina rolled her eyes and let out a sigh.

"I'll get them," Bisa said as she turned around to head out the door.

Bisa had just stepped outside when she realized the door to the car had been left open, the groceries were still there and she could hear the sound of another vehicle running. She walked out and jumped in shock.

"Nina!" Bisa cried out.

Someone slammed the door of a large truck shut, and Bisa saw Mitch flailing around in the back of a pickup as Bowie held him down. The rest of the coven spilled out onto the front yard and watched the truck speed off down the driveway and onto the main road. Without a second thought, Leo jumped into the front seat of the car, turned the key, which was still in the ignition, and peeled out down the driveway with the trunk still open. He could see the truck down the road, and if he kept his eye on it, he could catch up. He hadn't had time to think about what he was going to do if he caught up with it. He didn't want to use any of his powers, not with Mitch in the truck. It was too risky, and he had indulged in enough risky behavior for one day.

He rounded the first corner at a speed that left tire marks on the pavement. He was catching up to them quickly. Leo pressed on the gas pedal, an all-too-familiar act, and closed the gap between them. He could see the fear in Mitch's eyes as the wind whipped through his hair and the knife at his throat pressed against his skin. Leo accelerated again. Only a few feet now.

Before Leo could make another decision, Bowie kicked out a large railroad tie from the back of the truck and watched it clatter around the road like a butter knife on a kitchen floor. Leo swerved to the right to avoid hitting it, and the tires screeched in response. The car spun and spread across the road, leaving a trail of smoke and the smell of burnt rubber in the air. He anxiously gripped the wheel, trying to regain control of the vehicle as he spun into the woods. Then, all the motion stopped as the trunk of the car smashed into the side of a large tree. The roaring of the truck's muffler grew fainter as Leo tried to collect himself. His neck was aching like all hell. Slowly, Leo lifted his head and looked down at his arm. *Blood.* His vision was a little fuzzy, and he could taste blood on his tongue.

When he felt up to it, he opened the door (*The window busted out. That must be how I cut my arm.*) and swung his legs out onto the ground, more slowly than he expected to. He reached up to his head and felt around for bruises or cuts. *Just my arm and my lip.* He turned off the car, took the keys and abandoned the wreck to head back toward the house. He didn't care about the crash; he cared about finding Mitch.

Shortly after he rounded the corner, he met up with the rest of the coven. Nina wrapped his bloody arm around her for support, and Bisa took his other side. Together they helped him back to the house where they could properly care for him and figure out what to do next.

Nina did her best to soothe Leo's mind so that Avery could administer some physical healing. She had practiced it enough that it actually seemed to work better than the Aleve. Nina, Ollie and Bisa did a triple attack so they could ease his anxiety and rage. It didn't matter if he was injured; he was angry, and he was going to get on his bike and ride out after them. At least he planned on it until Nina cast a small spell on him to calm his mind. When he was pacified to rest, Nina noticed she hadn't even taken the time to wash his blood off her arm.

She set a glass of water next to Leo's bed and headed to the bathroom to wash up. The faucet was on and the washrag was wet, but Nina hesitated at the last minute. Even amid all the chaos, she hadn't forgotten about Leo potentially being a Corporeal, and she had never ruled it out one way or the other. She held the washcloth with one hand. With the other she extended her index finger over the blood on her arm—still wet, still fresh. Nina hadn't made it through Yale by forgetting everything she'd read. It was right then, with her finger above the blood, that she remembered what Rosemary had said when she'd boldly sniffed Leo's dirty laundry. She said it smelled *gold.* It wasn't likely that she would experience the same sort of synesthesia through Leo's blood, but what if she did? Rosemary had been concerned, for lack of a better word, when she declared the scent gold. Was that a sign of a Corporeal?

In one unsettling moment, Nina dipped her finger into Leo's blood on her arm and brought it to her mouth. She slipped her finger inside and rubbed the blood against her tongue. She felt her tongue curve along the roof of her mouth as she experienced the unexpected flavor. *Gold.* Rosemary's claims were now fully validated. Surely if witches had a certain and distinct smell, it was only logical to assume their blood would have a specific flavor as well. Nina rubbed her lips together and tried to swirl the flavor over her tongue once more. She hadn't been able to figure out Leo's smell originally, and now this peculiar characteristic—this…flavor—could only be described as not blood, but gold.

It had to be something special. So special that it reminded her of a section of her studies many years ago that she had thought was legend. The world of witches was magical enough, so if something was deemed to be legend, it probably was. Nevertheless, Nina stored it in her memory, because that was what she was good at. She wiped up Leo's blood with some toilet paper and squeezed a few drops out onto the bathroom counter. She stared at the tiny pool of blood and held her hand over it.

"*Quid est rubrum, potest esse aurum,*" Nina whispered, her eyes concentrated on the blood.

It wasn't a complete surprise, but it was enough to steal Nina's breath. Leo's blood turned translucent under the spell. *What is red can be gold.* It wasn't just legend. If there was another type of witch, now known as a Corporeal, their blood would run translucent under the spell. No one had ever talked about it, included it in their teachings or even thought about it, because it seemed like nothing more than a piddly fairy tale in the witch world. Clearly, it was not. Leo was a Corporeal, the prophesied type of witch with extraordinary powers that was said to emerge during another shift. There had been plenty of shifts in the past, and plenty of people had tried the spell, but not once had it turned out to be correct. Not until now, years and years after it had already become legend. The genes were not specific to certain witches. Everyone had the gene to become a Corporeal, but it activated only in those people whose cells were susceptible to that kind of magical alteration in their makeup. It was much like mosaicism, where certain cells in the body have different genetic expression.

Leo had just awakened from a short nap when Nina entered the room fresh from a hot shower that gave her some time to think. Although her arm was clean of his blood and still warm from the water she had used to wash it off, the sight of him gave her gooseflesh.

CHAPTER 54

Nina entered the Symposium room to meet with the Advisory. She arrived a little later than she'd planned. It was the first time Nix was early, perhaps the first time in his entire history.

"Thank you all for coming. I know it was on short notice," Nina said as she pulled out a chair at the table.

"Can we make this quick, if possible?" Per asked. "We've already met more times than I ever thought would be necessary, and I've only just now started to binge *Game of Thrones* and I'm all the way into season three now, so if we can get this rollin', that would be great."

"This is very important," Nina said. "I have something I need to tell you—tell all of you."

"I'm afraid I have something I'd like to share with the Advisory as well," Nix thundered.

Nina flinched at the sudden interruption. "Which we can address directly afterward," she said, her voice cracking. It surprised her. She wasn't a nervous speaker, but she was a little on edge.

"I apologize for speaking out of turn, since I wasn't the one to call this Symposium, but I do believe this is an extremely urgent matter," Nix said.

Rosemary rolled her eyes. "Oh, for heaven's sake, what is it now, Nix?"

"I'd like to propose that Nina be investigated for the murder of witches Andy Campbell and Blake Summerfield and further for the disappearance of their fellow coven member Maisie and their Proctor Merlot—"

Nina flew back in her seat with such force that the chair squeaked on the floor. "Excuse me?" she snapped.

"What in the bloody hell is this?" Rosemary asked. "What are you going on about?"

"I'm sorry to report that not only are two witches in our Houston coven dead, but two are missing," Nix declared as he crossed his legs and folded his arms.

"Yes, I'm aware of that," Nina said sharply.

Rosemary raised her eyebrows in surprise. "What? How do you know this? When did this happen?"

Before Nina could respond, Nix answered. "Nina has had some beef with the Houston coven, specifically the Proctor, Merlot, with whom she has some history."

"I'm aware of their relationship," Rosemary jabbed. "What of these deaths?"

"Nina, for reasons unknown, deliberately provoked the coven, stirred up some drama."

"Provoked?" Nina said, her eyes full of shock.

"There has been some friction between you ever since you took the position at the Advisory. Some competitive rivalry, yes?"

"Rivalry? No. We have different perspectives," Nina said. "Tell me, Nix, how is it that you even know I went to 'provoke' them, as you say?"

Nix smiled but tried to hide it. "A little bird told me."

"Look, we aren't here to play chicken," Per added.

"No, we're not. This is insane," Nina said.

"So you deny that you paid the coven a visit?" Nix asked.

"I did, yes. That's hardly out of the ordinary. I invited the coven over for dinner shortly before that. Why would I go there to stir up some drama?"

"But you did visit them?" Nix spat.

Nina sighed in a way that sounded as though she were trying to calm herself. "Yes. But it was only to warn them of the dangerous path they were treading. They attacked my coven with an exhauriat worm spell. That's why I went there. To stop their bullying. To do some damage control and talk some sense into them and Merlot."

"Why didn't you seek the help of the full Advisory after the spell?" Per asked, slightly suspicious.

"I didn't think it was something worth calling a Symposium about. Nothing I couldn't handle." Nina had her emotions back under control.

"We have no proof of your intentions for going over there," Nix said. "And the fact that you said nothing of it to any of us makes it a little suspicious."

Nina smoothed her hair away from her face. "What exactly are you trying to say?"

"The chickens are coming home to roost."

Right then, Per leaned forward to insert himself into the conversation again. "What does that mean? I could never figure out what that phrase meant."

"Maisie can attest to my innocence. These charges are absurd."

Rosemary fluttered her eyes as she pondered the predicament. "Where is this Maisie who can clear you of these—yes, I agree—absurd charges?"

"I don't know. How would I know that?"

"How do you know she would be able to clear you of the charges then?" Nix asked.

"They attacked us again. A second time. Maisie was with them, but she didn't attack. Later, after they fled, she stayed behind to tell us about her coven. Merlot had been drugging them with some sort of potent magic drug. We took her in."

"Where is she now?" Rosemary asked.

"She left. No one saw her; it was in the middle of the night."

Nix laughed. "So, the only person who could shed some light on this situation and attest to your truth is missing, and not only that, went missing under your care? Probably for the best. She was probably concerned about her safety while she was under your roof. Attacked twice…Can you blame her for not feeling safe?"

"I do everything to protect my coven! Being a Proctor isn't as easy as you might think, Nix." Nina threw her arms up in frustration. "Why don't you meet with *my* coven? Why don't you question them about my intentions and ask them what happened? They weren't eyewitnesses to what I saw at Merlot's, but they knew what I was doing and why." She turned to Rosemary. "I am not guilty of what he accuses me of. Nothing about my character even suggests in the slightest that I would be capable of something like that."

Rosemary dropped her eyes to the wad of what looked to be bloody tissue on the table in front of Nina. "What the bloody hell is that?" Rosemary said, pointing. She had a certain way of saying *bloody*, a stretched enunciation with an elongated *y*. It always made Nina want to both smile and recoil, because she could never figure out if she was amused or scornful.

"It's what I came here to talk about," Nina answered.

"I wasn't finished," Nix said.

"Oh, stop it," Rosemary said. "Just because you were the early bird this one time in the history of ever doesn't mean that you get the worm indefinitely." She believed in Nina, no matter how hard she was on her. It was also fair that Nina be able to speak about the reason she'd called the meeting without being smothered with allegations.

"It's blood. Leo's blood. He cut his arm, and while I helped patch him up, some of it got onto my arm. I brought it here to show you what I discovered." Nina held her hand over the tissue and recited the spell she had used earlier in the bathroom. The blood turned translucent in front of them.

Per shook his head in confusion. "Where did it go? I don't get it. What are you showing us? That would do wonders for laundry detergent. You should find a way to market that. You could make millions. Tide wouldn't have a chance."

Rosemary was stunned. "He's a Corporeal. It's true."

Nina nodded.

A look of frightful bliss crossed Nix's face. "My God…"

"That is why I called this meeting. To be advised. To let you know that it's not just legend, it's real. Corporeals are real."

Nix sat forward and swung his finger in the air as though reprimanding a naughty dog. "That is all the more reason why she shouldn't be Proctor! She can't be trusted to lead a coven, especially not one with such extraordinary gifts as Leo's. I stand by my call for her to be investigated—"

Rosemary cut him off. "I won't hear any more about that. It's ridiculous."

Nix placed both hands on the table and leaned over it. "I think you will, Rosemary."

"Excuse me?" Rosemary nipped.

"With the utmost respect, I am the Advisory's Keeper of Books and Assets, and the home that Nina resides in is in fact listed in my name. Under the decree set forth by the Advisory at the genesis of my position, the Keeper may evict a tenant—

in this case, Proctor—if the tenant violates the lease terms set forth by the Keeper."

"What terms? I've never heard of this," Nina declared.

Rosemary slowly closed her eyes and sighed.

Nix turned his attention to Nina. "The Keeper may choose to enforce or not enforce lease terms."

"What is he talking about? Per? Do you know about this?"

"It's a valid agreement," Per said.

"What? Since when? I never signed or agreed to anything!"

Rosemary puffed a sigh. "You don't exactly have to. It's always been custom for the Keeper to decide the terms a tenant must abide by when it concerns any of the Advisory's properties."

"What the hell? Why is this the first time I'm hearing about this?"

"I assume because Nix never told you," Rosemary said. "Don't get too upset. It's not something that's commonly talked about. It's more of an antiquated formality now, as things have become very casual when it comes to Proctors as tenants."

"Except of course when it's convenient," Nina said, glowering at Nix.

"You don't pay rent, and the Keeper is responsible for and has sole control over housing assets," Nix said.

"So what am I in violation of?"

"Your actions regarding the Houston coven are highly suspect," Nix said, "and I don't think you are fit to lead a coven, and not one with a Corporeal. I have already arranged for you to be taken in by another coven in New Mexico—"

"New Mexico!" Nina shouted.

Nix closed his eyes, regained his patience, then opened them again. "They run a small metaphysical shop. They have agreed to initiate you into their coven. You hereby have two weeks to vacate. I will arrange for your relocation, and you will have no further contact with your coven."

"This is bullshit!" Nina said.

Rosemary straightened her spine and sat up tall. "You have no right to banish her to another state," she said to Nix. "Or to forbid her from communicating with her own coven. That resides with the Advisory and needs a unanimous vote. I'm sorry—I draw the line there."

"Then I request for her to be put on probation," Nix said. "Until we know more about what happened to Merlot and until we can determine what to do about this new Corporeal who may or may not know the strength of his powers yet."

"And who will take over as Proctor temporarily?" Rosemary asked. "You…I imagine?"

"Yes. I volunteer."

"Per?" Rosemary asked.

"Sorry, I have no interest in leading a coven. Just don't."

Rosemary pressed her fingers to her temple, closed her eyes and mumbled a clandestine sentence under her breath. Her hesitation in passing a ruling was a relief to Nina. Perhaps it was because Rosemary believed in her, or maybe it was just because Rosemary was also a woman, but whatever the reason, she knew Rosemary wouldn't let the worst happen. "We will arrange accommodation for you outside of the house for two weeks. Pick where—I don't care…"

"Within our budget," Nix said.

"Oh, fuck your budget!" Rosemary said. "She can stay in the penthouse at the Ritz-Carlton for all I care! I don't foresee her staying there for very long. Nix will act as substitute Proctor while we try to uncover some details about the Houston coven, and then—as a group—we can decide what to do about the Corporeal. I don't want a single word about what he is uttered to Leo. Do you understand me, Nix?" Rosemary's eyes were blisteringly serious.

Nix nodded.

"Don't nod like a querulous teenager—say it."

Nix glanced into Rosemary's eyes, trying to decide if he wanted to slap her or respect her. Then he smiled. "I understand."

"Good." Rosemary scanned Nix's face for signs of insolence, and when she was satisfied that he had gotten the point, she turned to Nina. "This isn't a punishment, and it won't last long. It's not even immediate. Per wants to finish *Game of Thrones*, and I have to feed my cat. Relax tonight. Tomorrow morning I'll arrange everything—and Nix, don't rush anything. We have no proof of anything. Tomorrow evening. Same time. Let's say around eight. Can you do that? Can you make eight o'clock, Nix, or is that against some rule?"

"Eight. I'll be there."

Nina was on fire. "I'm not changing the sheets. I won't be gone long."

CHAPTER 55

Maisie sat in Edie's office, her arms and legs free from restraints for the first time.

"Do you want some pie?" Edie asked as she picked a pecan off the top of a pie on the counter.

Maisie responded only with a blank stare.

"No? How about some water? When's the last time you had something to drink?" Edie turned around, poured some water into a glass, spit into it and added the last of her potion. She turned her head so she could see Maisie.

Maisie nodded.

"Good. We can't survive long without water. I know it's been a minute. I'm sorry about that. My boys aren't exactly bred to be pillars of hospitality. But I'm a southern girl and manners cost me nothing, and if I don't have manners, I might as well have nothing at all if I'm going to be a southern girl." She set the glass of water in Maisie's hand. "Go on now, don't be shy. There's plenty more where that came from."

Maisie took a sip, waited, and then took a few more. She hadn't been given much food or water since being abducted in the middle of the night at Nina's. She was listless and cataclysmically thirsty. The antidote to the ant bites that Nina had administered had sapped her of her powers temporarily as it removed the drug from her system.

"What do you want?" Maisie asked.

"Well, I want to lose about fifteen pounds." Edie laughed with a sort of hammering intensity. For a brief moment, she thought about getting a slice of pecan pie from the counter, but she changed her mind when she rubbed her belly and felt the buttons on her jacket being stretched to their very limits. "Well, in all seriousness, I want to help you."

"How?"

"I can tell that you are in desperate need of some help."

"Abduction is a strange way of trying to help."

"Listen, the world is crazy. Sometimes extreme measures are necessary to achieve goals. I haven't always been the strong woman and leader that I am today. I had a rough childhood, and my early teenage years, which I have tried with all my might to erase, still haunt me every now and then. I'll be honest with you, and what I tell you can never leave this room, okay?"

Maisie nodded. She continued to sip on the sweating glass of water.

"I had a drug problem when I was fifteen. I'm not proud of that. I know it's hard to believe when you look at me now. You're probably thinking, *How in the world could someone like this ever have a problem with something like drugs?*, right? My daddy was not a happy man. In fact he was quite the opposite. I was afraid of him. I was afraid of his drinking and his violence, and even though I kinda liked his gun collection, I was afraid what would happen on the nights where his drinking got real bad and he and his collection mixed. He was a mean drunk. Really mean. I tried to find a way to deal with it however I could. Typical numb-the-pain type of scenario. I could've turned out like him, but I truly sought to better myself. To live a life rich with God's glory. And I did it. I want to help others who are teetering on that line of self-destruction, people like you, and show you that you too can be cleansed and reeducated. You can start fresh. I can show you the benefit of tradition and worship and Christianity."

"I'm not a traditional person. Tradition, in a way, has always felt like peer pressure from beyond the grave."

Edie smiled and dismissed her statement with the batting of her eyelashes. "I want to help you."

"I don't need your help," Maisie said, and she set down the glass of water, feeling slightly more relaxed than she should have.

"Well, then, why don't you help me?" Edie asked.

"What do you need?"

Edie smiled wickedly, a sinister glitter in her eyes. "Tell me everything I need to know about the witches."

"What do you want to know?" Maisie responded freely, and she shot Edie a pleasant look, as if she would do anything to oblige.

Edie asked several questions and learned about the powers of the Primordial and Transcendent witches. Maisie willingly told her how to determine whether someone is an actual witch by conducting an experiment with their blood. The blood of Primordial witches would go through a chemical reaction under the spell, although she was uncertain what would happen to the blood of Transcendent witches.

Once Edie had all the information she felt would be useful, she ordered Maisie to stay on the premises and wait for further instructions. Among all the commotion, she had almost forgotten about the little event she had organized, the Sin Drop. It was the best name she could come up with, and it made sense with the main attraction of the event. She thought of it like an ice cream social, but with a purpose (although there would be ice cream, too). Guests would start arriving within the hour, and she had a lot of finishing touches to attend to.

Edie had been looking forward to it ever since Mitch's abduction. She had a lot to celebrate, and the best way to do it while she was nearly broke was with the financial support of her followers. They covered the cost of the ice cream, the live band, the fireworks and the hasty construction of the Plexiglas box that Mitch would be stuffed inside before being hoisted into the air for everyone to witness. *Oh, I have to find time to squeeze in Mr. Marcy, too. Don't forget that.* Just before the fireworks, she had agreed to let Mr. Marcy do a demonstration of his new gun since he was the runner-up for the Guinness World Record for most clay pigeons shot within an hour. She was proud of that.

An hour and a half later, the party was in full swing. After everyone had a chance to eat some Blue Bell ice cream, listen to the honky-tonk band and watch Mr. Marcy shoot his gun, Edie announced that it was time for the main event, the one everyone had come to see. In the middle of the yard, next to a large rental crane, was a large white sheet covering a mysterious rectangular object. At the count of three, Edie ripped off the sheet to reveal Mitch inside the Plexiglas box. A set of three holes had been drilled into the top of each side for air, and the edges of the box were lined with white Christmas lights. She had spared no expense.

"All of you here know what we're up against, and I'm proud to say we have caught our very own dirty, stinky ol' witch!" Newly invigorated, she signaled for Buckshot to raise the box. For a moment, Edie thought perhaps she had been overly ambitious in her attempt to organize the Sin Drop, but all those thoughts slipped away as the box rose off the ground and into the air.

Mitch was still wearing the clothes from the day of his abduction. The only difference was that now he was barefoot and gagged and had a broken arm, a result of a failed attempt to escape being sealed into the box. His arm was throbbing with pain, but the pain wasn't half as great as the fear in his eyes. He pressed his hands against the sides of the Plexiglas as he looked over the hateful crowd, who cheered as the box was lifted higher into the air. It wobbled back and forth. The twangy guitar and crispy rhythm of the cymbals and drumming continued into an eerie crescendo. The cymbals went *ting ting ting.* If words were being sung, Mitch couldn't hear them over the thoughts in his head. *I'm going to die…I'm going to die!* If he were to scream, the music would overwhelm the sound, and if he were to cry out for help through his gag, the shrill cheers of the crowd would surely drown it out.

Edie stood near the crane, smiling and applauding herself as she watched the box rise higher and higher.

A cup sailed through the air, smacked the side of the box and plopped onto the ground below, leaving a splotch of melted ice cream and streaks of hot fudge. A few more followed. Edie watched the crowd cheer as she ducked away from the falling cups and drips of ice cream.

Mitch peered down at Edie from up in the air. He saw only a look of utter craziness in return. His heart beat louder than the drums on the stage: *bumbum-bumbum-bumbum-bumbum.* Thoughts raced through his mind amid the chaos. *I have to get out…I can't get out.* A tall man in a baseball hat raised a plastic cup in the air like it was a pitchfork. Mitch urinated down his leg as he looked down at the crowd cheering and chanting, "Higher, higher, higher!" Urine sloshed around the bottom of the box, slipped through a crack in the poorly constructed seams and dripped down to the grass below.

Edie raised her hand to catch the attention of the crowd. The band stopped and then began a dramatic kettledrum roll. She signaled to Buckshot to cease raising the box. Mitch would surely die once they released it. She began to count back from ten. The crowd joined in as if it were New Year's Eve. Edie ignored the mess of urine and ice cream and the foul scent of Buckshot's cigarette smoke and continued to count.

The crowd closed in. "Six…Five…Four…"

Edie backed up a few paces. "Three…Two…"

Mitch closed his eyes. This was it. He was going to die here, too scared to think or to unleash any power.

Edie dropped her hand and signaled to Buckshot to let it rip. "One!" everyone screamed in unison.

The rope loosened, and the box dropped. The drumroll swelled. Buckshot switched the lever, and the box stopped a couple of feet from the ground. Mitch smacked against the bottom of the Plexiglas and knocked his head on the box. The crowd, dozens and dozens, cheered wildly. Arms held high, voices even higher. The box swung back and forth over the yard. Mitch bellowed in pain through his gag and closed his eyes for half of a booming heartbeat. Then, without warning, Buckshot released the box, and it plunged down and crashed. Bowie and Buckshot looked each other in the eye and admired their construction of the box, which they were sure was going to break upon collision. Only it hadn't. It remained intact.

"Come forward and accept the gift of God's holy light!" Edie shouted to the crowd as she revealed a pitcher of grape drink laced with the very last bit of her potion. "Only a splash per person. There sure are a lot of y'all. Come on now, grab a shot glass!" They would soon all be her own private toy set. *I'm in business now,* Edie thought. In a way, she was a remarkable businesswoman. She wasn't in the business of salvation or community service; rather, she was in the business of delivering ideas to the masses in such an influential way that people no longer knew what their beliefs were, so they adopted hers. She inspired just enough hope to gain people's trust but not enough for them to question her intentions. That's what her success was contingent on, and there were no signs of failure in the near future.

After everyone had swallowed their serving, Edie said the party was over and ordered them to clean up the yard before they separated into groups. Buckshot would take half of them to the fountain, and the rest would stay at the church.

"Not you," Edie said, pointing to Bowie. "You..." She wagged her head to the right, clearly a nonverbal signal for him to carry out a task they had spoken of earlier. She entered the church and met with Maisie, who had been patiently waiting for her in the hallway.

"Maisie, dear—for your last act of atonement before I release you, I would like you to do something for me. Something that I can't do myself. You'll do it for me, won't you?" Edie asked politely as if she didn't already know the answer.

"Of course."

Edie guffawed. "Super duper. I'm going to have you make a phone call and ask to speak to Nina. You will speak only with her. It's all right for you to say who you are if they ask. I'd actually prefer it if you did. Tell her that if she wants to see you and Mitch alive, she'll do as you say. Don't let her suggest anything else. Say if she tries anything else, you and Mitch will both be killed. Tell her that a car will park outside her house at midnight tonight. She needs to follow it. Just her alone. Tell her it's just to have a discussion. Nothing more. Then hang up! That's all you have to do."

"I can do that," Maisie replied, her mind flipping from compliance to curiosity. "What do you want with Nina?"

"That's none of your concern. Remember?" Edie squinted and squeezed Maisie's chin.

"Yes." Maisie nodded. "Would you like me to call now? I can use my phone. That way she'll know it's me and she'll pick up."

"Look at you. Being all helpful when everyone thought you were just a useless hostage."

Edie retrieved Maisie's cell phone from the office, switched it on and dialed Nina.

"Maisie? Where did you go?" Nina asked.

"I need you to be quiet and listen."

"Maisie, what's going on? Where are you? Are you in trouble?"

"What you need to know is that tonight at midnight, a car will drive up to your house. Get in your car and follow it. Just you. No one else. If you try anything, both Mitch and I will be killed."

"What? Maisie tell—"

"Nina, please. Just do as you're told. They just want to talk. Please just do as they say. They've agreed to let us go afterward."

"That sounds like a trap to me—"

Edie grabbed the phone from Maisie's ear just as Maisie slipped in a final word. "Please just do it."

Edie ended the call and switched off the cell phone. She was filled with a potent sense of exhilaration. "Very, very good, Maisie. Thank you for handling that for me."

"Now you'll let me go?" Maisie said, her voice quivering slightly.

Edie looked over her face and thought that perhaps the effects of the potion worked differently on witches. Maybe it wasn't everlasting as she had thought. Maybe it was wearing off. "You are not my prisoner." Edie reached up and held the sides of Maisie's head and released a heavy breath. "You are hereby cleansed with God's holy light. The door is right over there if you want to leave. I won't stop you. I promise you I'll stay right here." Edie watched Maisie struggle with whether to believe her before she nodded and decided that Edie was honorable, maybe.

Maisie stood up from the bench and hustled toward the front entrance, looking back at Edie every few steps to make sure she was holding her promise. As she reached the doors, her hand only a couple of feet away from the handle, Maisie looked back one final time. The door opened, and Bowie blocked the path outside. Maisie stopped in her tracks and stared at the glowering man before her. She whipped her head around to take another look at Edie.

Edie waved her index finger back and forth in the air as she smirked. "I said *I* wouldn't stop you."

Maisie whipped around and dashed through the space between Bowie and the door. He reached down and grabbed her neck, pulling her hair in the process. She struggled like a mouse being held upside down by its tail.

"Tie her up. Gag her. Keep her quiet. All that," Edie said as she stood up from the bench and looked at her manicure. "Do it now!"

Bowie nodded, and with the ease of a child stepping on a tiny ant, swung Maisie's head into the door.

Thud!

"Good Lord!" Edie said. "This isn't a barn! Watch the doors, come on now." She sighed and rolled her eyes. "When you're done, put her and the other one up on stage. I want it to be a spectacle."

CHAPTER 56

Nina looked at herself in the mirror and trusted that the summoning spell she had cast would be more than just a fancy warning sign, like the shaking of a rattlesnake's tail. This time, her aura was infused with the power of her Transcendent ancestors. It came with a lot of perks. Almost instantly, she had a stronger understanding of how fragile the scales of balance were. Her empathy and compassion for human life radiated at a high frequency, even for her. It immediately made her think back to when Leo had asked shortly after they had all agreed to stay: "What would you have done if one of us had turned out to be a nasty-ass racist?" It was a legitimate question, because the gene that allowed witches to have their power didn't discriminate. Now she was flooded with responses and ideas about how she would have challenged perceptions and provided awakening results that may or may not have included psychic and mental role reversals.

All the perks were great, but none of them were as necessary as the main power she now possessed, the gift of mental communication. She had a plan to find and save Mitch, but she told no one. All she said was that she had to leave temporarily while Nix assumed her role. It was a very unpopular topic, to say the least.

Nina gave each member of her coven a hug and assured them she wouldn't be gone long. There were more sighs of anger and worry than there were tears.

"How can they ask you to leave when Mitch was kidnapped?" Bisa snapped.

Nix stood still, trying desperately to cling to a sense of stoicism. He watched from the back of the room as if he were in the front row of a dramatic play.

Nina reached for Bisa and gave her a second embrace, this time lingering long enough to elicit a suspicious response from the rest of the coven.

Bisa...don't react. Keep hugging me. I have a plan...I'm going to get Mitch back. Just trust me. Please. Just wait, Nina telepathically communicated before she released Bisa from her arms.

Nix took a few galumphing steps toward Nina, clearly trying to bring the sentimental goodbye to an end.

Nina turned to Nix and looked at him apprehensively. He stopped walking and stood directly in front of her. Nina extended her hand, and Nix shook it firmly. A vision flashed before Nina, activated by touch—but not just any touch. It was the touch of the one responsible for the gris-gris bag. The spell she had cast on the bag just before she'd revealed its presence to the coven was to alert her of its creator whenever she came in contact with them. Now it all came rushing in. Nix had planted the bag, he had murdered Blake and Andy, he had been plotting against them the entire time.

Bisa...walk behind him. Slowly.

Then she entered the minds of Leo, Ollie and Avery. *Surround him. Wait for my signal...*

Nina pulled her hand away from Nix as if she had just stuck it into a spider's web. Nina may have been a great witch, but she wasn't exactly the best actor. Her face told the story that she knew something was awry. She took a deep breath and smiled, and when a decent amount of silence had passed, she looked into Nix's eyes. She raised her eyebrows to suggest emotions that weren't there.

"Nix, Nix…I wish I could stay and share a big glass of good cabernet…" Nina began.

Nix nodded and shot her a benign smile.

"But it's time to go. Yet, there are things you should know."

Get ready…

Nix peered into Nina's eyes as he suddenly discerned a specific pattern in her words. Something was peculiar.

Nina tightened her lips and locked her eyes on Nix. "I know what you've done, and as you sow, so shall you reap…"

Nix's eyes widened as the realization struck him: *this is a spell.* He looked around at the coven closing in around him, a detail he had failed to pay attention to in his arrogance. There was no time to react, not now. His eyes darted to the front door, so far, far away from where he stood. How could he not have foreseen this?

"At the mercy of five, we bid you now…" Nina raised her hand to head height, fingers outstretched.

Nix spun on his heels in an attempt to run, but he had no chance. He had been seized by Nina's chant.

Now!

The coven all spoke in unison. "Sleep!"

Nina wrapped each finger in toward her palm in succession, from her pinky to her index finger. There was a snapping noise.

Nix's eyelids drifted shut as his knees gave out beneath him. He fell to the floor as if all his bones had dissolved. As his body slammed onto the ground, he slipped out of consciousness.

Ollie looked up from Nix's body, his jaw slightly unhinged. "Okay, what's going on?"

Avery pulled her hair back, and the skin on her face tightened. "This doesn't feel right!"

Nina nodded anxiously. "I don't have a lot of time to explain⁻that spell won't keep him out for long. He's the one who placed the amulet in our house to break our protection spell."

"Why would he do that? He's part of the Advisory!" Ollie replied.

"He's not!" Nina said frantically. "Now, I need you all to listen to me. If we are going to get Mitch and Maisie back, you have to do what I say. There's not much time."

"Maisie?" Leo asked.

"Where's Mitch?" Avery questioned.

A flurry of other questions hailed down upon Nina as she tried to deflect them.

"I'm going to need your help if this is going to work! So please, just do as I say. I can explain later when we get Mitch back."

"If we get him back!" Leo snapped.

"We *will* get him back!" Nina retorted.

"My God, what the fuck is happening?" Leo said heatedly. "I'm so tired of you answering everything like you are all-knowing! Like we should always listen to you because you're more intuitive, and we should always trust your judgment because your vibrations are higher and you're this super-powerful *manifestor*! Like, 'maybe you don't need anything from Amazon today' or 'let's eat something besides pizza'…'I have a feeling it's not going to be good today.' Just let us live our lives! Shit!"

Nina shook her head to try to clear his words from her head. "That is not what I'm saying. I have *never* said anything like that! I'm not trying to control anybody's life!"

"Mitch is gone and who knows if he's even alive," Leo said. "Don't you think we should do this together?"

"That's exactly what I'm saying, Leo!" Nina stepped up to face his anger.

Ollie and Avery stood close by, trying to pull Leo away from the argument with light tugs at his clothing.

"This is serious, Leo! This is dangerous!" Nina said. Her finger pointed down at the floor as if she were marking an exclamation point.

"Of course it is! We're not blind! Everything we've done since we've gotten here is dangerous! How many dangerous situations have we been in since we all got here, huh?"

Avery stepped up to Leo and held up her hand like a referee. "Leo, you need to calm down. You're in no position to lecture anyone about dangerous situations."

"What the hell is that supposed to mean, Avery?"

"You know what it means. You're a risk junkie, and you're not helping."

Leo scoffed. "I'm not helping? I'm doing more than Ollie is!" He pointed at Ollie without even looking at him.

Ollie frowned and shrugged, confused by the random insult.

"Do you think picking fights here and now is going to do a damn thing?" Avery said. "All you do is bitch and mock and tear people down, and if you're not doing that, you're feeling so damn hopeless and sorry for yourself, which only makes you take it out on everyone else—"

Nina inserted herself between them. "All right, stop. Both of you, just stop."

Avery raised her finger toward Nina to insist she back off as she continued to talk over her. "So don't you just stand there in front of Nina and tear her down like she hasn't given you more of a reason to live than anything in your entire life, while Mitch—who is in love with you for reasons I'll never understand—is probably dying. You want to talk about danger? What the hell is safe about you? You had sex with some random girl who just showed up at the house! If that sounds like someone in their right mind, let me know."

Bisa looked over at Leo, then back at Avery, then back at Leo. "What?"

Nina closed her eyes. The moment she heard Avery say it, she could feel the truth of it in the ether with her temporary psychic amplification.

"Yeah!" Avery said delightedly. "You think I couldn't smell that? And I'm not just talking about the physical sex, which, by the way, was very much a thing that happened."

"So, you're just gonna bring up all my shit now, huh?" Leo said "To what? Prove your point?"

"Who? That…girl…who was at the house the other day asking for Nina?" Bisa asked, her voice quivering. She hoped it wasn't true.

"Mmm-hmm," Avery said, on fire.

Leo turned to Bisa, and a stream of stutters and gasps came out of his mouth as he tried to figure out what to say.

Ollie walked over to Nina and whispered to her, "Are you gonna do something?"

Nina dropped her voice and closed her eyes. "We don't have time," she said, long and drawn out.

"Fuck off, Nina!" Leo shouted.

"No, fuck *you*!" Avery barked back. Her fingers sparked.

Albeit illuminating and dramatic, the argument was ill-timed, and Nina was only getting more impatient, more frustrated.

"Jesus Christ, you guys! Fuck all of you!" Ollie said, having become infested with the insanity.

Nina doubled over, opened her mouth as wide as she could and shouted, "Stop!" There was a quick hitch in the coven's movement, like they'd been electrocuted, just before they dropped to the floor. Nina hovered over Nix and looked around at the coven, all reeling from the psychic blow. "All of you listen…This is what's gonna happen…We are gon—"

Nina was interrupted by the ripping sound of a loud muffler outside the house. She turned toward the door. It roared again.

"There's no time. Listen to me now and do exactly as I say. I swear on my life if you do anything different, I will kill you myself. I'm taking the car and I'm following that car to wherever it leads me. You guys take Nix's car and follow me," she said, digging Nix's keys out from his jacket pocket. "Stay on my tail. Stay out of sight. Don't act until I say so. You'll hear my voice, just like before."

CHAPTER 57

Nina entered New Orleans City Park and pulled into the parking lot outside of Popp Fountain. The man she followed parked in front of the gate, unlocked it, swung the metal doors open and walked inside. The lot was empty apart from the other vehicle, and from the looks of it, the area around the fountain was vacant and dark. Nina left her car and began to walk toward the entrance, feeling—knowing—it was a trap. She continued on, knowing it was the only card she had to play. The borrowed power was beginning to take its toll on her body, and a headache and severe nausea set in. Soon it would be gone and she would be without any psychic protection other than her own, which was in no way weaponized.

Nina passed through the gate and pressed on dazedly, shaking her head at the jackhammer behind her eyes. Borrowed power had side effects sometimes, just like drugs. She could feel her coven's presence. They were close, and doing a fine job of staying inconspicuous. Then, the darkness ahead of her brightened under the light of two freshly lit torches.

Torches? These people have a flair for drama.

Nina walked down the stone walkway and proceeded up the set of steps to the fountain. She had never been there during the day, but she was certain it would have been a sight to see. She kept her pace as she passed under a trellis of leafless vines and entered the circular upper promenade that surrounded the fountain. A woman and a tall brute of a man stood blocking the view of the bronze sculpture in the fountain's center. Nina stopped and looked around the area. Suddenly, there were footsteps. People began to appear from behind the vine-dressed Corinthian columns that encircled the fountain. More torches were lit. Now she could see not only the majesty of the mysterious fountain but also that she was completely surrounded. There was an overwhelming feeling of hate, xenophobia and arrogance. Edie and Bowie emerged from the group and stood in front of the fountain. A beanpole of a man strolled up to meet them. Buckshot.

"You're that woman from the commercial," Nina said.

Edie chuckled, pleased to be recognized. "So, you know who I am!" Edie's smile dissolved to a chillingly vacant expression. "Who are you?" Her eyes were unreadable.

"I think you know," Nina said, bracing herself for a debate. "Where's Mitch? Maisie?"

Torches flared to life like tiny matches in the nearby grounds amidst the trees and shrubs, each one held by a member of Edie's church. They closed in like mice, each guided by a torch in one hand and hammers, machetes or other hillbilly weapons in the other. Nina half expected there to be a rope, seeing them as the lynching type.

Not yet. Stay back...

"Oh, they're not here."

"Why am I not surprised?" Nina said.

"I'd be shocked if you were!"

Nina looked around at the group of cult-y followers closing off any means of escape. "What is this then? Why am I here?"

"Surely you must have figured that out by now. You don't strike me as your typical dumb nigger. Cut off the head and the body dies. Snip those roots before it spreads. You're basically the Obama of the local witches and, well, let's face it, things are changing. Remove you from power, the rest will be easier to pick off than a muscadine grape!"

"You've either got some guts of steel or you're tremendously stupid to corner and challenge a witch. Either way, you're playing with one nasty fire."

Edie smiled and laughed in a darling sort of way. "I know all about you and your powers. Maisie told me everything I ever wanted to know about your kind. Primordials and Transcendents…all o' that. So, don't threaten me and say that I'm playing with fire when you've got none." Edie sounded condescending when she had meant to sound intimidating, a tone that she quickly tried to change before she spoke again. "I think you need to reevaluate who exactly is in danger here. You're outnumbered by, good Lord, I don't even know how many. You can threaten me with powers you don't have all you want, but take a look around you. You're surrounded."

"So, I'm just supposed to surrender? Go quietly?" Nina asked.

"That was the general idea, yeah."

"What will you do with Mitch and Maisie?"

"If you *lay down your arms*, like they say in the movies, I can guarantee they'll die quick. All I have to do is give the order."

"And if I refuse?"

"Well, I hope I don't get any of your blood on my shoes."

Nina took a few steps toward Edie, ignoring the armed forces around her. "You expect me to just come quietly when I know you have two of mine? Would you do something like that?"

Edie snickered and covered her smile with her chubby fingers. "For who? All of them?" She waved her hands at her crew as if she were indicating a coop of sickly chickens. "They're loyal, but they're a dime a dozen. Ain't that right, everyone? Y'all are a dime a dozen and you'll do anything I say even if it endangers your life, won't ya?" Edie locked eyes with Nina.

"Yes, ma'am!" roared the surrounding torch-yielding crowd.

Not yet…not just yet…Wait…

"You must be just another dumb nigger all dressed up with a fancy degree. Do you actually know who I am? I'm the co-founder, well"—Edie cleared her throat—"founder of the Whole Truth and True Light Assembly of God, the largest church in all of Louisiana with over fifty-four hundred members now, with a campus in Houma and a brand-new one in Baton Rouge! Darlin', I've got the manpower, the size, the publicity and the range, and as soon as I get my finances back in order—the one final severance gift from my husband—I'll have the means to wipe out every single witch in this world and this country and even a few stars in the sky if they're shining too bright for me to sleep. Make no mistake about it, darlin', y'all are goin' extinct. It's just God's plan. Cold hard truth right there. Honey, this is a losing battle if I've *ever* seen one."

Nina had split her concentration between Edie and her coven, who were advancing toward the fountain among the shadows.

Ready…?

"You know what's ironic?" Nina asked.

"What's that?"

"Your choice of setting." Nina opened her arms to indicate the fountain. "Many years ago, a coven used to meet right here in this very spot."

"And now it's just you." Edie cocked her head and signaled to her crew.

"Bitch, please."

"Get her!" Edie snarled.

NOW!

Nina ducked down and slammed her palms against the concrete, sending a groundswell of psychic energy out around her. The surge washed over Edie's men like a flood wave, knocked them off their feet and snuffed out their torches. Edie lost her footing on her wedge heel and fell backward into the fountain.

Avery, Ollie, Leo and Bisa raced through the entrance gates and up beside Nina. As they reached her, a couple of men caught them off guard and smacked Leo in the back of the head with the butt of a gun. He fell to the ground. The other stocky man reached out to grab Bisa, but Avery set his jacket on fire and left him to burn. Bisa tended to Leo, and Ollie helped Nina up. Nina's borrowed power had run its course, and nothing was left but fatigue and a headache.

"We have to get to the church, now," Nina breathed.

Bisa turned Leo's head and inspected his scalp. There was a slice in the side of his head where the gun had made contact. His eyes were angry but confused. Bisa ran her fingers over his blood-soaked hair and tried to encourage him to stand. His legs were limp, like old carrots.

"Leo, get up!" Bisa said.

She then felt something in the air, an assault on her skin that made the hair on the back of her neck stick up. She had felt this before under different circumstances, more natural ones. Bisa looked over at Avery, whose hands were outstretched. Bursts of fog ruptured around the grounds like pieces of popcorn. Bisa quickly gazed over the surroundings and wished that they had thought of that before they actually entered the gardens.

"Get them to the car!" Avery shouted.

"We're not gonna leave you here! Come on!" Bisa said.

Buckshot emerged from the thick fog and grabbed Ollie by the throat, his dirty, jagged fingernails scratching Ollie's neck. They struggled for control until Ollie lifted his knee into Buckshot's crotch and they both tumbled back to the ground.

"Go, now! Go!" Avery shouted.

Ollie picked Nina up from the ground, extended his free hand to Bisa and pulled her and Leo up simultaneously.

Avery turned to the crowd that was running straight at her from all angles, machetes glinting in the moonlight. She heard the voice of her spirit rise inside her. With a lungful of air, she expelled a shrilling groan as she fashioned a twisting tube of fire with a flourish of her hands. The fire soared away, landed on the concrete and encircled the coven as if following a path of kerosene. The flames rose from the ground in a blanket of impenetrable fire.

Bowie pulled out his knife, flipped the handle into the air and grabbed hold of the blade. In a single, efficient swing, he chucked the knife through the air and watched it dig through the mist, past Avery and into Leo's leg.

Leo shouted out in agony and fell deeper into Bisa's arms. As Ollie reached down to remove the knife, Avery turned her attention back to Bowie. His cold Slavic eyes glistened in the roaring flames, taunting her. His sly smile begged for a reaction. Avery looked at the ring of fire and commanded it to attack. The talent had always been there: an attribute of unlimited potential. The possibilities were countless, yet she chose hostility. She had never anticipated being provoked in such a way that would elicit such a violent response. Yet it seemed appropriate. One can do only so much to pacify a tyrant before strength of character is seen as weakness. The flames spat out from the ring and pelted Bowie like bullets. As he caught fire, Edie lifted her head out of the fountain. Avery seized the next opportunity and commanded the water to seal Edie's head beneath the surface. It splashed up around her head, formed a sheet and pulled her head back down into the water.

Then, a gunshot. Avery ducked and lost her control over the water holding Edie in the fountain. Not seeing where the shot had come from, she backed away toward the entrance. Another gunshot echoed through the park, and a bullet found its way into a column just behind her. She looked back to see how far her coven had made it. They weren't far, but they weren't in the clear just yet. Avery brought her palms together in front of her chest, the fingers of her left hand pointed to the right and vice versa. There wasn't a moment of indecisiveness. She acted on instinct. She felt the swelling of the power build up between her hands like a hot air balloon being filled. *I can do this*, she thought. She was too angry to leave and too frightened to stay. This was her last option, the last one she could think of amidst the chaos. The unassailable reality of her strength intensified, shaking her hands. For a split second she wasn't even certain what unleashing the power that she barely contained in her hands would do. But they needed to get away. They needed to escape, or they would all die. Avery pulled her hands apart, and there was a ripple of bright orange energy as an explosion of pyrotechnics rocketed out across the park. The grounds were covered in a shower of golden light as the violent, deafening boom shattered the columns. Stone, grass and debris shot into the air as showers of red sparks and black smoke rained down and fizzled out on the ground.

She marveled at the extent of her own power for only a second before she ran to catch up with the coven. There were no more gunshots, as the blast had ignited every bullet inside every gun all at once.

"How the hell did you do that?" Ollie asked.

"I have no idea!" Avery said quickly as she helped shove Leo into the back seat.

Ollie hopped into the driver's seat and peeled away from the park. Avery let her hands hover over Leo's leg, like a knife spreading butter over toast. Slowly the cut began to seal itself, leaving only a wet scratch. She would have continued, but she was exhausted and was starting to feel as hot as the fire she had left behind.

"Is everyone okay?" Nina asked as she built her grit back up through a series of deep breaths.

With everyone safe and healed, they headed to the church, hoping they would reach Mitch and Maisie before it was too late…if it wasn't already.

CHAPTER 58

The parking lot was filled with vehicles—far too many pickup trucks and Toyota Camrys for the church to be empty. Nina guided them toward the building, keeping an eye out for any suspicious movement.

"I can't believe the church is doing this," Avery said.

Nina scoffed. "Avery, just because they worship God it doesn't make them free from sin, no matter what they believe. Don't forget it was the church that condemned witches, or anyone they thought was a witch, to die."

"What if they're dead?" Bisa asked.

"Then that woman will be praying for her life," Nina answered.

The lights were on, but when they peeked through the windows, they couldn't see anyone inside.

"Nina, how did you get that power?" Avery asked. "I thought Transcendents had more useless kind of powers. Well, not useless, but, you know…"

"Passive?"

"Yeah."

"It's a type of magic I haven't told any of you about. You can invoke a spirit or spirits into your outer aura and their power is on loan to you. Their power is linked to you psychically, so it functions as if you actually had the power yourself. It wears you down and it doesn't last long. But it can be pretty handy for those of us who aren't gifted with more…functional kinds of magic."

Nina knew that she would one day have to explain how she harnessed that power, but she was hoping it wouldn't be as soon as now. She saw a flash of interest in Leo's eyes and knew she had something to worry about. It made her anxious for only a moment, and then she opened the door to the church.

"There's no one here," Avery said.

"Oh no, they're here. We just haven't seen them yet," Nina declared as she stepped farther into the church. "Avery…Leo…I hate to put this on you, but you two have the physical powers, so I need you to be on guard."

Bisa felt a surge of energy run through her body. She could sense Mitch nearby. "I can feel him," she said as she opened the door to the sanctuary.

Mitch and Maisie were in front, on the chancel, both bloody and unconscious. Leo pushed through the rest of the coven and began to run to their aid.

"Leo, wait!" Nina shouted as softly as she could.

Within a few seconds, Leo had run down the aisle, scaled the chancel and knelt down next to Mitch.

"He's still breathing. What do we do?" Leo asked.

The coven proceeded farther inside. When they were halfway down the aisle, the door behind them closed. A click followed. The lights began to dim, and soon the room was shrouded in darkness.

"Avery…" Nina said, indicating she needed some light.

Right then, the lights turned back up and the chancel filled with more of Edie's cronies. Then more entered from other doors until every last one of them was inside, all of them armed.

"Leo, get back here now," Nina shouted.

He looked at Nina and then back at the angry mob. Before he could do anything, Edie arrived on the upper balcony just above the entrance on the ground floor.

"I don't know why you'd think I wouldn't be prepared for something like this," Edie said. "I always get my way. I told you this was a battle you can't win. The only reason you're not already dead is that I draw the line at guns inside church. Anywhere else, they're welcome." She waved the order to kill.

Avery produced another ring of fire around them for protection. Flames licked the chairs and ignited the carpet. Leo turned to the group on the chancel, dropped his head and raised his arm along with a cyclone of fire. The flames ripped through a group of eight and landed uncontrollably on the chancel. Leo lifted his other hand to the air, detached the large decorative cross from the wall and let it fall on another group of crazed zealots. Screams filled the room, in contrast with the usual voices of the Sunday choir.

Blood began to flow from Leo's ear as he brought both of the poles holding the American flags up out of their stands and pierced the remaining four men on the chancel, as though he were running a wooden skewer through raw meat.

The unit on the ground floor tried to pass through Avery's fire ring, but backed away as she forced it to burn hotter and spread.

"Good luck gettin' out, motherfuckers!" Edie screamed from above as she scampered through the door, slammed it shut and locked it.

A couple of stinky, unshowered men busted through the ring of fire, their pants carrying pieces of flame. Ollie elbowed one in the face, and Nina held the other one under her influence, causing him to remain still. The man's eyes looked terrified as he realized his body was unable to move. Bisa grabbed hold of him and shoved him back through the fire, taking more flames with him.

A loud boom came from the chancel area. Nina turned around to see a large chunk of the wall missing. *Leo...* she thought. Her eyes whipped back to the chancel. Mitch was gone, but Maisie was not.

"Nina, we have to get out of here. I can't control the fire anymore," Avery said with a sense of dread.

A crack above the hole in the wall climbed up toward the ceiling and spread out across it. The fire soared up the curtains and met the cracks in the ceiling. Nina turned toward the door. There was just enough of her borrowed power left, she could feel it. She dutifully lifted her hand, and a gust of wind blew through the fire and knocked the doors off the hinges.

The loyal followers caught fire. *Edie wasn't kidding. They must be a dime a dozen,* Nina thought as they passed through the doorway and spilled out into the hall. The sanctuary was engulfed in flames, and the fire had a liquid-like quality to it, almost like it was alive. The view of the chancel dissolved into a mess of smoke and flame as the ceiling began to collapse.

The coven, minus Leo and Mitch, ran out of the church and toward the car. Edie stood outside a few feet away. There was a lot wrapped up in the church, but surely there would be some sort of insurance relief. When she thought about Josh now, or the church, even, it felt like someone else's life—much like the life she'd had as a rambunctious teenager. She was changing, evolving, and she was going to have to leave some things behind if she was going to make way for the new and improved Edie Bonner.

She watched the flames destroying what was left of what she thought was her life's purpose until she caught the coven running through the lot out of the corner of her eye. Her heart pounded. There was no way in hell she was going to let them get away. They simply couldn't. She was possessed with God's holy light, and it was her mission and purpose on earth to stop them, at all costs. Failure was such an unflattering color on her. Emotions of all kinds rose up in her throat as she watched the coven scurry to the car. There was no way she could run. She was one pie too heavy in those shoes to ever catch up to them in time. There were also way too many of them. The witches were like a virus: they were stronger when there were more of them.

Edie dropped to her knees right there in the parking lot. She hadn't done anything like that since she was a teenager, albeit under very different circumstances. However, if she could pull this off, the result would be the same. It would end with a bang. She clasped her hands together in prayer and looked up toward the starry heavens.

"Oh Lord, I ask you, give me the strength to stop your enemies. Empower me, illumine the light in my heart and my soul…" A single tear dripped down from her left eye. She was moved by the grace of her own prayer, captivated by her own captivation. She chuckled as she imagined God's hands enhancing her soul with his blessings. "O Lord, the almighty, I am your vessel, a vessel for your powerful light. I am your warrior and I will stop this calamity." She turned her attention back to the coven members who were in the car and beginning to pull away. Her eyes were silly and irrational like a carnival clown. "With your holy light, I serve you," Edie finally whispered as she outstretched her hands as if offering bread to a starving child.

The car lifted from the ground as if it had been catapulted, and overturned in the air. Edie smiled at the magnificence of the light as her ears began to seep blood, and she fell unconscious on the pavement. The car began to fall back to earth with the speed of a falling meteorite.

Nina was too weak to stop it. Avery had no other tricks up her sleeve, and even if she had, she was bouncing off the roof of the car. In the moments before the car hit the ground, Nina thought of all she had accomplished only to fail at the last minute. They tumbled and tumbled, like rags in the wash. There was no time for goodbyes, there was nothing more they could do. It was time to die. But in the quick moments of the rolling car, Bisa felt something besides fear. She felt a presence inside her emotions.

They all slammed into the car's seats, but they hadn't crashed. The roof was intact, and they were unharmed, apart from a few scrapes and bruises—small injuries that could be treated with some Advil and Netflix. Nina lifted her head. She wasn't dead. No one was. She beamed with wonder as she looked out the window to see that they were less than two feet from the ground. If she had been the fainting type, she would have fainted right then and there. But there was no time for that. Bisa wasn't capable of something so miraculous. Avery was a Primordial and lacked the delicate skills to do whatever this was. Ollie had other gifts, and this was not one of them. Her eyes found a figure on the lawn just off the side of the burning church. It was Leo. He had felt Bisa's panic and had arrived to rescue them.

Leo's hand was spread out before him, shaking as though he had the chills. He had stopped the car, with whatever power he possessed. He *was* a Corporeal. His eyes fell bloodshot, and a searing pain shot through his head. Like a migraine. Like electrocution. He lifted his other hand, and the car bobbed like a passenger car of a Ferris wheel upon stopping. A stream of blood poured out from his ear, and the sounds of the world were drowned away. He lowered his hands and the car sank another foot. Then without any warning, the car fell another foot to the ground, smashing the windows out but leaving the coven unharmed.

Mitch, who had been dropped by Leo's side on the ground, watched from his horizontal position. He was injured, but there was no mistaking what he saw. Leo was something special, something different. Sure, he had been mildly obsessed with Leo in a way that all gay men have a straight crush. But it wasn't his attraction talking. Leo *was* different.

Leo let out a painful gasp as he lowered his arms to scoop Mitch up off the ground. "Come on, buddy, time to go," he said wearily.

The two of them didn't exchange another word as they hobbled across the parking lot toward the car. If Leo could make it without fainting from exhaustion, that would be a bonus. If the car still worked, that would be a real phenomenon. Leo and Mitch battled with their wounds and through their fatigue until they arrived at the car. Mitch half expected, even in the heat of the crisis, for Leo to crack some kind of joke, or whine or stir up some drama, but he didn't.

Ollie maneuvered himself back into the driver's seat and took control of the wheel. The car had seen a night, that was for sure. When they were safely inside, they sped off in the opposite direction of the whirring sirens, leaving Edie unconscious in the lot where she dreamed of a heaven without witches, a throne next to God, and all the pecan pie she could ever eat. She drifted further into her dreams as her blood began to ooze out of her ears, mouth and nose. Soon, there was only pie, hundreds upon hundreds of uneaten pies, sticky, glazed, sweet like sex. It was sweet, so sweet, but suddenly it became nothing but an abstract idea and there were only sensations and strange feelings that swirled into one another, catching themselves like fishhooks, until the pie was sliced and sliced, becoming nothing but crumbs as everything faded, crumbled and dwindled away like dying embers, into black, barren nothingness. And just then, her heart stopped. The last subtle heartbeat echoed—vibrated—out into the world around her. So began the echo of mental balance.

CHAPTER 59

During the drive back home, Avery healed everyone's physical wounds. They chatted extensively for a few minutes about what had happened and what was going to happen next—Nix was still at the house. There was a flurry of suggestions from each of them until Nina closed the topic with a simple "We'll handle it together…as a coven." After that, the car fell quiet, the kind of silence that puzzled Nina. Were they quiet because they had come to accept that they needed to act as a unit, or because they disagreed?

Then, Leo spoke. "About earlier…what I said at the house?"

Nina's puzzled expression changed. She knew what was coming next. Before he even spoke, she knew the silence was caused by their unspoken commitment to the coven. She turned her head to face him. Then she waited.

"I get angry sometimes, and I say things. I'm not always proud of the things I do or have done, and it may not seem like it, but I really am trying to get better. I'm trying to work on that." He stared into his palms for a moment, picking at the rough calluses. Oh, how those hands had more than calluses on them. He took a deep breath and forcefully blew it out into the air that was rushing in from the open window. When he spoke again, his voice was different—softer.

"Sometimes I think I just hate myself and everything I do or say is just…all I've ever known. It's hard trying to be different from how you've always been. Especially now. When everything is so different. My whole world has been turned upside down. And I've never been around people like you before. Any friends, or people I called friends, were never anything like any of y'all." There was a distinct humility and calmness to his voice. "This has all been really fucking confusing from the very start. My life was so different. When I stopped to actually look at my future, which wasn't often, because it made me feel worse, I didn't really see one. I'd see people all the time and think, *I wish I could have that...Why can't I have that?* All I ever saw was my life how it was, on this endless loop, never changing, never getting any easier, only getting older. Then this happened, and I got thrown into this coven, and you said I was attuned, that we all were. And things started to change, but sometimes I wonder if I can't change, and I wonder if y'all are better off without me, or I think that you regret my being a part of all this—"

Nina interrupted. "I stand by my choice. I don't regret admitting you into this coven. It hasn't been easy, but what is? What I would regret is failing you. Letting you feel that you have no future or no home."

Ollie rolled the window up as they pulled onto their street. Nina smiled and left the conversation at that.

Avery turned to Leo. "So, this may be a bad time to bring this up, but...can we talk about what you did back there? I've never seen any of us do anything even remotely close to that. Is that even possible? What is that? Telekinesis?"

Leo could feel an avalanche of anxiety as he tried to think of how to explain what he was capable of.

Ollie looked into the rearview mirror and into Leo's eyes. "Yeah, what kind of magic was that? He's a Primordial, right?" he asked Nina.

Nina shook her head. "He's more than that. He's a Corporeal."

Her statement blew about in the air like dust waiting for a place to land.

"What's that?" Avery asked excitedly.

"Evolution," Nina replied as Ollie parked the car in front of the house.

The conversation would have to wait. Now that they were home, they had to figure out what to do about Nix.

"I don't know how his body will respond to our spell," Nina said. "He might still be out. He might be awake."

"Or he could be waiting to kill us all on the other side of the door!" Mitch said.

Bisa closed her eyes and scanned her hand across the front of the house. "I think he's gone."

"Are you sure?" Mitch said.

"I don't smell him," Avery said. "I mean, I don't smell anything…like there's no intent to harm or anything like that. I know that sounds stupid, but that's how it comes. It's like this weird synesthesia."

Nina stepped up toward the door. It was unlocked. Before she could grab hold of the handle, she felt a breeze of energy, a gust that carried the smell of gold. The handle twisted, but not from her own hand. The door opened. A few inches at first, and then farther and farther. Nina smiled and turned around. Leo was lowering his hand. He had opened the door for her, like a gentleman.

"That. Is. Amazing," Mitch said as he processed the magic that had just occurred before his very eyes.

When the door had opened as far as it could go, the coven huddled up behind Nina and they entered as a team. Nothing was out of the ordinary, all the lights were left on, and everything was in its place, but Nix was gone.

"Maybe he's somewhere in the house," Avery suggested as she looked around.

"No, he's gone," Nina said.

"Should we be worried? What's going on? I thought he was on our side," Mitch said plainly.

"I thought so too. But he's not. That I do know. What I don't know…is why," Nina said.

After the house was secured physically, Nina sat everyone down in the great room and told them the story of the Corporeals before she explained everything she knew about Nix. It was Bisa who suggested that they call upon the Advisory immediately to explain the situation. If they got to them first, it would be much easier for them to explain. Only they arrived without notice and without being summoned.

Nina answered the door, surprised to see Per and Rosemary standing before her. Nix, however, was nowhere in sight. Naturally. He wasn't just late this time, he was long gone.

"I was hoping you hadn't left yet! We have astounding news!" Rosemary said as Nina beckoned her and Per inside the house. "I know it's late—"

"Nix—" Nina began.

"You and your coven did it! You set in motion the systematic balance! Whatever you did, the indicators that mental balance has begun have started to reverberate!"

The satisfaction of their success was delayed as Nina explained everything she knew about Nix. She told them everything, about his amulet, his involvement with the other coven and his escape from their home. Shortly after that, Rosemary suggested the obvious, that Nina be reinstated as Proctor of the coven. Per elected Rosemary to take over the position of Keeper of Books and Assets. She was far more qualified than he was, and she actually enjoyed numbers. It only made sense.

Nina accepted the offer. Her first act as the newly reinstated Proctor was a decision that affected her entire coven. They were going to move.

"Why would you move? You've built a home here. Your coven's home is here," Per said.

"This is a house. It's not home. Home is us. The coven makes this house a home. And I would like to take credit for the idea, but I feel our time is done here, and that comes straight from the divine. I can ask Mitch to do a spread and we can take a look at what his cards tell us?"

"That won't be necessary. I believe you. I believe *in* you, Nina," Rosemary said. "I trust you will do whatever is best for the coven, wherever you will be. Give me a little time and I will organize a new home of your choosing. Secured with all that you had here."

A month passed. It was the new moon, in Aries. While the Whole Truth and True Light Assembly of God Church suddenly and bizarrely went bankrupt as a result of Edie's puzzling cardiac arrest and the devastating hundreds of thousands of dollars in property damage at the church due to the fire, their remaining campuses were seized by the bank and ended up being slated for auction. It wouldn't be long before they would look no different from the rest of the abandoned buildings throughout the state that were left unrepaired after Katrina. The Bonners would be talked about for a while. How could they not be? With their commercials airing posthumously for months after their death and the legacy of their outrageous churches. Their campuses would attract the occasional tourist and became a hot target for curious urban explorers or local pillagers, and would soon suffer the same fate as the abandoned Six Flags theme park in New Orleans East, an unsightly reminder of what once was with an eerie reminder still up on the front sign that read *closed for storm*. The church would cycle through the channels for bankruptcy, and filter down through the insurance policies (or lack thereof) until it became nothing but an eyesore, one that would trigger someone to say, "Hey, do you remember their commercials?"

The coven had spent their time packing and preparing themselves for a new adventure, although Leo still had plans of his own. Ollie packed up his plants and Avery said goodbye to the beehive. The last spell that was cast in the house was one that they did together as a coven. It took two weeks to prepare, and pulled from the talents of each of them. If they were going to leave Louisiana, they would have to leave it a little better than they had found it. Nina had been slightly inspired by Nix, and she felt an amulet would be an appropriate magical item to leave behind. After the coven shared a magical strawberry risotto* to inspire love and creativity, Nina asked for suggestions from Bisa and Avery, the most artistic members of the group. Together, they infused a long red section of fabric— a shroud—with many types of positive energy: steeped in a tea of herbs and left out under the moonlight, drizzled with various essences and elixirs and left out in the sun to dry, magically altered and infused with magic, the magic and divine love that the coven manifested.

"Let's go!" Leo shouted from the front seat of the moving van.

Nina stood in the window of the study, the red shroud wrapped around her wrists like a handwarmer. She nodded to

Leo, took one final look around the room and then unfolded the shroud to reveal its length. *It's gonna be okay. Everything is going to be okay.*

Nina tossed the shroud out the window and let the fabric unroll in the wind. She held one end over the windowsill and reached up to the window and dug her hands into the groove where the paint had begun to peel away. In a single, smooth movement, she lowered the window and sealed the shroud onto the windowsill. She leaned forward, barely pressing her forehead to the glass, and looked down. Now the shroud hung, exposed to the world and billowing under the breeze like the surface of the ocean.

"So shall it be," Nina said triumphantly.

It was more than an amulet—more than a shroud, even. It was the start of a new form of vibration, their first effort and last spell in the house to begin the energetic reversal of hate. The pearly undertones of the deep red cloth glistened in the sun, sending healing energy rippling out into the world with each billowing wave.

It was time to begin a new chapter and search for ways to balance the emotional and spiritual energies in the world. It was also time to tell the coven about the Union of the Divine Dualities.

THE

ESOTERIC COMPENDIUM

A collection of key terms, places, spells & recipes

TERMS & PLACES

Astral Fluid: AFD for short. An organic substance present in all beings. A witch's powers and lifeforce are embedded in it. It can be extracted and used.

Corporeal: The most recent type of witch to emerge, once thought to be legend. They can sometimes control the elements but cannot summon them. They are the energy alchemists, able to manipulate energy and matter. They possess varying levels of telekinesis, shapeshifting and auric manipulation.

The Land of Perpetual Midnight: The shadow realm. Existing under an open sky with more stars than one could ever see from even the most remote parts Earth, but no moon. There are occasional celestial activities in the sky that provide some additional light, with open fields of prairie-like grass, forests of evergreen and birch and a single mountain. There are no boundaries, no beginning and no end to its vastness. Access to the land, as well as other astral planes, can be achieved through ritual drug use, sexual trance, deep meditation, and repetition of words believed to contain power.

Lunastaterum: A mystical, bowl-shaped device created by witches that monitors the earth's gravitational pull and lunar rhythm in addition to indicating the direction of the closest witch, like a compass. It was created to locate other witches during times of persecution.

Primordial: The first type of witch to emerge, sometimes referred to as the Elementals. They can light fire, call storms, lightning and can manipulate water. They are especially gifted at using the elements for divinatory purposes. Heightened senses, can detect slight variations in voice pitch, mood and smell. They are physical healers and can communicate, summon and control animals to some degree.

Rafkolite: A vitreous silica projectile rock, silvery green with swirls of smoky purple bubbles that resemble moss. This rock fell to the earth as a meteor around 15 million years ago and is rumored to have many powers but especially known for its ability to create a butterfly effect of positive energy, when used by the right person or group.

Somnium plane: The plane where dreams manifest and take place. If one is skilled at lucid dreaming, they can access other areas of this plane where they can practice magic, learn its secrets and connect with ancestral spirits.

Starseed: Souls that have origins in the stars and are all cosmically linked to one another. Similar to the energy of a Twin Flame, in which a soul has been split into two bodies and can exist at varying stages of spiritual evolution.

Transcendent: The second type of witch to emerge, sometimes referred to as the Spirit Witches. The empathic clairvoyants and the most in touch with the divine. They can communicate with spirits, astral project, and heal emotional wounds and trauma. Their strongest skill is their power to influence others.

The Union of the Divine Dualities: An esoteric ritual designed to invoke the presence of the nigrum pullum.

SPELLS

Ab Initio Talisman:

This talisman meaning, "from the beginning," is designed to inspire its owner to shift their perspective to see the positive developments in one's life through the use of an inkblot. When the talisman ritual is complete, the inkblot is to be hung as art where it will be seen every single day. The talisman is most effective when created on the first new moon of the new year.

You will need:

Parchment or other plain paper

Ink

A few drops of a full or dark moon elixir

Garnet (to amplify the energies and characteristics of the other stones)

Herkimer diamond (to encourage you to be what you strive to become, healing)

Lepidolite (to aid in stressful environments)

Petrified wood (transformation and new beginnings)

- Cleanse the space and all objects, charge with intent.
- Place stones around the parchment and recite your mantra.
- With the intention to see a new beginning, squeeze ink onto one side of the parchment in a random fashion.
- Drizzle a few drops of the chosen elixir over the ink, then quickly fold the paper over itself and press firmly.
- Let it sit in the light of the new moon to charge and fully dry.
- Look at the talisman everyday throughout the year to see what you see differently.

Bisa's Okra Bath:

Used to remove negativity received throughout the day, washing away energetic blockages or to remove hexes, spells and toxicity or absorbed from other people or situations. Given to Bisa by a Babalawo in Chicago.

You will need:

Large bowl of water, enough to coat your entire body

20   okra, sliced

1   bottle of Florida water

½ c.   angelica root (to remove hexes and protect from evil intentions)

1 c.   sea salt

½ c.   rum (an offering to the ancestors)

2   white candles

Salt

White Sage

Van Van Oil (for anointing)

Oil of choice (I prefer amber)

White or light-colored clothing for after the bath

- Slice okra into small chunks and add to a large bowl of water as you visualize your intention. Recite, "Ancestors, angels and all higher beings of love and light, I ask that you please consume me and shower me in your energy. Assist me as I cleanse my body and spirit. Bless and energize this bathwater and allow truth and wisdom to emerge. Give me clarity and protect me from negativity. For the highest good of all I ask that you guide me away from negative energies I may encounter and bring in light, joy and love. Give me the confidence and stamina to overcome any obstacles in my path. Help me help others. Allow me to speak the truth, see the truth and hear the truth of all around me."

- Add Florida water, rum, sea salt, and angelica root to the bowl of okra water. Squeeze and crush the okra pieces in the water with your hands. Let the mixture sit for three hours. You may place in the sunlight or the moonlight depending on your intention.

- Strain the mixture through a colander and capture in another bowl. Discard solids outside near a tree.

- Anoint candle with van van oil. Roll candle in pulverized salt and white sage. Place a candle at either end of the tub. Visualize your intention and white light pouring in through your crown chakra and spilling through your entire body as you pour the bathwater over your head and rub over every inch of the body. The negative elements are trapped by the sticky okra bath. Shower yourself with clean water and be certain that the tub and shower area are clear of all residue that may contain negative energy. Dry yourself and anoint yourself with intention using an oil of your choice.

RECIPES

Nina's Bucatini all'Amatriciana:

1/2 lb	pancetta, coarsely chopped
¼ c.	olive oil
1	red onion, medium dice
4	garlic cloves
1 T	tomato paste
18	basil leaves, chiffonade
3	sprigs thyme, chopped
1 t.	red pepper flakes
1 ½ lb	canned, imported, Italian tomatoes
¾ c.	Parmigiano-Reggiano, grated
½ c.	flat-leaf parsley

Salt

Pepper

- Separate garlic cloves from the head, but do not peel. Place into a hot pan and dry roast them over medium high heat, turning occasionally, for about 8-10 minutes. Remove from heat, cool slightly, peel, chop and set aside.

- Heat the olive oil in a large pot or deep skillet. Add the pancetta and cook 12-15 minutes, until all the fat has rendered out. Remove the meat and set aside. Add the onion and sauté over medium heat for about 4 minutes. Add garlic, cook 30 seconds. Add tomato paste and cook for an additional minute. Drain the tomatoes, chop them and add to pot along with the red pepper flakes, basil and thyme. Reduce to a simmer and cook for 15-20 minutes, stirring occasionally. Adjust seasoning.

- Bring a pot of salted water, as salty as the Mediterranean, and cook the bucatini until al dente. Drain pasta.

•   Add the pasta and cooked pancetta to the pot with the sauce. Cook over medium high heat for one minute until the pasta is fully coated. Remove the pot from the heat, add in the cheese and mix well to combine. Transfer pasta to a serving bowl and garnish with freshly chopped parsley.

Nina's Chicken Piccata:

4	chicken breasts
2 oz.	flour
½ t.	kosher salt
½ t.	black pepper
3 T	butter
2 T	olive oil
2	shallots, sliced
2	sprigs thyme, chopped
6	garlic cloves, sliced
½ c.	dry white wine
¾ c.	low-sodium chicken broth
3 T	lemon juice
2 T	capers
½ c.	flat-leaf parsley, chopped

• Place the chicken breast between two pieces of heavy-duty plastic wrap. Pound out flat using a meat mallet or a rolling pin. Season with salt and pepper and then dredge fully in the flour, shaking off any excess.

• Melt the 2 T butter and 1 T of oil in a pan over medium high heat. Add chicken to pan, cooking 4 minutes on each side. Remove from pan and set aside.

• Add remaining oil to the pan, heat for 30 seconds and then add the sliced shallots and thyme. Stirring often. Add the garlic and continue to cook for another minute. Pour in the wine and bring to a boil. Keep cooking until almost all the liquid is gone. Add the broth and return to a boil and cook until reduced by about half. Next, whisk in 1 T of fresh flour and cook for 1 minute. Remove from the heat, add the remaining butter, lemon juice and capers. Plate the chicken, top with the sauce and garnish with a hefty amount of parsley.

Avery and Mitch's Cornbread:

1 ½ c.	coarse-grind yellow cornmeal
1 ½ t.	sugar
¾ t.	baking soda
1 t	kosher salt
2	eggs
1 ¾ c.	buttermilk
2 oz.	bacon fat
3 T	Enchanted Honey Butter, room temp

• Combine 1-2 teaspoons of Avery's enchanted honey with room temperature butter. Set aside.

• Preheat the oven to 400° and place a 10" cast-iron skillet in the oven to preheat.

• Combine all dry ingredients in a bowl, whisk to distribute really well. In a separate bowl, combine eggs and buttermilk with a fork.

• Remove hot skillet from the oven and add in the bacon fat, tilting to swirl around and coat the sides and bottom of the pan. Whisk the hot bacon fat into the buttermilk mixture and return skillet to the oven.

• Combine the dry mixture with the buttermilk mixture until evenly moistened, but still a little lumpy. Transfer batter into the hot skillet and bake until the edges are golden brown and the top is golden and slightly cracked in places. It should be firm to the touch, this takes about 20-25 minutes.

• Remove from oven, brush with enchanted butter and let cool 5-10 minutes before slicing.

Nina and Leo's Jambalaya:

4	strips of thick-cut, peppered bacon
2 c.	yellow onion, diced
2 c.	celery, diced
1 c.	green bell pepper
1 c.	red bell pepper
6	garlic cloves, minced
5	sprigs rosemary
1 ½ c.	andouille sausage
1 c.	beer (Yuengling or other pale lager)
1 ½ lb.	shrimp, peeled, deveined, tail-on
1 c.	chopped tomatoes
1	can diced tomatoes
1 c.	cherry tomatoes, halved
1 T	tomato paste
1	jalapeno, roasted and diced
1 c.	flat-leaf parsley, chopped
1 c.	green onion, sliced
5	bay leaves
2 t.	smoked paprika
2 t.	thyme
2 t.	oregano
1 t.	basil
2 t.	kosher salt
1 t.	black pepper, freshly ground
½ t.	cayenne pepper
4 c.	long grain brown rice
4 c.	chicken stock, low sodium (or a nice vegetable stock)

•   Preheat the oven to 375°. Place a cast-iron pot over medium high heat. Cook the bacon until crispy. Remove the bacon from the pan, drain on paper towels and chop. Set aside.

•   Pour out most of the bacon fat, and add in the onions, celery and bell peppers and cook 5-6 minutes. Add the garlic, rosemary and andouille, and cook until the meat begins to brown slightly.

•   Pour in the beer and deglaze the pot. Add the bacon back into the pot. Add the shrimp, tomatoes, paste, jalapeno, parsley, green onion and bay leaves. Next, add in the paprika, thyme, oregano, basil, salt, black pepper and cayenne.

•   Add the rice to the pot and stir to incorporate. Add in the chicken stock. Cover and bake in the oven for 1 hour or until most of the liquid has been absorbed into the dish. Check if the rice is cooked. If it's ready, turn off the oven and let the pot rest inside for another 10-15 minutes.

Bisa and Ollie's Okra Salad:

1 lb	okra
1	ear of fresh corn
1	red bell pepper, roasted and diced
1	jalapeno, roasted and diced
1	red onion, diced
2 T	apple cider vinegar
12	cherry tomatoes, halved
3 T	olive oil
¼ c.	lemon juice
¼ t.	cumin

Sea salt

Black pepper

- Add the diced red onion to a bowl with the vinegar. Set aside.
- Blanch the okra in heavily salted water until it's as bright as an emerald, about 30-45 seconds. Drain and let cool. Cut into ½ inch chunks and discarding the stems.
- Fire roast the red pepper and jalapeno. Cool slightly and dice, removing any seeds, unless you want to surprise someone.
- To a large mixing bowl, add the okra, corn, bell pepper, jalapeno, red onion, tomatoes, olive oil, lemon juice, cumin, salt and pepper and toss gently to coat. Chill the salad for 30 minutes or until ready to serve.

Ms. Boudreaux's Pecan Pie: (makes one 9-inch pie)

Filling:

175 g.   pecan pieces, toasted

60 g.   butter

100 g.   vanilla sugar

35 g.   dark muscovado sugar

¾ t.   kosher salt (add a full teaspoon for Edie's pies, she likes a salty sweet)

3   eggs

155 g.   steen's cane syrup

155 g.   Grade B maple syrup (I know it's not Southern, but that's the secret)

1 T   vanilla

1 T   apple brandy

•   Chop up pecan pieces (I like to use pecans from Della Hamilton's tree) and spread out over the bottom of a blind-baked pie shell. Set aside.

•   Melt the butter on the stove, set aside. Blend the sugars and the salt in a large bowl, then add the melted butter to combine. Stir in the vanilla and apple brandy.

•   Add the eggs 3 at a time, whisking after each addition.

•   Whisk in the syrups and strain into a clean container. Pour mixture over the prepared pie shell, tapping the pie plate lightly to release any air gaps between the nuts.

•   Bake for about 45-55 minutes, depending on your oven. The pie should be a little puffy but should be completely set.

•   Cool fully to room temperature before serving.

Pie Dough:

24 oz.	Pastry Flour
½ oz.	Kosher Salt
16 oz.	Butter, cubed
8 oz.	Cold Water
1 T.	Apple Cider Vinegar

• Blend the cold butter in with the flour and salt. Add the liquids and knead to a shaggy dough. Adjust hydration level if necessary but do not overmix. Chill for 30 minutes.

• Dust rolling surface with flour. Flatten the dough with your hand or rolling pin. Roll out from the center, turning a quarter turn after each roll. Add more flour underneath if necessary. Roll until the dough is about 1/8 inch thick.

• Coat a pie shell with nonstick spray. Place the dough into the pie shell taking care to press into the corners. Crimp corners. Chill 30 minutes. Preheat oven to 400°.

• Place a large piece of plastic wrap over the pie shell and dump in enough baking beans to rise to the edge of the shell. Bake for 15-20 minutes. The edges should be dry and golden. Remove the plastic containing the baking beans and bake for another 3-5 minutes. Cool to room temperature.

Poached Salmon with Tarragon Cream Sauce:

2	shallots, diced
¾ c.	dry white wine
¾ c.	fish stock
15	black peppercorns
10	pink peppercorns
1	lemon, sliced
1	orange, zested
½ t.	chopped thyme
3	bay leaves
2	ea 4 oz salmon steaks
1 c.	heavy cream
2 T	tarragon, roughly chopped
Salt	

• In a large sauté pan, cook shallots in 1 T oil for 1-2 min. Then add the wine, stock, peppercorns, lemon slices, orange zest, thyme and bay leaves, and bring to a boil. Reduce to a simmer and add the salmon. Cover the contents with buttered parchment. Poach until medium. Remove the salmon and keep warm.

• Strain out the remaining liquid, pour back into pan and whisk in cream and salt over medium low heat. Reduce until thickened slightly. Add the tarragon. Adjust seasoning to taste and serve with salmon.

Harmonizing Strawberry Risotto:

6 c.	whole milk
¼ c.	granulated sugar
¼ c.	light brown sugar
½ t.	black pepper
1 ¼ t	kosher salt
1	orange, zested and juiced (friendship and prosperity)
1	rose quartz
1 T	vanilla (love)
¼ t.	rosewater (love and serenity)
½ t.	elderflower liqueur (healing and prosperity)
2 T	unsalted butter
1 c.	arborio rice
1 c.	coconut milk
1 qt.	strawberries, 4 sliced, remaining chopped and macerated
2 T	basil, chiffonade (harmonized relationships and unity)

- Charge each ingredient before beginning.
- In a medium sized pot, heat the milk, sugars, black pepper, salt, orange zest and rose quartz. Reduce the heat to low, keep hot and covered.
- In another medium pot, melt the butter, then add the rice and cook, stirring occasionally, until toasted, 1-2 minutes. Add the orange juice and continue to cook until the juice is absorbed.
- Add 1 cup of the milk mixture to the rice and continue to simmer, stirring clockwise constantly, until almost all of the liquid is absorbed. Visualize the mood of your intention to infuse it into the dish. Keep repeating this process until all of the milk has been added, remove the rose quartz. The dish should be very thick and creamy by this point. Remove from the heat, stir in the vanilla, rosewater,

elderflower liqueur and coconut milk in a figure 8. Let sit untouched for 5 minutes.

•	Spoon some of the chopped and macerated strawberries into the bottom of a bowl, then top with the risotto and garnish with sliced strawberries and threads of basil. Serve immediately.

ABOUT THE AUTHOR

Ryan Kurr is an author, pastry chef, and mystic practitioner.
His work has been published by Witches Magazine.